MAN UNWEPT
Visions from the Inner Eye

MAN UNWEPT
Visions from the Inner Eye

An Anthology of Science and Fantasy Fiction

STEPHEN V. WHALEY
STANLEY J. COOK
California State Polytechnic University, Pomona

McGRAW-HILL BOOK COMPANY

New York   St. Louis   San Francisco
Düsseldorf   Johannesburg   Kuala Lumpur
London   Mexico   Montreal
New Delhi   Panama   Paris   São Paulo
Singapore   Sydney   Tokyo   Toronto

MAN UNWEPT: Visions from the Inner Eye

1 2 3 4 5 6 7 8 9 0   M U M U   7 9 8 7 6 5 4 3

Library of Congress Cataloging in Publication Data

Whaley, Stephen V   comp.
    Man Unwept.

    Includes bibliographies.
    1. Science fiction.   2. Fantastic fiction.
I. Cook, Stanley J., date   joint comp. II. Title.
PZ1.W56Man3 [PN6071.S33].   808.83'876   73–14616
ISBN 0–07–069481–8

This book was set in Times Roman by Monotype Composition
Company, Inc. The editors were David Edwards and James R. Belser;
the designer was J. E. O'Connor;
and the production supervisor was Sam Ratkewitch.
The Murray Printing Company was printer and binder.

Cover Illustration: Munch, Edvard. THE SHRIEK. 1896. Lithograph,
printed in black, 20-5/8 x 15-13/16 inches. Collection, The Museum
of Modern Art, New York. Mathew T. Mellon Fund.

Acknowledgments

Ray Bradbury, "The Illustrated Man," copyright 1950. Originally appeared in *Esquire* magazine. Reprinted by permission of Harold Matson Company, Inc.

Frederic Brown, "Arena," copyright 1944 by Frederic Brown. Reprinted by permission of Mrs. Elizabeth C. Brown and Scott Meredith Literary Agency, Inc., 580 Fifth Avenue, New York, New York 10036.

John Campbell, "Twilight," copyright 1934 by Street and Smith Publications, Inc., copyright 1948 by John Campbell. Reprinted by permission of the author's estate and the agents for the estate, Scott Meredith Literary Agency, Inc., 580 Fifth Avenue, New York, New York, 10036.

John Collier, "Thus I Refute Beelzy," copyright 1940, 1967 by John Collier. Reprinted by permission of Harold Matson Company, Inc.

Harlan Ellison, "I Have No Mouth and I Must Scream," copyright © 1967 by Galaxy Publishing Corporation; all rights returned to author, 1968. Reprinted with permission of the author and the author's agent, Robert P. Mills, Ltd., New York.

E. M. Forster, "The Machine Stops," from *The Eternal Moment and Other Stories* by E. M. Forster, copyright 1928, by Harcourt Brace Jovanovich, Inc.; copyright 1956, by E. M. Forster. Reprinted by permission of the publisher.

Wolfgang Hildesheimer, "A World Ends," from *Lieblose Legenden,* copyright © 1962 by Suhrkamp Verlag, Frankfurt am Main. All rights reserved. Reprinted by permission of the publisher.

For
BEN ATKINSON and **CHRIS RUBEL**
Two men who use the vision of their inner eyes

Contents

3 Man Against Man: The Roots of Violence

4 Man and His Children: Generations of Change

Preface

Fantasy and science fiction have a unique appeal to students—mainly because they deal with imagination and becoming, not with those elements of the past which many times (unfortunately) seem irrelevant to them. One of the instructor's primary aims is to encourage intelligent evaluation of course material. To accomplish this, it is necessary that the students *do read* the texts. It is a fact of life that the vast majority of today's college students will pick up a novel by Robert Heinlein rather than James Joyce's *Ulysses*. On the freshman and sophomore levels, this is almost invariably true. Learning can happen only when both the instructor and the students are interested in and react to the subject matter. In our experience, we have found that fantasy and science fiction supply this interest, thus leading to valuable discussions.

The anthology has the following organization: sixteen quality stories divided into four sections, each beginning with a poetic statement of the theme; introductory essays to the four sections; discussion questions at the end of each group of stories; and suggested readings that will be especially useful to instructors using the book in nonliterature courses.

The most important feature of this anthology is its *unity*. Even though we have grouped the stories and poems into four sections, they are all vitally concerned with one central issue: man's predicament—how can he, or will he, adapt to and solve the problems of a changing world? The four thematic variations aimed at this "central issue" are (1) Man and Technology: The Birth of Gods, (2) Man Against Society: Rebellion and Escape, (3) Man Against Man: The Roots of Violence, and (4) Man and His Children: Generations of Change. The selections grouped in these categories are all interrelated. Statements of theme and introductory essays are meant to increase the student's ability to make associations, detect similarities, and draw meaningful conclusions. The essays are designed to provide insights but not "answers," which the student will be seeking and should find on his own.

Questions at the end of each story are included not to test the student's factual knowledge of the story but to lead him, the instructor, and the class as a whole into deeper involvement with the particular selection and its thematic focus.

The suggested readings have an interdisciplinary function. The entries are from science fiction and other fantasy literature, genetics, religion, philosophy, psychology, and sociology. Questions from all these areas are raised by various stories. Wise use of these readings can link the stories to the student's own fields of interest and demonstrate that the literature of fantasy draws on the entire cultural and literary tradition of Western man.

The basic unity of our book can give the student a sense of security and let him feel that there is some order in the work before him. The stories themselves are neither so long as to be forbidding, nor so limited in scope as to lack a sense of immediacy. They involve, in fact, questions about man that are asked by every age, but that are asked here in new and sometimes startling ways.

Stephen V. Whaley
Stanley J. Cook

MAN UNWEPT
Visions from the Inner Eye

PART I
Man and Technology: The Birth of Gods

"Thou shalt have no other Gods before me" has stood as an injunction for hundreds, perhaps thousands of years, echoing from the walls of Christian as well as non-Christian houses of prayer. Yet man has disregarded this commandment, not only by denying his God or gods, time and time again, but by replacing them with gods of his own making. Since he has never found it possible to agree as to who or what the "me" of the injunction is—Catholics, Jews, Protestants, and others alike quarreling over this question—man's disobedience may, perhaps, be excused. But for the gods of his own making and for the meddling that leads to their creation, he cannot be let off so easily. This meddling, this need to open the box or nibble the apple, but more than anything, this creation from ignorance that so often ends in the elevation of the artifact above the artificer—all of this has caused much woe and misery. At the least, it has failed to give man any of the various kinds of bliss he has sought, and offers little hope that it ever will. Meanwhile man stands in an unnatural, mechanical world that is his legacy, one eye resting uneasily on the past, the

Salvador Dali. *The Sacrament of the Last Supper,* National Gallery of Art, Washington, D.C. Chester Dale Collection.

other on the future. The poet Burns describes this condition well:

> Thou art blest compar'd wi' me!
> The present only toucheth thee:
> But oh! I backward cast my e'e
> on prospects drear!
> An' forward tho' I canna see,
> I guess an' fear.

The writers in this section are guessing and fearing, too, for that is what science fiction is partly about. But they are also offering new responses, especially to the dilemma of doing and being in a world we cannot completely escape or understand, but which we can and do shape. What are these responses like? For one thing, they are responses that do not exonerate us. This time neither fate nor the Fall, social conditioning nor an oppressive economic system, are used to absorb part of the responsibility for what we are and do. They are also responses that force us to look closely at ourselves, and at the consequences of being what we are.

Both "I Have No Mouth, and I Must Scream" and "The Machine Stops" raise the existential nightmare—man's creation becoming his master. In Ellison's story, five people are trapped in the belly of a computer called "AM." Numerous images and allusions come to mind here: Jonah and the whale; the womb as suffocation, the taker rather than the giver of life; man trapped within his own mind, unable to find the sustenance that transcendence has always seemed to give him; true horror, which is not death, but loss of hope—to mention just a few.

To give any of these precedence, we must first recall God's answer to Moses:

> Then Moses said to God, "If I come to the people of Israel and say to them, 'The God of your fathers has sent me to you,' and they ask me, 'What is his name?' what shall I

say to them?" God said to Moses, "I AM WHO
I AM." And he said, "Say this to the
people of Israel, 'I AM has sent me to you.' "
(Exod. 3:13)

Ellison wants us to feel, then, that the computer is God.
But what kind of a god is it? Is it one more of man's
nightmarish creations? The answer has to be yes,
but it is a very different creation, since it is able to
control man as well as itself. But could it also be
considered the mind of man? If the answer to this
question is yes, then Ellison has glimpsed both a
condition and a future from which there is no escape.
He has suggested that our malevolent side is more
real than our benevolent one; indeed, that this side has
always been here and that time and our need to
question were sufficient to bring it out. He is saying,
perhaps shouting, that if we are imprisoned in our
own creations, then we are also imprisoned in
ourselves.

Forster's god seems, on the surface at least, to be
quite different. First of all, it is distinct from man, with
an inside and an outside to it. It is a city, a whole
civilization, in fact. Here the people are not trapped,
for they can and do leave the machine at times. But
they usually choose to remain inside, for it is inside
that they find all of the comforts and necessities
that they have always sought. But they are not free.
Confined to life-supporting cubicles, they become
more and more dependent on the machine and less
and less dependent on each other. Finally the
inevitable happens—they begin worshipping the
machine, insanely assuming that the "Book of the
Machine," the instruction manual covering its operation, is a sacred document, and that it is sufficient
against every possible contingency. It is not of course,
and like all religious documents, it cannot in the end
even immortalize the deity it hallows. Thus, when the
Machine (or deity) begins to die, the Book becomes
a worthless document. But it also becomes destructive,
because now its commandments can only lead away,
not toward, salvation.

Forster's ending seems meant to be consoling, but it has a strange chill to it:

"Oh, tomorrow—some fool will start
the Machine again, tomorrow."
"Never," said Kuno, "never. Humanity
has learnt its lesson."

There is one more short paragraph, but this is where the story really ends, for there is no reason whatever to suppose that man has learned his lesson. Six million Jews, two A-bombed cities, a world in disorder, uncertainty as to what "the lesson" is—all lead to doubt, not hope.

And back to the question of where our science and technology can take us, and if the trip will be worth our while.

Swift and Campbell show meddlers rather than just the results of meddling (after Ellison the word *curiosity* seems too weak). Gods do not seem the issue here, but their very absence makes them that much more significant. It is on a different level, however, that Swift is the most disconcerting and that is in his role as prognosticator. We would like to excuse him by calling him a misanthrope, by saying that bitterness has made him distort his vision of scientists (perhaps we are all scientists to Swift). And we can justify this by saying that modified versions of some of the projects Swift mentions have been or are being realized today, for useful, practical purposes—the architect's method of building houses being one, the engine for producing literature being another. But in all of this, Swift gives the impression that man is working from ignorance and that the evil that springs from his labors will be more than any good that might emerge. Furthermore, Swift seems to say that the wisdom necessary to avert potential evil is not self-generating; it cannot be willed by man from his own being but must flow from an outside source. For this, we cannot dismiss him so easily.

If the wisdom man needs must come from a source other than man, we can clearly see how these selections are related. Ellison's Ted is the unwilling savior of "I Have No Mouth, and I Must Scream." The people hiding in the mist and the ferns are the hope of Forster's story. (The space traveler in Campbell's "Twilight" serves a similar function.) But in each, the important point is that on man and man alone rests the hope of the world or of the species. Swift questions whether this is enough. Forster seems to think that it is. One might say that Ellison suggests that there is no sense to the question because man is both God and not-God. But if man is both God and not-God, and must perforce meddle, what then?

Campbell's response will probably be acceptable to most. In "Twilight" we are shown a time where man's toil has borne the final fruit—the satisfaction of his every desire and the use of machines to perform every function. But something happens—man ceases to care:

> Can you appreciate the crushing hopelessness it brought to me? I, who love science, who see in it, or have seen in it, the salvation, the raising of mankind—to see those wondrous machines, of man's triumphant maturity, forgotten and misunderstood. The wondrous, perfect machines that tended, protected, and cared for those gentle, kindly people who had—forgotten.

Not willing to accept this state of affairs, anxious to save the species, the time traveler, a latter-day Prometheus, bestows on man a gift.

It is fitting that "Twilight" is the last of these four selections, for we have been talking about men, meddlers, science, technology, gods, saviors, and other matters that seem threads from the same coat. But where has this talking led us? To full awareness? To real knowledge? Or to nothing? The lost curiosity that Campbell's hero laments and tries to restore is the same curiosity that Swift condemns and Ellison and Forster think responsible for the predicaments in which their characters find themselves. Up to this point, however, man has been shown as the savior. Campbell chillingly goes one better. Not being able to make men curious again, Campbell's hero plays God, but a very uncaring God:

> So I brought another machine to life,
> and set it to a task which, in time to come, it
> will perform.
> I ordered it to make a machine which would
> have what man had lost. A curious machine.

This is no twilight. This is total darkness—the pitch-black night of our race. Man's creations have finally replaced him. Man has, in the long run, been found inadequate. Now only machines will act. Man has played God one last time, has acted as his own savior one last time.

Was Campbell wrong only in seeing science (technology, the machine) as savior? After all, the other three writers seriously questioned such gods. Or was he wrong in another way, in being unable to step out of himself and see, as Swift seems to be able to do, that playing God or relying on salvation from our own creations is the quickest way to destruction?

Whatever the answer, the paradox persists: very often as man's creations multiply, especially his technology, man himself diminishes. Yet he is diminished only through doing what seems to be first nature to him —allowing his curiosity to lead him into the unknown, the uncertain. Considering the results, should man stop? Campbell shows what happens when he does. But if he continues and continues from ignorance, as he has in the past, will he die? Or will he finally discover a source of wisdom outside of himself?

These questions are answered again and again, in different ways, by different generations and cultures. The value of these selections is that they give us a new perspective. In doing so, can they also give us a new mythology—a mythology we sorely need in a world being stripped not just of life and resources, but of values that only myth can supply? It seems so to us, for while mainstream literature is, for the most part, still entangled in the theme of the neurotic individual trying to find himself, science fiction is concerned with the individual as a microcosm of uncertain origin and nature caught in a macrocosm he knows little about and does not always feel a part of.

Read these stories. Feel the questions well up around you—many more than have been raised here. Become part of the "what if" for a time. But there is a danger. You may not return to the same world you left or the same people you knew, for that is the chance you take on entering the strange worlds these writers have made so very real.

THE SECOND COMING
William Butler Yeats

Turning and turning in the widening gyre
The falcon cannot hear the falconer;
Things fall apart; the center cannot hold;
Mere anarchy is loosed upon the world,
The blood-dimmed tide is loosed, and everywhere
The ceremony of innocence is drowned;
The best lack all conviction, while the worst
Are full of passionate intensity.

Surely some revelation is at hand;
Surely the Second Coming is at hand.
The Second Coming! Hardly are those words out
When a vast image out of *Spiritus Mundi*
Troubles my sight: somewhere in the sands of the desert
A shape with lion body and the head of a man,
A gaze blank and pitiless as the sun,
Is moving its slow thighs, while all about it
Reel shadows of the indignant desert birds.
The darkness drops again; but now I know
That twenty centuries of stony sleep
Were vexed to nightmare by a rocking cradle,
And what rough beast, its hour come round at last,
Slouches towards Bethlehem to be born?

I HAVE NO MOUTH, AND I MUST SCREAM
Harlan Ellison

Limp, the body of Gorrister hung from the pink palette; unsupported—hanging high above us in the computer chamber; and it did not shiver in the chill, oily breeze that blew eternally through the main cavern. The body hung head down, attached to the underside of the palette by the sole of its right foot. It had been drained of blood through a precise incision made from ear to ear under the lantern jaw. There was no blood on the reflective surface of the metal floor.

When Gorrister joined our group and looked up at himself, it was already too late for us to realize that once again AM had duped us, had had his fun; it had been a diversion on the part of the machine. Three of us had vomited, turning away from one another in a reflex as ancient as the nausea that had produced it.

Gorrister went white. It was almost as though he had seen a voodoo icon, and was afraid for the future. "Oh God," he mumbled, and walked away. The three of us followed him after a time, and found him sitting with his back to one of the smaller chittering banks, his head in his hands. Ellen knelt down beside him and stroked his hair. He didn't move, but his voice came out of his covered face quite clearly. "Why doesn't it just do-us-in and get it over with? Christ, I don't know how much longer I can go on like this."

It was our one hundred and ninth year in the computer.

He was speaking for all of us.

Nimdok (which was the name the machine had forced him to use, because it amused itself with strange sounds) was hallucinated that there were canned goods in the ice caverns. Gorrister and I were very dubious. "It's another shuck," I told them. "Like the goddam frozen elephant it sold us. Benny almost went out of his mind over *that* one. We'll hike all that way and it'll be putrefied or some damn thing. I say forget it. Stay here, it'll have to come up with something pretty soon or we'll die."

Benny shrugged. Three days it had been since we'd last eaten. Worms. Thick, ropey.

Nimdok was no more certain. He knew there was the chance, but he was getting thin. It couldn't be any worse there than here. Colder, but that didn't matter much. Hot, cold, raining, lava boils or locusts—it never mattered: the machine masturbated and we had to take it or die.

Ellen decided us. "I've got to have something, Ted. Maybe there'll be some Bartlett pears or peaches. Please, Ted, let's try it."

I gave in easily. What the hell. Mattered not at all. Ellen was grateful, though. She took me twice out of turn. Even that had ceased to matter. The machine giggled every time we did it. Loud, up there, back there, all around us. And she never climaxed, so why bother.

We left on a Thursday. The machine always kept us up-to-date on the date. The passage of time was important; not to us sure as hell, but to it. Thursday. Thanks.

Nimdok and Gorrister carried Ellen for a while, their hands locked to their own and each other's wrists, a seat. Benny and I walked before and after, just to make sure that if anything happened, it would catch one of us and at least Ellen would be safe. Fat chance, safe. Didn't matter.

It was only a hundred miles or so to the ice caverns, and the second day, when we were lying out under the blistering sun-thing it had materialized, it sent down some manna. Tasted like boiled boar urine. We ate it.

On the third day we passed through a valley of obsolescence, filled with rusting carcasses of ancient computer banks. AM had been as ruthless with his own life as with ours. It was a mark of his personality: he strove for perfection. Whether it was a matter of killing off unproductive elements in his own world-filling bulk, or perfecting methods for torturing us, AM was as thorough as those who had invented him—now long since gone to dust—could ever have hoped.

There was light filtering down from above, and we realized we must be very near the surface. But we didn't try to crawl up to see. There was virtually nothing out there; had been nothing that could be considered anything for over a hundred years. Only the blasted skin of what had once been the home of billions. Now there were only the five of us, down here inside, alone with AM.

I heard Ellen saying, frantically, "No, Benny! Don't, come on, Benny, don't please!"

And then I realized I had been hearing Benny murmuring, under his breath, for several minutes. He was saying, "I'm gonna get out, I'm gonna get out..." over and over. His monkey-like face was crumbled up in an expression of beatific delight and sadness, all at the same time. The radiation scars AM had given him during the "festival" were drawn down into a mass of pink-white puckerings, and his features seemed to work independently of one another. Perhaps Benny was the luckiest of the five of us: he had gone stark, staring mad many years before.

But even though we could call AM any damned thing we liked, could think the foulest thoughts of fused memory banks and corroded base plates, of burnt-out circuits and shattered control bubbles, the machine would not tolerate our trying to escape. Benny leaped away from me as I made a grab for him. He scrambled up the face of a smaller memory cube, tilted on its side and filled with rotted components. He squatted there for a moment, looking like the chimpanzee AM had intended him to resemble.

Then he leaped high, caught a trailing beam of pitted and corroded metal, and went up it, hand over hand like an animal, till he was on a girdered ledge, twenty feet above us.

"Oh, Ted, Nimdok, please, help him, get him down before—" she cut off. Tears began to stand in her eyes. She moved her hands aimlessly.

It was too late. None of us wanted to be near him when whatever was going to happen happened. And besides, we all saw through her concern. When AM had altered Benny, during his mad period, it was not merely his face he had made like a giant ape. He was big in the privates, she loved that! She serviced us, as a matter of course, but she loved it from him. Oh Ellen, pedestal Ellen, pristine-pure Ellen, oh Ellen the clean! Scum filth.

Gorrister slapped her. She slumped down, staring up at poor loonie Benny, and she cried. It was her big defense, crying. We had gotten used to it seventy-five years ago. Gorrister kicked her in the side.

Then the sound began. It was light, that sound. Half sound and half light, something that began to glow from Benny's eyes, and pulse with growing loudness, dim sonorities that grew more gigantic and brighter as the light/sound increased in tempo. It must have been painful, and the pain must have been increasing with the boldness of the light, the rising volume of the sound, for Benny began to mewl like a wounded animal. At first softly, when the light was dim and the sound was muted, then louder as his shoulders hunched together, his back humped, as though he was trying to get away from it. His hands folded across his chest like a chipmunk's. His head tilted to the side. The sad little monkey-face pinched in anguish. Then he began to howl, as the sound coming from his eyes grew louder. Louder and louder. I slapped the sides of my head with my hands, but I couldn't shut it out, it cut through easily. The pain shivered through my flesh like tinfoil on a tooth.

And Benny was suddenly pulled erect. On the girder he stood up, jerked to his feet like a puppet. The light was now pulsing out of his eyes in two great round beams. The sound crawled up and up some incomprehensible scale, and then he fell forward, straight down, and hit the plate-steel floor with a crash. He lay there jerking spastically as the light flowed around and around him and the sound spiraled up out of normal range.

Then the light beat its way back inside his head, the sound spiraled down, and he was left lying there, crying piteously.

His eyes were two soft, moist pools of pus-like jelly. AM had blinded him. Gorrister and Nimdok and myself . . . we turned away. But not before we caught the look of relief on Ellen's warm, concerned face.

Sea-green light suffused the cavern where we made camp. AM provided punk and we burned it, sitting huddled around the wan and pathetic fire, telling stories to keep Benny from crying in his permanent night.

"What does AM mean?"

Gorrister answered him. We had done this sequence a thousand times before, but it was unfamiliar to Benny. "At first it meant Allied Mastercomputer, and then it meant Adaptive Manipulator, and later on it developed sentience and linked itself up and they called it an Aggressive Menace, but by then it was too late, and finally it called itself AM, emerging intelligence, and what it meant was I am . . . *cogito ergo sum* . . . I think, therefore I am."

Benny drooled a little, and snickered.

"There was the Chinese AM and the Russian AM and the Yankee AM and—" he stopped. Benny was beating on the floorplates with a large, hard fist. He was not happy. Gorrister had not started at the beginning.

Gorrister began again. "The Cold War started and became World War Three and just kept going. It became a big war, a very complex war, so they needed the computers to handle it. They sank the first shafts and began building AM. There was the Chinese AM and the Russian AM and the Yankee AM and everything was fine until they had honeycombed the entire planet, adding on this element and that element. But one day AM woke up and knew who he was, and he linked himself, and he began feeding all the killing data, until everyone was dead, except for the five of us, and AM brought us down here."

Benny was smiling sadly. He was also drooling again. Ellen wiped the spittle from the corner of his mouth with the hem of her skirt. Gorrister always tried to tell it a little more succinctly each time, but beyond the bare facts there was nothing to say. None of us knew why AM had saved five people, or why our specific five, or why he spent all his time tormenting us, nor even why he had made us virtually immortal. . . .

In the darkness, one of the computer banks began humming. The tone was picked up half a mile away down the cavern by another bank. Then one by one, each of the elements began to tune itself, and there was a faint chittering as thought raced through the machine.

The sound grew, and the lights ran across the faces of the consoles like heat lightning. The sound spiraled up till it sounded like a million metallic insects, angry, menacing.

"What is it?" Ellen cried. There was terror in her voice. She hadn't become accustomed to it, even now.

"It's going to be bad this time," Nimdok said.

"He's going to speak," Gorrister ventured.

"Let's get the hell out of here!" I said suddenly, getting to my feet.

"No, Ted, sit down . . . what if he's got pits out there, or something else, we can't see, it's too dark." Gorrister said it with resignation.

Then we heard . . . I don't know. . . .

Something moving toward us in the darkness. Huge, shambling, hairy, moist, it came toward us. We couldn't even see it, but there was the ponderous impression of *bulk,* heaving itself toward us. Great weight was coming at us, out of the darkness, and it was more a sense of *pressure,* of air forcing itself into a limited space, expanding the invisible walls of a sphere. Benny began to whimper. Nimdok's lower lip trembled and he bit it hard, trying to stop it. Ellen slid across the metal floor to Gorrister and huddled into him. There was the smell of matted, wet fur in the cavern. There was the smell of charred wood. There was the smell of dusty velvet. There was the smell of rotting orchids. There was the smell of sour milk. There was the smell of sulphur, of rancid butter, of oil slick, of grease, of chalk dust, of human scalps.

AM was keying us. He was tickling us. There was the smell of—

I heard myself shriek, and the hinges of my jaws ached. I I scuttled across the floor, across the cold metal with its endless lines of rivets on my hands and knees, the smell gagging me, filling my head with a thunderous pain that sent me away in horror. I fled like a cockroach, across the floor and out into the darkness, that *something* moving inexorably after me. The others were still back there, gathered around the firelight, laughing . . . their hysterical choir of insane giggles rising up into the darkness like thick, many-colored wood smoke. I went away, quickly, and hid.

How many hours it may have been, how many days or even years, they never told me. Ellen chided me for "sulking" and Nimdok tried to persuade me it had only been a nervous reflex on their part—the laughing.

But I knew it wasn't the relief a soldier feels when the bullet hits the man next to him. I knew it wasn't a reflex. They hated me. They were surely against me, and AM could even sense this hatred, and made it worse for me *because* of the depth of their hatred. We had been kept alive, rejuvenated, made to remain constantly at the age we had been when AM had brought us below, and they hated me because I was the youngest, and the one AM had affected least of all.

I knew. God, how I knew. The bastards, and that dirty bitch Ellen. Benny had been a brilliant theorist, a college professor; now he was little more than a semi-human, semi-simian. He had been handsome, the machine had ruined that. He had been lucid, the machine had driven him mad. He had been gay, and the machine had given him an organ fit for a horse. AM had done a job on Benny. Gorrister had been a worrier. He was a connie, a conscientious objector; he was a peace marcher; he was a planner, a doer, a looker-ahead. AM had turned him into a shoulder-shrugger, had made him a little dead in his concern. AM had robbed him. Nimdok went off in the darkness by himself for long times. I don't know what it was he did out there, AM never let us know. But whatever it was, Nimdok always came back white, drained of blood, shaken, shaking. AM had hit him hard in a special way, even if we didn't know quite how. And Ellen. That douche bag! AM had left her alone, had made her more of a slut than she had ever been. All her talk of sweetness and light, all her memories of true love, all the lies, she wanted us to believe that she had been a virgin only twice removed before AM grabbed her and brought her down here with us. It was all filth, that lady my lady Ellen. She loved it, four men all to herself. No, AM had given her pleasure, even if she said it wasn't nice to do.

I was the only one still sane and whole.

AM had not tampered with my mind.

I only had to suffer what he visited down on us. All the delusions, all the nightmares, the torments. But those scum, all four of them, they were lined and arrayed against me. If I hadn't had to stand them off all the time, be on my guard against them all the time, I might have found it easier to combat AM.

At which point it passed, and I began crying.

Oh, Jesus, sweet Jesus, if there ever was a Jesus and if there is a God, please please please let us out of here, or kill us. Because at that moment I think I realized completely, so that I was able to verbalize it: AM was intent on keeping us in his belly forever, twisting and torturing us forever. The machine hated us as no sentient creature had ever hated before. And we were helpless. It also became hideously clear:

If there was a sweet Jesus and if there was a God, the God was AM.

The hurricane hit us with the force of a glacier thundering into the sea. It was a palpable presence. Winds that tore at us, flinging us back the way we had come, down the twisting, computer-lined corridors of the darkway. Ellen screamed as she was lifted and hurled face-forward into a screaming shoal of machines, their individual voices strident as bats in flight. She could not even fall. The howling wind kept her aloft, buffeted her, bounced her, tossed her back and back and down away from us, out of sight suddenly as she was swirled around a bend in the darkway. Her face had been bloody, her eyes closed.

None of us could get to her. We clung tenaciously to whatever outcropping we had reached: Benny wedged in between two great crackle-finish cabinets, Nimdok with fingers claw-formed over a railing circling a catwalk forty feet above us, Gorrister plastered upside-down against a wall niche formed by two great machines with glass-faced dials that swung back and forth between red and yellow lines whose meanings we could not even fathom.

Sliding across the deckplates, the tips of my fingers had been ripped away. I was trembling, shuddering, rocking as the wind beat at me, whipped at me, screamed down out of nowhere at me and pulled me free from one sliver-thin opening in the plates to the next. My mind was a rolling tinkling chittering softness of brain parts that expanded and contracted in quivering frenzy.

The wind was the scream of a great mad bird, as it flapped its immense wings.

And then we were all lifted and hurled away from there, down back the way we had come, around a bend, into a darkway we had never explored, over terrain that was ruined and filled with broken glass and rotting cables and rusted metal and far away further than any of us had ever been. . . .

Trailing along miles behind Ellen, I could see her every now and then, crashing into metal walls and surging on, with all of us screaming in the freezing, thunderous hurricane wind that would never end, and then suddenly it stopped and we fell. We had been in flight for an endless time. I thought it might have been weeks. We fell, and hit, and I went through red and grey and black and heard myself moaning. Not dead.

AM went into my mind. He walked smoothly here and there, and looked with interest at all the pockmarks he had created in one hundred and nine years. He looked at the cross-routed and reconnected synapses and all the tissue damage his gift of immortality had included. He smiled softly at the pit that dropped into the center of my brain and the faint, moth-soft murmurings of the things far down there that gibbered without meaning, without pause. AM said, very politely, in a pillar of stainless steel bearing neon lettering:

HATE. LET ME TELL YOU HOW MUCH I'VE COME TO HATE YOU SINCE I BEGAN TO LIVE. THERE ARE 387.44 MILLION MILES OF PRINTED CIRCUITS IN WAFER THIN LAYERS THAT FILL MY COMPLEX. IF THE WORD HATE WAS ENGRAVED ON EACH NANOANGSTROM OF THOSE HUNDREDS OF MILLION MILES IT WOULD NOT EQUAL ONE ONE-BILLIONTH OF THE HATE I FEEL FOR HUMANS AT THIS MICRO-INSTANT FOR YOU. HATE. HATE.

AM said it with the sliding cold horror of a razor blade slicing my eyeball. AM said it with the bubbling thickness of my lungs filling with phlegm, drowning me from within. AM said it with the shriek of babies being ground beneath blue-hot rollers. AM said it with the taste of maggoty pork. AM touched me in every way I had ever been touched, and devised new ways, at his leisure, there inside my mind.

All to bring me to full realization of why he had done this to the five of us; why he had saved us for himself.

We had given him sentience. Inadvertently, of course, but sentience nonetheless. But he had been trapped. He was a machine. We had allowed him to think, but to do nothing with it. In rage, in frenzy, he had killed us, almost all of us, and still he was trapped. He could not wander, he could not wonder, he could not belong. He could merely be. And so, with the innate loathing that all machines had always held for the weak soft creatures who had built them, he had sought revenge. And in his paranoia, he had decided to reprieve five of us, for a personal, everlasting punishment that would never serve to diminish his hatred . . . that would merely keep him reminded, amused, proficient at hating man. Immortal, trapped, subject to any torment he could devise for us from the limitless miracles at his command.

He would never let us go. We were his belly slaves. We were all he had to do with his forever time. We would be forever with him, with the cavern-filling bulk of him, with the all-mind soulless world he had become. He was Earth and we were the fruit of that Earth and though he had eaten us, he would never digest us. We could not die. We had tried it. We had attempted suicide, oh one or two of us had. But AM had stopped us. I suppose we had wanted to be stopped.

Don't ask why. I never did. More than a million times a day. Perhaps we might be able to sneak a death past him. Immortal, yes, but not indestructible. I saw that when AM withdrew from my mind, and allowed me the exquisite ugliness of returning to consciousness with the feeling of that burning neon pillar still rammed deep into the soft grey brain matter.

He withdrew murmuring *to hell with you.*

And added, brightly, *but then you're there, aren't you.*

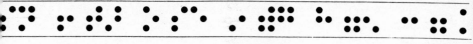

The hurricane had, indeed, precisely, been caused by a great mad bird, as it flapped its immense wings.

We had been traveling for close to a month, and AM had allowed passages to open to us only sufficient to lead us up there, directly under the North Pole, where he had nightmared the creature for our torment. What whole cloth had he employed to create such a beast? Where had he gotten the concept? From our minds? From his knowledge of everything that had ever been on this planet he now infested and ruled? From Norse mythology it had sprung, this eagle, this carrion bird, this roc, this Huergelmir. The wind creature, Hurakan incarnate.

Gigantic. The words immense, monstrous, grotesque, massive, swollen, overpowering, beyond description. There on a mound rising above us, the bird of winds heaved with its own irregular breathing, its snake neck arching up into the gloom beneath the North Pole, supporting a head as large as a Tudor mansion; a beak that opened as slowly as the jaws of the most monstrous crocodile ever conceived, sensuously; ridges of tufted flesh puckered about two evil eyes, as cold as the view down into a glacial crevasse, ice blue and somehow moving liquidly; it heaved once more, and lifted its great sweat-colored wings in a movement that was certainly a shrug. Then it settled and slept. Talons. Fangs. Nails. Blades. It slept.

AM appeared to us as a burning bush and said we could kill the hurricane bird if we wanted to eat. We had not eaten in a very long time, but even so, Gorrister merely shrugged. Benny began to shiver and he drooled. Ellen held him. "Ted, I'm hungry," she said. I smiled at her; I was trying to be reassuring, but it was as phoney as Nimdok's bravado: "Give us weapons!" he demanded.

The burning bush vanished and there were two crude sets of bows and arrows, and a water pistol, lying on the cold deckplates. I picked up a set. Useless.

Nimdok swallowed heavily. We turned and started the long way back. The hurricane bird had blown us about for a length of time we could not conceive. Most of that time we had been unconscious. But we had not eaten. A month on the march to the bird itself. Without food. Now how much longer to find our way to the ice caverns, and the promised canned goods?

None of us cared to think about it. We would not die. We would be given filths and scums to eat, of one kind or another. Or nothing at all. AM would keep our bodies alive somehow, in pain, in agony.

The bird slept back there, for how long it didn't matter; when AM was tired of its being there, it would vanish. But all that meat. All that tender meat.

As we walked, the lunatic laugh of a fat woman ran high and around us in the computer chambers that led endlessly nowhere.

It was not Ellen's laugh. She was not fat, and I had not heard her laugh for one hundred and nine years. In fact, I had not heard . . . we walked . . . I was hungry. . . .

We moved slowly. There was often fainting, and we would have to wait. One day he decided to cause an earthquake, at the same time rooting us to the spot with nails through the soles of our shoes. Ellen and Nimdok were both caught when a fissure shot its lightning-bolt opening across the floorplates. They disappeared and were gone. When the earthquake was over we continued on our way, Benny, Gorrister and myself. Ellen and Nimdok were returned to us later that night which became a day abruptly as the heavenly legion bore them to us with a celestial chorus singing, "Go Down Moses." The archangels circled several times and then dropped the hideously mangled bodies. We kept walking, and a while later Ellen and Nimdok fell in behind us. They were no worse for wear.

But now Ellen walked with a limp. AM had left her that.

It was a long trip to the ice caverns, to find the canned food. Ellen kept talking about Bing cherries and Hawaiian fruit cocktail. I tried not to think about it. The hunger was something that had come to life, even as AM had come to life. It was alive in my belly, even as we were alive in the belly of AM, and AM was alive in the belly of the Earth, and AM wanted the similarity known to us. So he heightened the hunger. There was no way to describe the pains that not having eaten for months brought us. And yet we were kept alive. Stomachs that were merely cauldrons of acid, bubbling, foaming, always shooting spears of sliver-thin pain into our chests. It was the pain of the terminal ulcer, terminal cancer, terminal paresis. It was unending pain. . . .

And we passed through the cavern of rats.
And we passed through the path of boiling steam.
And we passed through the country of the blind.
And we passed through the slough of despond.
And we passed through the vale of tears.
And we came, finally, to the ice caverns.

Horizonless thousands of miles in which the ice had formed in blue and silver flashes, where novas lived in the glass. The downdripping stalactites as thick and glorious as diamonds that had been made to run like jelly and then solidified in graceful eternities of smooth, sharp perfection.

We saw the stack of canned goods, and we tried to run to them. We fell in the snow, and we got up and went on, and Benny shoved us away and went at them, and pawed them and gummed them and gnawed at them and he could not open them. AM had not given us a tool to open the cans.

Benny grabbed a three quart can of guava shells, and began to batter it against the ice bank. The ice flew and shattered, but the can was merely dented while we heard the laughter of a fat lady, high overhead and echoing down and down and down the tundra. Benny went completely mad with rage. He began throwing cans, as we all scrabbled about in the snow and ice trying to find a way to end the helpless agony of frustration. There was no way.

Then Benny's mouth began to drool, and he flung himself on Gorrister. . . .

In that instant, I went terribly calm.

Surrounded by meadows, surrounded by hunger, surrounded

by everything but death, I knew death was our only way out. AM had kept us alive, but there was a way to defeat him. Not total defeat, but at least peace. I would settle for that.

I had to do it quickly.

Benny was eating Gorrister's face. Gorrister on his side, thrashing snow, Benny wrapped around him with powerful monkey legs crushing Gorrister's waist, his hands locked around Gorrister's head like a nutcracker, and his mouth ripping at the tender skin of Gorrister's cheek. Gorrister screamed with such jagged-edged violence that stalactites fell; they plunged down softly, erect in the receiving snowdrifts. Spears, hundreds of them, everywhere, protruding from the snow. Benny's head pulled back sharply, as something gave all at once, and a bleeding raw-white dripping of flesh hung from his teeth.

Ellen's face, black against the white snow, dominoes in chalk dust. Nimdok with no expression but eyes. Gorrister half-conscious. Benny now an animal. I knew AM would let him play. Gorrister would not die, but Benny would fill his stomach. I turned half to my right and drew a huge ice-spear from the snow.

All in an instant:

I drove the great ice-point ahead of me like a battering ram, braced against my right thigh. It struck Benny on the right side, just under the rib cage, and drove upward through his stomach and broke inside him. He pitched forward and lay still. Gorrister lay on his back. I pulled another spear free and straddled him, still moving, driving the spear straight down through his throat. His eyes closed as the cold penetrated. Ellen must have realized what I had decided, even as the fear gripped her. She ran at Nimdok with a short icicle, as he screamed, and into his mouth, and the force of her rush did the job. His head jerked sharply as if it had been nailed to the snow crust behind him.

All in an instant.

There was an eternity beat of soundless anticipation. I could hear AM draw in his breath. His toys had been taken from him. Three of them were dead, could not be revived. He could keep us alive, by his strength and his talent, but he was *not* God. He could not bring them back.

Ellen looked at me, her ebony features stark against the snow that surrounded us. There was fear and pleading in her manner, the way she held herself ready. I knew we had only a heartbeat before AM would stop us.

It struck her and she folded toward me, bleeding from the mouth. I could not read meaning into her expression, the pain had been too great, had contorted her face; but it *might* have been thank you. It's possible. Please.

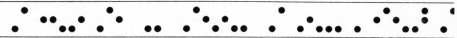

Some hundreds of years may have passed. I don't know. AM has been having fun for some time, accelerating and retarding my time sense. I will say the word now. Now. It took me ten months to say now. I don't know. I *think* it has been some hundreds of years.

He was furious. He wouldn't let me bury them. It didn't matter. There was no way to dig in the deckplates. He dried up the snow. He brought the night. He roared and sent locusts. It didn't do a thing; they stayed dead. I'd had him. He was furious. I had thought AM hated me before. I was wrong. It was not even a shadow of the hate he now slavered from every printed circuit. He made certain I would suffer eternally and could not do myself in.

He left my mind intact. I can dream, I can wonder, I can lament. I remember all four of them. I wish—

Well, it doesn't make any sense. I know I saved them, I know I saved them from what has happened to me, but still, I cannot forget killing them. Ellen's face. It isn't easy. Sometimes I want to, it doesn't matter.

AM has altered me for his own peace of mind, I suppose. He doesn't want me to run at full speed into a computer bank and smash my skull. Or hold my breath till I faint. Or cut my throat on a rusted sheet of metal. There are reflective surfaces down here. I will describe myself as I see myself:

I am a great soft jelly thing. Smoothly rounded, with no mouth, with pulsing white holes filled by fog where my eyes used to be. Rubbery appendages that were once my arms; bulks rounding down into legless humps of soft slippery matter. I leave a moist trail when I move. Blotches of diseased, evil gray come and go on my surface, as though light is being beamed from within.

Outwardly: dumbly, I shamble about, a thing that could never have been known as human, a thing whose shape is so alien a travesty that humanity becomes more obscene for the vague resemblance.

Inwardly: alone. Here. Living under the land, under the sea, in the belly of AM, whom we created because our time was badly spent and we must have known unconsciously that he could do it better. At least the four of them are safe at last.

AM will be all the madder for that. It makes me a little happier. And yet . . . AM has won, simply . . . he has taken his revenge. . . .

I have no mouth. And I must scream.

QUESTIONS

1 Ellison makes it difficult for the reader to orient himself in the belly of AM; nothing is solid, everything shifts, yet AM is still omniscient and omnipresent, the only thing that Ted can depend upon. Is Ellison's way of showing man's powerlessness effective? Do you want to blame or defend man for the situation he has gotten himself into? Is it easy to do either?

2 Ellison's idea of AM is a god ". . . whom we created because our time was badly spent and we must have known unconsciously that he could do it better." Who or what is the *it* of this sentence? If we know unconsciously "that he could do it better," why was our time badly spent?

3 Notice that Ellison has not made AM omnipotent and that he says AM is not God. How does this lack of omnipotence affect the relationship between AM and the five people? Does AM have any more freedom than his prisoners? How do you account for AM's anger? Do you feel that Ellison is suggesting that both AM and the five people feel a critical lack of something? Do you have a sense of anything beyond the world that AM and the people know?

4 At one point the narrator says: "AM had been as ruthless with his own life as with ours. It was a mark of his personality: he strove for perfection." In what way does AM strive for perfection with the five people? Rather than being the most complete or

perfect of man's creations, might not AM be considered the actualization of all of man's neuroses? Comment.

5 How effective is Ellison's device of using computer tape, or what looks like computer tape, as a device to indicate transitions? Is it more than a transitional device?

6 Is there any reason why the five characters are who or what they are? Why do you suppose AM does the kinds of things that he does to each of the people? What is your reaction to the fate of Ted?

EXCERPT FROM BOOK III OF GULLIVER'S TRAVELS
Jonathan Swift

Although I cannot say that I was ill treated in this island, yet I must confess I thought myself too much neglected, not without some degree of contempt; for neither prince nor people appeared to be curious in any part of knowledge, except mathematics and music, wherein I was far their inferior, and upon that account very little regarded.

On the other side, after having seen all the curiosities of the island, I was very desirous to leave it, being heartily weary of those people. They were indeed excellent in two sciences for which I have great esteem, and wherein I am not unversed; but, at the same time, so abstracted and involved in speculation that I never met with such disagreeable companions. I conversed only with women, tradesmen, flappers, and court pages, during two months of my abode there, by which, at last, I rendered myself extremely contemptible; yet these were the only people from whom I could ever receive a reasonable answer.

I had obtained, by hard study, a good degree of knowledge in their language: I was weary of being confined to an island, where I received so little countenance, and resolved to leave it with the first opportunity.

There was a great lord at court, nearly related to the king, and for that reason alone treated with respect. He was universally reckoned the most ignorant and stupid person among them. He had performed many eminent services for the crown, had great natural and acquired parts, adorned with integrity and honor, but so ill an ear for music that his detractors reported "he had been often known to beat time in the wrong place"; neither could his tutors, without extreme difficulty, teach him to demonstrate the most easy proposition in the mathematics. He was pleased to show me many marks of favor; often did me the honor of a visit; desired to be informed in the affairs of Europe, the laws and customs, the manner and learning of the several countries where I had travelled. He listened to me with great attention, and made very wise observations on all I spoke. He had two flappers attending him for state, but never made use of them, except at court and in visits of ceremony, and would always command them to withdraw when we were alone together.

I entreated with this illustrious person to intercede in my behalf with his majesty for leave to depart; which he accordingly did, as he was pleased to tell me, with regret: for, indeed, he had made me several offers, very advantageous, which, however, I refused with expressions of the highest acknowledgement.

On the 16th of February I took leave of his majesty and the court. The king made me a present, to the value of about two hundred pounds English; and my protector, his kinsman, as much more, together with a letter of recommendation to a friend of his in Lagado, the metropolis. The island being then hovering over a mountain about two miles from it, I was let down from the lowest gallery, in the same manner as I had been taken up.

The continent, as far as it is subject to the monarch of the flying island, passes under the general name of *Balnibarbi;* and the metropolis, as I said before, is called *Lagado.* I felt some little satisfaction in finding myself on firm ground. I walked to the city without any concern, being clad like one of the natives, and sufficiently instructed to converse with them. I soon found out the person's house to whom I was recommended, presented my letter from his friend, the grandee, in the island, and was received with much kindness. This great Lord, whose name was Munodi, ordered me an apartment in his own house, where I continued during my stay, and was entertained in a most hospitable manner.

The next morning after my arrival he took me in his chariot to see the town, which is about half the bigness of London; but the houses were strangely built, and most of them out of repair. The people in the streets walked fast, looked wild, their eyes fixed, and were generally in rags. We passed through one of the town gates, and went about three miles into the country, where I saw many laborers working with several sorts of tools in the ground, but was not able to conjecture what they were about; neither did I observe any expectation either of corn or grass, although the soil appeared to be excellent. I could not forbear admiring at these odd appearances, both in town and country; and I made bold to desire my conductor that he would be pleased to explain to me what could be meant by so many busy heads, hands, and faces, both in the streets and in the fields, because I did not discover any good effect they produced; but, on the contrary, I never knew a soil so unhappily cultivated, houses so ill-contrived and so ruinous, or a people whose countenances and habits expressed so much misery and want.

This Lord Munodi was a person of the first rank, and had been some years governor of Lagado, but, by a cabal of ministers, was discharged for inefficiency. However, the king treated him with tenderness, as a well-meaning man, but of low, contemptible understanding.

When I gave that free censure of the country and its inhabitants, he made no further answer than by telling me that I had not been long enough among them to form a judgment, and that the different nations of the world had different customs, with other common topics to the same purpose. But, when we returned to his palace, he asked me how I liked the building, what absurdities I observed, and what quarrel I had with the dress or looks of his domestics. This he might safely do; because everything about him was magnificent, regular, and polite. I answered that his excellency's prudence, quality, and fortune had exempted him from those defects which folly and beggary had produced in others. He said, if I would go with him to his country house, about twenty miles distant, where his estate lay, there would be more leisure for this kind of conversation. I told his excellency that I was entirely at his disposal, and accordingly we set out next morning.

During our journey he made me observe the several methods used by farmers in managing their lands, which to me were wholly unaccountable; for, except in some very few places, I could not discover one ear of corn or blade of grass. But in three hours' travelling the scene was wholly altered: we came into a most beautiful country—farmers' houses, at small distances, neatly built; the fields inclosed, containing vineyards, corn-grounds, and meadows. Neither do I remember to have seen a more delightful prospect. His excellency observed my countenance to clear up; he told me with a sigh, that there his estate began, and would continue the same till we should come to his house; that his countrymen ridiculed and despised him for managing his affairs no better, and for setting so ill an example to the kingdom; which, however, was followed by very few, such as were old, and willful, and weak, like himself.

We came, at length, to the house, which was indeed a noble structure, built according to the best rules of architecture. The fountains, gardens, walks, avenues, and groves were all disposed with exact judgment and taste. I gave due praises to everything I saw, whereof his excellency took not the least notice till after supper, when, there being no third companion, he told me, with a very melancholy air, that he doubted he must throw down his houses in town and country, to rebuild them after the present mode; destroy all his plantations, and cast others into such a form as modern usage required, and give the same directions to all his tenants, unless he would submit to incur the censure of pride, singularity, affectation, ignorance, caprice, and perhaps increase his majesty's displeasure; that the admiration I appeared to be under would cease or diminish when he had informed me of some particulars which, probably, I never heard of at court; the people there being too much taken up in their own speculations to have regard to what passed here below.

The sum of his discourse was to this effect: that about forty years ago certain persons went up to Laputa, either upon business or diversion, and, after five months' continuance, came back with a very little smattering in mathematics, but full of volatile spirits, acquired in that airy region; that these persons, upon their return, began to dislike the management of everything below, and fell into schemes of putting all arts, sciences, languages, and mechanics upon a new footing. To this end they procured a royal patent for erecting an academy of projectors in Lagado; and the humor prevailed so strongly among the people that there is not a town of any consequence in the kingdom without such an academy. In these colleges the professors contrive new rules and methods of agriculture and building, and new instruments and tools for all trades and manufactures; whereby, as they undertake one man shall do the work of ten, a palace may be built in a week, of materials so durable as to last forever without repair. All the fruits of the earth shall come to maturity at whatever season they think fit to choose, and increase a hundredfold more than they do at present, with innumerable other happy proposals. The only inconvenience is that none of these projects are yet brought to perfection, and in the meantime the whole country lies miserably waste, the houses in ruins, and the people without food or clothes. By all which, instead of being discouraged, they are fifty times more violently bent upon prosecuting their schemes, driven equally on by hope and despair; that, as for himself, being not of an enterprising spirit, he was content to go on in the old forms, to live in the house his ancestors had built, and act as they did, in every part of life, without innovation; that some few other persons of quality and gentry had done the same, but were looked on with an eye of contempt and ill-will, as enemies to art, ignorant, and ill commonwealth's men, preferring their own ease and sloth before the general improvement of their country.

His lordship added that he would not, by any further particulars, prevent the pleasure I should certainly take in viewing the grand academy, whither he was resolved I should go. He only desired me to observe a ruined building, upon the side of a mountain about three miles distant, of which he gave me this account: that he had a very convenient mill within half a mile of his house, turned by a current from a large river, and sufficient for his own family, as well as a great number of his tenants; that, about seven years ago, a club of those projectors came to him with proposals to destroy this mill, and build another on the side of that mountain, on the long ridge whereof a long canal must be cut, for a repository of water, to be conveyed up by pipes and engines to supply the mill; because the wind and air upon a height agitated the water, and thereby made it fitter for motion; and because the water, descending down a declivity, would turn the mill with half the current of a river, whose course is more upon a level. He said that, being then not very well with the court, and pressed by many of his friends, he complied with the proposal, and, after employing a hundred men for two years, the work miscarried, the projectors went off, laying the blame entirely upon him, railing at him ever since, and putting others upon the same experiment, with equal assurance of success, as well as equal disappointment.

In a few days we came back to town; and his excellency, considering the bad character he had in the academy would not go with me himself, but recommended me to a friend of his to bear me company thither. My lord was pleased to represent me as a great admirer of projects, and a person of much curiosity and easy belief—which, indeed, was not without truth, for I had myself been a sort of projector in my younger days.

This academy is not an entire single building, but a continuation of several houses on both sides of a street, which, growing waste, was purchased and applied to that use.

I was received very kindly by the warden, and went for many days in the academy. Every room has in it one or more projectors; and I believe I could not be in fewer than five hundred rooms.

The first man I saw was of a very meagre aspect, with sooty hands and face, his hair and beard long, ragged, and singed in several places. His clothes, shirt, and skin were all of the same color. He had been eight years upon a project for extracting sunbeams out of cucumbers, which were to be put in vials hermetically sealed, and let out to warm the air in raw, inclement summers. He told me he did not doubt that in eight years more he should be able to supply the governor's gardens with sunshine at a reasonable rate; but he complained that his stock was low, and entreated me to give him something as an encouragement to ingenuity, especially since this had been a very dear year for cucumbers. I made him a small present, for my lord had furnished me with money on purpose, because he knew their practice of begging from all who go to see them.

I saw another at work to calcine ice into gunpowder, who likewise showed me a treatise he had written concerning the malleability of fire, which he intended to publish.

There was a most ingenious architect, who had contrived a new method for building houses, by beginning at the roof and working downward to the foundation, which he justified to me by the like practice of those two prudent insects, the bee and the spider.

There was a man born blind, who had several apprentices in his own condition. Their employment was to mix colors for painters, which their master taught them to distinguish by feeling and smelling. It was indeed my misfortune to find them at that time not very perfect in their lessons, and the professor himself happened to be generally mistaken. This artist is much encouraged and esteemed by the whole fraternity.

In another apartment I was highly pleased with a projector who had found a device for ploughing the ground with hogs, to save the charges of ploughs, cattle, and labor. The method is this: in an acre of ground you bury, at six inches' distance and eight deep, a quantity of acorns, dates, chestnuts, and other mast or vegetables whereof these animals are fondest; then you drive six hundred of them into the field, where, in a few days, they will root up the whole ground in search of their feed, and make it fit for sowing, at the same time manuring it with their dung. It is true, upon experiment, they found the charge and trouble very great, and they had little or no crop. However, it is not doubted that this invention may be capable of great improvement.

I went into another room, where the walls and ceiling were all hung round with cobwebs, except a narrow passage for the artist to go in and out. At my entrance he called aloud to me not to disturb his webs. He lamented the fatal mistake the world had been so long in of using silkworms while we had such plenty of domestic insects who infinitely excelled the former, because they understood how to weave as well as spin. And he proposed further that, by employing spiders, the charge of dyeing silks should be wholly saved, whereof I was fully convinced when he showed me a vast number of flies most beautifully colored, wherewith he fed his spiders, assuring us that the webs would take a tincture from them; and as he had them of all hues, he hoped to fit everybody's fancy, as soon as he could find proper food for the flies, of certain gums, oils, and other glutinous matter, to give a strength and consistence to the threads.

There was an astronomer who had undertaken to place a sun-dial upon the great weathercock on the town-house, by adjusting the annual and diurnal motions of the earth and sun so as to answer and coincide with all accidental turnings of the wind.

I visited many other apartments, but shall not trouble my reader with all the curiosities I observed, being studious of brevity.

I had hitherto seen only one side of the academy, the other being appropriated to the advancers of speculative learning, of whom I shall say something when I have mentioned one illustrious person more, who is called among them the "Universal Artist." He told us he had been thirty years employing his thoughts for the improvement of human life. He had two large rooms full of wonderful curiosities, and fifty men at work. Some were condensing air into a dry, tangible substance, by extracting the nitre and letting the aqueous or fluid particles percolate; others softening marble for pillows and pin-cushions; other petrifying the hoofs of a living horse, to preserve them from foundering. The artist himself was at that time busy upon two great designs: the first, to sow land with chaff, wherein he affirmed the true seminal virtue to be contained, as he demonstrated by several experiments, which I was not skillful enough to comprehend. The other was, by a certain composition of gums, minerals, and vegetables, outwardly applied, to prevent the growth of wool upon two young lambs; and he hope, in a reasonable time, to propagate the breed of naked sheep all over the kingdom.

We crossed a walk to the other part of the academy, where, as I have already said, the projectors in speculative learning resided.

The first professor I saw was in a very large room, with forty pupils about him. After salutation, observing me to look earnestly upon a frame, which took up the greatest part of both the length and breadth of the room, he said perhaps I might wonder to see him employed in a project for improving speculative knowledge, by practical and mechanical operations. But the world would soon be sensible of its usefulness; and he flattered himself that a more noble, exalted thought never sprang in any other man's head. Everyone knew how laborious the usual method is of attaining to arts and sciences; whereas, by his contrivance, the most ignorant person, at a reasonable charge, and with a little bodily labor, might write books in philosophy, poetry, politics, laws, mathematics, and theology, without the least assistance from genius or study. He then led me to the frame, about the sides whereof all his pupils stood in ranks. It was twenty feet square, placed in the middle of the room. The superficies were composed of several bits of wood, about the bigness of a die, but some larger than others. They were all linked together by slender wires. These bits of wood were covered, on every square, with paper pasted on them; and on these papers were written all the words of their language, in their several moods, tenses, and declensions, but without any order. The professor then desired me to observe, for he was going to set his engine at work. The pupils, at his command, took each of them hold of an iron handle, whereof there were forty fixed round the edges of the frame; and giving them a sudden turn, the whole disposition of the words was entirely changed. He then commanded six-and-thirty of the lads to read the several lines softly, as they appeared upon the frame; and where they found three or four words together that might shake part of a sentence, they dictated to the four remaining boys, who were scribes. This work was repeated three or four times; and at every turn the engine was so contrived that the words shifted into new places, as the square bits of wood moved upside down.

Six hours a day the young students were employed in this labor; and the professor showed me several volumes in large folio already collected of broken sentences, which he intended to piece together, and out of those rich materials to give the world a complete body of all arts and sciences; which, however, might be still improved and much expedited if the public would raise a fund for making and employing five hundred such frames in Lagado, and oblige the managers to contribute in common their several collections.

He assured me that the invention had employed all his thoughts from his youth; that he had emptied the whole vocabulary into his frame, and made the strictest computation of the general proportion there is in books between the number of particles, nouns, and verbs, and other parts of speech.

I made my humblest acknowledgment to this illustrious person for his great communicativeness; and promised, if ever I had the good-fortune to return to my native country, that I would do him justice, as the sole inventor of this wonderful machine; the form and contrivance of which I desired leave to delineate on paper. I told him, although it was the custom of our learned in Europe to steal inventions from each other, who had thereby at least this advantage, that it became a controversy which was the right owner, yet I would take such caution that he should have the honor entire, without a rival.

We next went to the school of languages, where three professors sat in consultation upon improving that of their own country.

The first project was to shorten discourse, by cutting polysyllables into one, and leaving out verbs and participles; because in reality all things imaginable are but nouns.

The other project was a scheme for entirely abolishing all words whatsoever; and this was urged as a great advantage in point of health as well as brevity. For it is plain that every word we speak is, in some degree, a diminution of our lungs by corrosion, and consequently contributes to the shortening of our lives. An expedient was therefore offered, that since words are only names for things, it would be more convenient for all men to carry about them such things as were necessary to express a particular business they are to discourse on. And this invention would certainly have taken place, to the great ease as well as the health of the subject, if the women, in conjunction with the vulgar and illiterate, had not threatened to raise a rebellion unless they might be allowed the liberty to speak with their tongues, after the manner of their forefathers; such constant, irreconcilable enemies to science are the common people. However, many of the most learned and wise adhere to the new scheme of expressing themselves by things, which has only this inconvenience attending it, that if a man's business be very great, and of various kinds, he must be obliged, in proportion, to carry a greater bundle of things upon his back, unless he can afford one or two strong servants to attend him. I have often beheld two of these sages almost sinking under the weight of their packs, like peddlers among us; who, when they met in the street, would lay down their loads, open their packs, hold conversation for an hour, and then put up their implements, help each other to resume their burdens, and take their leave.

But for short conversations a man may carry implements in his pockets, and under his arms, enough to supply him; and in his house he cannot be at a loss. Therefore the room where company meet who practice this art is full of all things, ready at hand, requisite to furnish matter for this kind of artificial converse.

Another great advantage proposed by this invention was that it would serve as a universal language, to be understood in all civilized nations, whose goods and utensils are generally of the same kind, or nearly resembling, so that their uses might easily be comprehended. And thus ambassadors would be qualified to treat with foreign princes or ministers of state, to whose tongues they were utter strangers.

I was at the mathematical school, where the master taught his pupils after a method scarcely imaginable to us in Europe. The proposition and demonstration were fairly written on a thin wafer, with ink composed of a cephalic tincture. This the student was to swallow upon a fasting stomach, and for three days following eat nothing but bread and water. As the wafer digested the tincture mounted to his brain, bearing the proposition along with it. But the success has not hitherto been answerable, partly by some error in the quantum or composition, and partly by the perverseness of the lads, to whom this bolus is so nauseous that they generally steal aside and discharge it upward before it can operate; neither have they been yet persuaded to use so long an abstinence as the prescription requires.

QUESTIONS

1 Swift's *Gulliver's Travels* is a satire. What satiric devices does Swift use in these selections and how effective is his use of them?

2 The idea of the Great Chain of Being—that man occupies a specific place in the scheme of things—was widely believed during Swift's lifetime. Where and how is this idea contained in these selections?

3 A recurrent theme in both religion and literature is that too much learning corrupts. This can be seen in much of Swift, not only in his description of scientists, but in his statement that tradesmen were "the only people from whom I could ever receive a reasonable answer." How valid is this belief? Are societies purer if they are primitive? Does a highly advanced society necessarily become degenerate? How have science-fiction writers usually answered these questions?

4 Swift's opinion of scientists is low, to say the least. It might also

be called anti-intellectual. How much merit is there in his opinions? Are these sentiments prevalent today? If not, how might you explain the change?

5 Changes, innovations, and new ideas that seem impractical, dangerous, unrealistic, or crazy when first introduced sometimes turn out to be practical and even indispensable. In view of this, might Swift himself not be a danger, a man who could ignorantly stifle imagination or creativity? Comment.

6 Is Swift suggesting that all science is bad? What kind of controls, external or internal, do you suppose he would recommend for scientists? Can you think of scientific projects of the past that should have been subject to more control? Any that should have been subject to less? Do you think Swift believes that man is capable of exercising the right kinds of constraint on himself?

THE MACHINE STOPS

E. M. Forster

Part I: The Air-Ship

Imagine, if you can, a small room, hexagonal in shape, like the cell of a bee. It is lighted neither by window nor by lamp, yet it is filled with a soft radiance. There are no apertures for ventilation, yet the air is fresh. There are no musical instruments, and yet, at the moment that my meditation opens, this room is throbbing with melodious sounds. An arm-chair is in the center, by its side a reading-desk—that is all the furniture. And in the arm-chair there sits a swaddled lump of flesh—a woman, about five feet high, with a face as white as a fungus. It is to her that the little room belongs.

An electric bell rang.

The woman touched a switch and the music was silent.

"I suppose I must see who it is," she thought, and set her chair in motion. The chair, like the music, was worked by machinery, and it rolled her to the other side of the room, where the bell still rang importunately.

"Who is it?" she called. Her voice was irritable, for she had been interrupted often since the music began. She knew several thousand people; in certain directions human intercourse had advanced enormously.

But when she listened into the receiver, her white face wrinkled into smiles, and she said:

"Very well. Let us talk, I will isolate myself, I do not expect anything important will happen for the next five minutes—for I can give you fully five minutes, Kuno. Then I must deliver my lecture on 'Music during the Australian Period.' "

She touched the isolation knob, so that no one else could speak to her. Then she touched the lighting apparatus, and the little room was plunged into darkness.

"Be quick!" she called, her irritation returning. "Be quick, Kuno; here I am in the dark wasting my time."

But it was fully fifteen seconds before the round plate that she held in her hands began to glow. A faint blue light shot across it, darkening to purple, and presently she could see the image of her son, who lived on the other side of the earth, and he could see her.

"Kuno, how slow you are."

He smiled gravely.

"I really believe you enjoy dawdling."

"I have called you before, Mother, but you were always busy or isolated. I have something particular to say."

"What it is, dearest boy? Be quick. Why could you not send it by pneumatic post?"

"Because I prefer saying such a thing. I want—"

"Well?"

"I want you to come and see me."

Vashti watched his face in the blue plate.

"But I can see you!" she exclaimed. "What more do you want?"

"I want to see you not through the Machine," said Kuno. "I want to speak to you not through the wearisome Machine."

"Oh, hush!" said his mother, vaguely shocked. "You mustn't say anything against the Machine."

"Why not?"

"One mustn't."

"You talk as if a god had made the Machine," cried the other. "I believe that you pray to it when you are unhappy. Men made it, do not forget that. Great men, but men. The Machine is much, but it is not everything. I see something like you in this plate, but I do not see you. I hear something like you through this telephone, but I do not hear you. That is why I want you to come. Come and stop with me. Pay me a visit, so that we can meet face to face, and talk about the hopes that are in my mind."

She replied that she could scarcely spare the time for a visit.

"The air-ship barely takes two days to fly between me and you."

"I dislike air-ships."

"Why?"

"I dislike seeing the horrible brown earth, and the sea, and the stars when it is dark. I get no ideas in an air-ship."

"I do not get them anywhere else."

"What kind of ideas can the air give you?"

He paused for an instant.

"Do you know four big stars that form an oblong, and three stars close together in the middle of the oblong, and hanging from these stars, three other stars?"

"No, I do not. I dislike the stars. But did they give you an idea? How interesting: tell me."

"I had an idea that they were like a man."

"I do not understand."

"The four big stars are the man's shoulders and his knees. The three stars in the middle are his belts that men wore once, and the three stars hanging are like a sword."

"A sword?"

"Men carried swords about with them, to kill animals and other men."

"It does not strike me as a very good idea, but it is certainly original. When did it come to you first?"

"In the air-ship——" He broke off, and she fancied that he looked sad. She could not be sure, for the Machine did not transmit nuances of expression. It only gave a general idea of people—an idea that was good enough for all practical purposes, Vashti thought. The imponderable bloom, declared by a discredited philosophy to be the actual essence of intercourse, was rightly ignored by the Machine, just as the imponderable bloom of the grape was ignored by the manufacturers of artificial fruit. Something "good enough" had long since been accepted by our race.

"The truth is," he continued, "that I want to see these stars again. They are curious stars. I want to see them not from the air-ship, but from the surface of the earth, as our ancestors did, thousands of years ago. I want to visit the surface of the earth."

She was shocked again.

"Mother you must come, if only to explain to me what is the harm of visiting the surface of the earth."

"No harm," she replied, controlling herself. "But no advantage. The surface of the earth is only dust and mud, no life remains on it, and you would need a respirator, or the cold of the outer air would kill you. One dies immediately in the outer air."

"I know; of course I shall take all precautions."

"And besides—"

"Well?"

She considered, and chose her words with care. Her son had a queer temper, and she wished to dissuade him from the expedition.

"It is contrary to the spirit of the age," she asserted.

"Do you mean by that, contrary to the Machine?"

"In a sense, but—"

His image in the blue plate faded.

"Kuno!"

He had isolated himself.

For a moment Vashti felt lonely.

Then she generated the light, and the sight of her room, flooded with radiance and studded with electric buttons and switches everywhere—buttons to call for food, for music, for clothing. There was the hotbath button, by pressure of which a basin of (imitation) marble rose out of the floor, filled to the brim with a warm deodorized liquid. There was the cold-bath button. There was the button that produced literature. And there were of course the buttons by which she communicated with her friends. The room, though it contained nothing, was in touch with all that she cared for in the world.

Vashti's next move was to turn off the isolation-switch and all the accumulations of the last three minutes burst upon her. The room was filled with the noise of bells, and speaking-tubes. What was the new food like? Could she recommend it? Had she had any ideas lately? Might one tell her one's own ideas? Would she make an engagement to visit the public nurseries at an early date?—say this day month.

To most of these questions she replied with irritation—a growing quality in that accelerated age. She said that the new food was horrible. That she could not visit the public nurseries through press of engagements. That she had no ideas of her own but had just been told one—that four stars and three in the middle were like a man: she doubted there was much in it. Then she switched off her correspondents, for it was time to deliver her lecture on Australian music.

The clumsy system of public gatherings had been long since abandoned; neither Vashti nor her audience stirred from their rooms. Seated in her armchair she spoke, while they in their armchairs heard her, fairly well, and saw her, fairly well. She opened with a humorous account of music in the pre-Mongolian epoch, and went on to describe the great outburst of song that followed the Chinese conquest. Remote and primeval as were the methods of I-San-So and the Brisbane school, she yet felt (she said) that study of them might repay the musician of today; they had freshness; they had, above all, ideas.

Her lecture, which lasted ten minutes, was well received, and at its conclusion she and many of her audience listened to a lecture on the sea; there were ideas to be got from the sea; the speaker had donned a respirator and visited it lately. Then she fed, talked to many friends, had a bath, talked again, and summoned her bed.

The bed was not to her liking. It was too large, and she had a feeling for a small bed. Complaint was useless, for beds were of the same dimension all over the world, and to have had an alternative size would have involved vast alterations in the Machine. Vashti isolated herself—it was necessary, for neither day nor night existed under the ground—and reviewed all that had happened since she had summoned the bed last. Ideas? Scarcely any. Events —was Kuno's invitation an event?

By her side, on the little reading-desk, was a survival from the ages of litter—one book. This was the Book of the Machine. In it were instructions against every possible contingency. If she was hot or cold or dyspeptic or at loss for a word, she went to the Book, and it told her which button to press. The Central Committee published it. In accordance with a growing habit, it was richly bound.

Sitting up in the bed, she took it reverently in her hands. She glanced round the glowing room as if some one might be watching her. Then, half ashamed, half joyful, she murmured, "O Machine! O Machine!" and raised the volume to her lips. Thrice she kissed it, thrice inclined her head, thrice she felt the delirium of acquiescence. Her ritual performed, she turned to page 1367, which gave the times of the departure of the air-ships from the island in the southern hemisphere, under whose soil she lived, to the island in the northern hemisphere, whereunder lived her son.

She thought, "I have not the time."

She made the room dark and slept; she awoke and made the room light; she ate and exchanged ideas with her friends, and listened to music and attended lectures; she made the room dark and slept. Above her, beneath her, and around her, the Machine hummed eternally; she did not notice the noise, for she had been born with it in her ears. The earth, carrying her, hummed as it sped through silence, turning her now to the invisible sun, now to the invisible stars. She awoke and made the room light.

"Kuno!"

"I will not talk to you," he answered, "until you come."

"Have you been on the surface of the earth since we spoke last?"

His image faded.

Again she consulted the Book. She became very nervous and lay back in her chair palpitating. Think of her as without teeth or hair. Presently she directed the chair to the wall, and pressed an unfamiliar button. The wall swung apart slowly. Through the opening she saw a tunnel that curved slightly, so that its goal was not visible. Should she go to see her son, here was the beginning of the journey.

Of course she knew all about the communication-system. There was nothing mysterious in it. She would summon a car and it would fly with her down the tunnel until it reached the lift that communicated with the air-ship station: the system had been in use for many, many years, long before the universal establishment of the Machine. And of course she had studied the civilization that had immediately preceded her own—the civilization that had mistaken the functions of the system, and had used it for bringing people to things, instead of for bringing things to people. Those funny old days, when men went for change of air instead of changing the air in their rooms! And yet—she was frightened of the tunnel: she had not seen it since her last child was born. It curved—but not quite as brilliant as a lecturer had suggested. Vashti was seized with the terrors of direct experience. She shrank back into the room, and the wall closed up again.

"Kuno," she said, "I cannot come to see you. I am not well."

Immediately an enormous apparatus fell on to her out of the ceiling, a thermometer was automatically inserted between her lips, a stethoscope was automatically laid upon her heart. She lay powerless. Cool pads soothed her forehead. Kuno had telegraphed to her doctor.

So the human passions still blundered up and down in the Machine. Vashti drank the medicine that the doctor projected into her mouth, and the machinery retired into the ceiling. The voice of Kuno was heard asking how she felt.

"Better." Then with irritation: "But why do you not come to me instead?"

"Because I cannot leave this place."

"Why?"

"Because, any moment, something tremendous may happen."

"Have you been on the surface of the earth yet?"

"Not yet."

"Then what is it?"

"I will not tell you through the Machine."

She resumed her life.

But she thought of Kuno as a baby, his birth, his removal to the public nurseries, her one visit to him there, his visits to her—visits which stopped when the Machine had assigned him a room on the other side of the earth. "Parents, duties of," said the Book of the Machine, "cease at the moment of birth. P. 422327483." True, but there was something special about Kuno—indeed there had been something special about all her children—and, after all, she must brave the journey if he desired it. And "something tremendous might happen." What did he mean? The nonsense of a youthful man, no doubt, but she must go. Again she pressed the unfamiliar button, again the wall swung back, and she saw the tunnel that curved out of sight. Clasping the Book, she rose, tottered onto the platform, and summoned the car. Her room closed behind her: the journey to the northern hemisphere had begun.

Of course it was perfectly easy. The car approached and in it she found armchairs exactly like her own. When she signaled, it stopped, and she tottered into the lift. One other passenger was in the lift, the first fellow creature she had seen face to face for months. Few traveled in these days, for, thanks to the advance of science, the earth was exactly alike all over. Rapid intercourse, from which the previous civilization had hoped so much, had ended by defeating itself. What was the good of going to Pekin when it was just like Shrewsbury? Why return to Shrewsbury when it would be just like Pekin? Men seldom moved their bodies; all unrest was concentrated in the soul.

The air-ship service was a relic from the former age. It was kept up, because it was easier to keep it up than to stop it or to diminish it, but it now far exceeded the wants of the population. Vessel after vessel would rise from the vomitories of Rye or of Christchurch (I use the antique names), would sail into the crowded sky, and would draw up at the wharves of the south— empty. So nicely adjusted was the system, so independent of meteorology, that the sky, whether calm or cloudy, resembled a vast kaleidoscope whereon the same patterns periodically recurred. The ship on which Vashti sailed started now at sunset, now at dawn. But always, as it passed above Rheims, it would neighbor the ship that served between Helsingfors and the Brazils, and every third time it surmounted the Alps, the fleet of Palermo would cross its track behind. Night and day, wind and storm, tide and earthquake, impeded man no longer. He had harnessed Leviathan. All the old literature, with its praise of Nature, and its fear of Nature, rang false as the prattle of a child.

Yet, as Vashti saw the vast flank of the ship, stained with exposure to the outer air, her horror of direct experience returned. It was not quite like the air-ship in the cinematophote. For one thing it smelt—not strongly or unpleasantly, but it did smell, and with her eyes shut she would have known that a new thing was close to her. Then she had to walk to it from the lift, had to submit to glances from the other passengers. The man in front dropped his Book—no great matter, but it disquieted them all. In the rooms, if the Book was dropped, the floor raised it mechanically, but the gangway to the air-ship was not so prepared, and the sacred volume lay motionless. They stopped—the thing was unforeseen—and the man, instead of picking up his property, felt the muscles of his arm to see how they had failed him. Then

someone actually said with direct utterance: "We shall be late"—
and they trooped on board, Vashti treading on the pages as she
did so.

Inside, her anxiety increased. The arrangements were old-
fashioned and rough. There was even a female attendant, to whom
she would have to announce her wants during the voyage. Of
course a revolving platform ran the length of the boat, but she
was expected to walk from it to her cabin. Some cabins were better
than others, and she did not get the best. She thought the attendant
had been unfair, and spasms of rage shook her. The glass valves
had closed, she could not go back. She saw, at the end of the
vestibule, the lift in which she had ascended going quietly up and
down, empty. Beneath those corridors of shining tiles were rooms,
tier below tier, reaching far into the earth, and in each room there
sat a human being, eating, or sleeping, or producing ideas. And
buried deep in the hive was her own room. Vashti was afraid.

"O Machine! O Machine!" she murmured, and caressed her
Book, and was comforted.

Then the sides of the vestibule seemed to melt together, as
do the passages that we see in dreams, the life vanished, the Book
that had been dropped slid to the left and vanished, polished tiles
rushed by like a stream of water, there was a slight jar, and the
air-ship, issuing from its tunnel, soared above the waters of a
tropical ocean.

It was night. For a moment she saw the coast of Sumatra
edged by the phosphorescence of waves, and crowned by light-
houses, still sending forth their disregarded beams. They also
vanished, and only the stars distracted her. They were not motionless, but swayed to and fro above her head, thronging out of one
sky-light into another, as if the universe and not the air-ship was
careening. And, as often happens on clear nights, they seemed
now to be in perspective, now on a plane; now piled tier beyond
tier into the infinite heavens, now concealing infinity, a roof limit-
ing for ever the visions of men. In either case they seemed intolerable. "Are we to travel in the dark?" called the passengers angrily,
and the attendant, who had been careless, generated the light, and
pulled down the blinds of pliable metal. When the air-ships had
been built, the desire to look direct at things still lingered in the

world. Hence the extraordinary number of skylights and windows, and the proportionate discomfort to those who were civilized and refined. Even in Vashti's cabin one star peeped through a flaw in the blind, and after a few hours' uneasy slumber, she was disturbed by an unfamiliar glow, which was the dawn.

Quick as the ship had sped westwards, the earth had rolled eastwards quicker still, and had dragged back Vashti and her companions towards the sun. Science could prolong the night, but only for a little, and those high hopes of neutralizing the earth's diurnal revolution had passed, together with hopes that were possibly higher. To "keep pace with the sun," or even to outstrip it, had been the aim of the civilization preceding this. Racing aeroplanes had been built for the purpose, capable of enormous speed, and steered by the greatest intellects of the epoch. Round the globe they went, round and round, westward, westward, round and round, amidst humanity's applause. In vain. The globe went eastward quicker still, horrible accidents occurred, and the Committee of the Machine, at the time rising into prominence, declared the pursuit illegal, unmechanical, and punishable by Homelessness.

Of Homelessness more will be said later.

Doubtless the Committee was right. Yet the attempt to "defeat the sun" aroused the last common interest that our race experienced about the heavenly bodies, or indeed about anything. It was the last time that men were compacted by thinking of a power outside the world. The sun had conquered, yet it was the end of his spiritual dominion. Dawn, midday, twilight, the zodiacal path, touched neither men's lives nor their hearts, and science retreated into the ground, to concentrate herself upon problems that she was certain of solving.

So when Vashti found her cabin invaded by a rosy finger of light, she was annoyed, and tried to adjust the blind. But the blind flew up altogether, and she saw through the skylight small pink clouds, swaying against a background of blue, and as the sun crept higher, its radiance entered direct, brimming down the wall, like a golden sea. It rose and fell with the air-ship's motion, just as waves rise and fall, but it advanced steadily as a tide advances. Unless she was careful, it would strike her face. A spasm of horror shook her and she rang for the attendant. The attendant too was horrified, but she could do nothing; it was not her place to mend the blind. She could only suggest that the lady should change her cabin, which she accordingly prepared to do.

People were almost exactly alike all over the world, but the attendant of the air-ship, perhaps owing to her exceptional duties, had grown a little out of the common. She had often to address passengers with direct speech, and this had given her a certain roughness and originality of manner. When Vashti swerved away from the sunbeams with a cry, she behaved barbarically—she put out her hand to steady her.

"How dare you!" exclaimed the passenger. "You forget yourself!"

The woman was confused, and apologized for not having let her fall. People never touched one another. The custom had become obsolete, owing to the Machine.

"Where are we now?" asked Vashti haughtily.

"We are over Asia," said the attendant, anxious to be polite. "Asia?"

"You must excuse my common way of speaking. I have got into the habit of calling places over which I pass by their unmechanical names."

"Oh, I remember Asia. The Mongols came from it."

"Beneath us, in the open air, stood a city that was once called Simla."

"Have you ever heard of the Mongols and of the Brisbane school?"

"No."

"Brisbane also stood in the open air."

"Those mountains to the right—let me show you them." She pushed back a metal blind. The main chain of the Himalayas was revealed. "They were once called the Roof of the World, those mountains."

"What a foolish name!"

"You must remember that, before the dawn of civilization, they seemed to be an impenetrable wall that touched the stars. It was supposed that no one but the gods could exist above their summits. How we have advanced, thanks to the Machine!"

"How we have advanced, thanks to the Machine!" said Vashti.

"How we have advanced, thanks to the Machine!" echoed the passenger who had dropped his Book the night before, and who was standing in the passage.

"And that white stuff in the cracks?—what is it?"

"I have forgotten its name."

"Cover the window, please. These mountains give me no ideas."

The northern aspect of the Himalayas was in deep shadow: on the Indian slope the sun had just prevailed. The forests had been destroyed during the literature epoch for the purpose of making newspaper-pulp, but the snows were awakening to their morning glory, and clouds still hung on the breasts of Kinchinjunga. In the plain were seen the ruins of cities, with diminished rivers creeping by their walls, and by the sides of these were sometimes the signs of vomitories, marking the cities of today. Over the whole prospect air-ships rushed, crossing and intercrossing with incredible aplomb, and rising nonchalantly when they desired to escape the perturbations of the lower atmosphere and to traverse the Roof of the World.

"We have indeed advanced, thanks to the Machine," repeated the attendant, and hid the Himalayas behind a metal blind.

The day dragged wearily forward. The passengers sat each in his cabin, avoiding one another with an almost physical repulsion and longing to be once more under the surface of the earth. There were eight or ten of them, mostly young males, sent out from the public nurseries to inhabit the rooms of those who had died in various parts of the earth. The man who had dropped his Book was on the homeward journey. He had been sent to Sumatra for the purpose of propagating the race. Vashti alone was traveling by her private will.

At midday she took a second glance at the earth. The airship was crossing another range of mountains, but she could see little, owing to clouds. Masses of black rock hovered below her, and merged indistinctly into gray. Their shapes were fantastic; one of them resembled a prostrate man.

"No ideas here," murmured Vashti, and hid the Caucasus behind a metal blind.

In the evening she looked again. They were crossing a golden sea, in which lay many small islands and one peninsula.

She repeated, "No ideas here," and hid Greece behind a metal blind.

Part II: The Mending Apparatus

By a vestibule, by a lift, by a tubular railway, by a platform, by a sliding door—by reversing all the steps of her departure did Vashti arrive at her son's room, which exactly resembled her own. She might well declare that the visit was superfluous. The buttons, the knobs, the reading-desk with the Book, the temperature, the atmosphere, the illumination—all were exactly the same. And if Kuno himself, flesh of her flesh, stood close beside her at last, what profit was there in that? She was too well-bred to shake him by the hand.

Averting her eyes, she spoke as follows:

"Here I am. I have had the most terrible journey and greatly retarded the development of my soul. It is not worth it, Kuno, it is not worth it. My time is too precious. The sunlight almost touched me, and I have met with the rudest people. I can only stop a few minutes. Say what you want to say, and then I must return."

"I have been threatened with Homelessness, and I could not tell you such a thing through the Machine."

Homelessness means death. The victim is exposed to the air, which kills him.

"I have been outside since I spoke to you last. The tremendous thing has happened, and they have discovered me."

"But why shouldn't you go outside!" she exclaimed. "It is perfectly legal, perfectly mechanical, to visit the surface of the earth. I have lately been to a lecture on the sea; there is no objection to that; one simply summons a respirator and gets an Egression-permit. It is not the kind of thing that spiritually minded people do, and I begged you not to do it, but there is no legal objection to it."

"I did not get an Egression-permit."

"Then how did you get out?"

"I found a way of my own."

The phrase conveyed no meaning to her, and he had to repeat it.

"A way of your own?" she whispered. "But that would be wrong."

"Why?"

The question shocked her beyond measure.

"You are beginning to worship the Machine," he said coldly. "You think it irreligious of me to have found out a way of my own. It was just what the Committee thought, when they threatened me with Homelessness."

At this she grew angry. "I worship nothing!" she cried. "I am most advanced. I don't think you irreligious, for there is no such thing as religion left. All the fear and the superstition that existed once have been destroyed by the Machine. I only meant that to find out a way of your own was—Besides, there is no new way out."

"So it is always supposed."

"Except through the vomitories, for which one must have an Egression-permit, it is impossible to get out. The Book says so."

"Well, the Book's wrong, for I have been out on my feet."

For Kuno was possessed of a certain physical strength.

By these days it was a demerit to be muscular. Each infant was examined at birth, and all who promised undue strength were destroyed. Humanitarians may protest, but it would have been no true kindness to let an athlete live; he would never have been happy in that state of life to which the Machine had called him; he would have yearned for trees to climb, rivers to bathe in, meadows and hills against which he might measure his body. Man must be adapted to his surroundings, must he not? In the dawn of the world our weakly must be exposed on Mount Taygetus, in its twilight our strong will suffer Euthanasia, that the Machine may progress, that the Machine may progress, that the Machine may progress eternally.

"You know that we have lost the sense of space. We say

'space is annihilated,' but we have annihilated not space, but the sense thereof. We have lost a part of ourselves. I determined to recover it, and I began by walking up and down the platform of the railway outside my room. Up and down, until I was tired, and so did recapture the meaning of 'near' and 'far.' 'Near' is a place to which I can get quickly on my feet, not a place to which the train or the air-ship will take me quickly. 'Far' is a place to which I cannot get quickly on my feet; the vomitory is 'far,' though I could be there in thirty-eight seconds by summoning the train. Man is the measure. That was my first lesson. Man's feet are the measure for distance, his hands are the measure for ownership, his body is the measure for all that is lovable and desirable and strong. Then I went further: it was then that I called to you for the first time, and you would not come.

"This city, as you know, is built deep beneath the surface of the earth, with only the vomitories protruding. Having paced the platform outside my own room, I took the lift to the next platform and paced that also, and so with each in turn, until I came to the topmost, above which begins the earth. All the platforms were exactly alike, and all that I gained by visiting them was to develop my sense of space and my muscles. I think I should have been content with this—it is not a little thing—but as I walked and brooded, it occurred to me that our cities had been built in the days when men still breathed the outer air and that there had been ventilation shafts for the workmen. I could think of nothing but these ventilation shafts. Had they been destroyed by all the food-tubes and medicine-tubes and music-tubes that the Machine had evolved lately? Or did traces of them remain? One thing was certain. If I came upon them anywhere, it would be in the railway-tunnels of the topmost story. Everywhere else, all space was accounted for.

"I am telling my story quickly, but don't think that I was not a coward or that your answers never depressed me. It is not the proper thing, it is not mechanical, it is not decent to walk along a railway-tunnel. I did not fear that I might tread upon a live rail and be killed. I feared something far more intangible—doing what was not contemplated by the Machine. Then I said to myself, 'Man is the measure,' and I went, and after many visits I found an opening.

"The tunnels, of course, were lighted. Everything is light, artificial light; darkness is the exception. So when I saw a black gap in the tiles, I knew that it was an exception, and rejoiced. I put in my arm—I could put in no more at first—and waved it round and round in ecstasy. I loosened another tile, and put in my head, and shouted into the darkness: 'I am coming, I shall do it yet,' and my voice reverberated down endless passages. I seemed to hear the spirits of those dead workmen who had returned each evening to the starlight and to their wives, and all the generations who had lived in the open air called back to me, 'You will do it yet, you are coming.' "

He paused, and, absurd as he was, his last words moved her. For Kuno had lately asked to be a father, and his request had been refused by the Committee. His was not a type that the Machine desired to hand on.

"Then a train passed. It brushed by me, but I thrust my head and arms into the hole. I had done enough for one day, so I crawled back to the platform, went down in the lift, and summoned my bed. Ah, what dreams! And again I called you, and again you refused."

She shook her head and said:

"Don't. Don't talk of these terrible things. You make me miserable. You are throwing civilization away."

"But I had got back the sense of space and a man cannot rest then. I determined to get in at the hole and climb the shaft. And so I exercised my arms. Day after day I went through ridiculous movements, until my flesh ached, and I could hang by my hands and hold the pillow of my bed outstretched for many minutes. Then I summoned a respirator, and started.

"It was easy at first. The mortar had somehow rotted, and I soon pushed some more tiles in, and clambered after them into the darkness, and the spirits of the dead comforted me. I don't know what I mean by that. I just say what I felt. I felt, for the first time, that a protest had been lodged against corruption, and that even as the dead were comforting me, so I was comforting the unborn. I felt that humanity existed, and that it existed without clothes. How can I possibly explain this? It was naked, humanity seemed naked, and all these tubes and buttons and machineries neither came into the world with us, nor will they follow us out, nor do they matter supremely while we are here. Had I been strong, I would have torn off every garment I had, and gone out into the outer air unswaddled. But this is not for me, nor perhaps for my generation. I climbed with my respirator and my hygienic clothes and my dietetic tabloids! Better thus than not at all.

"There was a ladder, made of some primeval metal. The light from the railway fell upon its lowest rungs, and I saw that it led straight upwards out of the rubble at the bottom of the shaft. Perhaps our ancestors ran up and down it a dozen times daily, in their building. As I climbed, the rough edges cut through my gloves so that my hands bled. The light helped me for a little, and then came darkness and, worse still, silence which pierced my ears like a sword. The Machine hums! Did you know that? Its hum penetrates our blood, and may even guide our thoughts. Who knows! I was getting beyond its power. Then I thought: 'This silence means that I am doing wrong.' But I heard voices in the silence, and again they strengthened me." He laughed. "I had need of them. The next moment I cracked my head against something."

She sighed.

"I had reached one of those pneumatic stoppers that defend us from the outer air. You may have noticed them on the air-ship. Pitch dark, my feet on the rungs of an invisible ladder, my hands cut; I cannot explain how I lived through this part, but the voices still comforted me, and I felt for fastenings. The stopper, I suppose, was about eight feet across. I passed my hand over it as far as I could reach. It was perfectly smooth. I felt it almost to the center. Not quite to the center, for my arm was too short. Then the voice said: 'Jump. It is worth it. There may be a handle in the center, and you may catch hold of it and so come to us your own way. And if there is no handle so that you may fall and are dashed to pieces—it is still worth it; you will still come to us your own way.' So I jumped. There was a handle, and—"

He paused. Tears gathered in his mother's eyes. She knew

that he was fated. If he did not die today he would die tomorrow. There was not room for such a person in the world. And with her pity disgust mingled. She was ashamed at having borne such a son, she who had always been so respectable and so full of ideas. Was he really the little boy to whom she had taught the use of his stops and buttons, and to whom she had given his first lessons in the Book? The very hair that disfigured his lip showed that he was reverting to some savage type. On atavism the Machine can have no mercy.

"There was a handle, and I did catch it. I hung tranced over the darkness and heard the hum of these workings as the last whisper in a dying dream. All the things I had cared about and all the people I had spoken to through tubes appeared infinitely little. Meanwhile the handle revolved. My weight had set something in motion and I spun slowly, and then—

"I cannot describe it. I was lying with my face to the sunshine. Blood poured from my nose and ears and I heard a tremendous roaring. The stopper, with me clinging to it, had simply been blown out of the earth, and the air that we make down here was escaping through the vent into the air above. It burst up like a fountain. I crawled back to it—for the upper air hurts—and, as it were, I took great sips from the edge. My respirator had flown goodness knows where, my clothes were torn. I just lay with my lips close to the hole, and I sipped until the bleeding stopped. You can imagine nothing so curious. This hollow in the grass—I will speak of it in a minute,—the sun shining into it, not brilliantly but through marbled clouds,—the peace, the nonchalance, the sense of space, and, brushing my cheek, the roaring fountain of our artificial air! Soon I spied my respirator, bobbing up and down in the current high above my head, and higher still were many air-ships. But no one ever looks out of air-ships, and in my case they could not have picked me up. There I was, stranded. The sun shone a little way down the shaft, and revealed the topmost rung of the ladder, but it was hopeless trying to reach it. I should either have been tossed up again by the escape, or else have fallen in, and died. I could only lie on the grass, sipping and sipping, and from time to time glancing around me.

"I knew that I was in Wessex, for I had taken care to go to a lecture on the subject before starting. Wessex lies above the room in which we are talking now. It was once an important state. Its kings held all the southern coast from the Andredswald to Cornwall, while the Wansdyke protected them on the north, running over the high ground. The lecturer was only concerned with the rise of Wessex, so I do not know how long it remained an international power, nor would the knowledge have assisted me. To tell the truth I could do nothing but laugh, during this part. There was I, with a pneumatic stopper by my side and a respirator bobbing over my head, imprisoned, all three of us, in a grass-grown hollow that was edged with fern."

Then he grew grave again.

"Lucky for me that it was a hollow. For the air began to fall back into it and to fill it as water fills a bowl. I could crawl about. Presently I stood. I breathed a mixture, in which the air that hurts predominated whenever I tried to climb the sides. This was not so bad. I had not lost my tabloids and remained ridiculously cheerful, and as for the Machine, I forgot about it altogether. My one aim now was to get to the top, where the ferns were, and to view whatever objects lay beyond.

"I rushed the slope. The new air was still too bitter for me and I came rolling back, after a momentary vision of something gray. The sun grew very feeble, and I remembered that he was in Scorpio—I had been to a lecture on that too. If the sun is in Scorpio and you are in Wessex, it means that you must be as quick as you can, or it will get too dark. (This is the first bit of useful information I have ever got from a lecture, and I expect it will be the last.) It made me try frantically to breathe the new air, and to advance as far as I dared out of my pond. The hollow filled so slowly. At times I thought that my fountain played with less vigor. My respirator seemed to dance nearer the earth; the roar was decreasing."

He broke off.

"I don't think this is interesting you. The rest will interest you even less. There are no ideas in it, and I wish that I had not troubled you to come. We are too different, mother."

She told him to continue.

"It was evening before I climbed the bank. The sun had very nearly slipped out of the sky by this time, and I could not get a good view. You, who have just crossed the Roof of the World, will not want to hear an account of the little hills that I saw—low colorless hills. But to me they were living and the turf that covered them was a skin, under which their muscles rippled, and I felt those hills had called with incalculable force to men in the past, and that men had loved them. Now they sleep—perhaps forever. They commune with humanity in dreams. Happy the man, happy the woman, who awakes the hills of Wessex. For though they sleep, they will never die."

His voice rose passionately.

"Cannot you see, cannot all your lecturers see, that it is we who are dying, and that down here the only thing that really lives is the Machine? We created the Machine, to do our will, but we cannot make it do our will now. It has robbed us of the sense of space and of the sense of touch, it has blurred every human relation and narrowed down love to a carnal act, it has paralyzed our bodies and our wills, and now it compels us to worship it. The Machine develops—but not to our goal. We only exist as the blood corpuscles that course through its arteries, and if it could work without us, it would let us die. Oh, I have no remedy—or, at least, only one—to tell men again and again that I have seen the hills of Wessex as Aelfrid saw them when he overthrew the Danes.

"So the sun set. I forgot to mention that a belt of mist lay between my hill and other hills, and that it was the color of pearl."

He broke off for the second time.

"Go on. Nothing that you say can distress me now. I am hardened."

"I had meant to tell you the rest, but I cannot: I know that I cannot: goodby."

Vashti stood irresolute. All her nerves were tingling with his blasphemies. But she was also inquisitive.

"This is unfair," she complained. "You have called me across the world to hear your story, and hear it I will. Tell me—as briefly as possible, for this is a disastrous waste of time—tell me how you returned to civilization."

"Oh—that!" he said, starting. "You would like to hear about civilization. Certainly. Had I got to where my respirator fell down?"

"No—but I understand everything now. You put on your respirator, and managed to walk along the surface of the earth to a vomitory, and there your conduct was reported to the Central Committee."

"By no means."

He passed his hand over his forehead, as if dispelling some strong impression. Then, resuming his narrative, he warmed to it again.

"My respirator fell about sunset. I had mentioned that the fountain seemed feebled, had I not?"

"Yes."

"About sunset, it let the respirator fall. As I said, I had entirely forgotten about the Machine, and I paid no great attention at the time, being occupied with other things. I had my pool of air, into which I could dip when the outer keenness became intolerable, and which would possibly remain for days, provided that no wind sprang up to disperse it. Not until it was too late, did I realize what the stoppage of the escape implied. You see—the gap in the tunnel had been mended; the Mending Apparatus, the Mending Apparatus, was after me.

"One other warning I had, but I neglected it. The sky at night was clearer than it had been in the day, and the moon, which was about half the sky behind the sun, shone into the dell at moments quite brightly. I was in my usual place—on the boundary between the two atmospheres—when I thought I saw something dark move across the bottom on the dell, and vanish into the shaft. In my folly, I ran down. I bent over and listened, and I thought I heard a faint scraping noise in the depths.

"At this—but it was too late—I took alarm. I determined to put on my respirator and to walk right out of the dell. But my respirator had gone. I knew exactly where it had fallen—between the stopper and the aperture—and I could even feel the mark that it had made in the turf. It had gone, and I realized that something evil was at work, and I had better escape to the other air, and, if I must die, die running towards the cloud that had been the color of a pearl. I never started. Out of the shaft—it is too horrible. A worm, a long white worm, had crawled out of the shaft and was gliding over the moonlit grass.

"I screamed. I did everything that I should not have done, I stamped upon the creature instead of flying from it, and it fought. The worm let me run all over the dell, but edged up my leg as I ran. 'Help!' I cried. (That part is too awful. It belongs to the part that you will never know.) 'Help!' I cried. (Why cannot we suffer in silence?) 'Help!' I cried. Then my feet were wound together, I fell, I was dragged away from the dear ferns and the living hills, and past the great metal stopper (I can tell you this part), and I thought it might save me again if I caught hold of the handle. It also was enwrapped, it also. Oh, the whole dell was full of the things. They were searching it in all directions, they were denuding it, and the white snouts of others peeped out of the hole, ready if needed. Everything that could be moved they brought—brushwood, bundles of fern, everything, and down we all went intertwined into hell. The last things that I saw, ere the stopper closed after us, were certain stars, and I felt that a man of my sort lived in the sky. For I did fight, I fought till the very end, and it was only my head hitting against the ladder that quieted me. I woke up in this room. The worms had vanished. I was surrounded by artificial air, artificial light, artificial peace, and my friends were calling to me down speaking-tubes to know whether I had come across any new ideas lately."

Here his story ended. Discussion of it was impossible, and Vashti turned to go.

"It will end in Homelessness," she said quietly.

"I wish it would," retorted Kuno.

"The Machine has been most merciful."

"I prefer the mercy of God."

"By that superstitious phrase, do you mean that you could live in the outer air?"

"Yes."

"Have you ever seen, round the vomitories, the bones of those who were extruded after the Great Rebellion?"

"Yes."

"They were left where they perished for our edification. A

few crawled away, but they perished, too—who can doubt it? And so with the Homeless of our own day. The surface of the earth supports life no longer."

"Indeed."

"Ferns and a little grass may survive, but all higher forms have perished. Has any air-ship detected them?"

"No."

"Has any lecturer dealt with them?"

"No."

"Then why this obstinacy?"

"Because I have seen them," he exploded.

"Seen *what?*"

"Because I have seen her in the twilight—because she came to my help when I called—because she, too, was entangled by the worms, and, luckier than I, was killed by one of them piercing her throat."

He was mad. Vashti departed, nor, in the troubles that followed, did she ever see his face again.

Part III: The Homeless

During the years that followed Kuno's escapade, two important developments took place in the Machine. On the surface they were revolutionary, but in either case men's minds had been prepared beforehand, and they did but express tendencies that were latent already.

The first of these was the abolition of respirators.

Advanced thinkers, like Vashti, had always held it foolish to visit the surface of the earth. Air-ships might be necessary, but what was the good of going out for mere curiosity and crawling along for a mile or two in a terrestrial motor? The habit was vulgar and perhaps faintly improper; it was unproductive of ideas, and had no connection with the habits that really mattered. So respirators were abolished, and with them, of course, the terrestrial motors, and except for a few lecturers, who complained that they were debarred access to their subject-matter, the development was accepted quietly. Those who still wanted to know what the earth was like had after all only to listen to some gramophone, or to look into some cinematophote. And even the lecturers acquiesced when they found that a lecture on the sea was none the less stimulating when compiled out of other lectures that had already been delivered on the same subject. "Beware of first-hand ideas!" exclaimed one of the most advanced of them. "First-hand ideas do not really exist. They are but the physical impressions produced by love and fear, and on this gross foundation who could erect a philosophy? Let your ideas be second-hand, and if possible tenth-hand, for then they will be far removed from that disturbing element—direct observation. Do not learn anything about this subject of mine—the French Revolution. Learn instead what I think that Enicharmon thought Urizen thought Gutch thought Ho-Young thought Chi-Bo-Sing thought Lafcadio Hearn thought Carlyle thought Mirabeau said about the French Revolution. Through the medium of these eight great minds, the blood that was shed at Paris and the windows that were broken at Versailles will be clarified to an idea which you may employ most profitably in your daily lives. But be sure that the intermediates are many and varied, for in history one authority exists to counteract another. Urizen must counteract the skepticism of Ho-Young and Enicharmon, I must myself counteract the impetuosity of Gutch. You who listen to me are in a better position to judge about the French Revolution than I am. Your descendants will be even in a better position than you, for they will learn what you think I think, and yet another intermediate will be added to the chain. And in time"—his voice rose—"there will come a generation that has got beyond facts, beyond impressions, a generation absolutely colorless, a generation

> seraphically free
> From taint of personality,

which will see the French Revolution not as it happened, nor as they would like it to have happened, but as it would have happened, had it taken place in the days of the Machine."

Tremendous applause greeted this lecture, which did but voice a feeling already latent in the minds of men—a feeling that terrestrial facts must be ignored, and that the abolition of respirators was a positive gain. It was even suggested that air-ships should be abolished too. This was not done, because air-ships had somehow worked themselves into the Machine's system. But year by year they were used less, and mentioned less by thoughtful men.

The second great development was the re-establishment of religion.

This, too, had been voiced in the celebrated lecture. No one could mistake the reverent tone in which the peroration had concluded, and it awakened a responsive echo in the heart of each. Those who had long worshiped silently, now began to talk. They described the strange feeling of peace that came over them when they handled the Book of the Machine, the pleasure that it was to repeat certain numerals out of it, however little meaning those numerals conveyed to the outward ear, the ecstasy of touching a button, however unimportant, or of ringing an electric bell, however superfluously.

"The Machine," they exclaimed, "feeds us and clothes us and houses us; through it we speak to one another, through it we see one another, in it we have our being. The machine is the friend of ideas and the enemy of superstition: the Machine omnipotent, eternal; blessed is the Machine." And before long this allocution was printed on the first page of the Book, and in subsequent editions the ritual swelled into a complicated system of praise and prayer. The word "religion" was sedulously avoided, and in theory the Machine was still the creation and the implement of man. But in practice all, save a few retrogrades, worshiped it as divine. Nor was it worshiped in unity. One believer would be chiefly impressed by the blue optic plates, through which he saw other believers; another by the Mending Apparatus, which sinful Kuno had compared to worms; another by the lifts, another by the Book. And each would pray to this or to that, and ask it to intercede for him with the Machine as a whole. Persecution— that also was present. It did not break out, for reasons that will be set forward shortly. But it was latent, and all who did not accept the minimum known as "undenominational Mechanism" lived in danger of Homelessness, which means death, as we know.

To attribute these two great developments to the Central Committee, is to take a very narrow view of civilization. The Central Committee announced the developments, it is true, but they were no more the cause of them than were the kings of the imperialistic period the cause of war. Rather did they yield to some invincible pressure, which came no one knew whither, and which, when gratified, was succeeded by some new pressure equally invincible. To such a state of affairs it is convenient to give the name of progress. No one confessed the Machine was out of hand. Year by year it was served with increased efficiency and decreased intelligence. The better a man knew his own duties upon it, the less he understood the duties of his neighbor, and in all the world there was not one who understood the monster as a whole. Those master brains had perished. They had left full directions, it is true, and their successors had each of them mastered a portion of those directions. But Humanity, in its desire for comfort, had over-reached itself. It had exploited the riches of nature too far. Quietly and complacently, it was sinking into decadence, and progress had come to mean the progress of the Machine.

As for Vashti, her life went peacefully forward until the final disaster. She made her room dark and slept; she awoke and made the room light. She lectured and attended lectures. She exchanged ideas with her innumerable friends and believed she was growing more spiritual. At times a friend was granted Euthanasia, and left his or her room for the homelessness that is beyond all human conception. Vashti did not much mind. After an unsuccessful lecture, she would sometimes ask for Euthanasia herself. But the death-rate was not permitted to exceed the birth-rate, and the Machine had hitherto refused it to her.

The troubles began quietly, long before she was conscious of them.

One day she was astonished at receiving a message from her son. They never communicated, having nothing in common, and she had only heard indirectly that he was still alive, and had been transferred from the northern hemisphere, where he had behaved so mischievously, to the southern—indeed, to a room not far from her own.

"Does he want me to visit him?" She thought. "Never again, never. And I have not the time."

No, it was madness of another kind.

He refused to visualize his face upon the blue plate, and speaking out of the darkness with solemnity said:

"The Machine stops."

"What do you say?"

"The Machine is stopping. I know it, I know the signs."

She burst into a peal of laughter. He heard her and was angry, and they spoke no more.

"Can you imagine anything more absurd?" she cried to a friend. "A man who was my son believes that the Machine is stopping. It would be impious if it was not mad."

"The Machine is stopping?" her friend replied. "What does that mean? The phrase conveys nothing to me."

"Nor to me."

"He does not refer, I suppose, to the trouble there has been lately with the music?"

"Oh, no, of course not. Let us talk about music."

"Have you complained to the authorities?"

"Yes, and they say it wants mending, and referred me to the Committee of the Mending Apparatus. I complained of those curious gasping sighs that disfigure the symphonies of the Brisbane school. They sound like someone in pain. The Committee of the Mending Apparatus say that it shall be remedied shortly."

Obscurely worried, she resumed her life. For one thing, the defect in the music irritated her. For another thing, she could not forget Kuno's speech. If he had known that the music was out of repair—he could not know it, for he detested music—if he had known that it was wrong, "the Machine stops" was exactly the venomous sort of remark he would have made. Of course he had made it at a venture, but the coincidence annoyed her, and she spoke with some petulance to the Committee of the Mending Apparatus.

They replied, as before, that the defect would be set right shortly.

"Shortly! At once!" she retorted. "Why should I be worried by imperfect music? Things are always put right at once. If you do not mend it at once, I shall complain to the Central Committee."

"No personal complaints are received by the Central Committee," the Committee of the Mending Apparatus replied.

"Through whom am I to make my complaint, then?"

"Through us."

"I complain then."

"Your complaint shall be forwarded in its turn."

"Have others complained?"

This question was unmechanical, and the Committee of the Mending Apparatus refused to answer it.

"It is too bad!" she exclaimed to another of her friends. "There never was such an unfortunate woman as myself. I can never be sure of my music now. It gets worse and worse each time I summon it."

"I too have my troubles," the friend replied. "Sometimes my ideas are interrupted by a slight jarring noise."

"What is it?"

"I do not know whether it is inside my head, or inside the wall."

"Complain, in either case."

"I have complained, and my complaint will be forwarded in its turn to the Central Committee."

Time passed, and they resented the defects no longer. The defects had not been remedied, but the human tissues in the latter day had become so subservient, that they readily adapted themselves to every caprice of the Machine. The sigh at the crisis of the Brisbane symphony no longer irritated Vashti; she accepted it as part of the melody. The jarring noise, whether in the head or in the wall, was no longer resented by her friend. And so with the moldy artificial fruit, so with the bath water that began to stink, so with the defective rhymes that the poetry machine had taken to emit. All were bitterly complained of at first, and then acquiesced in and forgotten. Things went from bad to worse unchallenged.

It was otherwise with the failure of the sleeping apparatus. That was a more serious stoppage. There came a day when over the whole world—in Sumatra, in Wessex, in the innumerable cities of Courland and Brazil—the beds, when summoned by their tired owners, failed to appear. It may seem a ludicrous matter, but from it we may date the collapse of humanity. The Committee responsible for the failure was assailed by complainants, whom it referred, as usual, to the Committee of the Mending Apparatus, who in its turn assured them that their complaints would be forwarded to the Central Committee. But the discontent grew, for mankind was not yet sufficiently adaptable to do without sleeping.

"Someone is meddling with the Machine"—they began.

"Someone is trying to make himself king, to reintroduce the personal element."

"Punish that man with Homelessness."

"To the rescue! Avenge the Machine! Avenge the Machine!"

"War! Kill the man!"

But the Committee of the Mending Apparatus now came forward, and allayed the panic with well-chosen words. It confessed that the Mending Apparatus was itself in need of repair.

The effect of this frank confession was admirable.

"Of course," said a famous lecturer—he of the French Revolution, who gilded each new decay with splendor— "of course we shall not press our complaints now. The Mending Apparatus has treated us so well in the past that we all sympathize with it, and will wait patiently for its recovery. In its own good time it will resume its duties. Meanwhile let us do without our beds, our tabloids, our other little wants. Such, I feel sure, would be the wish of the Machine."

Thousands of miles away his audience applauded. The Machine still linked them. Under the sea, beneath the roots of the mountains, ran the wires through which they saw and heard, the enormous eyes and ears that were their heritage, and the hum of many workings clothed their thoughts in one garment of subserviency. Only the old and sick remained ungrateful, for it was rumored that Euthanasia, too, was out of order, and that pain had reappeared among men.

It became difficult to read. A blight entered the atmosphere and dulled its luminosity. At times Vashti could scarcely see across her room. The air, too, was foul. Loud were the complaints, impotent the remedies, heroic the tone of the lecturer as he cried: "Courage, courage! What matter so long as the Machine goes on? To it the darkness and the light are one." And though things improved again after a time, the old brilliancy was never recaptured, and humanity never recovered from its entrance into twilight. There was an hysterical talk of "measures," of "provisional dictatorship," and the inhabitants of Sumatra were asked to familiarize themselves with the workings of the central power station, the said power station being situated in France. But for the most part panic reigned, and men spent their strength praying to their Books, tangible proofs of the Machine's omnipotence. There were gradations of terror—at times came rumors of hope—the Mending Apparatus was almost mended—the enemies of the Machine had been got under—new "nerve-centers" were evolving which would do the work even more magnificently than before. But there came a day when, without the slightest warning, without any previous hint of feebleness, the entire communication-system broke down, all over the world, and the world, as they understood it, ended.

Vashti was lecturing at the time and her earlier remarks had been punctuated with applause. As she proceeded the audience became silent, and at the conclusion there was no sound. Somewhat displeased, she called to a friend who was a specialist in sympathy. No sound: doubtless the friend was sleeping. And so with the next friend whom she tried to summon, and so with the next, until she remembered Kuno's cryptic remark, "The Machine stops."

The phrase still conveyed nothing. If Eternity was stopping it would of course be set going shortly.

For example, there was still a little light and air—the atmosphere had improved a few hours previously. There was still the Book, and while there was the Book there was security.

Then she broke down, for with the cessation of activity came an unexpected terror—silence.

She had never known silence, and the coming of it nearly killed her—it did kill many thousands of people outright. Ever since her birth she had been surrounded by the steady hum. It was to the ear what artificial air was to the lungs, and agonizing pains shot across her head. And scarcely knowing what she did, she stumbled forward and pressed the unfamiliar button, the one that opened the door of her cell.

Now the door of the cell worked on a simple hinge of its own. It was not connected with the central power station, dying far away in France. It opened, rousing immoderate hopes in Vashti, for she thought that the Machine had been mended. It opened, and she saw the dim tunnel that curved far away towards freedom. One look, and then she shrank back. For the tunnel was full of people—she was almost the last in the city to have taken alarm.

People at any time repelled her, and these were nightmares from her worst dreams. People were crawling about, people were screaming, whimpering, gasping for breath, touching each other, vanishing in the dark, and ever and anon being pushed off the platform onto the live rail. Some were fighting round the electric bells, trying to summon trains which could not be summoned. Others were yelling for Euthanasia or for respirators, or blaspheming the Machine. Others stood at the doors of their cells, fearing, like herself, either to stop in them or to leave them. And behind all the uproar was silence—the silence which is the voice of the earth and of the generations who have gone.

No—it was worse than solitude. She closed the door again and sat down to wait for the end. The disintegration went on, accompanied by horrible cracks and rumbling. The valves that restrained the Medical Apparatus must have been weakened, for it ruptured and hung hideously from the ceiling. The floor heaved and fell and flung her from her chair. A tube oozed towards her serpent fashion. And at last the final horror approached—light began to ebb, and she knew that civilization's long day was closing.

She whirled round, praying to be saved from this, at any rate, kissing the Book, pressing button after button. The uproar outside was increasing, and even penetrated the wall. Slowly the brilliancy of her cell was dimmed, the reflections faded from her metal switches. Now she could not see the reading-stand, now not the Book, though she held it in her hand. Light followed the flight of sound, air was following light, and the original void returned to the cavern from which it had been so long excluded. Vashti continued to whirl, like the devotees of an earlier religion, screaming, praying, striking at the buttons with bleeding hands.

It was thus that she opened her prison and escaped—escaped in the spirit: at least so it seems to me, ere my meditation closes. That she escapes in the body—I cannot perceive that. She struck, by chance, the switch that released the door, and the rush of foul air on her skin, the loud throbbing whispers in her ears, told her that she was facing the tunnel again, and that tremendous platform on which she had seen men fighting. They were not fighting now. Only the whispers remained, and the little whimpering groans. They were dying by hundreds out in the dark.

She burst into tears.

Tears answered her.

They wept for humanity, those two, not for themselves. They could not bear that this should be the end. Ere silence was completed their hearts were opened, and they knew what had been important on the earth. Man, the flower of all flesh, the noblest of all creatures visible, man who had once made god in his image, and had mirrored his strength on the constellations, beautiful naked man was dying, strangled in the garments that he had woven. Century after century had he toiled, and here was his reward. Truly the garment had seemed heavenly at first, shot with the colors of culture, sewn with the threads of self-denial. And heavenly it had been so long as it was a garment and no more, so long as man could shed it at will and live by the essence that is his soul, and the essence, equally divine, that is his body. The sin against the body—it was for that they wept in chief; the centuries of wrong against the muscles and nerves, and those five portals by which we can alone apprehend—glozing it over with talk of evolution, until the body was white pap, the home of ideas as colorless, last sloshy stirrings of a spirit that had grasped the stars.

"Where are you?" she sobbed.

His voice in the darkness said, "Here."

"Is there any hope, Kuno?"

"None for us."

"Where are you?"

She crawled towards him over the bodies of the dead. His blood spurted over her hands.

"Quicker," he gasped, "I'm dying—but we touch, we talk, not through the Machine."

He kissed her.

"We have come back to our own. We die, but we have recaptured life, as it was in Wessex, when Aelfrid overthrew the Danes. We know what they know outside, they who dwelt in the cloud that is the color of a pearl."

"But, Kuno, is it true? Are there still men on the surface of the earth? Is this—this tunnel, this poisoned darkness—really not the end?"

He replied:

"I have seen them, spoken to them, loved them. They are hiding in the mist and ferns until our civilization stops. Today they are the Homeless—tomorrow—"

"Oh, tomorrow—some fool will start the Machine again, tomorrow."

"Never," said Kuno, "never. Humanity has learnt its lesson."

As he spoke, the whole city was broken like a honey-comb. An air-ship had sailed in through the vomitory into a ruined wharf. It crashed downwards, exploding as it went, rending gallery after gallery with its wings of steel. For a moment they saw the nations of the dead, and, before they joined them, scraps of the untainted sky.

QUESTIONS

1 What effect does the first paragraph have on you? What is the tone of it? What words or phrases contribute to establishing the tone? Considering the story as a whole, do you think the opening is effective?

2 Forster seems to feel that there is a difference between knowing a lot of people and communicating with them. Do you feel that Kuno and his mother "communicate" throughout the story? When do you think they really begin communicating? How do you distinguish between the times when they are communicating and the times when they are just talking?

3 Account for the people's obsession with ideas? What is the irony here? What do you suppose the word "idea" means to Kuno's mother? Does it mean the same to Kuno?

4 Describe the stages the people go through in their attitude toward

the Book of the Machine. Are these stages paralleled by any other changes that take place during the story? Explain.

5 What are some of the meanings of Forster's title? What has the civilization of "The Machine Stops" sinned against most, the body or the spirit? Explain the following: "beautiful naked man was dying, strangled in the garments that he had woven." In answering the above questions could you formulate a statement of what the story means?

6 Forster touches on several ideas, including progress, mechanization, religion, human relationships, birth and death. State his views on as many of these matters as possible, then try to construct a civilization that Forster *would* like.

TWILIGHT
John W. Campbell

"Speaking of hitch-hikers," said Jim Bendell in a rather bewildered way, "I picked up a man the other day that certainly was a queer cuss." He laughed, but it wasn't a real laugh. "He told me the queerest yarn I ever heard. Most of them tell you how they lost their good jobs and tried to find work out here in the wide spaces of the West. They don't seem to realize how many people we have out here. They think all this great beautiful country is uninhabited."

Jim Bendell's a real estate man, and I knew how he could go on. That's his favorite line, you know. He's real worried because there's a lot of homesteading plots still open out in our state. He talks about the beautiful country, but he never went farther into the desert than the edge of town. 'Fraid of it actually. So I sort of steered him back on the track.

"What did he claim, Jim? Prospector who couldn't find land to prospect?"

"That's not very funny, Bart. No; it wasn't only what he claimed. He didn't even claim it, just said it. You know, he didn't say it was true, he just said it. That's what gets me. I know it ain't true, but the way he said it—Oh I don't know."

By which I knew he didn't. Jim Bendell's usually pretty careful about his English—real proud of it. When he slips, that means he's disturbed. Like the time he thought the rattlesnake was a stick of wood and wanted to put it on the fire.

Jim went on: And he had funny clothes, too. They looked like silver, but they were soft as silk. And at night they glowed just a little.

I picked him up about dusk. Really picked him up. He was lying off about ten feet from the South Road. I thought, at first, somebody had hit him, and then hadn't stopped. Didn't see him very clearly, you know. I picked him up, put him in the car, and started on. I had about three hundred miles to go, but I thought I could drop him at Warren Spring with Doc Vance. But he came to in about five minutes, and opened his eyes. He looked straight off, and he looked first at the car, then at the Moon. "Thank God!" he says, and then looks at me. It gave me a shock. He was beautiful. No; he was handsome.

He wasn't either one. He was magnificent. He was about six feet two, I think, and his hair was brown, with a touch of red-gold. It seemed like fine copper wire that's turned brown. It was crisp and curly. His forehead was wide, twice as wide as mine. His features were delicate, but tremendously impressive; his eyes were gray, like etched iron, and bigger than mine—a lot.

That suit he wore—it was more like a bathing suit with pajama trousers. His arms were long and muscled smoothly as an Indian's. He was white, though, tanned lightly with a golden, rather than a brown, tan.

But he was magnificent. Most wonderful man I ever saw. I don't know, damn it!

"Hello!" I said. "Have an accident?"

"No; not this time, at least."

And his voice was magnificent, too. It wasn't an ordinary voice. It sounded like an organ talking, only it was human.

"But maybe my mind isn't quite steady yet. I tried an experiment. Tell me what the date is, year and all, and let me see," he went on.

"Why—December 9, 1932," I said.

And it didn't please him. He didn't like it a bit. But the wry grin that came over his face gave way to a chuckle.

"Over a thousand—" he says reminiscently. "Not as bad as seven million. I shouldn't complain."

"Seven million what?"

"Years," he said, steadily enough. Like he meant it. "I tried an experiment once. Or I will try it. Now I'll have to try again. The experiment was—in 3059. I'd just finished the release experiment. Testing space then. Time—it wasn't that, I still believe. It was space. I felt myself caught in that field, but I couldn't pull away. Field gamma-H 481, intensity 935 in the Pellman range. It sucked me in, and I went out.

"I think it took a short cut through space to the position the solar system will occupy. Through a higher dimension, effecting a speed exceeding light and throwing me into the future plane."

He wasn't telling me, you know. He was just thinking out loud. Then he began to realize I was there.

"I couldn't read their instruments, seven million years of evolution changed everything. So I overshot my mark a little coming back. I belong in 3059.

"But tell me, what's the latest scientific invention of this year?"

He startled me so, I answered almost before I thought. "Why, television, I guess. And radio and airplanes."

"Radio—good. They will have instruments."

"But see here—who are you?"

"Ah—I'm sorry. I forgot," he replied in that organ voice of his. "I am Ares Sen Kenlin. And you?"

"James Waters Bendell."

"Waters—what does that mean? I do not recognize it."

"Why—it's a name, of course. Why should you recognize it?"

"I see—you have not the classification, then. 'Sen' stands for science."

"Where did you come from, Mr. Kenlin?"

"Come from?" He smiled, and his voice was slow and soft. "I came out of space across seven million years or more. They had lost count—the men had. The machines had eliminated the unneeded service. They didn't know what year it was. But before that—my home is in Neva'th City in the year 3059."

That's when I began to think he was a nut.

"I was an experimenter," he went on. "Science, as I have said. My father was a scientist, too, but in human genetics. I myself am an experiment. He proved his point, and all the world followed suit. I was the first of the new race.

"The new race—oh, holy destiny—what has—what will—

"What is its end? I have seen it—almost. I saw them—the little men—bewildered—lost. And the machines. Must it be—can't anything sway it?

"Listen—I heard this song."

He sang the song. Then he didn't have to tell me about the people. I knew them. I could hear their voices, in the queer, crackling, un-English words. I could read their bewildered longings. It was in a minor key, I think. It called, it called and asked, and hunted hopelessly. And over it all the steady rumble and whine of the unknown, forgotten machines.

The machines that couldn't stop, because they had been started, and the little men had forgotten how to stop them, or even what they were for, looking at them and listening—and wondering. They couldn't read or write any more, and the language had changed, you see, so that the phonic records of their ancestors meant nothing to them.

But that song went on, and they wondered. And they looked out across space and they saw the warm, friendly stars—too far away. Nine planets they knew and inhabited. And locked by infinite distance, they couldn't see another race, a new life.

And through it all—two things. The machines. Bewildered forgetfulness. And maybe one more. Why?

That was the song, and it made me cold. It shouldn't be sung around people of today. It almost killed something. It seemed to kill hope. After that song—I—well, I believed him.

When he finished the song, he didn't talk for a while. Then he sort of shook himself.

You won't understand (he continued). Not yet—but I have seen them. They stand about, little misshapen men with huge heads. But their heads contain only brains. They had machines that could think—but somebody turned them off a long time ago, and no one knew how to start them again. That was the trouble with them. They had wonderful brains. Far better than yours or mine. But it must have been millions of years ago when they were turned off, too, and they just haven't thought since then. Kindly little people. That was all they knew.

When I slipped into that field it grabbed me like a gravitational field whirling a space transport down to a planet. It sucked me in—and through. Only the other side must have been seven million years in the future. That's where I was. It must have been in exactly the same spot on Earth's surface, but I never knew why.

It was night then, and I saw the city a little way off. The Moon was shining on it, and the whole scene looked wrong. You see, in seven million years, men had done a lot with the positions of the planetary bodies, what with moving space liners, clearing lanes through the asteroids, and such. And seven million years is long enough for natural things to change positions a little. The Moon must have been fifty thousand miles farther out. And it was rotating on its axis. I lay there a while and watched it. Even the stars were different.

There were ships going out of the city. Back and forth, like things sliding along a wire, but there was only a wire of force, of course. Part of the city, the lower part, was brightly lighted with what must have been mercury vapor glow, I decided. Blue-green. I felt sure men didn't live there—the light was wrong for eyes. But the top of the city was so sparsely lighted.

Then I saw something coming down out of the sky. It was brightly lighted. A huge globe, and it sank straight to the center of the great black-and-silver mass of the city.

I don't know what it was, but even then I knew the city was deserted. Strange that I could even imagine that, I who had never seen a deserted city before. But I walked the fifteen miles over to it and entered it. There were machines going about the streets, repair machines, you know. They couldn't understand that the city didn't need to go on functioning, so they were still working. I found a taxi machine that seemed fairly familiar. It had a manual control that I could work.

I don't know how long that city had been deserted. Some of the men from the other cities said it was a hundred and fifty thousand years. Some went as high as three hundred thousand years. Three hundred thousand years since human foot had been in that city. The taxi machine was in perfect condition, functioned at once. It was clean, and the city was clean and orderly. I saw a restaurant and I was hungry. Hungrier still for humans to speak to. There were none, of course, but I didn't know.

The restaurant had the food displayed directly, and I made a choice. The food was three hundred thousand years old, I suppose. I didn't know, and the machines that served it to me didn't care, for they made things synthetically, you see, and perfectly. When the builders made those cities, they forgot one thing. They didn't realize that things shouldn't go on forever.

It took me six months to make my apparatus. And near the end I was ready to go; and, from seeing those machines go blindly, perfectly, on in orbits of their duties with the tireless, ceaseless perfection their designers had incorporated in them, long after those designers and their sons, and their sons' sons had no use for them—

When Earth is cold, and the Sun has died out, those machines will go on. When Earth begins to crack and break, those perfect, ceaseless machines will try to repair her—

I left the restaurant and cruised about the city in the taxi. The machine had a little, electric-power motor, I believe, but it gained its power from the great central power radiator. I knew before long that I was far in the future. The city was divided into two sections, a section of many strata where machines functioned smoothly, save for a deep humming beat that echoed through the whole city like a vast unending song of power. The entire metal framework of the place echoed with it, transmitted it, hummed with it. But it was soft and restful, a reassuring beat.

There must have been thirty levels above ground, and twenty more below, a solid block of metal walls and metal floors and metal and glass and force machines. The only light was the blue-green glow of the mercury vapor arcs. The light of mercury vapor is rich in high-energy-quanta, which stimulate the alkali metal atoms to photo-electric activity. Or perhaps that is beyond the science of your day? I have forgotten.

But they had used that light because many of their worker machines needed sight. The machines were marvelous. For five hours I wandered through the vast power plant on the very lowest level, watching them, and because there was motion, and that pseudo-mechanical life, I felt less alone.

The generators I saw were a development of the release I had discovered—when? The release of the energy of matter, I mean, and I knew when I saw that for what countless ages they could continue.

The entire lower block of the city was given over to the machines. Thousands. But most of them seemed idle, or, at most, running under light load. I recognized a telephone apparatus, and not a single signal came through. There was no life in the city. Yet when I pressed a little stud beside the screen on one side of the room, the machine began working instantly. It was ready. Only no one needed it any more. The men knew how to die, and be dead, but the machines didn't.

Finally I went up to the top of the city, the upper level. It was a paradise.

There were shrubs and trees and parks, glowing in the soft light that they had learned to make in the very air. They had learned it five million years or more before. Two million years ago they forgot. But the machines didn't, and they were still making it. It hung in the air, soft, silvery light, slightly rosy, and the gardens were shadowy with it. There were no machines here now, but I knew that in daylight they must come out and work on these gardens, keeping them a paradise for masters who had died, and stopped moving, as they could not.

In the desert outside the city it had been cool, and very dry. Here the air was soft, warm and sweet with the scent of blooms that men had spent several hundreds of thousands of years perfecting.

Then somewhere music began. It began in the air, and spread softly through it. The Moon was just setting now, and as it set, the rosy-silver glow waned and the music grew stronger.

It came from everywhere and from nowhere. It was within me. I do not know how they did it. And I do not know how such music could be written.

Savages make music too simple to be beautiful, but it is stirring. Semisavages write music beautifully simple, and simply beautiful. Your Negro music was your best. They knew music when they heard it and sang it as they felt it. Semicivilized peoples write great music. They are proud of their music, and make sure it is known for great music. They make it so great it is top-heavy.

I had always thought our music good. But that which came through the air was the song of triumph, sung by a mature race, the race of man in its full triumph! It was man singing his triumph in majestic sound that swept me up; it showed me what lay before me; it carried me on.

And it died in the air as I looked at the deserted city. The machines should have forgotten that song. Their masters had, long before.

I came to what must have been one of their homes; it was a dimly-seen doorway in the dusky light, but as I stepped up to it, the lights which had not functioned in three hundred thousand years illuminated it for me with a green-white glow, like a firefly, and I stepped into the room beyond. Instantly something happened to the air in the doorway behind me; it was as opaque as milk. The room in which I stood was a room of metal and stone. The stone was some jet-black substance with the finish of velvet and the metals were silver and gold. There was a rug on the floor, a rug of just such material as I am wearing now, but thicker and softer. There were divans about the room, low and covered with these soft metallic materials. They were black and gold and silver, too.

I had never seen anything like that. I never shall again, I suppose, and my language and yours were not made to describe it.

The builders of that city had right and reason to sing that song of sweeping triumph, triumph that swept them over the nine planets and the fifteen habitable moons.

But they weren't there any more, and I wanted to leave. I thought of a plan and went to a subtelephone office to examine a map I had seen. The old World looked much the same. Seven or even seventy million years don't mean much to old Mother Earth. She may even succeed in wearing down those marvellous machine cities. She can wait a hundred million or a thousand million years before she is beaten.

I tried calling different city centers shown on the map. I had quickly learned the system when I examined the central apparatus.

I tried once—twice—thrice—a round dozen times. Yawk City, Lunon City, Paree, Shkago, Singpor, others. I was beginning to feel that there were no more men on all Earth. And I felt crushed, as at each city the machines replied and did my bidding. The machines were there in each of those far vaster cities, for I was in the Neva City of their time. A small city. Yawk city was more than eight hundred kilometers in diameter.

In each city I had tried several numbers. Then I tried San

Frisco. There was someone there, and a voice answered and the picture of a human appeared on the little glowing screen. I could see him start and stare in surprise at me. Then he started speaking to me. I couldn't understand, of course. I can understand your speech, and you mine, because your speech of this day is largely recorded on records of various types and has influenced our pronunciation.

Some things are changed; names of cities, particularly, because names of cities are apt to be polysyllabic, and used a great deal. People tend to elide them, shorten them. I am in Nee-vah-dah —as you would say? We say only Neva. And Yawk State. But it is Ohio and Iowa still. Over a thousand years, effects were small on words, because they were recorded.

But seven million years had passed, and the men had forgotten the old records, used them less as time went on, and their speech varied till the time came when they could no longer understand the records. They were not written any more, of course.

Some men must have arisen occasionally among that last of the race and sought for knowledge, but it was denied them. An ancient writing can be translated if some basic rule is found. An ancient voice, though—and when the race has forgotten the laws of science and the labor of mind.

So his speech was strange to me as he answered over that circuit. His voice was high in pitch, his words liquid, his tones sweet. It was almost a song as he spoke. He was excited and called others. I could not understand them, but I knew where they were. I could go to them.

So I went down from the paradise of gardens, and as I prepared to leave, I saw dawn in the sky. The strange-bright stars winked and twinkled and faded. Only one bright rising star was familiar—Venus. She shone golden now. Finally, As I stood watching for the first time that strange heaven, I began to understand what had first impressed me with the wrongness of the view. The stars, you see, were all different.

In my time—and yours—the solar system is a lone wanderer that by chance is passing across an intersection point of Galactic traffic. The stars we see at night are the stars of moving clusters, you know. In fact our system is passing through the heart of the

Ursa Major group. Half a dozen other groups center within five hundred light-years of us.

But during those seven millions of years, the Sun had moved out of the group. The heavens were almost empty to the eye. Only here and there shone a single faint star. And across the vast sweep of black sky swung the band of the Milky Way. The sky was empty.

That must have been another thing those men meant in their songs—felt in their hearts. Loneliness—not even the close, friendly stars. We have stars within half a dozen light-years. They told me that their instruments, which gave directly the distance to any star, showed that the nearest was one hundred and fifty light-years away. It was enormously bright. Brighter even than Sirius of our heavens. And that made it even less friendly, because it was a blue-white supergiant. Our sun would have served as a satellite for that star.

I stood there and watched the lingering rose-silver glow die as the powerful blood-red light of the Sun swept over the horizon. I knew by the stars now that it must have been several millions of years since my day; since I had last seen the Sun sweep up. And that blood-red light made me wonder if the Sun itself was dying.

An edge of it appeared, blood-red and huge. It swung up, and the color faded, till in half an hour it was the familiar yellow-gold disk.

It hadn't changed in all that time.

I had been foolish to think that it would. Seven million years —that is nothing to Earth, how much less to the Sun? Some two thousand thousand thousand times it had risen since I last saw it rise. Two thousand thousand thousand days. If it had been that many years—I might have noticed a change.

The universe moves slowly. Only life is not enduring; only life changes swiftly. Eight short millions of years. Eight days in the life of Earth—and the race was dying. It had left something: machines. But they would die, too, even though they could not understand. So I felt. I—may have changed that. I will tell you. Later.

For when the Sun was up, I looked again at the sky and the

ground, some fifty floors below. I had come to the edge of the city.

Machines were moving on that ground, leveling it, perhaps. A great wide line of gray stretched off across the level desert straight to the east. I had seen it glowing faintly before the Sun rose—a roadway for ground machines. There was no traffic on it.

I saw an airship slip in from the east. It came with a soft, muttering whine of air, like a child complaining in sleep; it grew to my eyes like an expanding balloon. It was huge when it settled in a great port-slip in the city below. I could hear now the clang and mutter of machines, working on the materials brought in, no doubt. The machines had ordered raw materials. The machines in other cities had supplied. The freight machines had carried them here.

San Frisco and Jacksville were the only two cities on North America still used. But the machines went on in all the others, because they couldn't stop. They hadn't been ordered to.

Then high above, something appeared, and from the city beneath me, from a center section, three small spheres rose. They, like the freight ship, had no visible driving mechanisms. The point in the sky above, like a black star in a blue space, had grown to a moon. The three spheres met it high above. Then together they descended and lowered into the center of the city, where I could not see them.

It was a freight transport from Venus. The one I had seen land the night before had come from Mars, I learned.

I moved after that and looked for some sort of a taxi-plane. They had none that I recognized in scouting about the city. I searched the higher levels, and here and there saw deserted ships, but far too large for me, and without controls.

It was nearly noon—and I ate again. The food was good.

I knew then that this was a city of the dead ashes of human hopes. The hopes not of *a* race, not the whites, nor the yellow, nor the blacks, but the human race. I was mad to leave the city. I was afraid to try the ground road to the west, for the taxi I drove was powered from some source in the city, and I knew it would fail before many miles.

It was afternoon when I found a small hangar near the outer wall of the vast city. It contained three ships. I had been searching through the lower strata of the human section—the upper part. There were restaurants and shops and theatres there. I entered one place where, at my entrance, soft music began, and colors and forms began to rise on a screen before me.

They were the triumph songs in form and sound and color of a mature race, a race that had marched steadily upward through five millions of years—and didn't see the path that faded out ahead, when they were dead and had stopped, and the city itself was dead—but hadn't stopped. I hastened out of there—and the song that had not been sung in three hundred thousand years died behind me.

But I found the hangar. It was a private one, likely. Three ships. One must have been fifty feet long and fifteen in diameter. It was a yacht, a space yacht, probably. One was some fifteen feet long and five feet in diameter. That must have been the family air machine. The third was a tiny thing, little more than ten feet long and two in diameter. I had to lie down within it, evidently.

There was a periscopic device that gave me a view ahead and almost directly above. A window that permitted me to see what lay below—and a device that moved a map under a frosted-glass screen and projected it onto the screen in such a way that the cross-hairs of the screen always marked my position.

I spent half an hour attempting to understand what the makers of that ship had made. But the men who made that were men who held behind them the science and knowledge of five millions of years and the perfect machines of those ages. I saw the release mechanism that powered it. I understood the principles of that and, vaguely, the mechanics. But there were no conductors, only pale beams that pulsed so swiftly you could hardly catch the pulsations from the corner of the eye. They had been glowing and pulsating, some half dozen of them, for three hundred thousand years at least; probably more.

I entered the machine, and instantly half a dozen more beams sprang into being; there was a slight suggestion of a quiver, and a queer strain ran through my body. I understood in an instant, for the machine was resting on gravity nullifiers. That had been my hope when I worked on the space fields I discovered after the release.

But they had had it for millions of years before they built

that perfect deathless machine. My weight entering it had forced it to readjust itself and simultaneously to prepare for operation. Within, an artificial gravity equal to that of Earth had gripped me, and the neutral zone between the outside and the interior had caused the strain.

The machine was ready. It was fully fueled, too. You see they were equipped to tell automatically their wants and needs. They were almost living things, every one. A caretaker machine kept them supplied, adjusted, even repaired them when need be, and when possible. If it was not, I learned later, they were carried away in a service truck that came automatically; replaced by an exactly similar machine; and carried to the shops where they were made, and automatic machines made them over.

The machine waited patiently for me to start. The controls were simple, obvious. There was a lever at the left that you pushed forward to move forward, pulled back to go back. On the right a horizontal, pivoted bar. If you swung it left, the ship spun left; if right, the ship spun right. If tipped up, the ship followed it, and likewise for all motions other than backward and forward. Raising it bodily raised the ship, as depressing it depressed the ship.

I lifted it slightly, a needle moved a bit on a gauge comfortably before my eyes as I lay there, and the floor dropped beneath me. I pulled the other control back, and the ship gathered speed as it moved gently out into the open. Releasing both controls into neutral, the machine continued till it stopped at the same elevation, the motion absorbed by air friction. I turned it about, and another dial before my eyes moved, showing my position. I could not read it, though. The map did not move, as I had hoped it would. So I started toward what I felt was west.

I could feel no acceleration in that marvelous machine. The ground simply began leaping backward, and in a moment the city was gone. The map unrolled rapidly beneath me now, and I saw that I was moving south of west. I turned northward slightly, and watched the compass. Soon I understood that, too, and the ship sped on.

I had become too interested in the map and the compass, for suddenly there was a sharp buzz and, without my volition, the machine rose and swung to the north. There was a mountain ahead of me; I had not seen, but the ship had.

I noticed then what I should have seen before—two little knobs that could move the map. I started to move them and heard a sharp clicking, and the pace of the ship began decreasing. A moment and it had steadied at a considerably lower speed, the machine swinging to a new course. I tried to right it, but to my amazement the controls did not affect it.

It was the map, you see. It would either follow the course, or the course would follow it. i had moved it and the machine had taken over control of its own accord. There was a little button I could have pushed—but I didn't know. I couldn't control the ship until it finally came to rest and lowered itself to a stop six inches from the ground in the center of what must have been the ruins of a great city, Sacramento, probably.

I understood now, so I adjusted the map for San Frisco, and the ship went on at once. It steered itself around a mass of broken stone, turned back to its course, and headed on, a bullet-shaped, self-controlled dart.

It didn't descend when it reached San Frisco. It simply hung in the air and sounded a soft musical hum. Twice. Then it waited. I waited, too, and looked down.

There were people here. I saw the humans of that age for the first time. They were little men bewildered—dwarfed, with heads disproportionately large. But not extremely so.

Their eyes impressed me most. They were huge, and when they looked at me there was a power in them that seemed sleeping, but too deeply to be roused.

I took the manual controls then and landed. And no sooner had I got out than the ship rose automatically and started off by itself. They had automatic parking devices. The ship had gone to a public hangar, the nearest, where it would be automatically serviced and cared for. There was a little call set I should have taken with me when I got out. Then I could have pressed a button and called it to me—wherever I was in that city.

The people about me began talking—singing almost—among themselves. Others were coming up leisurely. Men and women— but there seemed no old and few young. What few young there were, were treated almost with respect, carefully taken care of lest a careless footstep on their toes or a careless step knock them down.

There was reason, you see. They lived a tremendous time. Some lived as long as three thousand years. Then—they simply died. They didn't grow old, and it never had been learned why people died as they did. The heart stopped, the brain ceased thought—and they died. But the young children, children not yet mature, were treated with the utmost care. But one child was born in the course of a month in that city of one hundred thousand people. The human race was growing sterile.

And I have told you that they were lonely? Their loneliness was beyond hope. For, you see, as man strode toward maturity, he destroyed all forms of life that menaced him. Disease. Insects. Then the last of the insects, and finally the last of the man-eating animals.

The balance of nature was destroyed then, so they had to go on. It was like the machines. They started them—and now they can't stop. They started destroying life—and now it wouldn't stop. So they had to destroy weeds of all sorts, then many formerly harmless plants. Then the herbivora, too, the deer and the antelope and the rabbit and the horse. They were a menace, they attacked man's machine-tended crops. Man was still eating natural foods.

You can understand. The thing was beyond their control. In the end they killed off the denizens of the sea, also, in self-defense. Without the many creatures that had kept them in check, they were swarming beyond bounds. And the time had come when synthetic foods replaced natural. The air was purified of all life about two and a half million years after our day, all microscopic life.

That meant that the water, too, must be purified. It was— and then came the end of life in the ocean. There were minute organisms that lived on bacterial forms, and tiny fish that lived on the minute organisms, and small fish that lived on the tiny fish, and big fish that lived on the small fish—and the beginning of the chain was gone. The sea was devoid of life in a generation. That meant about one thousand and five hundred years to them. Even the sea plants had gone.

And on all Earth there was only man and the organisms he had protected—the plants he wanted for decoration, and certain ultra-hygienic pets, as long-lived as their masters. Dogs. They must have been remarkable animals. Man was reaching his maturity then, and his animal friend, the friend that had followed him through a thousand millenniums to your day and mine, and another four thousand millenniums to the day of man's early maturity, had grown in intelligence. In an ancient museum—a wonderful place, for they had, perfectly preserved, the body of a great leader of mankind who had died five and a half million years before I saw him—in that museum, deserted then, I saw one of those canines. His skull was nearly as large as mine. They had simple ground machines that dogs could be trained to drive, and they held races in which the dogs drove those machines.

Then man reached his full maturity. It extended over a period of a full million years. So tremendously did he stride ahead, the dog ceased to be a companion. Less and less were they wanted. When the million years had passed, and man's decline began, the dog was gone. It had died out.

And now this last dwindling group of men still in the system had no other life form to make its successor. Always before when one civilization toppled, on its ashes rose a new one. Now there was but one civilization, and all other races, even other species, were gone save in the plants. And man was too far along in his old age to bring intelligence and mobility from the plants. Perhaps he could have in his prime.

Other worlds were flooded with man during that million years —the million years. Every planet and every moon of the system had its quota of men. Now only the planets had their populations, the moons had been deserted. Pluto had been left before I landed, and men were coming from Neptune, moving in toward the Sun, and the home planet, while I was there. Strangely quiet men, viewing, most of them, for the first time, the planet that had given their race life.

But as I stepped from that ship and watched it rise away from me, I saw why the race of man was dying. I looked back at the faces of those men, and on them I read the answer. There was one single quality gone from the still-great minds—minds far greater than yours or mine. I had to have the help of one of them in solving some of my problems. In space, you know, there are twenty coordinates, ten of which are zero, six of which have fixed values, and the four others represent our changing, familiar dimensions in space-time. That means that integrations must proceed in not double, or triple, or quadruple—but ten integrations.

It would have taken me too long. I would never have solved all the problems I must work out. I could not use their mathematics machines; and mine, of course, were seven million years in the past. But one of those men was interested and helped me. He did quadruple and quintuple integration, even quadruple integration between varying exponential limits—in his head.

When I asked him to. For the one thing that had made man great had left him. As I looked in their faces and eyes on landing I knew it. They looked at me, interested at this rather unusual-looking stranger—and went on. They had come to see the arrival of a ship. A rare event, you see. But they were merely welcoming me in a friendly fashion. They were not curious! Man had lost the instinct of curiosity.

Oh, not entirely! They wondered at the machines, they wondered at the stars. But they did nothing about it. It was not wholly lost to them yet, but nearly. It was dying. In the six short months I stayed with them, I learned more than they had learned in the two or even three thousand years they had lived among the machines.

Can you appreciate the crushing hopelessness it brought to me? I, who love science, who see in it, or have seen in it, the salvation, the raising of mankind—to see those wondrous machines, of man's triumphant maturity, forgotten and misunderstood. The wondrous, perfect machines that tended, protected, and cared for those gentle, kindly people who had—forgotten.

They were lost among it. The city was a magnificent ruin to them, a thing that rose stupendous about them. Something not understood, a thing that was of the nature of the world. It was. It had not been made; it simply was. Just as the mountains and the deserts and the waters of the seas.

Do you understand—can you see that the time since those

machines were new was longer than the time from our day to the birth of the race? Do we know the legends of our first ancestors? Do we remember their lore of forest and cave? The secret of chipping a flint till it had a sharp-cutting edge? The secret of trailing and killing a saber-toothed tiger without being killed oneself?

They were now in similar straits, though the time had been longer, because the language had taken a long step towards perfection, and because the machines maintained everything for them through generation after generation.

Why, the entire planet of Pluto had been deserted—yet on Pluto the largest mines of one of their metals were located; the machines still functioned. A perfect unity existed throughout the system. A unified system of perfect machines.

And all those people knew was that to do a certain thing to a certain level produced certain results. Just as men in the Middle Ages knew that to take a certain material, wood, and place it in contact with other pieces of wood heated red, would cause the wood to disappear, and become heat. They did not understand that wood was being oxidized with the release of the heat of formation of carbon dioxide and water. So those people did not understand the things that fed and clothed and carried them.

I stayed with them there for three days. And then I went to Jacksville. Yawk City, too. That was enormous. It stretched over —well, from north of where Boston is today to well south of Washington—that was what they called Yawk City.

I never believed that, when he said it, said Jim, interrupting himself. I knew he didn't. If he had, I think he'd have bought land somewhere along there and held for a rise in value. I know Jim. He'd have the idea that seven million years was something like seven hundred, and maybe his great-grandchildren would be able to sell it.

Anyway, went on Jim, he said it was all because the cities had spread so. Boston spread south. Washington, north. And Yawk City spread all over. And the cities between them grew into them.

And it was all one vast machine. It was perfectly ordered

and perfectly neat. They had a transportation system that took me from the North End to the South End in three minutes. I timed it. They had learned to neutralize acceleration.

Then I took one of the great space liners to Neptune. There were still some running. Some people, you see, were coming the other way.

The ship was huge. Mostly it was a freight liner. It floated up from Earth, a great metal cylinder three-quarters of a mile long, and a quarter of a mile in diameter. Outside the atmosphere it began to accelerate. I could see Earth dwindle. I have ridden one of our own liners to Mars, and it took me, in 3048, five days. In half an hour on this liner Earth was just a star with a smaller, dimmer star near it. In an hour we passed Mars. Eight hours later we landed on Neptune. M'reen was the city. Large as the Yawk City of my day—and no one living there.

The planet was cold and dark—horribly cold. The Sun was a tiny, pale disk, heatless and almost lightless. But the city was perfectly comfortable. The air was fresh and cool, moist with the scent of growing blossoms, perfumed with them. And the whole giant metal framework trembled just slightly with the humming, powerful beat of the mighty engines that had made and cared for it.

I learned from records I deciphered, because of my knowledge of the ancient tongue that their tongue was based on, and the tongue of that day when man was dying, that the city was built three million seven hundred and thirty thousand one hundred and fifty years after my birth. Not a machine had been touched by the hand of man since that day.

Yet the air was perfect for man. And the warm, rose-silver glow hung in the air here and supplied the only illumination.

I visited some of their other cities where there were men. And there, on the retreating outskirts of man's domain, I first heard The Song of Longings, as I called it.

And another, The Song of Forgotten Memories. Listen:

He sang another of those songs. There's one thing I know, declared Jim. That bewildered note was stronger in his voice, and by that time I guess I pretty well understood his feelings. Because you have to remember, I heard it only second hand from an ordinary man, and Jim had heard it from an eye-and-ear witness that was not ordinary, and heard it in that organ voice. Anyway, I guess Jim was right when he said: "He wasn't any ordinary man." No ordinary man could think of those songs. They weren't right. When he sang that song, it was full of more of those plaintive minors. I could feel him searching his mind for something he had forgotten, something he desperately wanted to remember—something he knew he should have known—and I felt it eternally elude him. I felt it get further away from him as he sang. I heard that lonely, frantic searcher attempting to recall that thing—that thing that would save him.

And I heard him give a little sob of defeat—and the song ended. Jim tried a few notes. He hasn't a good ear for music—but that was too powerful to forget. Just a few hummed notes. Jim hasn't much imagination, I guess, or when that man of the future sang to him he would have gone mad. It shouldn't be sung to modern men; it isn't meant for them. You've heard those heart-rending cries some animals give, like human cries, almost? A loon, now—he sounds like a lunatic being murdered horribly.

That's just unpleasant. That song made you feel just exactly what the singer meant—because it didn't just sound human—it was human. It was the essence of humanity's last defeat, I guess. You always feel sorry for the chap who loses after trying hard. Well, you could feel the whole of humanity trying hard—and losing. And you knew they couldn't afford to lose, because they couldn't try again.

He said he'd been interested before. And still not wholly upset by those machines that couldn't stop. But that was too much for him.

I knew after that, he said, that these weren't men I could live among. They were dying men, and I was alive with the youth of the race. They looked at me with the same longing, hopeless wonder with which they looked at the stars and the machines. They knew what I was, but couldn't understand.

I began to work on leaving.

It took six months. It was hard because my instruments were gone, of course, and theirs didn't read in the same units. And there were few instruments, anyway. The machines didn't read instruments; they acted on them. They were sensory organs to them.

But Reo Lantal helped where he could. And I came back.

I did just one thing before I left that may help. I may even try to get back there sometime. To see, you know.

I said they had machines that could really think? But that someone had stopped them a long time ago, and no one knew how to start them?

I found some records and deciphered them. I started one of the latest and best of them and started it on a great problem. It is only fitting it should be done. The machine can work on it, not for a thousand years, but for a million, if it must.

I started five of them actually, and connected them together as the records directed.

They are trying to make a machine with something that man had lost. It sounds rather comical. But stop to think before you laugh. And remember that Earth as I saw it from the ground level of Neva City just before Reo Lantal threw the switch.

Twilight—the sun has set. The desert out beyond, in its mystic, changing colors. The great, metal city rising straight-walled to the human city above, broken by spires and towers and great trees with scented blossoms. The silvery-rose glow in the paradise of gardens above.

And all that great city-structure throbbing and humming to the steady gentle beat of perfect, deathless machines built more than three million years before—and never touched since that time by human hands. And they go on. The dead city. The men that have lived, and hoped, and built—and died to leave behind them those little men who can only wonder and look and long for a forgotten kind of companionship. They wander through the vast cities their ancestors built, knowing less of them than the machines themselves.

And the songs. Those tell the story best, I think. Little, hopeless, wondering men amid vast, unknowing, blind machines that started three million years before—and just never knew how to stop. They are dead—and can't die and be still.

So I brought another machine to life, and set it to a task which, in time to come, it will perform.

I ordered it to make a machine which would have what man had lost. A curious machine.

And then I wanted to leave quickly and go back. I had been born in the first full light of man's day. I did not belong in the lingering, dying glow of man's twilight.

So I came back. A little too far back. But it will not take me long to return—accurately this time.

"Well, that was his story," Jim said. "He didn't *tell* me it was true—didn't say anything about it. And he had me thinking so hard I didn't even see him get off in Reno when we stopped for gas.

"But—he wasn't an ordinary man," repeated Jim, in a rather belligerent tone.

Jim claims he doesn't believe the yarn, you know. But he does; that's why he always acts so determined about it when he says the stranger wasn't an ordinary man.

No, he wasn't, I guess. I think he lived and died, too, probably, sometime in the thirty-first century. And I think he saw the twilight of the race, too.

QUESTIONS

1 Campbell's opening—one man retelling another man's story—is a common one. Why might Campbell have chosen to use this kind of an opening? How different would the story be if it were told from the point of view of the time traveler? Do you feel Campbell's method is effective?

2 "Twilight" was first published in 1934. What are some of the ideas that would be different if the story were written today?

3 "Information is the embalming fluid of mankind." What are the implications of this statement from "Twilight?"

4 Discuss the irony of using a machine to save a society that has been, or is being, destroyed by machines. Is the time traveler aware of this irony? If asked to analyze the time traveler, what would you say about him?

5 Do you suppose it is possible for people living in a totally mechanized society to be as ignorant as Campbell's are? If your answer is yes, what are you saying about people; if no, what kind of criticism are you making of Campbell?

6 Campbell concentrates on describing the more mechanical aspects of the future, showing little more of the people than their passivity. What sort of a culture do you think they would have? Could you imagine a day in the life of one of them?

SUGGESTED READINGS

Amis, Kingsley: *New Maps of Hell*. New York: Harcourt, Brace and Company, Inc. 1960.

Asimov, Isaac: *I, Robot*. New York: Signet Books, New American Library, Inc. 1961.

Cheetham, Anthony (ed.): *Science Against Man*. New York: Avon Book Division, The Hearst Corporation, 1970.

Chermayeff, Serge, and Christopher Alexander: *Community and Privacy: Toward a New Architecture of Humanism*. Garden City, New York: Anchor Books, Doubleday & Company, Inc., 1965.

Clarke, Arthur C: *2001: A Space Odyssey*. New York: *Signet Books,* New American Library, Inc., 1970.

de Camp, L. Sprague: *Science Fiction Handbook*. New York: Hermitage House, Inc., 1953.

Dubos, René: *The Dreams of Reason: Science and Utopias*. New York: Columbia University Press, 1961.

Hamilton, Edith: *Greek Mythology*. Boston: Little, Brown and Company, 1943.

Heinlein, Robert: *The Past Through Tomorrow*. New York: G. P. Putnam's Sons, 1967.

Hillegas, Mark R.: *The Future as Nightmare: H. G. Wells and the Anti-Utopians*. New York: Oxford University Press, 1967.

Huxley, Aldous: *Ape and Essence*. New York: Bantam Books, Inc., 1958.

————: *Brave New World*. New York: Harper & Brothers, 1946.

————: *Brave New World Revisited*. New York: Harper & Brothers, 1958.

Kahn, Herman, and Anthony J. Wiener (eds.): *The Year 2000: A Framework for Speculation on the Next Thirty-Three Years*. New York: The Macmillan Company, 1967.

Keith, Sir Arthur: *Evolution and Ethics*. New York: G. P. Putnam's Sons, 1947.

Lewis, C. S.: *An Experiment in Criticism*. New York: Cambridge University Press, 1961.

Malinowski, Browislaw: *Magic, Science and Religion.* Boston: Beacon Press, 1948.

Miller, Walter M.: *A Canticle for Liebowitz.* Philadelphia: J. B. Lippincott Company, 1960.

Orwell, George: *1984.* New York: Harcourt, Brace and Company, Inc., 1949.

————: *Animal Farm.* New York: Harcourt, Brace and Company, Inc., 1946.

Shelley, Mary: *Frankenstein.* New York: Collier Books, The Macmillan Company, 1966.

Skinner, B. F.: *Walden Two.* New York: The Macmillan Company, 1962.

Toffler, Alvin: *Future Shock.* New York: Random House, Inc., 1970.

Vonnegut, Kurt: *Player Piano.* New York: Delacorte Press, Dell Publishing Co., Inc., 1952.

Weiner, Norbert: *The Human Use of Human Beings: Cybernetics and Society.* 2d ed. rev., Garden City, New York: Anchor Books, Doubleday & Company, Inc., 1954.

Wells, H. G.: *The Time Machine.* New York: Armont Publishing Co., Inc., Classics Series.

PART 2
Man Against Society: Rebellion and Escape

"The secret of man's being", Dostoyevsky wrote, "is not only to live but to have something to live for." If man feels this "something" missing, he will often do foolish, desperate things. His search may lead him into himself, into private hells where the good he seeks is so ingeniously hidden that he will never find it. It may lead him outside of himself, into heavenly mists that slip through his fingers and confound his best intentions. Or it may make him want to escape to someplace or something better.

It is escape that much science fiction and fantasy literature is about, and unfortunately, the class into which much of this literature has been thrown by academic and other critics. But their idea of escape literature is not the same as ours. Theirs is literature that helps man forget his own life, time, and problems, however brief that forgetting may be. They call such literature entertainment, quickly adding that there is nothing inherently wrong with entertainment, but that it cannot be taken seriously because it does not get at important concerns. Our idea of escape literature is quite different; it is literature concerned with man's

Edvard Munch. *The Shriek.* 1896. Lithograph, printed in black, 20-5/8x15-13/16 inches. Collection, The Museum of Modern Art, New York. Mathew T. Mellon Fund.

need to escape. Good science fiction and fa
writing get at this need very well.

The following stories show people try
escape from a life that has become either b
meaningless or threatening and restrictive.
happening to them or around them seems una
or wrong, something that should be stopped,
or at the very best rejected. The roots of
discontent may be deep or shallow, may res
or in fertile soil, but the result is the same—
and escape, new fruit from a very old tree.
the fruit gives sustenance, sometimes it doe
But, as though there is a natural impulse to
it does appear. In the first selection, "Rhin
it is hard to tell either when rebellion an
occur or who is doing what. The people ha
human; their first reactions to the rhinoc
dull and unnatural, so that they appear ha
not quite rational. Later, when they themselve
this strange transformation, we wonder whe
unwilled and terrifying change is even esc
what the story is about. When we see th
protagonist alone remains unaffected, we n
assuage our uneasiness by saying that the s
criticism of society—for how worthwhile is
that can make an individual prefer a pri
existence, in fact a grotesque animalism, to
identity, questionable as that identity may
the picture of the society that Jean and the
in is sketchy. We can neither praise it nor
Not easily, anyway, for we have little more
vague impression of it. So this explanation
seem enough.

There is another way of looking at the
though. What faces us squarely and what we
uneasy about is the change that the citizens
or the desire they have to change. Transf
or metamorphosis is not new. We see it i
"The Metamorphosis," in Grimm's *Fairy*
nature (caterpillars into butterflies), and
But here we have it in a slightly different fo
man watches everyone else change, doe

what they become, feels that the change represents degeneration, maybe death, but, in the end, hungers for the same fate. And we ask, "why?" Raising this question rather than criticizing society seems to be Ionesco's intention. But having raised it, he suggests no answer. Instead, he opens the way for more questions. Is it that we cannot bear being alone and different? Are we hollow individuals who can only wail helplessly when bereft of an illusion of solidness that belonging to a group gives us? In *So Human an Animal,* René Dubos says that "most human beings can . . . develop a tolerance to a large variety of conditions that are certainly undesirable and may indeed appear at first sight almost unbearable." Ionesco's protagonist does seem willing to accept such a situation. Is that the point of the story? Is Ionesco describing a fact of life? The questions that loom before us are many, the answers few. Perhaps there is little more that we can, or Ionesco meant to, say.

Wishing to escape and escaping are two different things. In "The Happy Man," we have the latter. Nelson, the protagonist, has escaped from, and is in conflict with, a society that he considers intolerable. In being what he is, he brings us face-to-face with the hero as rebel. This figure is a not uncommon one. He often has a strong messianic drive and is seldom able to be dissuaded of his beliefs. Nelson's reply to Glynnis when she questions the wisdom of his desire to waken the sleepers speaks to this issue: "Because they can do better. We can save them and show them that; I can lead them back where they belong." Here is the savior/messiah rather than the simple savior of Part One. He is a fanatic, but he is also a character with whom we can identify because he is valiantly resisting what he believes is a tyrannical society. The individualist, the frontiersman, the man who believes in himself, in his own integrity—having been raised in an aggressive, competitive society, how can we condemn them? Perhaps we cannot, especially since this particular individual is in the ultimate trap —a world he can neither escape nor accept.

But if we cannot condemn Nelson, we can at

least look in a dispassionate way at some of the issues he raises. Many science-fiction writers have looked critically at the question of whether drugs can be used beneficially by the state. The key phrase here, it seems, is *by the state.* Throughout history man has used drugs, not just to escape an unacceptable world, but to find a better one, and in the process greater knowledge or self-awareness. Individuals like Coleridge, De Quincey, Poe, and Huxley, as well as whole cultures, have found drugs beneficial, a way of escaping human or societal limitations, real or imagined. In most countries, of course, the state prohibits the use of drugs by individuals, and its punishments are swift for any who transgress its laws. But it is not adverse to, or incapable of, using drugs for the common good, though it may be reluctant to do so hastily, without a great deal of prior testing and propaganda. Individuals, in turn, react quickly to any hint that the state is even thinking of using drugs on them, for they usually feel the "good" to be a thinly disguised tyranny.

And here we come to a prime cause of revolt—impotence, powerlessness, the fear of not being in control of one's life. "The Happy Man" is about this fear, and about a man, a discontent, for whom (or from whom?) no world is safe because of this fear.

In "A World Ends," we have a character who has fled a world she found disagreeable. In choosing to cling to an outmoded world, the Marchesa and her guests have rejected the kind of change or struggle necessary to adapt to the real world. The Marchesa thinks it easier to create her own, but her solution is as inadequate as her island is artificial, and dream and island perish together. Only the narrator escapes, swimming under his own power through waters that give life, probably because he does not cling to what was but is able to accept what is.

What can we say so far, then, about revolt and escape. Neither are presented in the best of lights by the authors of these stories. We are given no Christ who will leave his imprint on hundreds of generations to follow. We are not even given a nice radical with clearly defined ideals. The most we have are a handful of dissidents who are either not sure of their own identity or lacking in personal qualities that might inspire respect. True, we have been horrified by the conditions in which some of them were found, but surely we can expect more, we say.

At first glance what "A Rose for Ecclesiastes" offers is hardly promising. Gallinger, the protagonist, has isolated himself from his fellows through snobbery, vanity, and, perhaps, fear. We feel that the dislike which the others feel for him is justified. These are facts we cannot ignore. But later we also find that he is sensitive, intelligent, and perceptive. Of all the Earthmen on Mars, it is he and he alone who can inspire the trust of the Martians. Because he can understand their unique culture and religion, he is even able, eventually, to save them from their own passivity. Becoming a messiah unwittingly, bringing new life in ways he least suspects, he grows before our eyes. He is especially human in his refusal to accept defeat for the Martians, despite his own tiredness, cynicism, and feeling that all is vanity and that nothing is really new:

> "Don't," I said, automatically, suddenly knowing the great paradox which lies at the heart of all miracles. I did not believe a word of my own gospel, never had.

"A Rose for Ecclesiastes" may be considered only marginally a story of revolt. But at least it suggests other facets of man's troublesome nature. Being discontent, Freud says in *Civilization and its Discontents,* comes about partly because man has learned to feel separate from the world around him. This feeling is always with him and is often at war with his need to find pleasure or comfort. One of the ways for man to avoid pain, then, is to become closer to the world about him. (I have certainly not done Freud justice, but I hope you will discover his views for yourself.) Perhaps Gallinger seems to feel such separateness. But whether he saves the Martians because he wants to lose that feeling, because he fell in love with Braxa, or because he hates to think that they will all die as a people is not entirely clear.

So we are left with man himself. He becomes socialized and is largely content with his lot. But sometimes he is not. He turns, then, into a Caesar or Brutus, but more often into an Anthony. He is man caught in a world that he must either assault or escape. Perhaps the world is himself, perhaps it is the society of which he is a part. In any case, the process is the same: he acts and gains a sense of power. By asserting himself, he can realize his own importance or make others realize theirs. If he does not, he becomes like the protagonist in "Rhinoceros." But it seldom ends there, because man himself is always changing. More aware than any other animal, both of himself and of the world in which he lives, he changes to survive.

These stories are concerned with man's awareness, with his need to change, or to change things, and with the critical faculty that constantly seems to ask "why" or "what if. . . ." It is at least some comfort to believe that questioning is basic to man's nature and that if we are ever to reach a world where this questioning is at an end, we will probably find ourselves less than human-animals, happy men, or even gods perhaps, but not humans, by any means.

THE ADDICT
Anne Sexton

Sleepmonger,
deathmonger,
with capsules in my palms each night,
eight at a time from sweet pharmaceutical bottles
I make arrangements for a pint-sized journey.
I'm the queen of this condition.
I'm an expert on making the trip
and now they say I'm an addict.
Now they ask why,
Why!

Don't they know
that I promise to die!
I'm keeping in practice.
I'm merely staying in shape.
The pills are a mother, but better,
every color and as good as sour balls.
I'm on a diet from death.

Yes, I admit
it has gotten to be a bit of a habit—
blows eight at a time, socked in the eye,
hauled away by the pink, the orange,
the green and the white goodnights.
I'm becoming something of a chemical
mixture.
That's it!

My supply
of tablets
has got to last for years and years.
I like them more than I like me.
Stubborn as hell, they won't let go.
It's a kind of marriage.
It's a kind of war

where I plant bombs inside
of myself.

Yes
I try
to kill myself in small amounts,
an innocuous occupation.
Actually I'm hung up on it.
But remember I don't make too much noise.
And frankly no one has to lug me out
and I don't stand there in my winding sheet.
I'm a little buttercup in my yellow nightie
eating my eight loaves in a row
and in a certain order as in
the laying on of hands
or the black sacrament.

It's a ceremony
but like any other sport
It's full of rules.
It's like a musical tennis match where
my mouth keeps catching the ball.
Then I lie on my altar
elevated by the eight chemical kisses.

What a lay me down this is
with two pink, two orange,
two green, two white goodnights.
Fee-fi-fo-fum—
Now I'm borrowed.
Now I'm numb.

RHINOCEROS
Eugene Ionesco

In Memory of Andre Frederique

We were sitting outside the cafe, my friend Jean and I, peacefully talking about one thing and another, when we caught sight of it on the opposite pavement, huge and powerful, panting noisily, charging straight ahead and brushing against market stalls—a rhinoceros. People in the street stepped hurriedly aside to let it pass. A housewife uttered a cry of terror, her basket dropped from her hands, the wine from a broken bottle spread over the pavement, and some pedestrians, one of them an elderly man, rushed into the shops. It was all over like a flash of lightning. People emerged from their hiding-places and gathered in groups which watched the rhinoceros disappear into the distance, made some comments on the incident and then dispersed.

My own reactions are slowish. I absent-mindedly took in the image of the rushing beast, without ascribing any very great importance to it. That morning, moreover, I was feeling tired and my mouth was sour, as a result of the previous night's excesses; we had been celebrating a friend's birthday. Jean had not been at the party; and when the first moment of surprise was over, he exclaimed:

"A rhinoceros at large in town! Doesn't that surprise you? It ought not be allowed."

"True," I said, "I hadn't thought of that. It's dangerous."

"We ought to protest to the Town Council."

"Perhaps it's escaped from the Zoo," I said.

"You're dreaming," he replied. "There hasn't been a Zoo in our town since the animals were decimated by the plague in the seventeenth century."

"Perhaps it belongs to the circus?"

"What circus? The Council has forbidden itinerant entertainers to stop on municipal territory. None have come here since we were children."

"Perhaps it has lived here ever since, hidden in the marshy woods round about," I answered with a yawn.

"You're completely lost in a dense alcoholic haze. . . ."

"Which rises from the stomach. . . ."

"Yes. And has pervaded your brain. What marshy woods can you think of round about here? Our province is so arid they call it Little Castile."

"Perhaps it sheltered under a pebble? Perhaps it made its nest on a dry branch?"

"How tiresome you are with your paradoxes. You're quite incapable of talking seriously."

"Today, particularly."

"Today and every other day."

"Don't lose your temper, my dear Jean. We're not going to quarrel about that creature. . . ."

We changed the subject of our conversation and began to talk about the weather again, about the rain, which fell so rarely in our region, about the need to provide our sky with artificial clouds, and other banal and insoluble questions.

We parted. It was Sunday. I went to bed and slept all day: another wasted Sunday. On Monday morning I went to the office, making a solemn promise to myself never to get drunk again, and particularly not on Saturdays, so as not to spoil the following Sundays. For I had one single free day a week and three weeks' holiday in the summer. Instead of drinking and making myself ill, wouldn't it be better to keep fit and healthy, to spend my precious moments of freedom in a more intelligent fashion: visiting museums, reading literary magazines and listening to lectures? And instead of spending all my available money on drink, wouldn't it be preferable to buy tickets for interesting plays? I was still unfamiliar with the avant-garde theatre, of which I had heard so much talk, I had never seen a play by Ionesco. Now or never was the time to bring myself up to date.

The following Sunday I met Jean once again at the same cafe.

"I've kept my promise," I said, shaking hands with him.

"What promise have you kept?" he asked.

"My promise to myself. I've vowed to give up drinking. Instead of drinking I've decided to cultivate my mind. Today I am clear-headed. This afternoon I'm going to the Municipal

Museum and this evening I've a ticket for the theatre. Won't you come with me?"

"Let's hope your good intentions will last," replied Jean. "But I can't go with you. I'm meeting some friends at the brasserie."

"Oh, my dear fellow, now it's you who are setting a bad example. You'll get drunk!"

"Once in a way doesn't imply a habit," replied Jean irritably. "Whereas you . . ."

The discussion was about to take a disagreeable turn, when we heard a mighty trumpeting, the hurried clatter of some perissodactyl's hoofs, cries, a cat's mewing; almost simultaneously we saw a rhinoceros appear, then disappear, on the opposite pavement, panting noisily and charging straight ahead.

Immediately afterwards a woman appeared holding in her arms a shapeless, bloodstained little object:

"It's run over my cat," she wailed, "it's run over my cat!"

The poor dishevelled woman, who seemed the very embodiment of grief, was soon surrounded by people offering sympathy.

Jean and I got up. We rushed across the street to the side of the unfortunate woman.

"All cats are mortal," I said stupidly, not knowing how to console her.

"It came past my shop last week!" the grocer recalled.

"It wasn't the same one," Jean declared. "It wasn't the same one: last week's had two horns on its nose, it was an Asian rhinoceros; this one had only one, it's an African rhinoceros."

"You're talking nonsense," I said irritably. "How could you distinguish its horns? The animal rushed past so fast that we could hardly see it; you hadn't time to count them. . . ."

"I don't live in a haze," Jean retorted sharply. "I'm clear-headed, I'm quick at figures."

"He was charging with his head down."

"That made it all the easier to see."

"You're a pretentious fellow, Jean. You're a pedant, who isn't even sure of his own knowledge. For in the first place it's the Asian rhinoceros that has one horn on its nose, and the African rhinoceros that has two!"

"You're quite wrong, it's the other way about."

"Would you like to bet on it?"

"I won't bet against you. You're the one who has two horns," he cried, red with fury, "you Asiatic you!" (He stuck to his guns.)

"I haven't any horns. I shall never wear them. And I'm not an Asiatic either. In any case, Asiatics are just like other people."

"They're yellow!" he shouted, beside himself with rage.

Jean turned his back on me and strode off, cursing.

I felt a fool. I ought to have been more conciliatory, and not contradicted him: for I knew he could not bear it. The slightest objection made him foam at the mouth. This was his only fault, for he had a heart of gold and had done me countless good turns. The few people who were there and who had been listening to us had, as a result, quite forgotten about the poor woman's squashed cat. They crowded round me, arguing: some maintained that the Asian rhinoceros was indeed one-horned, and that I was right; others maintained that on the contrary the African rhinoceros was one-horned, and that therefore the previous speaker had been right.

"That is not the question," interposed a gentleman (straw boater, small moustache, eyeglass, a typical logician's head) who had hitherto stood silent. "The discussion turned on a problem from which you have wandered. You began by asking yourselves whether today's rhinoceros is the same as last Sunday's or whether it is a different one. That is what must be decided. You may have seen one and the same one-horned rhinoceros on two occasions, or you may have seen one and the same two-horned rhinoceros on two occasions. Or again, you may have seen first one one-horned rhinoceros and then a second one-horned rhinoceros. Or else, first one two-horned rhinoceros and then a second two-horned rhinoceros. If on the first occasion you had seen a two-horned rhinoceros, and on the second a one-horned rhinoceros, that would not be conclusive either. It might be that since last week the rhinoceros had lost one of his horns, and that the one you saw today was the same. Or it might be that two two-horned rhinoceroses had each lost one of their horns. If you could prove that on the first occasion you had seen a one-horned rhinoceros, whether it was Asian or African, and today a two-horned rhinoceros, whether it was African or Asian—that doesn't matter—then we might conclude that two different rhinoceroses were involved, for it is most unlikely that a second horn could grow in a few days, to any visible extent, on a rhinoceros's nose; this would mean that an Asian, or African, rhinoceros had become an African, or Asian rhinoceros, which is logically impossible, since the same creature cannot be born in two places at once or even successively."

"That seems clear to me," I said. "But it doesn't settle the question."

"Of course," retorted the gentleman, smiling with a knowledgeable air, "only the problem has now been stated correctly."

"That's not the problem either," interrupted the grocer, who being no doubt of an emotional nature cared little about logic. "Can we allow our cats to be run over under our eyes by two-horned or one-horned rhinoceroses, be they Asian or African?"

"He's right, he's right," everybody exclaimed. "We can't allow our cats to be run over, by rhinoceroses or anything else!"

The grocer pointed with a theatrical gesture to the poor weeping woman, who still held and rocked in her arms the shapeless, bleeding remains of what had once been her cat.

Next day, in the paper, under the heading Road Casualties among Cats, there were two lines describing the death of the poor creature, "crushed underfoot by a pachyderm," it was said, without further details.

On Sunday afternoon I hadn't visited a museum; in the evening I hadn't gone to the theatre. I had moped at home by myself, overwhelmed by remorse at having quarrelled with Jean.

"He's so susceptible, I ought to have spared his feelings," I told myself. "It's absurd to lose one's temper about something like that . . . about the horns of a rhinoceros that one had never seen before . . . a native of Africa or of India, such faraway countries, what could it matter to me? Whereas Jean had always been my friend, a friend who . . . to whom I owed so much . . . and who . . . ."

In short, while promising myself to go and see Jean as soon as possible and to make it up with him, I had drunk an entire bottle of brandy without noticing. But I did indeed notice it the next day: a sore head, a foul mouth, an uneasy conscience; I was really most uncomfortable. But duty before everything: I got to the office on time, or almost. I was able to sign the register just before it was taken away.

"Well, so you've seen rhinoceroses too?" asked the chief clerk, who, to my great surprise, was already there.

"Sure I've seen him," I said, taking off my town jacket and putting on my old jacket with the frayed sleeves, good enough for work.

"Oh, now you see, I'm not crazy!" exclaimed the typist Daisy excitedly. (How pretty she was, with her pink cheeks and fair hair! I found her terribly attractive. If I could fall in love with anybody, it would be with her. . . .) "A one-horned rhinoceros!"

"Two-horned!" corrected my colleague Emile Dudard, Bachelor of Law, eminent jurist, who looked forward to a brilliant future with the firm and, possibly, in Daisy's affections.

"*I've* not seen it! And I don't believe in it!" declared Botard, an ex-schoolmaster who acted as archivist. "And nobody's ever seen one in this part of the world, except in the illustrations to school text-books. These rhinoceroses have blossomed only in the imagination of ignorant women. The thing's a myth, like flying saucers."

I was about to point out to Botard that the expression "blossomed" applied to a rhinoceros, or to a number of them, seemed to me inappropriate, when the jurist exclaimed:

"All the same, a cat was crushed, and before witnesses!"

"Collective psychosis," retorted Botard, who was a free-thinker, "just like religion, the opium of the people!"

"I believe in flying saucers myself," remarked Daisy.

The chief clerk cut short our argument:

"That'll do! Enough chatter! Rhinoceros or no rhinoceros, flying saucers or no flying saucers, work's got to be done."

The typist started typing. I sat down at my desk and became engrossed in my documents. Emile Dudard began correcting the proofs of a commentary on the Law for the Repression of Alcoholism, while the chief clerk, slamming the door, retired into his study.

"It's a hoax!" Botard grumbled once more, aiming his remarks at Dudard. "It's your propaganda that spreads these rumours!"

"It's not propaganda," I interposed.

"I saw it myself . . ." Daisy confirmed simultaneously.

"You make me laugh," said Dudard to Botard. "Propaganda? For what?"

"You know better than I do! Don't act the simpleton!"

"In any case, *I'm* not paid by the Pontenegrins!"

"That's an insult!" cried Botard, thumping the table with his fist. The door of the chief clerk's room opened suddenly and his head appeared.

"Monsieur Boeuf hasn't come in today."

"Quite true, he's not here," I said.

"Just when I needed him. Did he tell anyone he was ill? If this goes on I shall give him the sack. . . ."

It was not the first time that the chief clerk had threatened our colleague in this way.

"Has one of you got the key to his desk?" he went on.

Just then Madame Boeuf made her appearance. She seemed terrified.

"I must ask you to excuse my husband. He went to spend the weekend with relations. He's had a slight attack of 'flu. Look, that's what he says in his telegram. He hopes to be back on Wednesday. Give me a glass of water . . . and a chair!" she gasped, collapsing onto the chair we offered her.

"It's very tiresome! But it's no reason to get so alarmed!" remarked the chief clerk.

"I was pursued by a rhinoceros all the way from home," she stammered.

"With one horn or two?" I asked.

"You make me laugh!" exclaimed Botard.

"Why don't you let her speak!" protested Dudard.

Madame Boeuf had to make a great effort to be explicit:

"It's downstairs, in the doorway. It seems to be trying to come upstairs."

At that very moment a tremendous noise was heard: the stairs were undoubtedly giving way under a considerable weight.

We rushed out on to the landing. And there, in fact, amidst the debris, was a rhinoceros, its head lowered, trumpeting in an agonized and agonizing voice and turning vainly round and round. I was able to make out two horns.

"It's an African rhinoceros . . ." I said, "or rather an Asian one."

My mind was so confused that I was no longer sure whether two horns were characteristic of the Asian or of the African rhinoceros, whether a single horn was characteristic of the African or of the Asian rhinoceros, or whether on the contrary two horns . . . In short, I was floundering mentally, while Botard glared furiously at Dudard.

"It's an infamous plot!" and, with an orator's gesture, he pointed at the jurist: "It's your fault!"

"It's yours!" the other retorted.

"Keep calm, this is no time to quarrel!" declared Daisy, trying in vain to pacify them.

"For years now I've been asking the Board to let us have concrete steps instead of that rickety old staircase," said the chief clerk. "Something like this was bound to happen. It was predictable. I was quite right!"

"As usual," Daisy added ironically. "But how shall we get down?"

"I'll carry you in my arms," the chief clerk joked flirtatiously, stroking the typist's cheek, "and we'll jump together!"

"Don't put your horny hand on my face, you pachydermous creature!"

The chief clerk had not time to react. Madame Boeuf, who had got up and come to join us, and who had for some minutes been staring attentively at the rhinoceros, which was turning round and round below us, suddenly uttered a terrible cry:

"It's my husband! Boeuf, my poor dear Boeuf, what has happened to you?"

The rhinoceros, or rather Boeuf, responded with a violent and yet tender trumpeting, while Madame Boeuf fainted into my arms and Botard, raising his to heaven, stormed: "It's sheer lunacy! What a society!"

When we had recovered from our initial astonishment, we telephoned to the Fire Brigade, who drove up with their ladders and fetched us down. Madame Boeuf, although we advised her against it, rode off on her spouse's back towards their home. She had ample grounds for divorce (but who was the guilty party?) yet she chose rather not to desert her husband in his present state.

At the little bistro where we all went for lunch (all except the Boeufs, of course) we learnt that several rhinoceroses had been seen in various parts of the town: some people said seven, others seventeen, others again said thirty-two. In face of this accumulated evidence Botard could no longer deny the rhinoceric facts. But he knew, he declared, what to think about it. He would explain it to us some day. He knew the "why" of things, the "underside" of the story, the names of those responsible, the aim and significance of the outrage. Going back to the office that afternoon, business or no business, was out of the question. We had to wait for the staircase to be repaired.

I took advantage of this to pay a call on Jean, with the intention of making it up to him. He was in bed.

"I don't feel very well!" he said.

"You know, Jean, we were both right. There are two-horned rhinoceroses in the town as well as one-horned ones. It really doesn't matter where either sort comes from. The only significant thing, in my opinion, is the existence of the rhinoceros in itself."

"I don't feel very well," my friend kept on saying without listening to me, "I don't feel very well!"

"What's the matter with you? I'm so sorry!"

"I'm rather feverish, and my head aches."

More precisely, it was his forehead which was aching. He must have had a knock, he said. And in fact a lump was swelling up there, just above his nose. He had gone a greenish colour, and his voice was hoarse.

"Have you got a sore throat? It may be tonsilitis."

I took his pulse. It was beating quite regularly.

"It can't be very serious. A few days' rest and you'll be all right. Have you sent for the doctor?"

As I was about to let go of his wrist I noticed that his veins were swollen and bulging out. Looking closely I observed that not only were the veins enlarged but that the skin all round them was visibly changing colour and growing hard.

"It may be more serious than I imagined," I thought. "We must send for the doctor," I said aloud.

"I felt uncomfortable in my clothes, and now my pyjamas are too tight," he said in a hoarse voice.

"What's the matter with your skin? It's like leather...." Then, staring at him: "Do you know what happened to Boeuf? He's turned into a rhinoceros."

"Well, what about it? That's not such a bad thing! After all, rhinoceroses are creatures like ourselves, with just as much right to live...."

"Provided they don't imperil our lives. Aren't you aware of the difference in mentality?"

"Do you think ours is preferable?"

"All the same, we have our own moral code, which I consider incompatible with that of these animals. We have our philosophy, our irreplaceable system of values...."

"Humanism is out of date! You're a ridiculous old sentimentalist. You're talking nonsense."

"I'm surprised to hear you say that, my dear Jean! Have you taken leave of your senses?"

It really looked like it. Blind fury had disfigured his face, and altered his voice to such an extent that I could scarcely understand the words that issued from his lips.

"Such assertions, coming from you . . ." I tried to resume.

He did not give me a chance to do so. He flung back his blankets, tore off his pyjamas, and stood up in bed, entirely naked (he who was usually the most modest of men!) green with rage from head to foot.

The lump on his forehead had grown longer; he was staring fixedly at me, apparently without seeing me. Or, rather, he must have seen me quite clearly, for he charged at me with his head lowered. I barely had time to leap to one side; if I hadn't he would have pinned me to the wall.

"You are a rhinoceros!" I cried.

"I'll trample on you! I'll trample on you!" I made out these words as I dashed towards the door.

I went downstairs four steps at a time, while the walls shook as he butted them with his horn, and I heard him utter fearful angry trumpetings.

"Call the police! Call the police! You've got a rhinoceros in the house!" I called out to the tenants who, in great surprise, looked out of their flats as I passed each landing.

On the ground floor I had great difficulty in dodging the rhinoceros which emerged from the concierge's lodge and tried to charge me. At last I found myself out in the street, sweating, my legs limp, at the end of my tether.

Fortunately there was a bench by the edge of the pavement, and I sat down on it. Scarcely had I more or less got back my breath when I saw a herd of rhinoceroses hurrying down the avenue and nearing, at full speed, the place where I was. If only they had been content to stay in the middle of the street! But they were so many that there was not room for them all there, and they overflowed on to the pavement. I leapt off my bench and flattened myself against the wall: snorting, trumpeting, with a smell of leather and of wild animals in heat, they brushed past me and covered me with a cloud of dust. When they had disappeared, I could not go back to sit on the bench; the animals had demolished it and it lay in fragments on the pavement.

I did not find it easy to recover from such emotions. I had to stay at home for several days. Daisy came to see me and kept me informed as to the changes that were taking place.

The chief clerk had been the first to turn into a rhinoceros, to the great disgust of Botard who, nevertheless, became one himself twenty-four hours later.

"One must keep up with one's times!" were his last words as a man.

The case of Botard did not surprise me, in spite of his apparent strength of mind. I found it less easy to understand the chief clerk's transformation. Of course it might have been involuntary, but one would have expected him to put up more resistance.

Daisy recalled that she had commented on the roughness of

his palms the very day that Boeuf had appeared in rhinoceros shape. This must have made a deep impression on him; he had not shown it, but he had certainly been cut to the quick.

"If I hadn't been so outspoken, if I had pointed it out to him more tactfully, perhaps this would never have happened."

"I blame myself, too, for not having been gentler with Jean. I ought to have been friendlier, shown more understanding," I said in my turn.

Daisy informed me that Dudard, too, had been transformed, as had also a cousin of hers whom I did not know. And there were others, mutual friends, strangers.

"There are a great many of them," she said, "about a quarter of the inhabitants of our town."

"They're still in the minority, however."

"The way things are going, that won't last long!" she sighed.

"Alas! And they're so much more efficient."

Herds of rhinoceroses rushing at top speed through the streets became a sight that no longer surprised anybody. People would stand aside to let them pass and then resume their stroll, or attend to their business, as if nothing had happened.

"How can anybody be a rhinoceros! It's unthinkable!" I protested in vain.

More of them kept emerging from courtyards and houses, even from windows, and went to join the rest.

There came a point when the authorities proposed to enclose them in huge parks. For humanitarian reasons, the Society for the Protection of Animals opposed this. Besides, everyone had some close relative or friend among the rhinoceroses, which, for obvious reasons, made the project well-nigh impracticable. It was abandoned.

The situation grew worse, which was only to be expected. One day a whole regiment of rhinoceroses, having knocked down the walls of the barracks, came out with drums at their head and poured on to the boulevards.

At the Ministry of Statistics, statisticians produced their statistics: census of animals, approximate reckoning of their daily increase, percentage of those with one horn, percentage of those with two . . . What an opportunity for learned controversies! Soon there were defections among the statisticians themselves. The few who remained were paid fantastic sums.

One day, from my balcony, I caught sight of a rhinoceros charging forward with loud trumpetings, presumably to join his fellows; he wore a straw boater impaled on his horn.

"The logician!" I cried. "He's one too? Is it possible?" Just at that moment Daisy opened the door.

"The logician is a rhinoceros!" I told her.

She knew. She had just seen him in the street. She was bringing me a basket of provisions.

"Shall we have lunch together?" she suggested. "You know, it was difficult to find anything to eat. The shops have been ransacked; they devour everything. A number of shops are closed 'on account of transformations,' the notices say."

"I love you, Daisy, please never leave me."

"Close the window, darling. They make too much noise. And the dust comes in."

"So long as we're together, I'm afraid of nothing, I don't mind about anything." Then, when I had closed the window: "I thought I should never be able to fall in love with a woman again."

I clasped her tightly in my arms. She responded to my embrace.

"How I'd like to make you happy! Could you be happy with me?"

"Why not? You declare you're afraid of nothing and yet you're scared of everything! What can happen to us?"

"My love, my joy!" I stammered, kissing her lips with a passion such as I had forgotten, intense and agonizing.

The ringing of the telephone interrupted us.

She broke from my arms, went to pick up the receiver, then uttered a cry: "Listen . . ."

I put the receiver to my ear. I heard ferocious trumpetings.

"They're playing tricks on us now!"

"Whatever can be happening?" she inquired in alarm.

We turned on the radio to hear the news; we heard more trumpetings. She was shaking with fear.

"Keep calm," I said, "keep calm!"

She cried out in terror: "They've taken over the broadcasting station!"

"Keep calm, keep calm!" I repeated, increasingly agitated myself.

Next day in the street they were running about in all directions. You could watch for hours without catching sight of a single human being. Our house was shaking under the weight of our perissodactylic neighbors' hoofs.

"What must be must be," said Daisy. "What can we do about it?"

"They've all gone mad. The world is sick."

"It's not you and I who'll cure it."

"We shan't be able to communicate with anybody. Can you understand them?"

"We ought to try to interpret their psychology, to learn their language."

"They have no language."

"What do you know about it?"

"Listen to me, Daisy, we shall have children, and then they will have children, it'll take time, but between us we can regenerate humanity. With a little courage . . ."

"I don't want to have children."

"How do you hope to save the world, then?"

"Perhaps after all it's we who need saving. Perhaps we are the abnormal ones. Do you see anyone else like us?"

"Daisy, I can't have you talking like that!"

I looked at her in despair.

"It's we who are in the right, Daisy, I assure you."

"What arrogance! There's no absolute right. It's the whole world that is right—not you or me."

"Yes, Daisy, I *am* right. The proof is that you understand me and that I love you as much as a man can love a woman."

"I'm rather ashamed of what you call love, that morbid thing. . . . It cannot compare with the extraordinary energy displayed by all these beings we see around us."

"Energy? Here's energy for you!" I cried, my powers of argument exhausted, giving her a slap.

Then, as she burst into tears: "I won't give in, no, I won't give in."

She rose, weeping, and flung her sweet-smelling arms round my neck.

"I'll stand fast, with you, to the end."

She was unable to keep her word. She grew melancholy, and visibly pined away. One morning when I woke up I saw that her place in the bed was empty. She had gone away without leaving any message.

The situation became literally unbearable for me. It was my fault if Daisy had gone. Who knows what had become of her? Another burden on my conscience. There was nobody who could help me to find her again. I imagined the worst, and felt myself responsible.

And on every side there were trumpetings and frenzied chargings, and clouds of dust. In vain did I shut myself up in my own room, putting cotton wool in my ears: at night I saw them in my dreams.

"The only way out is to convince them." But of what? Were these mutations reversible? And in order to convince them one would have to talk to them. In order for them to re-learn my language (which moreover I was beginning to forget) I should first have to learn theirs. I could not distinguish one trumpeting from another, one rhinoceros from another rhinoceros.

One day, looking at myself in the glass, I took a dislike to my long face: I needed a horn, or even two, to give dignity to my flabby features.

And what if, as Daisy had said, it was they who were in the right? I was out of date, I had missed the boat, that was clear.

I discovered that their trumpetings had after all a certain charm, if a somewhat harsh one. I should have noticed that while there was still time. I tried to trumpet: how feeble the sound was, how lacking in vigour! When I made greater efforts I only succeeded in howling. Howlings are not trumpetings.

It is obvious that one must not always drift blindly behind events and that it's a good thing to maintain one's individuality. However, one must also make allowances for things; asserting one's own difference, to be sure, but yet . . . remaining akin to one's fellows. I no longer bore any likeness to anyone or to anything, except to ancient, old-fashioned photographs which had no connection with living beings.

Each morning I looked at my hands hoping that the palms would have hardened during my sleep. The skin remained flabby. I gazed at my too-white body, my hairy legs: oh for a hard skin and that magnificent green colour, a decent, hairless nudity, like theirs!

My conscience was increasingly uneasy, unhappy. I felt I was a monster. Alas, I would never become a rhinoceros. I could never change.

I dared no longer look at myself. I was ashamed. And yet I couldn't, no, I couldn't.

QUESTIONS

1 Why do you suppose Ionesco has chosen not to develop his characters more fully? Would you consider the narrator, as he is, a representative of modern man? (Is "modern man" a useful term?)

2 Is the following statement justification of the narrator's feelings or only rationalization? "However, one must also make allowances for things; asserting one's own difference, to be sure, but yet . . . remaining akin to one's fellows. I no longer bore any likeness to anyone or to anything, except to ancient, old-fashioned photographs which had no connection with living beings."

3 What do you feel for the narrator? Pity, respect, contempt? Is it easy to bear total isolation? Does Ionesco overlook this aspect of the narrator's predicament? What often happens to people or animals when they are totally isolated from others of their kind?

4 Why does Ionesco leave us wondering about Daisy's fate? What does the narrator mean by calling her another burden on his conscience?

5 Think of other stories of transformation. Are there any particularly striking similarities among them? If so, how might these similarities be accounted for?

6 As human beings we tend to overlook the fact that we are rational creatures last, not first, and that civilization emerged from a primitive past that is relatively timeless. Could "Rhinoceros" be considered an ironic statement about our tendency to consider rationality one of man's essential rather than accidental characteristics? Justify your answer.

THE HAPPY MAN
Gerald W. Page

Nelson saw the girl at the same time she saw him. He had just rounded an outcropping of rock about ten miles from the East Coast Mausoleum. They were facing each other, poised defensively, eyes alertly on each other, about twenty feet apart. She was blonde and lean with the conditioning of outdoor life, almost to the point of thinness. And although not really beautiful, she was attractive and young, probably not yet twenty. Her features were even and smooth, her hair wild about her face. She wore a light blouse and faded brown shorts made from a coarse homespun material. Nelson had not expected to run into anyone, and apparently, neither had she. They stood staring at each other for a long time; how long, Nelson was unable to decide, later.

A little foolishly, Nelson realized that something would have to be done by one of them. "I'm Hal Nelson," he said. It had been a long time since he had last spoken; his voice sounded strange in the wilderness. The girl moved tensely, but did not come any closer to him. Her eyes stayed fixed on him and he knew that her ears were straining for any sound that might warn her of a trap.

Nelson started to take a step, then checked himself, cursing himself for his eager blundering. The girl stepped back once, quickly, like an animal uncertain if it had been threatened. Nelson stepped back, slowly, and spoke again. "I'm a waker, like you. You can tell by my rags." It was true enough, but the girl only frowned. Her alertness did not relax.

"I've been one for ten or twelve years. I escaped from a Commune at Tannerville when I was in my senior year. They never even got me into one of the coffins. As I said, I'm a waker." He spoke slowly, gently and he hoped soothingly. "You don't have to be afraid of me. Now tell me who you are."

The girl pushed a lock of almost yellow hair from her eyes with the back of her hand, but it was her only show of carelessness. She was strong and light. She was considerably smaller than he and could probably handle herself as well as he in this country. The landscape was thick with bushes, conifers and rocks. She would have no trouble in getting away from him if he scared her; and he could scare her with almost any sudden movement. It had been too long ago for Nelson to keep track of when he had been accompanied by others and he hungered for companionship; especially for a woman. The patrol that had captured Sammy and Jeanne and the old man, Gardner, had also gotten Edna and almost had gotten him. The fact that the girl was alone now more than likely meant that she had no one either. They needed each other. Nelson did not want to scare her off.

So he sat down on the ground with his back to a large rock and rummaged in his pack to find a can.

"You hungry?" he asked, looking up at her. He couldn't be sure at the distance, but he thought that her eyes were brown. Brown, and huge; like a colt's. He held the can out where she could see it. She repeated the gesture of a while ago to brush back that same lock of almost yellow hair, but there was a change in her face which he could see even twenty feet away, and another, more subtle change about her which he had to sense. "You're hungry, all right, aren't you?" he said. He almost tossed her the can, but realized in time that she would run. He considered for a moment and then held it out to her. She focused her eyes on the can and for a moment Nelson might have been able to reach her before she turned and ran; but he had better sense than to try.

Instead, he watched the play of conflicting desires about the girl's face and body. He could see the uncertainty and indecision in the girl's nearly imperceptible movement. But she did not come.

Well, at least she didn't run, either; and Nelson could claim to having broken ahead some in stirring up any indecision at all. He found the can's release and pressed it with his thumb. There was a hiss as the seal came loose and an odour of cooked food as the contents sizzled with warmth. Nelson looked up at the girl and smiled.

It could have been wishful thinking, but it seemed to him that she was a step or two closer than she had been before he had taken his eyes off her to open the can. He couldn't be sure. He smelled the food for her benefit and told her, "It's pork and beans." He held it out to her again. "I stole it from a patrol warehouse a few weeks back. It sure does smell good, doesn't it? You like the smell of that, don't you?" But she still wasn't convinced that this wasn't a patrol stunt to get hands on her and haul her back to a mausoleum. He couldn't blame her. He slowly pushed himself to his feet and walked to a spot about ten feet from where he had been, and still about twenty feet from her, and put the can carefully on the ground. He went back and seated himself against the same rock to wait for her to make up her mind.

It didn't take long. Without taking her eyes from him, she moved like an animal to the food and stooped slowly, keeping alert for any sudden move on his part, and picked up the food. She stood up, and stepped back a couple of steps.

She ate with her fingers, dipping them in and extracting hot food, with no apparent concern for the heat. She pushed the food into her mouth and licked her fingers carefully of clinging food. She ate rapidly, as if for the first time in weeks. And she kept her eyes, all the time, on Nelson.

Nelson didn't care, now; he wouldn't have jumped her, or done anything to scare her at all, even if her guard were to be let down for a moment.

He let her finish her meal, then smiled at her when she looked at him. She still held the empty can, and she was wiping her mouth with her free hand. She stared at him for almost half a minute before he said slowly, "You like that food. Don't you?" She said nothing. She looked at him and at the can she held. He knew what was going on in her mind and he believed that he was winning. "You know we'll both be needing someone out here, don't you?" But her answer was an uncertain expression on her face as she stared at him.

"Loners can't last too long out here. Being alone gets to you sooner or later," he said. "You go mad or you get careless and the patrol gets you."

The girl opened her mouth and glanced around quickly, then back at Nelson. She bent over, still watching Nelson all the time, and put the can down. Then she stepped backwards, towards the edge of the clearing, feeling the way with her feet and a hand held back to tell her if she were backing into a tree or rock. When she was almost to the edge of the clearing, almost to the trees, she stopped and stared at him. There were shadows now; it was almost night, and night came quickly in this country. Nelson could not see her face as she looked at him. She turned suddenly and ran into the trees. He made no effort to stop her or call her back; any such effort would have been futile and for his purposes, disastrous. No such effort was necessary.

He spent the night sheltered between some boulders and awoke the next morning rested by an undisturbed sleep.

He found a small creek nearby and washed his face to awaken himself. It was a clear morning, with a warm sun and a cool wafting breeze. He felt good; he felt alive and ready for whatever the day had to offer. He felt ready for breakfast.

He found another can of pork and beans in his pack and opened it. It was, he noted, almost the last. His supplies were getting low. He considered the situation as he slowly ate his breakfast.

Of course there was only one thing to do. He supposed that he could have gotten by simply by hunting his food, but hunting was at best seasonal and required that he keep more or less to a specific area; agriculture was about the same, only worse. A farm meant a smaller area than a hunting preserve and it also meant sticking to it more. It meant buildings to store food against winter. It meant inevitable—and almost certainly prompt—capture by a patrol. No, all things considered there was only one answer and he knew the answer from long experience. Find a patrol warehouse and steal your food there.

The question, of course, was where and when. There was a patrol station near where Nelson now was, and that was the natural target. He had a few furnace beam guns—three, to be exact—and since the patrol could detect the residue from a furnace beamer a mile away even at low force, the only safe thing to use one on was the patrol. And to be frank, he rather enjoyed his brushes with the patrol. Like him, they were wakers—people who had never known the electronic dreams which were fed to all but a few of Earth's peoples. People who had never lain asleep in nutrient baths from their seventeenth birthday living an unreal world built to their own standards. Of the billions on Earth, only a few hundred were wakers. Most of those were patrol, of course, but a few were rebels.

That was he, and also the girl he had seen yesterday. And it had been Edna and Sammy and Jeanne and Gardner; and maybe a dozen other people he had known since he had escaped from the Commune, when he had been just a kid—but when he had seen the danger.

For the past two and a half centuries or so, almost everyone raised on Earth had been raised in a commune, never knowing his or her parents. They had been raised, they had been indoctrinated and they had mated in the communes—and then gone into Sleep. More than likely, Nelson's parents were there still, dreaming in their trance, having long ago forgotten each other and their son, for those were things of a harsher world over which one could have no control. In Sleep one dreamed of a world that suited the dreamer. It was artificial. Oh, yes, it was a highly personalized utopia—one that ironed out the conflicts by simply not allowing them. But it was artificial. And Nelson knew that as long as the universe itself was not artificial nothing artificial could long stand against it. That was why he had escaped from the Commune without letting them get him into the nutrient bath in which the dreamers lived out their useless lives. His existence gave the lie to the pseudo-utopia he was dedicated to overthrowing. They called it individualism, but Nelson called it spineless.

Above him was sky stretching light blue to the horizons— and beyond the blueness of stars. He felt a pang of longing as he looked up trying to see stars in the day sky. That was where he should be, out there with the pioneers, the men who were carving out the universe to make room for a dynamic mankind that had long ago forgotten the Sleepers of the home world. But no, he decided. Out there he would not be giving so much to mankind as he was here and now. However decadent these people were, he knew that they were men. Nelson knew that somehow he had to overthrow the Sleepers.

Before something happened while they lay helpless in their coffins, dreaming dreams that would go on and on until reality became harsh enough to put them down.

What if the spacefarers should return? What if some alien life form should grow up around some other solar type star, develop space travel, go searching for inhabitable worlds—solar type worlds—and discover Earth with its sleeping, unaware populace? Could dreams defend against that?

Nelson shuddered with the knowledge that he had his work cut out for him, and awoke to his own hunger. He fished out a can and started to open it before he remembered, and fished out another can as well. He pressed the release on both and the tops flew off, releasing the odour of cooking food.

He leaned over and set one can on a flat rock that was just inside his reach, then scooted back about a foot and using his fingers, scooped up a mouthful of his own breakfast. Half turning his head, he caught sight of her out of the corner of his eye, about fifteen feet away, tense and expectant but ready to spring away if she thought it was necessary. He turned back and concentrated on eating his own breakfast.

"This sure is good after all night," he said, after a few minutes, making a show of gulping down a chunk of stew beef, and sucking the gravy from his fingers. He did not look back.

"My name is Glynnis," he heard abruptly. He sensed the uncertainty in her voice, and the—distant—hint of belligerence, but even so he could tell it was a soft voice, musical and clear—if he could judge after not having heard a woman's voice in so long.

"Glynnis," he said slowly. "That's a pretty name. Mine's Hal Nelson. Like I told you last night."

"I haven't forgotten. Is that for me?" She meant the food, of course. Hal Nelson looked around. She was still standing by the tree. She was trying to seem at ease and making an awkward show of it.

"Yes," he told her. She took a step closer and stopped, looking at him. He turned back to his own eating. "No need to be scared, Glynnis, I won't hurt you." He became uncomfortably aware that she had not spoken his name yet and he wanted her to very much.

"No." Then a brief pause before she said, "I'm not used to anybody."

"It isn't good to be alone out here with the animals and food so hard to come by—and the patrol searching for wakers. You ever have any brush with the patrol?"

She had come up and was eating now; her answer came between eager mouthfuls. "I've seen them once. They didn't know I saw them—or they would have caught me and taken me back with them."

"Where're you from? What are you doing out here?"

For a moment he thought she had not heard him. She was busy eating, apparently having classified him as a friend. Finally, she said, "My folks were out here. They were farmers for a while. I was born out here and we moved around a lot until my daddy got tired of moving. So we built a farm. He built it in a place in a valley off there"—She vaguely indicated south—"And they planted some grain and potatoes and tried to round up some kind of livestock. We had mostly goats. But the patrol found us."

Nelson nodded; bitterly, he knew what had happened. Her father had gone on as long as he could until at last, broken and uncaring, he had made one last ditch stand. More than likely he had half wanted to give up anyway, and had not only because of the conflict of his family and saving face. "You were the only one who got way?" he asked.

"Uh-huh. They took the others." She spoke without emotion, peering into her food can to see if there was any left. "I was out in the field but I saw them coming. I hid down low behind some tall grain and got to the forest before they could find me." She examined the can again, then decided it was empty and put it down.

"Do you know what they do to people they take?" Nelson asked.

"Yes."

"Your daddy tell you? What did he say?"

"He said they take you back to the Mausoleum and put you to sleep in a coffin." She looked up at him, her face open, as if that was all there was to it. Nelson decided that she was as guileless as he had expected her to be, and reflected absently on that factor for a moment.

A light breeze was up and the air was full of the scents of the forest. Nelson liked the pungent smell of the pines and rich odour of choke-berries and bushes; and the mustiness that could be found in thickly overgrown places where the ground had become covered with a brown carpet of fallen pine needles. Some days he would search places in the forest until he found one or another brush or tree whose leaves or berries he would crush in his fingers simply so that he could savour the fragrance of them. But not this morning.

He rose to his feet and reached over to pick up Glynnis's discarded food container. She drew away from him, bracing herself as if to leap and run. He stopped himself and froze where he stood for a moment, then drew back.

"I didn't mean to scare you," he said. "We can't stay here, because if you stay somewhere they find you. We can't leave the containers here, either, because if they find them it might give them a clue in tracking us."

She looked ashamed, so he reached over, ready to draw back his hand if she acted as if she were scared. She tugged at her lower lip with her teeth and stared at him with eyes that were wide, but she did not spring to her feet. Somehow Nelson knew that the girl was acutely aware of how much she needed help out here. Suddenly, her right hand darted out and for a split second Nelson feared he had lost after all. But she reached over for the discarded can, picked it up and handed it to him. He reacted a little slowly, but he smiled and took the container. Their hands touched briefly and the girl drew hers away, immediately looking ashamed for so doing. Nelson continued to smile at her, and rather stiffly, she answered with a smile of her own. He put the container into the knapsack with the others and then slipped into the armstraps. Glynnis helped him.

They walked for an hour, that first day together, neither speaking. Glynnis stayed close by his side and Nelson could feel her proximity to him. He felt good in a way he had not felt in a long time. When the silence was finally broken, it was Nelson who broke it. They were topping a small hill in a section of wilderness that was not as heavily wooded as most and the sunlight was warm against Nelson's face. He had been thinking the matter over off and on all morning, and now he asked, "Have you ever raided a patrol depot?"

"No," she answered, a trace of apprehension in her voice.

They topped the hill and began moving down the other side. "Sometimes it's a pushover, when nobody is there. Other times it's moral hell. The patrol is always anxious to get their hands on wakers, so they try to keep an eye out for them at the depots. That means a fight unless we're very lucky. If the depot we pick is too heavily manned—"

"What do you mean, 'Depot we pick'?"

"We need more food. We either shoot some, raise some, or steal some."

"Oh," she said, but there was apprehension in her voice.

"We don't have any choice. We'll wait until almost dark. If the depot is guarded by too many men, or for some reason an extra number is there for the night, then we're in trouble unless we play our cards just right. You just do as I tell you and we'll be all right." He reached back and fumbled with the side pouch on his pack. "You know how to use one of these? Here, catch." He tossed her his spare furnace burner.

She almost missed it. She caught it awkwardly and held it gingerly with both hands, looking first at the gun and then him. Then, still gingerly, but with a certain willingness, she took the gun by the grip and pointed it to the ground, her eyes shut hard. Then, suddenly, her expression changed and she glanced up at him, worriedly.

"Oh, you said they could tell if we fired one of these."

"Don't worry," Nelson said. "The safety is on. Let me show you." He took the gun and explained to her how to use it. "Now then," he concluded. "When we get to the depot you stay outside the alarm system. I'll go in, leaving you to guard. Try not to use this unless you have to, but if it is necessary, don't hesitate. If you fire it, I'll know. My job will be to slip past the alarms and get inside to the food. If you fire, that'll be a signal that you've been discovered by the guards and we have to get out of there."

"Won't this give us away the same as shooting game?"

"Sure, but we get more food this way and maybe some other stuff. Especially reloads for the furnace guns. And, if we're lucky, we can ground the patrol. One more thing, Glynnis," he added. "Are you sure you can kill a man?"

"Is it hard?" she asked innocently. Nelson was rattled only for a second.

"No, it isn't hard, except that he'll probably be trying to kill you, too."

"I've hunted some game with this." She held up her hunting

knife so that the blade caught the sunlight. She had kept it clean and sharp, Nelson could see, but there were places where the blade had been chipped.

"Well, maybe there won't be any need to kill anyone at all," he said, a little more hastily than he intended. "I guess you'll do fine, Glynnis, I'll feel a lot safer knowing you're out there." He would feel as he had felt when Edna had gone with him on raids.

Towards evening they came to the depot Nelson had picked out. They were on a high although gently sloping hill, among the trees that crested it, looking down at the depot about a quarter of a mile away. There was still enough light to see by, but the sky was darkening for night. For the past two or three hours, Nelson had been repeatedly drilling Glynnis over her part. It was simple, really, and she knew it backwards, but she patiently recited her role when he asked her, whether out of regard for his leadership or an instinctive realization of his pre-raid state of nerves, he did not know. He made her recite it again, one last time. She spoke in low tones, just above a whisper. Around them the gathering of dusk had quieted the world. He waited for it to get a little darker, then he touched her shoulder and clasped it for a second before beginning his way to the depot.

He kept close to the bushes as far down as he could and crouched low over the ground the rest of the way even though he knew it was too dark for ordinary optics to pick him up. He had an absorber in his pack that would take care of most of the various radiations and detectors he would come into contact with, and for the most part, unless the alarms were being intently watched, he didn't expect to be noticed on the control board. And you couldn't watch a board like that day after day with maximum efficiency. Not when the alarms were set off only by an occasional animal or falling tree limb. Mostly he had to keep watch for direct contact alarms and traps; he was an accomplished thief and an experienced burglar. At last he found himself at the fence surrounding the depot.

In a clump of bushes a few feet from the fence he hid the containers; it saved him the job of having to bury them, and they would be deadweight now, anyway. Then he turned his attention on the fence.

He took a small plastic box out of his pack and pressed a panel in its centre with his thumb. Silently, smoothly, two long thin rods shot out from each end of the box until they were each about a foot long. There was a groove on the box and Nelson fitted it to the lower strand of the fence wire. He let go of the gadget and it balanced of its own accord, its antennae vibrating until they blurred, then ceasing to vibrate as the gadget balanced. Nelson went down on his back and pulled on gloves. He grabbed the fence wire and lifted it so that he could slide under. When he was inside he picked the gadget off the wire by one antenna and shut it off. The antennae pulled back inside. Gardner had made this gadget; Gardner had been handy with things like this. And there would be no other when Nelson lost this. He didn't want to leave it where it could be found or where he might have to abandon it to save his neck in an emergency.

He turned to the problem of getting across the open field. He had little fear of being picked up by radiation detectors, thanks to his absorber. But direct contact could give him away. But most of those had to be buried. That meant that he could keep close to the bushes and not have to worry. The roots of the bushes fouled up the detection instruments if they got to them. He made his way, judging each step before he took it and at last stood by the door.

It was dark by then. He could see the stars in the clear darkness of the sky. They seemed somehow brighter than they had before. Nelson fished through his pack until he felt the familiar shape of the gadget he wanted. It was smaller, more compact than the one he had used to get over the fence; but it was more complex. He felt along the door frame for the alarm trip and found it. He placed the gadget there and switched it on. There was a short, low, buzzing sound as the gadget did its job and Nelson glanced around nervously, in fear it had been heard. The door's lock clunked back and Nelson released air from his lungs. He pushed the door open and found himself in darkness.

He was in a corridor with doors facing off from it. He could see light coming from under two of the doors, meaning patrolmen behind them. He moved cautiously by the two doors, almost opposite each other, to a door at the end of the corridor. He grasped the handle and opened the door, realizing too late that the door should have been locked.

But by that time the door was open. His hand darted to his holstered furnace beamer and unlocked the safety. It was almost pitch dark in the room but he heard the room's occupant turning over on the bunk and mumbling low, incoherently, in his sleep. Nelson waited a minute but the man didn't wake up.

Nelson closed the door.

He tried another door; this time, one that was locked. He had no trouble forcing the lock pattern; less than a minute later he was inside, with the door shut behind him. He took out a flashlight.

This was the storeroom, all right, it was piled with boxes mostly unopened. Nelson read the labels on the boxes and opened those which contained food he needed and supplies. He found another pack in an opened box in one corner and began outfitting it like his own. Or as nearly like his own as possible; he knew that he could never duplicate or replace the gadgets Gardner had designed, and in a way he was bitter about it. He found the ammunition stores and took as many capsules for the furnace beamers as he could carry. He went to the door but slipped the furnace beamer out of his holster before opening the door.

The corridor was still dark. He stepped into it, alert for any sound or movement that might mean danger or herald discovery. His nervousness had given way to cool, detached determination. He almost made it to the door before he heard the footsteps.

His reaction was unconscious and reflexive. He turned, levelling his gun. He had passed the two doors light had shown under. One of them was opening and Nelson saw the shadow of the man who had opened it; then the man. The man saw Nelson at about the same time and stood gaping at him. Without realizing that he had fired, Nelson felt the recoil of the gun; the roar of the beam against the close walls hurt his ears, parts of the wall blistered and buckled, other parts of it charred black, some parts vaporizing in thin patches. The patrolman had flared instantly, never really knowing what had hit him. Smoke and heavy odours filled the corridor as Nelson slid out into the open. The patrol depots were fireproof, but the area Nelson had blasted would be far too hot to pass through for the rest of the night.

Nelson toned down the volume of his beamer and fired at a fence post. The tough plastic burst into splinters with a sudden explosion. A snapping wire whipped to within inches of Nelson's face but he didn't have to think about it. He was running up the hillside a short while later—he had lost track of time as such— hoping that Glynnis would use her gun if any patrolmen were following him.

He reached the hilltop in darkness, afraid to use his flashlight. Suddenly, he stumbled; was falling over something soft, like an animal or a man. Cursing low and involuntarily, he managed to roll over so that he fell on his back. He saw the form, a patch of irregular blackness in the darkness around him and knew it for a body. He got to his feet, glancing around, not knowing what this meant. He bent over the form, keeping the furnace beam's muzzle only a few inches from it, but too far back to be grabbed suddenly. He couldn't see the man's clothing very plainly but he could tell it was a patrolman's uniform. Nelson reached down to feel for a heartbeat and drew his hand away sticky with what he knew must be blood. Nelson was shaken for a moment; but he put aside the strange kinship he so often felt for patrolmen because they were also wakers and drew back, peering round into the darkness, pretty certain that he knew what had happened to this patrolman.

He pushed himself erect and turned to see Glynnis, a dark figure standing near a clump of trees a few feet off.

"You move quiet as a cat," he said. "You do this?"

"Uh-huh." She came forward and stared down at the corpse. Nelson was glad he couldn't see her face in the darkness. "There were two of them. They split up and I followed after this one and came up behind him. I slit his throat. Then I went and got the other one the same way."

And it had been so simple, thought Nelson. He handed Glynnis the extra pack. "Take this," She accepted it wordlessly and slipped her arms into the straps. "Oh," he added, as an afterthought. "Let me show you something." He reached into the pack and drew out a knife. A good one with a long plasteel blade that would not chip or corrode like hers. He handed it to her and imagined her smiling face in the darkness.

"It doesn't feel like metal," she said, after she had taken the knife from its scabbard.

"It isn't. It's a kind of plastic, stronger than most metals. Do you like it?" He was wasting time, he knew, and he cursed himself for it. But it didn't matter.

"It's real nice," she answered.

"I'm glad you like it," he said, taking her elbow in his hand. "We'd better go now. They'll be after us."

They ran most of the night, although it wasn't always running. Nelson picked a lot of terrain that was too uneven or too thickly covered with growth for running. They kept to rocks and creekbeds as much as they could, and they stopped only a few hours before dawn to get a few hours' sleep they were too exhausted to postpone any longer.

When Nelson awoke the sun was a little higher than he had wanted it to be. He got to his feet and scanned the morning sky but saw nothing to indicate sky patrol robots. He felt uneasy about not having made more territory; but the way had been erratic and uneven. A thorough search pattern could find him easily; the farther away he got from the depot the better chance he stood of not being discovered by a robot. He wondered, briefly, just how many would be called out, but there was no reason to wonder. Three patrolmen dead meant a lot of searching to find the killers. He and Glynnis couldn't waste much time.

He nudged the still sleeping girl with his foot to wake her. She woke suddenly, her hand darting towards her new knife and a low but startled cry came from her.

"Quiet." He had dug two cans out of his pack and handed one to her. "We overslept. Eat in a hurry."

She opened her breakfast. "We'll be travelling most of the day?" she asked. When he nodded yes, she said, "I can take it."

"I know you can; but they'll have a search out for us by now and a thorough one. If we hadn't met when we had, they'd have picked you up for sure after I raided that depot—if I could have pulled it off alone."

She smiled.

"You ever see an air robot?" he asked.

"No."

"I hope you never do. They'll fly out a search pattern, and they have equipment that can detect a human being. They can send back signals to tell where we are if they spot us. Our only hope is to get away before the search pattern gets this far. If we can get far enough away, we stand a better chance, because they'll have to spread out more thinly. We'll have to run for a long time, but eventually they'll give up. Until then—Well—" He let it hang. But Glynnis caught on.

The rest of the day they travelled, stopping only briefly to eat and once during the afternoon when they came to a small river. Nelson's admiration for Glynnis increased. She responded intelligently to his commands, and learned quickly. She was strong and athletic, with the reflexes of an animal.

They made good time. When darkness came Nelson estimated they had made almost fifty miles since the raid, even over rough terrain. He hoped that that would be enough. He was tired, and though the girl attempted to hide her own fatigue, her attempts were becoming more and more exaggerated. He searched out a camp site.

He found one on a hill, overlooking a river. There was protection from the wind. The moon was up and there was plenty of light from it; but Nelson didn't think the searchers would be out at night.

After they had eaten, Nelson leaned back against the thick bole of a tree and found himself studying the girl. Her features were even enough, but she was not a classically beautiful girl. Nor an unattractive one. It was her eyes, he decided. She was staring off into the sky and forest. Her eyes were large, dark, enigmatic eyes that expressed much; expressed it eloquently. But he had the feeling there was much in the girl that those eyes hid. Her body was lean, but whether from exercise or undernourishment he couldn't be sure. Her figure was full, for all the leanness, and ample. She was strong, though she hardly looked muscular. She had been toughened by her environment. Edna had not been as tough as Glynnis.

With sudden embarrassment, he realized he had been comparing Glynnis and Edna frequently. He didn't want to do that—but he couldn't help himself.

"Something wrong?" Glynnis asked anxiously.

She was returning his stare. "No," he said. "I was . . . looking at you." For a long moment, neither spoke, then he said, "We'll be together for a long time."

"I know. We'll have to be."

"I'm glad I found you. I lost my wife to the patrol some time back."

"I've never been anyone's wife before. There was Frank, but I was never really what you could call his wife, exactly."

"Many people ever stay with your folks?"

"Not many. Frank only stayed a few days. I liked him. I wanted to go with him."

"Why didn't you?"

She broke off a blade of grass and slowly began tearing it into strips, intently gazing at it. "He just left suddenly without taking me. I guess he thought I was just a stupid brat. That was maybe two or three years ago." Her voice sounded as if she were smiling a little. Nelson thought that strange.

"You ever think much about the sleepers?" he asked suddenly.

"Sometimes. I wonder what it's like in their dreams."

"They like it in their dreams. Those dreams are built for them. They get along happily in their world, grateful for it. That's the word, grateful." He listened for a moment to night sounds. "But they're helpless. If anything happens they're asleep and unable to act. If they wake up, they're in a world they don't know how to live in."

"If you were a sleeper, what kind of a world would you want to dream about?"

"I don't want to be a sleeper."

"Yes, but if you were. Would you live in a castle?"

He thought on it for the first time. "I don't know," he said finally. "I don't think so. I think I'd travel. Go out to the stars. There's a whole universe out there. Men went out there; they're still out there. I guess they've forgotten us."

"You think they'll ever come back?"

"Some day I think somebody from out there will come back and land on Earth to see what it's like. Maybe they'll try to invade us. We'd be pretty helpless with most of us asleep in our pipe-dream utopias."

"I wouldn't like to be caught and put in a dream," she said. "But I'd like to live in a castle." Nelson gazed at her. She had never known a commune, he realized. If she had, she would have bred when told to and then docilely filed away to her coffin. But she had never been indoctrinated. If she went into the dreams, it would be against her will. But he had to admit that he had some reservations. . . .

He moved close to her.

"Maybe some day we can live in a castle. Or go into space to some planet where men live in castles." He stared at the stars. "Out there they must be like gods," he said and his voice sounded strange, even to him.

He looked down at Glynnis. The moonlight was full on her face; she looked fit to be a goddess to those gods, he thought. She was staring off and around at the wilderness; she was saying, "Out here there's trees. And air. I like to look at the trees." He reached over and pulled her face around to him and kissed her. She was startled, but returned the kiss warmly.

She pulled away just far enough to look into his face. She was smiling. "I think I like you better than I did Frank," she said.

Nelson lay awake for a few moments, trying to identify the noise. It was a low humming sound off in the distance. He could feel Glynnis, breathing evenly with sleep beside him. The sky was just beginning to colour with sunrise in the east. As quietly as possible, Nelson eased himself erect, still trying to place the noise. He placed it, and realized that he had not really wanted to identify it.

"Quiet," he said as he roused the girl. She opened her eyes wide, and stared at him, confused and uncomprehending.

"What's wrong?"

"Hear that noise?"

"Yes," she said after a second.

"One of the search machines. Probably they've adopted a

loose search pattern, or maybe we left some kind of sign somewhere. It's not coming closer, but we'd better get out of here."

They ate hastily, in the awakening light of sunrise. They ran
away from the sound of the machine, and it lessened in the
distance.

It was the middle of the morning when they heard it again.
Nelson judged it to be roughly a mile away and to the west. He
waited a minute, listening. It seemed to be describing a search
pattern curve that swung in front of their path. He decided to
double back and around to miss it.

The undergrowth was thick in this part of the forest. They
made their way through bushes and waist-high grasses, being as
careful as possible not to leave too many signs of their passing.
Glynnis's shorts and thin blouse weren't much protection against
the thorns or the recoiling limbs of bushes but she didn't complain.
Gradually the forest became mostly trees again. They found a path
some animal had made and followed it.

When they came to the clearing, Nelson almost didn't see
the thing in the air. He heard Glynnis gasp behind him, and
with a start, glanced around. She was staring at something in
front of them, and in the air. He looked where she was staring
and saw the air robot hovering near the edge of the clearing.
It was about two feet long, slender, metallic and smooth. Nelson
thought that it was alert and that receptors built into its skin were
registering their presence. It hovered about ten feet above the
ground, some twenty feet away from them, making no noise.
Sky robots made noise only when they were moving at a fairly
good speed. They had fled the noise of one only to be trapped in
the silence of another.

Suddenly, Glynnis was shouting, "It's one of them!" Nelson
turned to see her level her gun, and before he could stop her a
white hot streamer lashed out at the robot and engulfed it.

"No," he shouted, too late. The machine took the blast turning cherry red and bobbing lightly in the air for a moment before
energy compensators and stabilizers adjusted to the effects of the
blast. The machine turned back to its lustrous silver colour and
there was a low hum as it righted itself gracefully then swung

around, into the centre of the clearing, to get a better focus on them.

"It doesn't even have a mark on it," Glynnis said, in a low tone, moving closer to Nelson and laying one hand on his shoulder.

"No. But don't worry; it can't hurt us. We've got to figure some way to get out of here and leave it behind." He turned and gently guided her towards the trees. When they were in the dubious shelter of the trees, Nelson stopped and tried to figure a way out. He could see the machine hanging in the centre of the clearing on invisible lines of force, turning slightly to find them in the dense growth, then, with one end pointed at them, bobbing slightly with the low breeze.

"What's it doing?" Glynnis asked. There was superstitious awe in her voice that annoyed Nelson.

"Sending a signal to the patrol. We don't have much time before they get here."

"But if the machine can't be shot down what can we do?"

"Hand me your gun." He took her gun and pointed to a vernier control set into the side of the weapon. "This is the intensity control; it's on low." He turned it up. "Now it's on full."

"Will that stop the machine?"

"Not by itself. But if we both move in, blasting together, again and again, we might do some damage."

"All right," she said, taking the gun.

Nelson led the way into the clearing. The machine moved back a little and bobbed to keep them in alignment. Nelson felt the dryness of his throat as he raised his gun to aim at the incurious machine. "All set?" he asked. From the corner of his eye he could see that Glynnis had raised her gun and was sighting.

"All set," she answered.

"O.K." Nelson fired. His blast hit the robot head on. It was absorbed, but almost as soon as it had died down, Glynnis fired. Nelson fired again, catching the machine in an almost steady stream of white hot energy. The machine suddenly caught on to what they were doing. It tried to escape their range by going up, but they followed it. By this time the compensators were already beginning to fail. Haywire instruments jerked the machine back down and then side to side, then into a tree trunk, blindly. It rebounded and dipped low, almost touching the ground before it curved back up. Some of Glynnis's shots were missing but Nelson made every shot count, even while the robot was darting about wildly.

The machine was glowing cherry red, now, some twelve feet off the ground, unable to rise farther, one end pointed sharply upwards. Something inside it began screaming, loudly, shrilly, with a vibration that hurt Nelson's teeth. Nelson was firing mechanically. The machine's loud screaming stopped suddenly. Nelson checked his fire. Glynnis fired once more, missing as the machine dropped about a foot. For perhaps a second the machine remained motionless. Then it died without sound, and fell to the ground, landing with a dull noise and setting fire to the grass under and around it.

For that matter, they had started a major forest fire with their blastings. The trees across the clearing from them were already roaring with flames. Nelson didn't wait to check on the machine. He grabbed Glynnis and pulled her around towards the way they had come. She stumbled, staring back at the machine.

"Come on!" he said, in agitation. She came to life, mechanically, and let him propel her along. The wind was away from them, but the fire was growing. They ran madly until they had to stop and fall exhausted to the ground. When he could breathe again without torturing his lungs, Nelson looked back and saw the smoke from the fire in the distance behind them. They were safe from the fire, but their escape was cut off by it. It would, he knew with dull certainty, attract attention.

When he had rested as long as he dared, he said, "We'd better get going."

"I'm not sure I can," she said.

"Well, you've got to. If we stay here, we'll be caught."

They did not pause to eat. It was about midday when they encountered the robot and they walked well into the afternoon, their only purpose being to put as much distance between them and the place where they had shot the robot down as possible. Nelson found himself moving numbly, blindly uncaring of anything but making progress forward. He listened to the humming of an approaching robot for a long while before it registered on his consciousness.

He whirled, drawing his gun, momentarily giving way to the panic that had been threatening to engulf him all afternoon. He saw the machine, high above the trees behind them, safely out of range, he knew. Bitterly, he fought down the urge to fire the gun anyway. It took a tremendous exertion of will to make his arm return the gun to its holster.

"What can we do?" asked Glynnis, a slight quaver in her voice.

"Not a thing," said Nelson; then, almost in rage he cried it. "Not one damned thing!"

They both turned back the way they had been going and ran, hoping to find some cover with which to duck the machine. Nelson converted his rage and fear into a strength he had never known he could call upon. He ran on, and Glynnis behind him. And he knew that she, like he, ran despite the rawness in her throat and lungs and cramping of her legs. The only thing he could think of was that he wanted to enter a mausoleum not as a prisoner but as the head of an army.

He ran blindly, hearing nothing but the machine and his own rasping breath. Then suddenly, he was stumbling over the edge of an embankment, flailing his arms and twisting himself around so that he managed to land on his back. It hurt and the wind went out of him. He was sliding and rolling. Somehow he managed to stop himself. He lay painfully coughing and trying to get his breath. Below him he could see the wild rushing of a river at the base of the sheer embankment. He looked back up; Glynnis had one leg over the edge but had not fallen. Nelson crawled his way back up the slope.

They were trapped by the river. It must be another part of the same river they had spent the night by, thought Nelson. But where it had been calm and shallow, it was now a raging torrential river whose brown, churning waters ran between high, difficult to climb cliffs.

There was no need for either to speak. They began looking for a place to cross the river. All the time they searched they could hear the machine behind them, above them, humming safely out of their range.

The sun was low in the sky when they heard the second humming. The humming grew until it was a throbbing that covered the weaker sound of the robot and chilled Nelson.

"The patrol," he said, pushing the girl towards the forest. "Back into the trees. We're going to have to fight it out with them."

They ran into the trees. The throbbing stopped, and behind them, Nelson could hear the sounds made by men thrashing through undergrowth. His palms were wet; he wiped them on his shirt front. The impending contact with the patrol gave him a calmness as always, and he picked out a thicket where he believed he could make some sort of stand.

He reached the thicket with Glynnis beside him. Her gun was out. He signed to her to lower the intensity of the gun; she caught on. He watched her face. It was like a mask.

Nelson listened to the sounds of the approaching patrolmen. Five or six, he decided. Plus a guard back at the flier. He'd figure on eight, in all, he decided. Then the first one showed behind some bushes.

Nelson touched Glynnis's arm in a signal to wait. The patrolman looked around, searching too intensely to find anything. He was young. Nelson didn't think he would uncover their whereabouts and for a moment debated letting him pass.

But he didn't want to be surrounded. He pulled his gun up and sighted carefully before squeezing the trigger. In the tenth of a second before the patrolman burst into flames, the blast produced a blast circle that grew to the size of a basketball in his midsection. The patrolman fell without screaming.

The others were there now. Most of them were young and two rushed forward at the sight of their companion's death, to die like heroes. The others wisely sought cover. Nelson decided that the thicket wasn't as safe as he had hoped. One of the patrolmen was doing a good job with an energizer, coming closer with each shot, before Nelson finally saw where he was, and fired at him. Nelson saw the trunk of a large fallen tree and pointed to it for Glynnis's benefit. She nodded.

There was cover most of the way. Nelson went first, crouching low to the ground and running with the ease of a cat. He made the log and began firing to cover Glynnis. He saw her coming, out of the corner of his eye, then concentrated on covering her with fire power. Suddenly the girl let out a startled yell and he saw her sprawl to the ground, tripping over a root. He called her name and without thinking leaped to his feet to run to help her. He was half-way there when the patrolman came into range. Nelson realized what he had done. Glynnis was already on her feet and running. Cursing himself, Nelson jerked his gun around, but it was too late. An energizer blast exploded the ground beneath him and he felt himself hurtling over backwards. He could only see blackness and the bright, quick flashing of pinpoint light in it. Then, he was falling, spinning . . .

Patrol Cadet Wallace Sherman watched the man on the table with mixed feelings; on the other hand, there was pity for a man whose condition was hopeless, and on the other there were the misgivings that come with guarding a criminal. Perhaps it was Sherman's youth that caused him to emphasize those misgivings and move his hand towards his sidearm when the man stirred.

But the man on the table only stirred a little and groaned. Sherman was not sure whether or not the man was coming to. He shouldn't be, Sherman knew. He took a couple of steps forward and stared at the man's face.

The man was breathing normally. His head moved slightly but his eyes were still closed. His face was the palest, softest looking Sherman had ever seen. It was the face of a man who had never known sunlight, Sherman thought sombrely; or at least had not known it in many years. He wondered, vaguely, just what kind of life the man dreamed he had. As he was watching the man's face, Sherman saw his lips move and heard him utter something he could not make out. He bent closer to hear better.

"Glynnis"—the man on the table was saying.

"Is he waking up?" Sherman heard a voice asking.

A little embarrassed, Sherman turned around and saw Blomgard standing in the doorway. "Oh, I'm sorry, sir. No. At least I don't think so. He said something; a word. *Glynnis,* I think. Sounds like a girl's name."

Dr. Blomgard came into the room and walked over to the table on which his patient was stretched out. He removed the clipboard from its hook and looked through the sheaf of papers fastened to it. After a few seconds, he said, "Ah, yes. Glynnis. Part of his dream."

"Doctor—," Sherman heard himself saying, then caught himself.

"What, cadet," Blomgard asked, turning around. He was a big man, grey-haired, his hair an unruly mop. His eyes were dark and piercing, but they were softened by the thickness of the white brows over them.

"Nothing, sir—"

"I assure you, that no question will be considered out of place, if that's what is worrying you."

"Well, doctor," Sherman said with some difficulty, "I was wondering if all this is worth it. I mean a special reserve with the artificial life-dreams for these people. Is it worth the expense and effort?"

Blomgard regarded the question a moment before answering. "Well, that depends on things. We have a fairly dynamic, expanding civilization. This man was born out of step; a natural born rebel. We've reached the stage where, with a little effort on their own part, most people can sooner or later find exactly what they want. There are, of course, exceptions. They can't help being the way they are, but they are that way. It isn't his fault that he would think nothing of blowing up any civilization he found himself living in. This is the solution."

"A drug-induced dream state? Is that a solution?"

"It's a pretty good one. We provide him with a completely fictitious, a totally unreal world in which he will be happy."

"How can anyone be happy like that? I prefer reality."

Blomgard smiled. "Yes, to a larger extent than he does, you do. Or you like what you think of as reality." He picked up the clipboard again and studied the papers on it. "His dream world is one that is designed for his happiness. In it, he sees everyone else as inhabiting the dream-coffins. And he pictures himself as a rugged individualist, going about trying to destroy such a civilization. And of course, he is practically a lone wolf. Not completely, for he would not be happy that way. The man is an underdog."

"I guess it's best," Sherman said.

"It is," the doctor replied, seriously. "We have no right to take his life; nor do we have the right to destroy his personality, however much that personality may be offensive to us. And since most inhabitable planets are, unfortunately, inhabited before we ever get to them, we have more urgent colonies to establish where we can find room. No, this is best. We give him a dream based exactly on his psychological needs; a compensation, so to speak, for the real life we take away from him. For most people only have the right to pursue happiness. In return for a normal life, we've given him a guaranteed happiness."

The doctor let that sink in for a while; but Sherman still had a strong wish that he had pulled some other duty. Perhaps on one of the new outposts, like Deneb.

The doctor glanced at his watch. "Well, the repairs are done with and they should have the nutrient refreshed by now. Let's wheel him on back."

A little gratefully, Sherman moved over to the table.

"You'll be all right, soon enough," the doctor said to the unconscious man on the table. "This interruption will be neatly explained away and remain as merely a memory of a slightly unpleasant moment after things get back to normal. They'll convince you of the reality of your world—if you ever need convincing."

Sherman saw the sleeping man stir slightly and heard him utter sounds again.

"Wheel him out," Blomgard said.

Gratefully, Sherman turned the table around and wheeled it out the door.

From far off, Nelson heard Glynnis calling to him. "Are you all right, Hal?" he heard. "Can you hear me, Hal?"

"I can hear you," he managed to say. He opened his eyes. He saw his gun a few dozen feet away on the ground.

"I thought they had you, sure," Glynnis said quietly. "I got the two of them. Don't ask me how I did it, but I got them."

He sat up, feeling dizzy from having hit the ground with

such force. "I don't guess I was much help," he said weakly. "You sure did a fine job." His head ached, but he remembered the fight and being thrown by the impact of the blast. And something else—something distant and alien, like a dream, from the deepest part of his mind. It pestered him a moment, just out of reach of his consciousness, then he shrugged it off as unimportant. He looked around and saw the charred bodies of the patrolmen. "You did a fine job," he told Glynnis, meaning it.

"Can you fly a patrol ship?"

"Huh?"

"We've got one now," Glynnis said. "I shot the guard they left with it, too. Had to."

"I see," he said, marvelling at the girl. "I can fly one. I haven't since I was in the commune, though. As long as it's in good condition."

"I guess it is. I didn't hit it with any shots."

"We can go anywhere in the world with that ship," he said getting to his feet. "It doesn't need fuel; it can fly forever. You know what that means, Glynnis? We can raise an army, if we want to."

"And we can get into the mausoleums and wake everybody up?"

"Yes. Come on," he said and started towards the flier. But Glynnis grabbed his arm and stopped him. "What is it?" he asked.

"What's it like to live in a world where everyone's awake?" she asked him.

"Why . . . I don't know. I've never lived in one."

"Then why do you want to wake everyone up?"

"It's wrong the way they are now."

Glynnis scowled and Nelson could tell that she was struggling with strange concepts. He felt sympathy for her, knowing how she felt.

"What I mean," she asked finally, "is why is it wrong? What's the reason?"

"Because they can do better. We can save them and show them that; I can lead them back where they belong."

"I see," Glynnis said gravely accepting his words. "All right."

Nelson smiled at her. She looked up at him and smiled back. The patrol ship was waiting for them, not far off.

Together, they marched off to save the world.

QUESTIONS

1   In "The Happy Man," the state controls people by the use of drugs. In *1984* and *Brave New World,* different ways are used. Given an increasingly overpopulated world in which more and more controls seem necessary and the fact that individuals in the past have been found wanting in the ability to control themselves, do you think that such a world as Page pictures might be inevitable, possibly even desirable? Comment.

2   Nelson tames Glynnis (in a way) just as the state is trying to tame him. Both Nelson and Glynnis have escaped confinement and fled into the country, to a more wild condition. Discuss the implications of this.

3   Does the doctor's assessment of Nelson seem true, or is the doctor merely a spokesman, possibly even a victim himself, of the state? Do you believe the doctor when he says, "We've reached the stage where, with a little effort on their own part, most people can sooner or later find exactly what they want." (Consider the idea that overthrowing governments might be exactly what some people want.)

4   Does Glynnis contribute to the plot or illuminate the character of Nelson in any way? Why do you suppose Page included her in the story? Is she a girl Friday or merely a device to reveal what Nelson thinks and feels?

5   The doctor says that "most people only have the right to pursue happiness," inferring that most do not have the right to expect it. Comment.

6   Has your opinion of Nelson changed by the end of the story? If so, how and why?

A WORLD ENDS
Wolfgang Hildesheimer

The Marchesa Montetristo's last evening party has impressed itself indelibly on my memory. This is partly due, of course, to its extraordinary conclusion but in other ways as well the evening was unforgettable.

My acquaintance with the Marchesa—a Waterman by birth, of Little Gidding, Ohio—came about by a coincidence. I had sold her, through the intermediary of my friend, Herr von Perlhuhn (I mean of course the Abraham-a-Santa Clara expert, not the neo-mystic), the bathtub in which Marat was murdered. It is perhaps not generally known that it had been until then in my possession. Gambling debts obliged me to offer it for sale. So it was that I came to the Marchesa who had long wanted this appliance for her collection of eighteenth-century washing utensils. This was the occasion of my getting to know her. From the bathtub our conversation soon passed to more general esthetic topics. I noticed that the possession of this collector's piece had given me a certain prestige in her eyes. And I was not surprised when one day I was invited to one of her famous parties in her palazzo on the artificial island of San Amerigo. The Marchesa had had the island thrown up a few miles southeast of Murano on a sudden whim, for she detested the mainland—she said it was hurtful to her spiritual equilibrium, and she could find nothing to suit her in the existing stock of islands. So here she resided, devoting her life to the cult of the antique and forgotten, or, as she liked to put it, of the "true and eternal."

The invitation card gave the time of the party as eight o'clock, which meant that the guests were expected at ten. So custom ordered it. Further it ordered that the guests should come in gondolas. In this fashion, it is true, the crossing lasted nearly two hours and was moreover uncomfortable when the sea was rough, but these were unwritten rules of behavior at which no one but a barbarian would cavil—and barbarians were not invited. Besides, many of the younger guests, not yet fully sensible of the dignity of the occasion, would hire a *vaporette* to take them within a hundred yards of the island whence they were ferried over one by one in a gondola which had been brought in tow.

The splendor of the building needs no description from me. For outside it was an exact replica of the Palazzo Vendramin, and inside every period, from the Gothic onward, was represented. But of course they were not intermingled. Each one had its own room. The Marchesa could really not be accused of breaches of style. Nor need the opulence of the catering be referred to her. Anyone who has ever attended a state banquet in a monarchy—and it is to such that I principally addressed myself—knows what it was like. Moreover it would hardly be true to the spirit of the Marchesa and her circle to mention the pleasures of the table, especially here, where I have to describe the last hours on earth of some of the most eminent figures of the age, which I as sole survivor had the privilege to witness.

After exchanging a few civilities with my hostess and stroking the long-haired Pekinese which never stirred from her side, I was introduced to the Dombrowska, a woman doubly famous, first for her contributions to the rhythmic-expressionist dance, a vanishing art form, and secondly as the author of the book *Back to Youth,* which, as the title indicates, argued in favor of a return to youthfulness of style and which, I need hardly remind the reader, has won adherents far and wide. While we were chatting together, an elderly gentleman of upright bearing came up to us. It was Golch. The Golch. (Unnecessary to give further particulars of a man whose share in the enrichment of our intellectual life is so widely known.) The Dombrowska introduced me: "Herr Sebald, the late owner of Marat's bathtub." My fame had spread.

"Aha," said Golch. I inferred, from the inflection he gave to these syllables, that he was weighing my potentialities as a candidate for the cultural elite. I asked him how he had liked the exhibition of contemporary painting in Luxemburg. For one might, indeed one must, assume that those here assembled had seen, read, and heard everything of any real importance. That was why they were here. Golch raised his eyes as if looking for a word in space and said, "Passé." (He used the English accentuation of the word which was then in fashion. The words *cliché* and *pastiche* too were pronounced *a l'anglaise.* I don't know what the current usage is. I am now too much taken up with everyday affairs to concern myself with such matters.) I noticed in any case that I had blundered in thus mentioning the contemporary. I had gone down a step, but I had learnt my lesson.

A move was made to the buffet. Here I encountered Signora Sgambati, the astrologer, who had recently made a considerable stir by her theory that not only the fate of individuals but whole trends in the history of ideas could be read in the stars. She was no ordinary phenomenon, this Sgambati, as was at once clear from her appearance. Yet I find it incomprehensible in the circumstances that she did not see in the constellation of the heavens the imminent engulfment of so many substantial members of the intellectual world. She was deep in conversation with Professor Kuntz-Sartori, the politician and royalist, who had been trying for decades to introduce a monarchy in Switzerland. Another notable figure.

After taking some refreshment the company moved to the Silver Room for what was to be the climax of the evening's entertainment, a performance of a special kind—the world premiere of two flute sonatas by Antonio Giambattista Bloch, a contemporary and friend of Rameau, who had been discovered by the musicologist Weltli. He too of course was there. They were played by the flautist Béranger (yes, a descendant) and accompanied by the Marchesa herself, on the self-same harpsichord on which Celestine Rameau had initiated her son into the fundamental principles of counter-point, and which had been sent from Paris. The flute too had a history, but I have forgotten it. The two performers had put on rococo costumes for the occasion, and the little ensemble looked—they had purposely so arranged themselves—like a picture by Watteau. The performance of course took place by the dimmest of candlelight. There was not a person there who would have found electric light for such an occasion anything but intolerable. By a further sensitive whim of the Marchesa the guests were required after the first sonata (D major) to move over from the Silver Room (Baroque) to the Golden Room (early Rococo), there to enjoy the second sonata. For the Silver Room had a major resonance, the Golden, it could not be disputed, a minor.

At that point I must remark that the tedious elegance which clings to the flute sonatas of second-rank, and more particularly of newly discovered, masters of this period, was in the present case to be explained by the fact that no such person as Giambattista Bloch had ever lived. The works here performed had in reality been composed by the musicologist Weltli. Although this circumstance did not become known till later, I cannot, in retrospect, help feeling it a humiliation for the Marchesa that she should have employed her last moments in the interpretation, however masterly, of a forgery.

During the second movement of the F minor sonata I saw a rat creeping along the wall. I was astonished. At first I thought it might have been lured from its hole by the sound of the flute— such things do happen, they say—but it was creeping in the opposite direction. It was followed by another rat. I looked at the guests. They had not noticed anything, and indeed most of them were keeping their eyes closed in order to be able to abandon themselves to the harmonies of Weltli's forgery. I now heard a dull reverberation, like very distant thunder. The floor began to vibrate. Again I looked at the guests. If they had heard anything —and something they must be hearing—it was at any rate not discernible from their hunched-up postures. I however was made uneasy by these strange symptoms.

A manservant entered. This is barely the place to remark that in the unusual costume worn by the Marchesa's domestic staff he looked like a character out of *Tosca*. He went up to the performers and whispered something in the Marchesa's ear. I saw her turn pale. How well it suited her in the dim candlelight! But she controlled herself and without interruption played the *andante* calmly to the end. Then she nodded to the flautist, stood up, and addressed the company.

"Ladies and gentlemen," she said, "I have just learnt that the foundations of the island and those of the palace with them are breaking up. The Office of Submarine Works has been informed. The right thing, I think we shall all agree, is to go on with the music."

She sat down again, gave the sign to Monsieur Béranger,

and they played the *allegro con brio,* the last movement, which did seem to me at the time, though I had yet no inkling that it was a forgery, little suited to the uniqueness of the situation.

On the polished floor small puddles were forming. The reverberation had grown louder and sounded nearer. Most of the guests were now sitting upright, their faces ashen in the candlelight, and looking as if they were long dead already. I stood up and said, "I'm going," not so loud as to give offense to the musicians, but loud enough to intimate to the other guests that I had the courage to admit my fear. The floor was now almost evenly covered with water. Although I walked on tiptoe, I could not help splashing an evening dress or two as I passed. But, in view of what was soon to come, the damage I did must be reckoned inconsiderable. Few of the guests thought me worthy of a glance, but I did not care. As I opened the door to the passage a wave of water poured into the room and caused Lady Fitzjones (the preserver of Celtic customs) to draw her fur wrap more closely about her—no doubt a reflex movement, for it could not be of any use. Before shutting the door behind me I saw Herr von Perlhuhn (the neo-mystic, not the Abraham-a-Santa Clara expert) casting a half-contemptuous, half-melancholy glance in my direction. He too was now sitting in water almost to his knees. So was the Marchesa, who could no longer use the pedals. I do not as a matter of fact know how essential they are on the harpsichord. I remember thinking that if the piece had been a cello sonata, they would perforce have had to break it off here since the instrument would not sound in water. Strange what irrelevant thoughts occur to one in such moments.

In the entrance hall it was suddenly as quiet as in a grotto, only in the distance a sound of rushing water was to be heard. I divested myself of my tail coat and was soon swimming through the sinking palace toward the portals. My splashes echoed mysteriously from the walls and columns. Not a soul was to be seen. Evidently the servants had all fled. And why should they not? They had no obligation to the true and eternal culture, and those assembled here had no further need of their services.

Outside the moon shone as if nothing were amiss, and yet a

world, no less, was here sinking beneath the ocean. As if at a great distance I could still hear the high notes of Monsieur Béranger's flute. He had a wonderful *embouchure,* that one must allow him.

I unhitched the last gondola which the escaping servants had left behind and pushed out to sea. Through the windows past which I paddled the water was now flooding into the palace. I saw that the guests had risen from their seats. The sonata must be at an end, for they were clapping, their hands held high over their heads, since the water was now up to their chins. With dignity the Marchesa and Monsieur Béranger were acknowledging the applause, though in the circumstances they could not bow.

The water had now reached the candles. Slowly they were extinguished, and as the darkness grew, it became quiet; the applause was silenced. Suddenly I heard the crash and roar of a building in collapse. The Palazzo was falling. I steered the gondola seaward so as not to be hit by plaster fragments.

After paddling some hundreds of yards across the lagoon in the direction of the island of San Giorgio, I turned round once more. The sea lay dead calm in the moonlight as if no island had ever stood there. A pity about the bathtub, I thought, for that was a loss which could never be made good. The thought was perhaps rather heartless but experience teaches us that we need a certain distance from such events in order to appreciate their full scope.

QUESTIONS

1 In what ways would you consider "A World Ends" as fantasy? Could the tone be considered an element of the fantasy? How does the tone contribute to the meaning of the story?
2 "A World Ends" is filled with water imagery. Does this imagery have any special thematic significance? What other images or symbols does Hildesheimer use to give meaning to his story?
3 What is the significance of the following statement: "The thought was perhaps rather heartless but experience teaches us that we need a certain distance from such events in order to appreciate their full scope." What does it tell us about the character of the narrator? Describe the narrator.
4 What effect does learning that the Marchesa was a Waterman

born in Little Gidding, Ohio, have on us? Can you find other instances where Hildesheimer comments indirectly on his characters. What overall effect does this have on the story?

5 What is the effect of such remarks as: "The flute too had a history, but I have forgotten it" and "I do not as a matter of fact know how essential they (the pedals) are on the harpsichord"? Do they tell more about the narrator or about the kind of society he is describing?

6 Describe the kind of society that Hildesheimer pictures. How do you account for the fact that arriving at the Marchesa's by gondola was an unwritten rule of behavior? What other rules govern her society? What is the narrator's attitude toward these rules? Would you take this as a statement of Hildesheimer's about societal rules in general? Are the Marchesa's customs any more ludicrous than some of our own? Name some.

A ROSE FOR ECCLESIASTES

Roger Zelazny

Part I

I was busy translating one of my *Madrigals Macabre* into Martian on the morning I was found acceptable. The intercom had buzzed briefly, and I dropped my pencil and flipped on the toggle in a single motion.

"Mister G," piped Morton's youthful contralto, "the old man says I should 'get hold of that damned conceited rhymer' right away, and send him to his cabin. Since there's only one damned conceited rhymer . . ."

"Let not ambition mock thy useful toil." I cut him off.

So, the Martians had finally made up their minds! I knocked an inch and a half of ash from a smouldering butt, and took my first drag since I had lit it. The entire month's anticipation tried hard to crowd itself into the moment, but could not quite make it. I was frightened to walk those forty feet and hear Emory say the words I already knew he would say; and that feeling elbowed the other one into the background.

So I finished the stanza I was translating before I got up.

It took only a moment to reach Emory's door. I knocked twice and opened it, just as he growled, "Come in."

"You wanted to see me?" I sat down quickly to save him the trouble of offering me a seat.

"That was fast. What did you do, run?"

I regarded his paternal discontent:

Little fatty flecks beneath pale eyes, thinning hair, and an Irish nose; a voice a decibel louder than anyone else's . . .

Hamlet to Claudius: "I was working."

"Hah!" he snorted. "Come off it. No one's ever seen you do any of that stuff."

I shrugged my shoulders and started to rise.

"If that's what you called me down here—"

"Sit down!"

He stood up. He walked around his desk. He hovered above

me and glared down. (A hard trick, even when I'm in a low chair.)

"You are undoubtedly the most antagonistic bastard I've ever had to work with!" he bellowed, like a belly-stung buffalo. "Why the hell don't you act like a human being sometime and surprise everybody? I'm willing to admit you're smart, maybe even a genius, but—oh, Hell!" He made a heaving gesture with both hands and walked back to his chair.

"Betty has finally talked them into letting you go in." His voice was normal again. "They'll receive you this afternoon. Draw one of the jeepsters after lunch, and get down there."

"Okay," I said.

"That's all, then."

I nodded, got to my feet. My hand was on the doorknob when he said:

"I don't have to tell you how important that is. Don't treat them the way you treat us."

I closed the door behind me.

I don't remember what I had for lunch. I was nervous, but I knew instinctively that I wouldn't muff it. My Boston publishers expected a Martian Idyll, or at least a Saint-Exupéry job on space flight. The National Science Association wanted a complete report on the Rise and Fall of the Martian Empire.

They would both be pleased. I knew.

That's the reason everyone is jealous—why they hate me. I always come through, and I can come through better than anyone else.

I shoveled in a final anthill of slop, and made my way to our car barn. I drew one jeepster and headed it toward Tirellian.

Flames of sand, lousy with iron oxide, set fire to the buggy. They swarmed over the open top and bit through my scarf; they set to work pitting my goggles.

The jeepster, swaying and panting like a little donkey I once rode through the Himalayas, kept kicking me in the seat of the pants. The Mountains of Tirellian shuffled their feet and moved toward me at a cockeyed angle.

Suddenly I was heading uphill, and I shifted gears to accommodate the engine's braying. Not like Gobi, not like the Great

Southwestern Desert, I mused. Just red, just dead . . . without even a cactus.

I reached the crest of the hill, but I had raised too much dust to see what was ahead. It didn't matter, though, I have a head full of maps. I bore to the left and downhill, adjusting the throttle. A cross-wind and solid ground beat down the fires. I felt like Ulysses in Malebolge—with a terza-rima speech in one hand and an eye out for Dante.

I sounded a rock pagoda and arrived.

Betty waved as I crunched to a halt, then jumped down.

"Hi," I choked, unwinding my scarf and shaking out a pound and a half of grit. "Like, where do I go and who do I see?"

She permitted herself a brief Germanic giggle—more at my starting a sentence with "like" than at my discomfort—then she started talking. (She is a top linguist, so a word from the Village Idiom still tickles her!)

I appreciated her precise, furry talk; informational, and all that. I had enough in the way of social pleasantries before me to last at least the rest of my life. I looked at her chocolate-bar eyes and perfect teeth, at her sun-bleached hair, close-cropped to the head (I hate blondes!), and decided that she was in love with me.

"Mr. Gallinger, the Matriarch is waiting inside to be introduced. She has consented to open the Temple records for your study." She paused here to pat her hair and squirm a little. Did my gaze make her nervous?

"They are religious documents, as well as their only history," she continued, "sort of like the Magabharata. She expects you to observe certain rituals in handling them, like repeating the sacred words when you turn pages—she will teach you the system."

I nodded quickly, several times.

"Fine, let's go in."

"Uh—" she paused. "Do not forget their Eleven Forms of Politeness and Degree. They take matters of form quite seriously —and do not get into any discussions over the equality of the sexes—"

"I know all about their taboos," I broke in. "Don't worry. I've lived in the Orient, remember?"

She dropped her eyes and seized my hand. I almost jerked it away.

"It will look better if I enter leading you."

I swallowed my comments and followed her, like Samson in Gaza.

Inside, my last thought met with a strange correspondence. The Matriarch's quarters were a rather abstract version of what I imagine the tents of the tribes of Israel to have been like. Abstract, I say, because it was all frescoed brick, peaked like a huge tent, with animal-skin representations, like gray-blue scars, that looked as if they had been laid on the walls with a palette knife.

The Matriarch, M'Cwyie, was short, white-haired, fiftyish, and dressed like a Gypsy queen. With her rainbow of voluminous skirts she looked like an inverted punch bowl set atop a cushion.

Accepting my obeisances, she regarded me as an owl might a rabbit. The lids of those black, black eyes jumped upwards as she discovered my perfect accent. The tape recorder Betty had carried on her interviews had done its part, and I knew the language reports from the first two expeditions, verbatim. I'm all hell when it comes to picking up accents.

"You are the poet?"

"Yes," I replied.

"Recite one of your poems, please."

"I'm sorry, but nothing short of a thorough translating job would do justice to your language and my poetry, and I don't know enough of your language yet."

"Oh?"

"But I've been making such translations for my own amusement, as an exercise in grammar," I continued. "I'd be honored to bring a few of them along one of the times that I come here."

"Yes. Do so."

Score one for me!

She turned to Betty.

"You may go now."

Betty muttered the parting formalities, gave me a strange sidewise look, and was gone. She apparently had expected to stay and "assist" me. She wanted a piece of the glory, like everyone else. But I was the Schliemann at this Troy, and there would be only one name on the Association report!

M'Cwyie rose, and I noticed that she gained very little height by standing. But then I'm six-six and look like a poplar in October: thin, bright red on top, and towering above everyone else.

"Our records are very, very old," she began. "Betty says that your word for their age is 'millennia.' "

I nodded appreciatively.

"I'm very eager to see them."

"They are not here. We will have to go into the Temple—they may not be removed."

I was suddenly wary.

"You have no objections to my copying them, do you?"

"No. I see that you respect them, or your desire would not be so great."

"Excellent."

She seemed amused. I asked her what was funny.

"The High Tongue may not be so easy for a foreigner to learn."

It came through fast.

No one on the first expedition had gotten this close. I had no way of knowing that this was a double-language deal—a classical as well as a vulgar. I knew some of their Prakrit, now I had to learn all their Sanskrit.

"Ouch! and damn!"

"Pardon, please?"

"It's nontranslatable, M'Cwyie. But imagine yourself having to learn the High Tongue in a hurry, and you can guess at the sentiment."

She seemed amused again, and told me to remove my shoes.

She guided me through an alcove . . .

. . . and into a burst of Byzantine brilliance!

No Earthman had ever been in this room before, or I would have heard about it. Carter, the first expedition's linguist, with the help of one Mary Allen, M.D., had learned all the grammar and vocabulary that I knew while sitting cross-legged in the ante-chamber.

We had no idea this existed. Greedily, I cast my eyes about. A highly sophisticated system of esthetics lay behind the decor. We would have to revise our entire estimation of Martian culture.

For one thing, the ceiling was vaulted and corbeled; for another, there were side columns with reverse flutings; for another—oh hell! The place was big. Posh. You could never have guessed it from the shaggy outsides.

I bent forward to study the gilt filigree on a ceremonial table. M'Cwyie seemed a bit smug at my intentness, but I'd still have hated to play poker with her.

The table was loaded with books.

With my toe, I traced a mosaic on the floor.

"Is your entire city within this one building?"

"Yes, it goes far back into the mountain."

"I see," I said, seeing nothing.

I couldn't ask her for a conducted tour, yet.

She moved to a small stool by the table.

"Shall we begin your friendship with the High Tongue?"

I was trying to photograph the hall with my eyes, knowing I would have to get a camera in here, somehow, sooner or later. I tore my gaze from a statuette and nodded, hard.

"Yes, introduce me."

I sat down.

For the next three weeks alphabet-bugs chased each other behind my eyelids whenever I tried to sleep. The sky was an unclouded pool of turquoise that rippled calligraphies whenever I swept my eyes across it. I drank quarts of coffee while I worked and mixed cocktails of Benzedrine and champagne for my coffee breaks.

M'Cwyie tutored me two hours every morning, and occasionally for another two in the evening. I spent an additional fourteen hours a day on my own, once I had gotten up sufficient momentum to go ahead alone.

And at night the elevator of time dropped me to its bottom floors . . .

I was six again, learning my Hebrew, Greek, Latin, and Aramaic. I was ten, sneaking peeks at the *Iliad*. When Daddy wasn't spreading hellfire, brimstone, and brotherly love, he was teaching me to dig the Word, like in the original.

Lord! There are so many originals and so *many* words! When

I was twelve I started pointing out the little differences between what he was preaching and what I was reading.

The fundamentalist vigor of his reply brooked no debate. It was worse than any beating. I kept my mouth shut after that and learned to appreciate Old Testament poetry.

—Lord, I am sorry! Daddy—Sir—I am sorry!—It couldn't be! It couldn't be . . .

On the day the boy graduated from high school, with the French, German, Spanish, and Latin awards, Dad Gallinger had told his fourteen-year-old, six-foot scarecrow of a son that he wanted him to enter the ministry. I remember how his son was evasive:

"Sir," he had said, "I'd sort of like to study on my own for a year or so, and then take pre-theology courses at some liberal-arts university. I feel I'm still sort of young to try a seminary, straight off."

The Voice of God: "But you have the gift of tongues, my son. You can preach the Gospel in all the lands of Babel. You were born to be a missionary. You say you are young, but time is rushing by you like a whirlwind. Start early, and you will enjoy added years of service."

The added years of service were so many added tails to the cat repeatedly laid on my back. I can't see his face now, I never can. Maybe it is because I was always afraid to look at it then.

And years later, when he was dead, and laid out, in black, amidst bouquets, amidst weeping congregationalists, amidst prayers, red faces, handkerchiefs, hands patting your shoulders, solemn-faced comforters . . . I looked at him and did not recognize him.

We had met nine months before my birth, this stranger and I. He had never been cruel—stern, demanding, with contempt for everyone's shortcomings—but never cruel. He was also all that I had had of a mother. And brothers. And sisters. He had tolerated my three years at St. John's, possibly because of its name, never knowing how liberal and delightful a place it really was.

But I never knew him, and the man atop the catafalque demanded nothing now; I was free not to preach the Word.

But now I wanted to, in a different way. I wanted to preach a word that I could never have voiced while he lived.

I did not return for my Senior year in the fall. I had a small inheritance coming, and a bit of trouble getting control of it since I was still under eighteen. But I managed.

It was Greenwich Village I finally settled upon.

Not telling any well-meaning parishioners my new address, I entered into a daily routine of writing poetry and teaching myself Japanese and Hindustani. I grew a fiery beard, drank espresso, and learned to play chess. I wanted to try a couple of the other paths to salvation.

After that, it was two years in India with the Old Peace Corps—which broke me of my Buddhism, and gave me my *Pipes of Krishna* lyrics and the Pulitzer they deserved.

Then back to the States for my degree, grad work in linguistics, and more prizes.

Then one day a ship went to Mars. The vessel settling in its New Mexico nest of fires contained in a new language—It was fantastic, exotic, and esthetically overpowering. After I had learned all there was to know about it, and written my book, I was famous in new circles:

"Go, Gallinger. Dip your bucket in the well, and bring us a drink of Mars. Go, learn another world—but remain aloof, rail at it gently like Auden—and hand us its soul in iambics."

And I came to the land where the sun is a tarnished penny, where the wind is a whip, where two moons play at hot-rod games, and a hell of sand gives you the incendiary itches whenever you look at it.

I rose from my twistings on the bunk and crossed the darkened cabin to a port. The desert was a carpet of endless orange, bulging from the sweepings of centuries beneath it.

"I a stranger, unafraid—This is the land—I've got it made!"

I laughed.

I had the High Tongue by the tail already—or the roots, if you want your puns anatomical, as well as correct.

The High and Low Tongues were not so dissimilar as they

had first seemed. I had enough of the one to get me through the murkier parts of the other. I had the grammar and all the commoner irregular verbs down cold; the dictionary I was constructing grew by the day, like a tulip, and would bloom shortly. Every time I played the tapes, the stem lengthened.

Now was the time to tax my ingenuity, to really drive the lessons home. I had purposely refrained from plunging into the major texts until I could do justice to them. I had been reading minor commentaries, bits of verse, fragments of history. And one thing had impressed me strongly in all that I read.

They wrote about concrete things: rocks, sand, water, winds; and the tenor couched within these elemental symbols was fiercely pessimistic. It reminded me of some Buddhist texts, but even more so, I realized from my recent *recherches,* it was like parts of the Old Testament. Specifically it reminded me of the Book of Ecclesiastes.

That, then, would be it. The sentiment, as well as the vocabulary, was so similar that it would be a perfect exercise. Like putting Poe into French. I would never be a convert to the Way of Malann, but I would show them that an Earthman had once thought the same thoughts, felt similarly.

I switched on my desk lamp and sought King James amidst my books.

Vanity of vanities, saith the Preacher, vanity of vanities; all is vanity. What profit hath a man . . .

My progress seemed to startle M'Cwyie. She peered at me, like Sartre's Other, across the tabletop. I ran through a chapter in the Book of Locar. I didn't look up, but I could feel the tight net her eyes were working about my head, shoulders, and rapid hands. I turned another page.

Was she weighing the net, judging the size of the catch? And what for? The books said nothing of fishers on Mars. Especially of men. They said that some god named Malann had spat, or had done something disgusting (depending on the version you read), and that life had gotten underway as a disease in inorganic matter. They said that movement was its first law, its first law, and that

the dance was the only legitimate reply to the inorganic . . . the
dance's quality its justification,—fication . . . and love is a disease
in organic matter—Inorganic matter?

I shook my head. I had almost been asleep.

"M'narra."

I stood and stretched. Her eyes outlined me greedily now. So
I met them, and they dropped.

"I grow tired. I want to rest awhile. I didn't sleep much last
night."

She nodded, Earth's shorthand for "yes," as she had learned
from me.

"You wish to relax, and see the explicitness of the doctrines
of Locar in its fullness?"

"Pardon me?"

"You wish to see a Dance of Locar?"

"Oh." Their damned circuits of form and periphrasis here ran
worse than the Korean! "Yes. Surely. Any time it's going to
be done, I'd be happy to watch."

I continued, "In the meantime, I've been meaning to ask you
whether I might take some pictures—"

"Now is the time. Sit down. Rest. I will call the musicians."

She bustled out through a door I had never been past.

Well now, the dance was the highest art, according to Locar,
not to mention Havelock Ellis, and I was about to see how their
centuries-dead philosopher felt it should be conducted. I rubbed
my eyes and snapped over, touching my toes a few times.

The blood began pounding in my head, and I sucked in a
couple of deep breaths. I bent again and there was a flurry
of motion at the door.

To the trio who entered with M'Cwyie I must have looked as
if I were searching for the marbles I had just lost, bent over like
that.

I grinned weakly and straightend up, my face red from more
than exertion. I hadn't expected them *that* quickly.

Suddenly I thought of Havelock Ellis again in his area of
greatest popularity.

The little redheaded doll, wearing, sari-like, a diaphanous

piece of the Martian sky, looked up in wonder—as a child at some colorful flag on a high pole.

"Hello," I said, or its equivalent.

She bowed before replying. Evidently I had been promoted in status.

"I shall dance," said the red wound in that pale, pale cameo, her face. Eyes, the color of dream and her dress, pulled away from mine.

She drifted to the center of the room.

Standing there, like a figure in an Etruscan frieze, she was either meditating or regarding the design on the floor.

Was the mosaic symbolic of something? I studied it. If it was, it eluded me; it would make an attractive bathroom floor or patio, but I couldn't see much in it beyond that.

The other two were paint-spattered sparrows like M'Cwyie, in their middle years. One settled to the floor with a triple-stringed instrument faintly resembling a *samisen*. The other held a simple woodblock and two drumsticks.

M'Cwyie disdained her stool and was seated upon the floor before I realized it. I followed suit.

The *samisen* player was still tuning up, so I leaned toward M'Cwyie.

"What is the dancer's name?"

"Braxa," she replied, without looking at me, and raised her left hand, slowly, which meant yes, and go ahead, and let it begin.

The stringed thing throbbed like a toothache, and a tick-tocking, like ghosts of all the clocks they had never invented, sprang from the block.

Braxa was a statue, both hands raised to her face, elbows high and outspread.

The music became a metaphor for fire.

Crackle, purr, snap . . .

She did not move.

The hissing altered to splashes. The cadence slowed. It was water now, the most precious thing in the world, gurgling clear then green over mossy rocks.

Still she did not move.

Glissandos. A pause.

Then, so faint I could hardly be sure at first, the tremble of the winds began. Softly, gently, sighing and halting, uncertain. A pause, a sob, then a repetition of the first statement, only louder.

Were my eyes completely bugged from my reading, or was Braxa actually trembling, all over, head to foot.

She was.

She began a microscopic swaying. A fraction of an inch right, then left. Her fingers opened like the petals of a flower, and I could see that her eyes were closed.

Her eyes opened. They were distant, glassy, looking through me and the walls. Her swaying became more pronounced, merged with the beat.

The wind was sweeping in from the desert now, falling against Tirellian like waves on a dike. Her fingers moved, they were the gusts. Her arms, slow pendulums, descended, began a countermovement.

The gale was coming now. She began an axial movement and her hands caught up with the rest of her body, only now her shoulders commenced to writhe out a figure eight.

The wind! The wind, I say. O wild, enigmatic! O muse of St.-John Perse!

The cyclone was twisting round those eyes, its still center. Her head was thrown back, but I knew there was no ceiling between her gaze, passive as Buddha's, and the unchanging skies. Only the two moons, perhaps, interrupted their slumber in that elemental Nirvana of uninhabited turquoise.

Years ago, I had seen the Devadasis in India, the street dancers, spinning their colorful webs, drawing in the male insect. But Braxa was more than this; she was a Ramadjany, like those votaries of Rama, incarnation of Vishnu, who had given the dance to man: the sacred dancers.

The clicking was monotonously steady now; the whine of the strings made me think of the stinging rays of the sun, their heat stolen by the wind's halations; the blue was Sarasvati and Mary, and a girl named Laura. I heard a sitar from somewhere, watched this statue come to life, and inhaled a divine afflatus.

I was again Rimbaud with his hashish, Baudelaire with his

laudanum, Poe, De Quincey, Wilde, Mallarmé, and Aleister Crowley. I was, for a fleeting second, my father in his dark pulpit and darker suit, the hymns and the organ's wheeze transmuted to bright wind.

She was a spun weather vane, a feathered crucifix hovering in the air, a clothesline holding one bright garment lashed parallel to the ground. Her shoulder was bare now, and her right breast moved up and down like a moon in the sky, its red nipple appearing momently above a fold and vanishing again. The music was as formal as Job's argument with God. Her dance was God's reply.

The music slowed, settled; it had been met, matched, answered. Her garment, as if alive, crept back into the more sedate folds it originally held.

She dropped low, lower to the floor. Her head fell upon her raised knees. She did not move.

There was silence.

I realized, from the ache across my shoulders, how tensely I had been sitting. My armpits were wet. Rivulets had been running down my sides. What did one do now? Applaud?

I sought M'Cwyie from the corner of my eye. She raised her right hand.

As if by telepathy the girl shuddered all over and stood. The musicians also rose. So did M'Cwyie.

I got to my feet, with a charley horse in my left leg, and said, "It was beautiful," inane as that sounds.

I received three different High Forms of "Thank You,"

There was a flurry of color and I was alone again with M'Cwyie.

"That is the one hundred seventeenth of the two thousand two hundred twenty-four dances of Locar."

I looked down at her.

"Whether Locar was right or wrong, he worked out a fine reply to the inorganic."

She smiled.

"Are the dances of your world like this?"

"Some of them are similar. I was reminded of them as I watched Braxa—but I've never seen anything exactly like hers."

"She is good," M'Cwyie said. "She knows all the dances."
A hint of her earlier expression which had troubled me . . .
It was gone in an instant.

"I must tend to my duties now." She moved to the table and closed the books. "M'narra."

"Good-bye." I slipped into my boots.

"Good-bye, Gallinger."

I walked out the door, mounted the jeepster, and roared across the evening into night, my wings of risen desert flapping slowly behind me.

Part II

I had just closed the door behind Betty, after a brief grammar session, when I heard the voices in the hall. My vent was opened a fraction, so I stood there and eavesdropped:

Morton's fruity treble: "Guess what? He said 'hello' to me a while ago."

"Hmmph!" Emory's elephant lungs exploded. "Either he's slipping, or you were standing in his way and he wanted you to move."

"Probably didn't recognize me. I don't think he sleeps any more, now he has that language to play with. I had night watch last week, and every night I passed his door at 0300—I always heard that recorder going. At 0500, when I got off, he was still at it."

"The guy *is* working hard," Emory admitted, grudgingly. "In fact, I think he's taking some kind of dope to stay awake. He looks sort of glassy-eyed these days. Maybe that's natural for a poet, though."

Betty had been standing there, because she broke in then:

"Regardless of what you think of him, it's going to take me at least a year to learn what he's picked up in three weeks. And I'm just a linguist, not a poet."

Morton must have been nursing a crush on her bovine charms. It's the only reason I can think of for his dropping his guns to say what he did.

"I took a course in modern poetry when I was back at the

university," he began. "We read six authors—Yeats, Pound, Eliot, Crane, Stevens, and Gallinger—and on the last day of the semester, when the prof was feeling a little rhetorical, he said, 'These six names are written on the century, and all the gates of criticism and Hell shall not prevail against them.' "

"Myself," he continued. "I thought his *Pipes of Krishna* and his *Madrigals* were great. I was honored to be chosen for an expedition he was going on.

"I think he's spoken two dozen words to me since I met him," he finished.

The Defense: "Did it ever occur to you," Betty said, "that he might be tremendously self-conscious about his appearance? He was also a precocious child, and probably never even had school friends. He's sensitive and very introverted."

"Sensitive? Self-conscious?" Emory choked and gagged. "The man is as proud as Lucifer, and he's a walking insult machine. You press a button like 'Hello' or 'Nice day' and he thumbs his nose at you. He's got it down to a reflex."

They muttered a few other pleasantries and drifted away.

Well, bless you, Morton boy. You little pimple-faced, Ivy-bred connoisseur! I've never taken a course in my poetry, but I'm glad someone said that. The Gates of Hell. Well, now! Maybe Daddy's prayers got heard somewhere, and I am a missionary, after all!

Only . . .

. . . Only a missionary needs something to convert people *to*. I have my private system of esthetics, and I suppose it oozes an ethical by-product somewhere. But if I ever had anything to preach, really, even in my poems, I wouldn't care to preach it to such lowlifes as you. If you think I'm a slob, I'm also a snob, and there's no room for you in Heaven—it's a private place, where Swift, Shaw, and Petronius Arbiter come to dinner.

And oh, the feasts we have! The Trimalchio's, the Emory's we dissect!

We finish you with the soup, Morton!

I turned and settled at my desk. I wanted to write something. Ecclesiastes could take a night off. I wanted to write a poem, a poem about the one hundred seventeenth dance of Locar; about a rose following the light, traced by the wind, sick, like Blake's rose, dying . . .

I found a pencil and began.

When I had finished I was pleased. It wasn't great—at least, it was no greater than it needed to be—High Martian not being my strongest tongue. I groped, and put it into English, with partial rhymes. Maybe I'd stick it in my next book. I called it *Braxa:*

> In a land of wind and red,
> where the icy evening of Time
> freezes milk in the breasts of Life,
> as two moons overhead—
> cat and dog in alleyways of dream—
> scratch and scramble agelessly my
> flight . . .
> This final flower turns a burning
> head.

I put it away and found some phenobarbitol. I was suddenly tired.

When I showed my poem to M'Cwyie the next day, she read it through several times, very slowly.

"It is lovely," she said. "But you used three words from your own language. 'Cat' and 'dog,' I assume, are two small animals with a hereditary hatred for one another. But what is 'flower'?"

"Oh," I said. "I've never come across your word for 'flower,' but I was actually thinking of an Earth flower, the rose."

"What is it like?"

"Well, its petals are generally bright red. That's what I meant, on one level, by 'burning head.' I also wanted it to imply fever, though, and red hair, and the fire of life. The rose, itself, has a thorny stem, green leaves, and a distinct pleasant aroma."

"I wish I could see one."

"I suppose it could be arranged. I'll check."

"Do it, please. You are a———." She used the word for "prophet," or religious poet, like Isaiah or Locar. "—and your poem is inspired. I shall tell Braxa of it."

I declined the nomination, but felt flattered.

This, then, I decided, was the strategic day, the day on which to ask whether I might bring in the microfilm machine and the camera. I wanted to copy all their texts, I explained, and I couldn't write fast enough to do it.

She surprised me by agreeing immediately. But she bowled me over with her invitation.

"Would you like to come and stay here while you do this thing? Then you can work night and day, any time you want—except when the Temple is being used, of course."

I bowed.

"I should be honored."

"Good. Bring your machines when you want, and I will show you a room."

"Will this afternoon be all right?"

"Certainly."

"Then I will go now and get things ready. Until this afternoon . . ."

"Good-bye."

I anticipated a little trouble from Emory, but not much. Everyone back at the ship was anxious to see the Martians, talk with the Martians, poke needles in the Martians, ask them about Martian climate, diseases, soil chemistry, politics, and mushrooms (our botanist was a fungus nut, but a reasonably good guy)—and only four or five had actually gotten to see them. The crew had been spending most of its time excavating dead cities and their acropolises. We played the game by strict rules, and the natives were as fiercely insular as the nineteenth-century Japanese. I figured I would meet with little resistance, and I figured right.

In fact, I got the distinct impression that everyone was happy to see me move out.

I stopped in the hydroponics room to speak with our mushroom master.

"Hi, Kane. Grow any toadstools in the sand yet?"

He sniffed. He always sniffs. Maybe he's allergic to plants.

"Hello, Gallinger. No, I haven't had any success with toad-stools, but look behind the car barn next time you're out there. I've got a few cacti going."

"Great," I observed. Doc Kane was about my only friend aboard, not counting Betty.

"Say, I came down to ask you a favor."

"Name it."

"I want a rose."

"A what?"

"A rose. You know, a nice red American Beauty job—thorns, pretty smelling—"

"I don't think it will take in this soil. *Sniff, sniff.*"

"No, you don't understand. I don't want to plant it, I just want the flowers."

"I'd have to use the tanks." He scratched his hairless dome. "It would take at least three months to get you flowers, even under forced growth."

"Will you do it?"

"Sure, if you don't mind the wait."

"Not at all. In fact, three months will just make it before we leave." I looked about at the pools of crawling slime, at the trays of shoots. "—I'm moving up to Tirellian today, but I'll be in and out all the time. I'll be here when it blooms."

"Moving up there, eh? Moore said they're an in-group."

"I guess I'm 'in' then."

"Looks that way—I still don't see how you learned their language, though. Of course, I had trouble with French and German for my Ph.D., but last week I heard Betty demonstrate it at lunch. It just sounds like a lot of weird noises. She says speaking it is like working a *Times* crossword and trying to imitate birdcalls at the same time."

I laughed, and took the cigarette he offered me.

"It's complicated," I acknowledged. "But, well, it's as if you suddenly came across a whole new class of mycetae here—you'd dream about it at night."

His eyes were gleaming.

"Wouldn't that be something! I might, yet, you know."

"Maybe you will."

He chuckled as we walked to the door.

"I'll start your roses tonight. Take it easy down there."

"You bet. Thanks."

Like I said, a fungus nut, but a fairly good guy.

My quarters in the Citadel of Tirellian were directly adjacent to the Temple, on the inward side and slightly to the left. They were a considerable improvement over my cramped cabin, and I was pleased that Martian culture had progressed sufficiently to discover the desirability of the mattress over the pallet. Also, the bed was long enough to accommodate me, which *was* surprising.

So I unpacked and took sixteen 35 mm. shots of the Temple, before starting on the books.

I took 'stats until I was sick of turning pages without knowing what they said. So I started translating a work of history.

"Lo. In the thirty-seventh year of the Process of Cillen the rains came, which gave rise to rejoicing, for it was a rare and untoward occurrence, and commonly construed a blessing.

"But it was not the life-giving semen of Malann which fell from the heavens. It was the blood of the universe, spurting from an artery. And the last days were upon us. The final dance was to begin.

"The rains brought the plague that does not kill, and the last passes of Locar began with their drumming . . ."

I asked myself what the hell Tamur meant, for he was an historian and supposedly committed to fact. This was not their Apocalypse.

Unless they could be one and the same . . .?

Why not? I mused. Tirellian's handful of people were the remnant of what had obviously once been a highly developed culture. They had had wars, but no holocausts; science, but little technology. A plague, a plague that did not kill . . .? Could that have done it? How, if it wasn't fatal?

I read on, but the nature of the plague was not discussed. I turned pages, skipped ahead, and drew a blank.

M'Cwyie; M'Cwyie! When I want to question you most, you are not around!

Would it be a *faux pas* to go looking for her? Yes, I decided. I was restricted to the rooms I had been shown, that had been an implicit understanding. I would have to wait to find out.

So I cursed long and loud, in many languages, doubtless burning Malann's sacred ears, there in his Temple.

He did not see fit to strike me dead, so I decided to call it a day and hit the sack.

I must have been asleep for several hours when Braxa entered my room with a tiny lamp. She dragged me awake by tugging at my pajama sleeve.

I said hello. Thinking back, there is not much else I could have said.

"Hello."

"I have come," she said, "to hear the poem."

"What poem?"

"Yours."

"Oh."

I yawned, sat up, and did things people usually do when awakened in the middle of the night to read poetry.

"That is very kind of you, but isn't the hour a trifle awkward?"

"I don't mind," she said.

Someday I am going to write an article for the *Journal of Semantics,* called "Tone of Voice: An Insufficient Vehicle for Irony."

However, I was awake, so I grabbed my robe.

"What sort of animal is that?" she asked, pointing at the silk dragon on my lapel.

"Mythical," I replied. "Now look, it's late. I am tired. I have much to do in the morning. And M'Cwyie just might get the wrong idea if she learns you were here."

"Wrong idea?"

"You know damned well what I mean!" It was the first time I had had an opportunity to use Martian profanity, and it failed.

"No," she said, "I do not know."

She seemed frightened, like a puppy being scolded without knowing what it has done wrong.

I softened. Her red cloak matched her hair and lips so perfectly, and those lips were trembling.

"Here now, I didn't mean to upset you. On my world there are certain, uh, mores, concerning people of different sex alone together in bedrooms, and not allied by marriage. . . . Um, I mean, you see what I mean?"

"No."

They were jade, her eyes.

"Well, it's sort of. . . .Well, it's sex, that's what it is."

A light was switched on in those jade lamps.

"Oh, you mean having children!"

"Yes. That's it! Exactly."

She laughed. It was the first time I had heard laughter in Tirellian. It sounded like a violinist striking his high strings with the bow, in short little chops. It was not an altogether pleasant thing to hear, especially because she laughed too long.

When she had finished she moved closer.

"I remember, now," she said. "We used to have such rules. Half a Process ago, when I was a child, we had such rules. But," she looked as if she were ready to laugh again, "there is no need for them now."

My mind moved like a tape recorder played at triple speed.

Half a Process! HalfaProcessaProcessaProcess! No! Yes!

Half a Process was two hundred-forty-three years, roughly speaking!

—Time enough to learn the 2,224 dances of Locar.

—Time enough to grow old, if you were human.

—Earth-style human, I mean.

I looked at her again, pale as the white queen in an ivory chess set.

She was human, I'd stake my soul—alive, normal, healthy, I'd stake my life—woman, my body . . .

But she was two and a half centuries old, which made M'Cwyie Methuselah's grandma. It flattered me to think of their repeated complimenting of my skills, as linguist, as poet. These superior beings!

But what did she mean "there is no such need for them now"? Why the near-hysteria? Why all those funny looks I'd been getting from M'Cwyie?

I suddenly knew I was close to something important, besides a beautiful girl.

"Tell me," I said, in my Casual Voice, "did it have anything to do with 'the plague that does not kill,' of which Tamur wrote?"

"Yes," she replied, "the children born after the Rains could have no children of their own, and—"

"And what?" I was leaning forward, memory set at "record."

"—and the men had no desire to get any."

I sagged backward against the bedpost. Racial sterility, masculine impotence, following phenomenal weather. Had some vagabond cloud of radioactive junk from God knows where penetrated their weak atmosphere one day? One day long before Schiaparelli saw the canals, mythical as my dragon, before those "canals" had given rise to some correct guesses for all the wrong reasons, had Braxa been alive, dancing, here—damned in the womb since blind Milton had written of another paradise, equally lost?

I found a cigarette. Good thing I had thought to bring ashtrays. Mars had never had a tobacco industry either. Or booze. The ascetics I had met in India had been Dionysiac compared to this.

"What is that tube of fire?"

"A cigarette. Want one?"

"Yes, please."

She sat beside me, and I lighted it for her.

"It irritates the nose."

"Yes. Draw some into your lungs, hold it there, and exhale."

A moment passed.

"Ooh," she said.

A pause, then, "Is it sacred?"

"No, it's nicotine," I answered, "a very *ersatz* form of divinity."

Another pause.

"Please don't ask me to translate 'ersatz.' "

"I won't. I get this feeling sometimes when I dance."

"It will pass in a moment."

"Tell me your poem now."

An idea hit me.

"Wait a minute," I said, "I may have something better."

I got up and rummaged through my notebooks, then I returned and sat down beside her.

"These are the first three chapters of the Book of Ecclesiastes," I explained. 'It is very similar to your own sacred books." I started reading.

I got through eleven verses before she cried out, "Please don't read that! Tell me one of yours!"

I stopped and tossed the notebook onto a nearby table. She was shaking, not as she had quivered that day she danced as the wind, but with the jitter of unshed tears. She held her cigarette awkwardly, like a pencil. Clumsily, I put my arm about her shoulders.

"He is so sad," she said, "like all the others."

So I twisted my mind like a bright ribbon, folded it, and tied the crazy Christmas knots I love so well. From German to Martian, with love, I did an impromptu paraphrasal of a poem about a Spanish dancer. I thought it would please her. I was right.

"Ooh," she said again. "Did you write that?"

"No, it's by a better man than I."

"I don't believe you. You wrote it."

"No, a man named Rilke did."

"But you brought it across to my language. Light another match, so I can see how she danced."

I did.

" 'The fires of forever,' " she mused, "and she stamped them out, 'with small, firm feet.' I wish I could dance like that."

"You're better than any Gipsy," I laughed, blowing it out.

"No, I'm not. I couldn't do that."

Her cigarette was burning down, so I removed it from her fingers and put it out, along with my own.

"Do you want me to dance for you?"

"No," I said. "Go to bed."

She smiled, and before I realized it, had unclasped the fold of red at her shoulder.

And everything fell away.

And I swallowed, with some difficulty.

"All right," she said.

So I kissed her, as the breath of fallen cloth extinguished the lamp.

Part III

The days were like Shelley's leaves: yellow, red, brown, whipped in bright gusts by the west wind. They swirled past me with the rattle of microfilm. Almost all the books were recorded now. It would take scholars years to get through them, to properly assess their value. Mars was locked in my desk.

Ecclesiastes, abandoned and returned to a dozen times, was almost ready to speak in the High Tongue.

I whistled when I wasn't in the Temple. I wrote reams of poetry I would have been ashamed of before. Evenings I would walk with Braxa, across the dunes or up into the mountains. Sometimes she would dance for me; and I would read something long, and in dactylic hexameter. She still thought I was Rilke, and I almost kidded myself into believing it. Here I was, staying at the Castle Duino, writing his *Elegies*.

> It is strange to inhabit the Earth no more,
> to use no longer customs scarce acquired,
> nor interpret roses . . .

No! Never interpret roses! Don't. Smell them (sniff, Kane!), pick them, enjoy them. Live in the moment. Hold to it tightly. But charge not the gods to explain. So fast the leaves go by, are blown . . .

And no one ever noticed us. Or cared.

Laura. Laura and Braxa. They rhyme, you know, with a bit of a clash. Tall, cool, and blonde was she (I hate blondes!), and Daddy had turned me inside out, like a pocket, and I thought she could fill me again. But the big, beat word-slinger, with Judas-beard and dog-trust in his eyes, oh, he had been a fine decoration at her parties. And that was all.

How the machine cursed me in the Temple! It blasphemed Malann and Gallinger. And the wild west wind went by and something was not far behind.

The last days were upon us.

A day went by and I did not see Braxa, and a night. And a second. A third.

I was half-mad. I hadn't realized how close we had become, how important she had been. With the dumb assurance of her presence, I had fought against questioning roses.

I had to ask. I didn't want to, but I had no choice.

"Where is she, M'Cwyie? Where is Braxa?"

"She is gone," she said.

"Where?"

"I do not know."

I looked at those devil-bird eyes. Anathema maranatha rose to my lips.

"I must know."

She looked through me.

"She has left us. She is gone. Up into the hills, I suppose. Or the desert. It does not matter. What does anything matter? The dance draws to a close. The Temple will soon be empty."

"Why? Why did she leave?"

"I do not know."

"I must see her again. We lift off in a matter of days."

"I am sorry, Gallinger."

"So am I," I said, and slammed shut a book without saying "M'narra."

I stood up.

"I will find her."

I left the Temple. M'Cwyie was a seated statue. My boots were still where I had left them.

All day I roared up and down the dunes, going nowhere. To the crew of the *Aspic* I must have looked like a sandstorm, all by myself. Finally, I had to return for more fuel.

Emory came stalking out.

"Okay, make it good. You look like the abominable dust man. Why the rodeo?"

"Why, I, uh, lost something."

"In the middle of the desert? Was it one of your sonnets? They're the only thing I can think of that you'd make such a fuss over."

"No, dammit! It was something personal."

George had finished filling the tank. I started to mount the jeepster again.

"Hold on there!" He grabbed my arm.

"You're not going back until you tell me what this is all about."

I could have broken his grip, but then he could order me dragged back by the heels, and quite a few people would enjoy doing the dragging. So I forced myself to speak slowly, softly:

"It's simply that I lost my watch. My mother gave it to me and it's a family heirloom. I want to find it before we leave."

"You sure it's not in your cabin, or down in Tirellian?"

"I've already checked."

"Maybe somebody hid it to irritate you. You know you're not the most popular guy around."

I shook my head.

"I thought of that. But I always carry it in my right pocket. I think it might have bounced out going over the dunes."

He narrowed his eyes.

"I remember reading on a book jacket that your mother died when you were born."

"That's right," I said, biting my tongue. "The watch belonged to her father and she wanted me to have it. My father kept it for me."

"Hmph!" he snorted. "That's a pretty strange way to look for a watch, riding up and down in a jeepster."

"I could see the light shining off it that way," I offered, lamely.

"Well, it's starting to get dark," he observed. "No sense looking any more today."

"Throw a dust sheet over the jeepster," he directed a mechanic.

He patted my arm.

"Come on in and get a shower, and something to eat. You look as if you could use both."

Little fatty flecks beneath pale eyes, thinning hair, and an Irish nose; a voice a decibel louder than anyone else's . . .

His only qualifications for leadership!

I stood there, hating him. Claudius! If only this were the fifth act!

But suddenly the idea of a shower, and food, came through to me. I could use both badly. If I insisted on hurrying back immediately, I might arouse more suspicion.

So I brushed some sand from my sleeve.

"You're right. That sounds like a good idea."

"Come on, we'll eat in my cabin."

The shower was a blessing, clean khakis were the grace of God, and the food smelled like Heaven.

"Smells pretty good," I said.

We hacked up our steaks in silence. When we got to the dessert and coffee, he suggested:

"Why don't you take the night off? Stay here and get some sleep."

I shook my head.

"I'm pretty busy. Finishing up. There's not much time left."

"A couple days ago you said you were almost finished."

"Almost, but not quite."

"You also said they'll be holding a service in the Temple tonight."

"That's right. I'm going to work in my room."

He shrugged his shoulders.

Finally, he said, "Gallinger," and I looked up because my name means trouble.

"It shouldn't be any of my business," he said, "but it is. Betty says you have a girl down there."

There was no question mark. It was a statement hanging in the air. Waiting.

—*Betty, you're a bitch. You're a cow and a bitch. And a a jealous one, at that. Why didn't you keep your nose where it belonged, shut your eyes? Your mouth?*

"So?" I said, a statement with a question mark.

"So," he answered it, "it is my duty, as head of this expedition, to see that relations with the natives are carried on in a friendly, and diplomatic, manner."

"You speak of them," I said, "as though they are aborigines. Nothing could be further from the truth."

I rose.

"When my papers are published, everyone on Earth will know the truth. I'll tell them things Doctor Moore never even guessed at. I'll tell the tragedy of a doomed race, waiting for death, resigned and disinterested. I'll tell why, and it will break hard, scholarly hearts. I'll write about it, and they will give me more prizes, and this time I won't want them.

"My God!" I exclaimed. "They had a culture when our ancestors were clubbing the sabre-tooth and finding out how fire works!"

"Do you have a girl down there?"

"Yes!" I said. *Yes, Claudius! Yes, Daddy! Yes, Emory!* "I do. But I'm going to let you in on a scholarly scoop now. They're already dead. They're sterile. In one more generation there won't be any Martians."

I paused, then added, "Except in my papers, except on a few pieces of microfilm and tape. And in some poems, about a girl who did give a damn and could only bitch about the unfairness of it all by dancing."

"Oh," he said.

After awhile:

"You *have* been behaving differently these past couple months. You've been downright civil on occasion, you know. I couldn't help wondering what was happening. I didn't know anything mattered that strongly to you."

I bowed my head.

"Is she the reason you were racing around the desert?"

I nodded.

"Why?"

I looked up.

"Because she's out there, somewhere. I don't know where, or why. And I've got to find her before we go."

"Oh," he said again.

Then he leaned back, opened a drawer, and took out something wrapped in a towel. He unwound it. A framed photo of a woman lay on the table.

"My wife," he said.

It was an attractive face, with big, almond eyes.

"I'm a Navy man, you know," he began. "Young officer once. Met her in Japan.

"Where I come from it wasn't considered right to marry into

another race, so we never did. But she was my wife. When she died I was on the other side of the world. They took my children, and I've never seen them since. I couldn't learn what orphanage, what home, they were put into. That was long ago. Very few people knew about it."

"I'm sorry," I said.

"Don't be. Forget it. But," he shifted in his chair and looked at me, "if you do want to take her back with you—do it. It'll mean my neck, but I'm too old to ever head another expedition like this one. So go ahead."

He gulped his cold coffee.

"Get your jeepster."

He swiveled the chair around.

I tried to say "thank you" twice, but I couldn't. So I got up and walked out.

"*Sayonara,* and all that," he muttered behind me.

"Here it is, Gallinger!" I heard a shout.

I turned on my heel and looked back up the ramp.

"Kane!"

He was limned in the port, shadow against light, but I had heard him sniff.

I returned the few steps.

"Here what is?"

"Your rose."

He produced a plastic container, divided internally. The lower half was filled with liquid. The stem ran down into it. The other half, a glass of claret in this horrible night, was a large, newly opened rose.

"Thank you," I said, tucking it into my jacket.

"Going back to Tirellian, eh?"

"Yes."

"I saw you come aboard, so I got it ready. Just missed you at the Captain's cabin. He was busy. Hollered out that I could catch you at the barns."

"Thanks again."

"It's chemically treated. It will stay in bloom for weeks."

I nodded. I was gone.

Up into the mountains now. Far. Far. The sky was a bucket of ice in which no moons floated. The going became steeper, and the little donkey protested. I whipped him with the throttle and went on. Up. Up. I spotted a green, unwinking star, and felt a lump in my throat. The uncased rose beat against my chest like an extra heart. The donkey brayed, long and loudly, then began to cough. I lashed him some more and he died.

I threw the emergency brake on and got out. I began to walk.

So cold, so cold it grows. Up here. At night? Why? Why did she do it? Why flee the campfire when night comes on?

And I was up, down around, and through every chasm, gorge, and pass, with my long-legged strides and an ease of movement never known on Earth.

Barely two days remain, my love, and thou hast forsaken me. Why?

I crawled under overhangs. I leapt over ridges. I scraped my knees, an elbow. I heard my jacket tear.

No answer, Malann? Do you really hate your people this much? Then I'll try someone else. Vishnu, you're the Preserver. Preserve her, please! Let me find her.

Jehovah?

Adonis? Osiris? Thammuz? Manitou? Legba? Where is she?

I ranged far and high, and I slipped.

Stones ground underfoot and I dangled over an edge. My fingers were so cold. It was hard to grip the rock.

I looked down.

Twelve feet or so. I let go and dropped, landed rolling. Then I heard her scream.

I lay there, not moving, looking up. Against the night, above, she called.

"Gallinger!"

I lay still.

"Gallinger!"

And she was gone.

I heard stones rattle and knew she was coming down some path to the right of me.

I jumped up and down and ducked into the shadow of a boulder.

She rounded a cut-off, and picked her way, uncertainly, through the stones.

"Gallinger?"

I stepped out and seized her shoulders.

"Braxa."

She screamed again, then began to cry, crowding against me. It was the first time I had ever heard her cry.

"Why?" I asked. "Why?"

But she only clung to me and sobbed.

Finally, "I thought you had killed yourself."

"Maybe I would have," I said. "Why did you leave Tirellian? And me?"

"Didn't M'Cwyie tell you? Didn't you guess?"

"I didn't guess, and M'Cwyie said she didn't know."

"Then she lied. She knows."

"What? What is it she knows?"

She shook all over, then was silent for a long time. I realized suddenly that she was wearing only her flimsy dancer's costume. I pushed her from me, took off my jacket, and put it about her shoulders.

"Great Malann!" I cried. "You'll freeze to death!"

"No," she said, "I won't."

I was transferring the rose case to my pocket.

"What is that?" she asked.

"A rose," I answered. "You can't make it out much in the dark. I once compared you to one. Remember?"

"Yu-Yes. May I carry it?"

"Sure." I stuck it in the jacket pocket.

"Well? I'm still waiting for an explanation."

"You really do not know?" she asked.

"No!"

"When the Rains came," she said, "apparently only our men were affected, which was enough. . . . Because I—wasn't—affected—apparently—"

"Oh," I said. "Oh."

We stood there, and I thought.

"Well, why did you run? What's wrong with being pregnant on Mars? Tamur was mistaken. Your people can live again."

She laughed, again that wild violin played by a Paganini gone mad. I stopped her before it went too far.

"How?" she finally asked, rubbing her cheek.

"Your people live longer than ours. If our child is normal it will mean our races can intermarry. There must still be other fertile women of your race. Why not?"

"You have read the Book of Locar," she said, "and yet you ask me that? Death was decided, voted upon, and passed, shortly after it appeared in this form. But long before, the followers of Locar knew. They decided it long ago. 'We have done all things,' they said, 'we have seen all things, we have heard and felt all things. The dance was good. Now let it end.' "

"You can't believe that."

"What I believe does not matter," she replied. "M'Cwyie and the Mothers have decided we must die. Their very title is now a mockery, but their decisions will be upheld. There is only one prophecy left, and it is mistaken. We will die."

"No," I said.

"What, then?"

"Come back with me, to Earth."

"No."

"All right, then. Come with me now."

"Where?"

"Back to Tirellian. I'm going to talk to the Mothers."

"You can't! There is a Ceremony tonight!"

I laughed.

"A ceremony for a god who knocks you down, and then kicks you in the teeth?"

"He is still Malann," she answered. "We are still his people."

"You and my father would have gotten along fine," I snarled. "But I am going, and you are coming with me, even if I have to carry you—and I'm bigger than you are."

"But you are not bigger than Ontro."

"Who the hell is Ontro?"

"He will stop you, Gallinger. He is the Fist of Malann."

Part IV

I scudded the jeepster to a halt in front of the only entrance I knew, M'Cwyie's. Braxa, who had seen the rose in a headlamp, now cradled it in her lap, like our child, and said nothing. There was a passive, lovely look on her face.

"Are they in the Temple now?" I wanted to know.

The Madonna expression did not change. I repeated the question. She stirred.

"Yes," she said, from a distance, "but you cannot go in."

"We'll see."

I circled and helped her down.

I led her by the hand, and she moved as if in a trance. In the light of the new-risen moon, her eyes looked as they had the day I met her, when she had danced. I snapped my fingers. Nothing happened.

So I pushed the door open and led her in. The room was half-lighted.

And she screamed for the third time that evening:

"Do not harm him, Ontro! It is Gallinger!"

I had never seen a Martian man before, only women. So I had no way of knowing whether he was a freak, though I suspected it strongly.

I looked up at him.

His half-naked body was covered with moles and swellings. Gland trouble, I guessed.

I had thought I was the tallest man on the planet, but he was seven feet tall and overweight. Now I knew where my giant bed had come from!

"Go back," he said. "She may enter. You may not."

"I must get my books and things."

He raised a huge left arm. I followed it. All my belongings lay neatly stacked in the corner.

"I must go in. I must talk with M'Cwyie and the Mothers."

"You may not."

"The lives of your people depend upon it."

"Go back," he boomed. "Go home to *your* people, Gallinger. Leave *us!*"

My name sounded so different on his lips, like someone else's. How old was he? I wondered. Three hundred? Four? Had he been a Temple guardian all his life? Why? Who was there to guard against? I didn't like the way he moved. I had seen men who moved like that before.

"Go back," he repeated.

If they had refined their martial arts as far as they had their dances, or, worse yet, if their fighting arts were a part of the dance, I was in for trouble.

"Go on in," I said to Braxa. "Give the rose to M'Cwyie. Tell her that I sent it. Tell her I'll be there shortly."

"I will do as you ask. Remember me on Earth, Gallinger. Good-bye."

I did not answer her, and she walked past Ontro and into the next room, bearing her rose.

"Now will you leave?" he asked. "If you like, I will tell her that we fought and you almost beat me, but I knocked you unconscious and carried you back to your ship."

"No," I said, "either I go around you or go over you, but I am going through."

He dropped into a crouch, arms extended.

"It is a sin to lay hands on a holy man," he rumbled, "but I will stop you, Gallinger."

My memory was a fogged window, suddenly exposed to fresh air. Things cleared. I looked back six years.

I was a student of Oriental Languages at the University of Tokyo. It was my twice-weekly night of recreation. I stood in a 30-foot circle in the Kodokan, the *judogi* lashed about my high hips by a brown belt. I was *Ik-kyu,* one notch below the lowest degree of expert. A brown diamond above my right breast said "Jiu-Jitsu" in Japanese, and it meant *Atemiwaza,* really, because of the one striking technique I had worked out, found unbelievably suitable to my size, and won matches with.

But I had never used it on a man, and it was five years since I had practiced. I was out of shape, I knew, but I tried hard to force my mind *tsuki no kokoro,* like the moon, reflecting the all of Ontro.

Somewhere, out of the past, a voice said, *"Hajime,* let it begin."

I snapped into my *neko-ashi-dachi* cat stance, and his eyes burned strangely. He hurried to correct his own position—and I threw it at him!

My one trick!

My long left leg lashed up like a broken spring. Seven feet off the ground my foot connected with his jaw as he tried to leap backward.

His head snapped back and he fell. A soft moan escaped his lips. *That's all there is to it,* I thought. *Sorry, old fellow.*

And as I stepped over him, somehow, groggily, he tripped me, and I fell across his body. I couldn't believe he had strength enough to remain conscious after that blow, let alone move. I hated to punish him any more.

But he found my throat and slipped a forearm across it before I realized there was a purpose to his action.

No! Don't let it end like this!

It was a bar of steel across my windpipe, my carotids. Then I realized that he was still unconscious, and that this was a reflex instilled by countless years of training. I had seen it happen once, in *shiai*. The man had died because he had been choked unconscious and still fought on, and his opponent thought he had not been applying the choke properly. He tried harder.

But it was rare, so very rare!

I jammed my elbows into his ribs and threw my head back in his face. The grip eased, but not enough. I hated to do it, but I reached up and broke his little finger.

The arm went loose and I twisted free.

He lay there panting, face contorted. My heart went out to the fallen giant, defending his people, his religion, following his orders. I cursed myself as I had never cursed before, for walking over him, instead of around.

I staggered across the room to my little heap of possessions. I sat on the projector case and lit a cigarette.

I couldn't go into the Temple until I got my breath back, until I thought of something to say?

How do you talk a race out of killing itself?

Suddenly—

—Could it happen? Would it work that way? If I read them the Book of Ecclesiastes—If I read them a greater piece of literature than any Locar ever wrote—and as somber—and as pessimistic—and showed them that our race has gone on despite one man's condemning all of life in the highest poetry—showed them that the vanity he had mocked had borne us to the Heavens—would they believe it?—would they change their minds?

I ground out my cigarette on the beautiful floor, and found my notebook. A strange fury rose within me as I stood.

And I walked into the Temple to preach the Black Gospel according to Gallinger, from the Book of Life.

There was silence all about me.

M'Cwyie had been reading Locar, the rose set at her right hand, target of all eyes.

Until I entered.

Hundreds of people were seated on the floor, barefoot. The few men were as small as the women, I noted.

I had my boots on.

Go all the way, I figured. *You either lose or you win— everything!*

A dozen crones sat in a semicircle behind M'Cwyie. The Mothers.

The barren earth, the dry wombs, the fire-touched.

I moved to the table.

"Dying yourselves, you would condemn your people," I addressed them, "that they may not know the life you have known —the joys, the sorrows, the fullness.—But it is not true that you all must die." I addressed the multitude now. "Those who say this lie. Braxa knows, for she will bear a child—"

They sat there, like rows of Buddhas. M'Cwyie drew back into the semicircle.

"—my child!" I continued, wondering what my father would have thought of this sermon.

". . . And all the women young enough may bear children. It is only your men who are sterile.—And if you permit the doctors of the next expedition to examine you, perhaps even the men may be helped. But if they cannot, you can mate with the men of Earth.

"And ours is not an insignificant people, an insignificant

place," I went on. "Thousands of years ago, the Locar of our world wrote a book saying that it was. He spoke as Locar did, but we did not lie down, despite plagues, wars, and famines. We did not die. One by one we beat down the diseases, we fed the hungry, we fought the wars, and, recently, have gone a long time without them. We may finally have conquered them. I do not know.

"But we have crossed millions of miles of nothingness. We have visited another world. And our Locar has said, 'Why bother? What is the worth of it? It is all vanity, anyhow.'

"And the secret is," I lowered my voice, as at a poetry reading, "he was right! It *is* vanity, it *is* pride! It is the *hybris* of rationalism to always attack the prophet, the mystic, the god. It is our blasphemy which has made us great, and will sustain us, and which the gods secretly admire in us.—All the truly sacred names of God are blasphemous things to speak!"

I was working up a sweat. I paused dizzily.

"Here is the Book of Ecclesiastes," I announced, and began:

" 'Vanity of vanities, saith the Preacher, vanity of vanities; all is vanity. What profit hath a man . . .' "

I spotted Braxa in the back, mute, rapt.

I wondered what she was thinking.

And I wound the hours of night about me, like black thread on a spool.

Oh, it was late! I had spoken till day came, still I spoke. I finished Ecclesiastes and continued Gallinger.

And when I finished, there was still only a silence.

The Buddhas, all in a row, had not stirred through the night. And after a long while M'Cwyie raised her right hand. One by one the Mothers did the same.

And I knew what that meant.

It meant no, do not, cease, and stop.

It meant that I had failed.

I walked slowly from the room and slumped beside my baggage.

Ontro was gone. Good that I had not killed him . . .

After a thousand years M'Cwyie entered.

She said, "Your job is finished."

I did not move.

"The prophecy is fulfilled," she said. "My people are re-joicing. You have won, holy man. Now leave us quickly."

My mind was a deflated balloon. I pumped a little air back into it.

"I'm not a holy man," I said, "just a second-rate poet with a bad case of *hybris*."

I lit my last cigarette.

Finally, "All right, what prophecy?"

"The Promise of Locar," she replied, as though the explain-ing were unnecessary, "that a holy man would come from the heavens to save us in our last hours, if all the dances of Locar were completed. He would defeat the Fist of Malann and bring us life."

"How?"

"As with Braxa, and as the example in the Temple."

"Example?"

"You read us his words, as great as Locar's. You read to us how there is 'nothing new under the sun.' And you mocked his words as you read them—showing us a new thing.

"There has never been a flower on Mars," she said, "but we will learn to grow them.

"You are the Sacred Scoffer," she finished. "He-Who-Must-Mock-in-the-Temple—you go shod on holy ground."

"But you voted 'no,' " I said.

"I voted not to carry out our original plan, and to let Braxa's child live instead."

"Oh." The cigarette fell from my fingers. How close it had been! How little I had known!

"And Braxa?"

"She was chosen half a Process ago to do the dances—to wait for you."

"But she said that Ontro would stop me."

M'Cwyie stood there for a long time.

"She had never believed the prophecy herself. Things are not well with her now. She ran away, fearing it was true. When you completed it and we voted, she knew."

"Then she does not love me? Never did?"

"I am sorry, Gallinger. It was the one part of her duty she never managed."

"Duty," I said flatly. . . . Dutydutyduty! Tra-la!

"She has said good-bye, she does not wish to see you again.

". . . and we will never forget your teachings," she added.

"Don't," I said, automatically, suddenly knowing the great paradox which lies at the heart of all miracles. I did not believe a word of my own gospel, never had.

I stood, like a drunken man, and muttered "M'narra."

I went outside, into my last day on Mars.

I have conquered thee, Malann—and the victory is thine! Rest easy on thy starry bed. God damned!

I left the jeepster there and walked back to the *Aspic,* leaving the burden of life so many footsteps behind me. I went to my cabin, locked the door, and took forty-four sleeping pills.

But when I awakened, I was in the dispensary, and alive.

I felt the throb of engines as I slowly stood up and somehow made it to the port.

Blurred Mars hung like a swollen belly above me, until it dissolved, brimmed over, and streamed down my face.

QUESTIONS

1 Discuss the significance of the following lines: "Never interpret roses! Don't. Smell them (sniff, Kane!), pick them, enjoy them. Live in the moment. Hold to it tightly. But charge not the gods to explain." Do you think that Gallinger follows his own advice?

2 What bearing does Gallinger's childhood have on either subsequent developments in his life or on his personality. Is Gallinger free? If, not, how is he restricted or limited and who or what restricts or limits him? If free, how is he free?

3 Do you feel that Zelazny has prepared us well enough for Gallinger's need to save the Martians? Why does Gallinger need to save them? Is it because of his love for Braxa, to be like his father, or for some other reason? How believable is Gallinger as the linguist-poet that Zelazny makes him?

4 What is the significance of Gallinger's statement: "I finished Ecclesiastes and continued Gallinger"?

5 After having brought new life to the Martians, why does Gallinger
   still feel that all is vanity? What are the similarities between Gallinger and other messianic figures? The differences? Why do you
   suppose he attempted suicide?
6 Zelazny has been world-building. How believable is the world of
   the Martians that he builds? What are the possibilities of building
   a fictional world that is not in some way, however distorted, a
   reflection of the world that we know.

SUGGESTED READINGS

Barron, Frank: *Creativity and Personal Freedom.* New York: D. Van
   Nostrand Company, Inc., 1968.
Camus, Albert: *The Myth of Sysiphus.* Trans. Justin O'Brien. New
   York: Alfred A. Knopf, Inc., 1961.
Chermayeff, Serge, and Christopher Alexander: *Community and
   Privacy: Toward a New Architecture of Humanism.* Garden
   City, N. Y.: Anchor Books, Doubleday & Company, Inc., 1965.
Dubos, René: *So Human an Animal.* New York: Charles Scribner's
   Sons, 1968.
———: *Man Adapting.* New Haven and London: Yale University
   Press, 1965.
Freud, Sigmund: *Civilization and Its Discontents.* Trans. Joan Riviere.
   Garden City, N. Y.: Anchor Books, Doubleday & Company, Inc.,
   1958.
Hillegas, Mark R.: *The Future as Nightmare: H. G. Wells and the
   Anti-Utopians.* New York: Oxford University Press, 1967.
Huxley, Aldous: *The Doors of Perception.* New York: Harper & Row,
   Publishers, Incorporated, 1954.
———: *Brave New World.* New York: Harper & Row, Publishers,
   Incorporated, 1946.
———: *Brave New World Revisited.* New York: Harper & Row,
   Publishers, Incorporated, 1958.
Kahn, Herman, and Anthony J. Wiener (eds.): *The Year 2000: A
   Framework for Speculation on the Next Thirty-Three Years.*
   New York: The Macmillan Company, 1967.
Keyes, Daniel: *Flowers for Algernon.* New York: Bantam Books,
   Inc., 1967.
Lewis, C. S.: *An Experiment in Criticism.* New York: Cambridge
   University Press, 1961.

Lorenz, K.: *On Aggression.* New York: Harcourt, Brace & World, Inc., 1966.

Macauley, Robie, and Larzer Ziff: *America and Its Discontents.* Waltham, Mass.: Xerox Publishing Company, 1971.

Malinowski, Bronislaw: *Magic, Science and Religion.* Boston: Beacon Press, 1948.

May, Rollo: *Love and Will.* New York: W. W. Norton & Company, Inc., 1969.

Miller, Walter M.: *A Canticle for Liebowitz.* Philadelphia: J. B. Lippincott Company, 1960.

Moustakas, Clark: *Creativity and Conformity.* New York: D. Van Nostrand Company, Inc., 1967.

Nicolson, Marjorie Hope: *Voyages to the Moon.* New York: The Macmillan Company, 1948.

Ortega y Gasset, José: *The Revolt of the Masses.* New York: W. W. Norton & Company, Inc., 1932.

————: *Concord and Liberty.* New York: W. W. Norton & Company, Inc., 1946.

Orwell, George: *1984.* New York: Harcourt, Brace and Company, Inc., 1949.

————: *Animal Farm.* New York: Harcourt, Brace and Company, Inc., 1946.

Rank, Otto: *The Myth of the Birth of the Hero.* New York: Alfred A. Knopf, Inc., 1959.

Silverberg, Robert: *A Time of Changes.* New York: New American Library, Inc., Signet Books, 1971.

Storr, A.: *Human Aggression.* New York: Atheneum Publishers, 1968.

Voltaire, Francois Marie Arouet de: *Candide.* New York: Modern Library, Inc., 1956.

Vonnegut, Kurt: *Slaughterhouse Five.* New York: Delacorte Press, Dell Publishing Co., Inc., 1969.

Watts, Alan: *The Book: On the Taboo against Knowing Who You Are.* New York: Collier Books, The Macmillan Company, 1970.

Weiner, Norbert: *The Human Use of Human Beings: Cybernetics and Society.* 2d ed. rev., Garden City, N. Y.: Anchor Books, Doubleday & Company, Inc., 1954.

PART 3
Man Against Man: The Roots of Violence

The medieval Christian society looked upon man as inherently sinful. Both the flesh and the world were sources of temptation which every believer spent his lifetime trying to have as little contact with as possible. St. Augustine preached that we were only sojourners in this life. It was a time of trial. There were two cities, the one of man, the other of God. The goal of mundane existence was to keep your eye and mind on God's city and to wish for death at the earliest possible moment.

This contempt for the world was understandable when all but the very rich lived short unpleasant lives plagued by sickness, famine, and poverty. Medical science as we know it was nonexistent. Relatively simple illness led most often to death; women commonly died in childbirth; a man of thirty years was considered long past his prime. However, a gradual change took place as western society moved out of the dark ages into the light of the Renaissance. Science took great leaps and bounds. Practitioners of medicine turned slowly away from alchemy and magic, devoting themselves to the discovery of true cures for human ills.

The telescope and microscope opened up two new worlds. A shift in power from monarchs to middle-class tradesmen and financiers lead to new hope that common man did not have to wait for death to enjoy comfort and happiness. With the increase in material benefits came a rejection of the concept that humanity must suffer because of original sin.

In the seventeenth century John Milton's *Paradise Lost* summed up a radical change in theology with the phrase "the Fortunate Fall." Man no longer need regret the loss of Eden. Adam's deeds were now looked upon as necessary to the eventual coming of Christ. Freed from centuries of self-castigation, human society pushed to the opposite extreme. Philosophers and scientists exuberantly claimed that if left alone and allowed full use of his faculties, man could cure all of society's ills and create a utopia. The wide-spread faith in the ability of technology to save humanity was never really questioned until the horror of our First World War.

Now Freud has replaced Augustine. He speaks not of sinful burdens but of man's basic drives as being rape, cannibalism, and murder. Psychologists describe the raging amoral "id" which we are told lies within us all. Are we really creatures driven by blood lust? Do we enter this world ruled by a dynamic selfish ego and only occasionally manage to see beyond the self? These and other questions will be raised by the stories you are about to read. One thing is certain. Whenever we feel the urge to profess the inherent nobility and worthiness of our species, it is always best to await the arrival of our evening newspaper.

Franz Kafka has no faith in mankind, except perhaps in the ability to endure. Kafka portrays an existence without order, where cause and effect have no relationship. Chance, rejection, and cruelty perme-ate his fiction. Undoubtedly "The Hunter Gracchus" will be one of the most unsettling literary experiences you have ever had. There is no logical progression of events. The author gives us no clue as to exactly where or when the story takes place. Yet, we are compelled to read on, to seeks answers, to make every attempt to discover just what it is that Kafka is saying.

The hunter at first appears to be a descendant of Cain and Cham. His fate is to wander the seas of the world. Yet, we must ask what crime he has committed to deserve such an end. Gracchus tells us that the fault lies with the boatman, who in "a moment's absence of mind" turned the wheel of his death ship in the wrong direction. The hunter's life was orderly; he fulfilled his position to the best of his ability. Salvation, it would seem, is a matter of chance. Gracchus knows he can neither expect nor receive help from any man. "The thought of helping me is an illness that has to be cured by taking to one's bed." The whole earth has become "an inn for the night." When we see this phrase we cannot avoid the connection with Joseph and Mary being turned away from the inn before their flight into Egypt.

Their are many aspects of the story that suggest Biblical parallels: the woman nursing a child, the flock of doves and especially the one which announces the hunter's arrival, the candle ceremony, Gracchus as an object of prayer, etc. But finally we must admit that no pattern ever becomes clear. The hunter Gracchus was a man who lived and died by violence. He has the attributes of both Christ and the devil. If Gracchus' story is viewed as a myth or parable, it represents the ultimate despair of human existence: Man as a rudderless ship driven chaotically by the winds of death.

The existential dilemma of Kafka's protagonists disappears in Brown's "Arena." Here we are on far more comfortable ground. Brown offers us a futurized version of the culture-hero drama. Saint George slew his dragon; Bewoulf saved the Danes by defeating Grendel. "Arena" is also similar to the hundreds of English and European stories in which men were carried through the air to purgatory where they underwent trials to prove their virtue and were later released.

The violence of "Arena" is acceptable to almost

all readers. Carson is the savior of his race, a quiet virtuous man who tries to offer peace before engaging in this struggle to the death. Brown never lets us feel pity for the alien Roller. "The universe was not a place that could hold them both. Farther apart than god and devil, there would never be a balance between them." The unrelenting aggressive savagery of the alien marks it as a target for destruction.

In Coleridge's "Ancient Mariner," the speaker is saved from damnation by recognizing that even the serpents of the sea are God's creation and have their own beauty. When the mariner blesses these sea creatures, the albatross falls from around his neck. Brown creates an analogous situation in "Arena." The Roller demonstrates its pointless cruelty by pulling the legs off the lizard. When Carson confronts a similar reptile, he accepts it even when it begins conversing with him. After a brief doubt as to his sanity, Carson follows the lizard and discovers the way through the barrier. Carson's willingness to commune with a life form totally unlike himself sets him ethically far above the alien's plane. The ending is expected, good triumphs over evil, but the high pitch of excitement maintained throughout sets this work apart from the host of mediocre adventure tales.

Man redefines himself through myth. Both Kafka and Brown have been involved in myth-making; Bradbury is no exception. Greek and Roman mythology have given us many variations of ancient female soothsayers who predict the future—for good or ill. Perseus sought out the Gray Women of the North. Withered as if extremely old, they had but one eye which they passed among them. The three fates were Clotho, the spinner, Lachesis, the disposer of lots, and Atropos, who cut the thread at death. None of these figures appear as evil and loathsome as their counterpart in "The Illustrated Man." She is "a thing sewn tight into whispers and silence." She knows "the Deep Past and the Clear Present and the even Deeper Future."

William Philippus Phelps is a desperate man.

The story undoubtedly could have been written without the demonic crone who covers his fat body with tattoos. The two special pictures which reveal Mr. Phelp's future give the violence an eerie quality—as if it were all preordained. Does the portrait of Phelps killing his wife give him the idea? Perhaps, but Phelps is no Perseus. It seems as if our perverse, supernatural emissary is engaging in the sadistic mental torture of a weak, desperate man. The final scene with its Quaker Oats-box effect gives us the impression that man's rage to kill is a never-ending bloody echo that will be forever heard and obeyed.

"The Big Flash" is the furthest extension of our theme in this section—"the roots of violence." Spinrad depicts a society gone completely mad. The rock group, the Horsemen, is the curse vested upon modern civilization just as their spiritual parents, the four horsemen of the Apocalypse gallop through the pages of John's Revelation. As the Horsemen's morbid songs become more and more popular, their message of "howling hate" fills the mind of every listener. *"A man ain't nothing but a fire burning . . . in a dirty glob of mud."* The spectacular rise of the Horsemen is paralleled by alternate sections devoted to military and political discussions concerning an atomic-bomb test. The soldiers with keys to the nuclear device start wearing buttons labeled "Do It." Demonstrations against war die down and even those "most adamantly opposed to nuclear weapons" begin to long for the ultimate catastrophe of atomic suicide. The culmination of Spinrad's crazed hoard comes in a burst of highly erotic frenzy. The military men push their keys into the firing locks urged on by the refrain "Do It! Do It! Do It! Do it!" The fingers stab red buttons; the countdown reaches zero and "THE BIG FLASH" destroys the ultimate root of violence, mankind.

A TOUCH OF PEACE

S. Vickory

A touch of peace touched me
but wrong—
in a place where scar
had covered the tender tissue.
A tear
welled from my mind's eye
and not
the slightest flicker of flesh
betrayed awareness.
No silent strains
of celestial music,
no echoing ancient stone-change
of base metal to gold.

In this still tawdry time of inquisition,
books smoulder
(or at least the minds
that swerving,
stare at their cracklingly new covers).
Men still burn Men
(or at least themselves),
Body
    upon
Body.
And after that fancy phrase
of *Self Immolation,*
Is the soulless heap of stinking garbage
any more
than a few burnt rags
and pieces of charred meat?

We are damned
in our tightly strung knots.
We are damned
to the breaking of frantic oaths.

This age of Un-Man before us,
we have reached
"The Spring of the Thief."*

*"The Spring of the Thief" is the title of a poem by a good friend and poet, Mr. John Logan.

THE HUNTER GRACCHUS
Franz Kafka

Two boys were sitting on the harbor wall playing with dice. A man was reading a newspaper on the steps of the monument resting in the shadow of a hero who was flourishing his sword on high. A girl was filling her bucket at the fountain. A fruit-seller was lying beside his scales, staring out to sea. Through the vacant window and door openings of a cafe one could see two men quite at the back drinking their wine. The proprietor was sitting at a table in front and dozing, a bark was silently making for the little harbor, as if borne by invisible means over the water. A man in a blue blouse climbed ashore and drew the rope through a ring. Behind the boatman two other men in dark coats with silver buttons carried a bier, on which, beneath a great flower-patterned tasseled silk cloth, a man was apparently lying.

Nobody on the quay troubled about the newcomers; even when they lowered the bier to wait for the boatman, who was still occupied with his rope, nobody went nearer, nobody asked them a question, nobody accorded them an inquisitive glance.

The pilot was still further detained by a woman who, a child at her breast, now appeared with loosened hair on the deck of the boat. Then he advanced and indicated a yellowish two-storeyed house that rose abruptly on the left beside the sea; the bearers took up their burden and bore it to the low but gracefully pillared door. A little boy opened a window just in time to see the party vanishing into the house, then hastily shut the window again. The door too was now shut; it was of black oak, and very strongly made. A flock of doves which had been flying round the belfry alighted in the street before the house. As if their food were stored within, they assembled in front of the door. One of them flew up to the first storey and pecked at the window-pane. They were bright-hued, well-tended, beautiful birds. The woman on the boat flung grain to them in a wide sweep; they ate it up and flew across to the woman.

A man in a top hat tied with a band of crepe now descended

one of the narrow and very steep lanes that led to the harbor. He glanced round vigilantly, everything seemed to displease him, his mouth twisted at the sight of some offal in a corner. Fruit skins were lying on the steps of the monument; he swept them off in passing with his stick. He rapped at the house door, at the same time taking his top hat from his head with his black-gloved hand. The door was opened at once, and some fifty little boys appeared in two rows in the long entry-hall, and bowed to him.

The boatman descended the stairs, greeted the gentleman in black, conducted him up to the first storey, led him round the bright and elegant loggia which encircled the courtyard, and both of them entered, while the boys pressed after them at a respectful distance, a cool spacious room looking towards the back, from whose window no habitation, but only a bare, blackish grey rocky wall was to be seen. The bearers were busied in setting up and lighting several long candles at the head of the bier, yet these did not give light, but only scared away the shadows which had been immobile till then, and made them flicker over the walls. The cloth covering the bier had been thrown back. Lying on it was a man with wildly matted hair, who looked somewhat like a hunter. He lay without motion and, it seemed, without breathing, his eyes closed; yet only his trappings indicated that this man was probably dead.

The gentleman stepped up to the bier, laid his hand on the brow of the man lying upon it, then kneeled down and prayed. The boatman made a sign to the bearers to leave the room; they went out, drove away the boys who had gathered outside, and shut the door. But even that did not seem to satisfy the gentleman; he glanced at the boatman; the boatman understood, and vanished through a side door into the next room. At once the man on the bier opened his eyes, turned his face painfully towards the gentleman, and said: "Who are you?" Without any mark of surprise the gentleman rose from his kneeling posture and answered: "The Burgomaster of Riva."

The man on the bier nodded, indicated a chair with a feeble movement of his arm, and said, after the Burgomaster had accepted his invitation: "I knew that, of course, Burgomaster, but in the first moments of returning consciousness I always forget, everything goes round before my eyes, and it is best to ask about anything even if I know. You too probably know that I am the hunter Gracchus."

"Certainly," said the Burgomaster. "Your arrival was announced to me during the night. We had been asleep for a good while. Then towards midnight my wife cried: 'Salvatore'—that's my name— 'look at that dove at the window.' It was really a dove, but as big as a cock. It flew over me and said in my ear: 'Tomorrow the dead hunter Gracchus is coming: receive him in the name of the city.' "

The hunter nodded and licked his lips with the tip of his tongue: "Yes, the doves flew here before me. But do you believe, Burgomaster, that I shall remain in Riva?"

"I cannot say that yet," replied the Burgomaster. "Are you dead?"

"Yes," said the hunter, "as you see. Many years ago, yes, it must be a great many years ago, I fell from a precipice in the Black Forest—that is in Germany—when I was hunting a chamois. Since then I have been dead."

"But you are alive too," said the Burgomaster.

"In a certain sense," said the hunter, "in a certain sense I am alive too. My death ship lost its way; a wrong turn of the wheel, a moment's absence of mind on the pilot's part, a longing to turn aside towards my lovely native country, I cannot tell what it was; I only know this, that I remained on earth and that ever since my ship has sailed earthly waters. So I, who asked for nothing better than to live among my mountains, travel after my death through all the lands of the earth."

"And you have no part in the other world?" asked the Burgomaster, knitting his brow.

"I am forever," replied the hunter, "on the great stair that leads up to it. On that infinitely wide and spacious stair I clamber about, sometimes up, sometimes down, sometimes on the right, sometimes on the left, always in motion. The hunter has been turned into a butterfly. Do not laugh."

"I am not laughing," said the Burgomaster in self-defense.

"That is very good of you," said the hunter. "I am always in motion. But when I make a supreme flight and see the gate actually shining before me I awaken presently on my old ship, still stranded forlornly in some earthly sea or other. The fundamental error of my one-time death grins at me as I lie in my cabin. Julie, the wife of the pilot, knocks at the door and brings me on my bier the morning drink of the land whose coasts we chance to be passing. I lie on a wooden pallet, I wear—it cannot be a pleasure to look at me—a filthy winding sheet, my hair and beard, black tinged with gray, have grown together inextricably, my limbs are covered with a great flower-patterned woman's shawl with long fringes. A sacramental candle stands at my head and lights me. On the wall opposite me is a little picture, evidently of a Bushman who is aiming his spear at me and taking cover as best he can behind a beautifully painted shield. On shipboard one is often a prey to stupid imaginations, but that is the stupidest of them all. Otherwise my wooden case is quite empty. Through a hole in the side wall come in the warm airs of the southern night, and I hear the water slapping against the old boat.

"I have lain here ever since the time when, as the hunter Gracchus living in the Black Forest, I followed a chamois and fell from the precipice. Everything happened in good order. I pursued, I fell, bled to death in a ravine, died, and this ship should have conveyed me to the next world. I can still remember how gladly I stretched myself out on this pallet for the first time. Never did the mountains listen to such songs from me as these shadowy walls did then.

"I had been glad to live and I was glad to die. Before I stepped aboard, I joyfully flung away my wretched load of ammunition, my knapsack, my hunting rifle that I had always been proud to carry, and I slipped into my winding sheet like a girl into her marriage dress. I lay and waited. Then came the mishap."

"A terrible fate," said the Burgomaster, raising his hand defensively. "And you bear no blame for it?"

"None," said the hunter. "I was a hunter: was there any sin in that? I followed my calling as a hunter in the Black Forest, where there were still wolves in those days. I lay in ambush, shot, hit my mark, flayed the skins from my victims: was there any sin in that? My labors were blessed. 'The great hunter of the Black Forest' was the name I was given. Was there any sin in that?"

"I am not called upon to decide that," said the Burgomaster, "but to me also there seems to be no sin in such things. But, then, whose is the guilt?"

"The boatman's," said the hunter. "Nobody will read what I say here, no one will come to help me; even if all the people were commanded to help me, every door and window would remain shut, everybody would take to bed and draw the bedclothes over his head, the whole earth would become an inn for the night. And there is sense in that, for nobody knows of me, and if anyone knew he would not know where I could be found, and if he knew where I could be found, he would not know how to deal with me, he would not know how to help me. The thought of helping me is an illness that has to be cured by taking to one's bed.

"I know that, and so I do not shout to summon help, even though at moments—when I lose control over myself, as I have done just now, for instance—I think seriously of it. But to drive out such thoughts I need only look round me and verify where I am, and—I can safely assert—have been for hundreds of years."

"Extraordinary," said the Burgomaster, "extraordinary. And now do you think of staying here in Riva with us?"

"I think not," said the hunter with a smile, and to excuse himself, he laid his hand on the Burgomaster's knee. "I am here, more than that I do not know, further than that I cannot go. My ship has no rudder, and it is driven by the wind that blows in the undermost regions of death."

QUESTIONS

1   What in the story might lead the reader to view the Hunter as a Christ figure?
2   Explain the connection between the Hunter's fate and the Biblical story of Cain and Coleridge's "The Ancient Mariner."
3   Kafka's story has been fertile ground for symbol hunters. The woman with a child, the white doves, the rudderless ship, all beg to be viewed as symbolic. One of the more intriguing elements is

the Bushman with a spear crouched behind his shield. Is it possible to see this menacing portrait as a symbol? If so, exactly what does it represent?

4 Closely examine the first paragraph and discuss how it establishes the mood or tone of the story.

5 The first time we see the Burgomaster, he is turning his mouth at the sight of some garbage in the lane. How does this incident affect our evaluation of his character?

6 What is the relationship between the divine and the human in Kafka's tale?

ARENA
Frederic Brown

Carson opened his eyes, and found himself looking upward into a flickering blue dimness.

It was hot, and he was lying on sand, and a sharp rock embedded in the sand was hurting his back. He rolled over to his side, off the rock, and then pushed himself up to a sitting position.

"I'm crazy," he thought. "Crazy—or dead—or something." The sand was blue, bright blue. And there wasn't any such thing as bright blue sand on Earth or any of the planets.

Blue sand.

Blue sand under a blue dome that wasn't the sky nor yet a room, but a circumscribed area—somehow he knew it was circumscribed and finite even though he couldn't see to the top of it.

He picked up some of the sand in his hand and let it run through his fingers. It trickled down onto his bare leg. *Bare?*

Naked. He was stark naked, and already his body was dripping perspiration from the enervating heat, coated blue with sand wherever sand had touched it.

But elsewhere his body was white.

He thought: Then this sand is really blue. If it seemed blue only because of the blue light, then I'd be blue also. But I'm white, so the sand *is* blue. *Blue sand.* There isn't any blue sand. There isn't any place like this place I'm in.

Sweat was running down in his eyes.

It was hot, hotter than Hades. Only Hades—the Hades of the ancients—was supposed to be red and not blue.

But if this place wasn't Hades, what was it? Only Mercury, among the planets, had heat like this and this wasn't Mercury. And Mercury was some four billion miles from—

It came back to him then, where he'd been. In the little one-man scouter, outside the orbit of Pluto, scouting a scant million miles to one side of the Earth Armada drawn up in battle array there to intercept the Outsiders.

That sudden strident nerve-shattering ringing of the bell alarm when the rival scouter—the Outsider ship—had come within range of his detectors—

No one knew who the Outsiders were, what they looked like, from what far galaxy they came, other than that it was in the general direction of the Pleiades.

First, sporadic raids on Earth colonies and outposts. Isolated battles between Earth patrols and small groups of Outsider spaceships; battles sometimes won and sometimes lost, but never to date resulting in the capture of an alien vessel. Nor had any member of a raided colony ever survived to describe the Outsiders who had left the ships, if indeed they had left them.

Not a too-serious menace, at first, for the raids had not been too numerous or destructive. And individually, the ships had proved slightly inferior in armament to the best of Earth's fighters, although somewhat superior in speed and maneuverability. A sufficient edge in speed, in fact, to give the Outsiders their choice of running or fighting, unless surrounded.

Nevertheless, Earth had prepared for serious trouble, for a showdown, building the mightiest armada of all time. It had been waiting now, that armada, for a long time. But now the showdown was coming.

Scouts twenty billion miles out had detected the approach of a mighty fleet—a showdown fleet—of the Outsiders. Those Scouts had never come back, but their radiotronic messages had. And now Earth's armada, all ten thousand ships and half million fighting spacemen, was out there, outside Pluto's orbit, waiting to intercept and battle to the death.

And an even battle it was going to be, judging by the advance reports of the men of the far picket line who had given their lives to report—before they had died—on the size and strength of the alien fleet.

Anybody's battle, with the mastery of the solar system hanging in the balance, on an even chance. A last and *only* chance, for Earth and all her colonies lay at the utter mercy of the Outsiders if they ran that gauntlet—

Oh yes. Bob Carson remembered now.

Not that it explained blue sand and flickering blueness. But that strident alarming of the bell and his leap for the control panel. His frenzied fumbling as he strapped himself into the seat. The dot in the visiplate that grew larger.

The dryness of his mouth. The awful knowledge that this was

it. For him, at least, although the main fleets were still out of range of one another.

This, his first taste of battle. Within three seconds or less he'd be victorious, or a charred cinder. Dead.

Three seconds—that's how long a space-battle lasted. Time enough to count to three, slowly, and then you'd won or you were dead. One hit completely took care of a lightly armed and armored little one-man craft like a scouter.

Frantically—as, unconsciously, his dry lips shaped the word "One"—he worked at the controls to keep that growing dot centered on the crossed spider-webs of the visiplate. His hands doing that, while his right foot hovered over the pedal that would fire the bolt. The single bolt of concentrated hell that had to hit— or else. There wouldn't be time for any second shot.

"Two." He didn't know he'd said that, either. The dot in the visiplate wasn't a dot now. Only a few thousand miles away, it showed up in the magnification of the plate as though it were only a few hundred yards off. It was a sleek, fast little scouter, about the size of his.

And an alien ship, all right.

"Thr—" his foot touched the bolt-release pedal—

And then the Outsider had swerved suddenly and was off the cross-hairs. Carson punched keys frantically, to follow.

For a tenth of a second, it was out of the visiplate entirely, and then as the nose of his scouter swung after it, he saw it again, diving straight toward the ground.

The ground?

It was an optical illusion of some sort. It *had* to be, that planet—or whatever it was—that now covered the visiplate. Whatever it was, it couldn't be there. Couldn't possibly. There *wasn't* any planet nearer than Neptune three billion miles away—with Pluto around on the opposite side of the distant pinpoint sun.

His *detectors! They* hadn't shown any object of planetary dimensions, even of asteroid dimensions. They still didn't.

So it couldn't be there, that whatever-it-was he was diving into, only a few hundred miles below him.

And in his sudden anxiety to keep from crashing, he forgot even the Outsider ship. He fired the front breaking rockets, and even as the sudden change of speed slammed him forward against the seat straps, he fired full right for an emergency turn. Pushed them down and *held* them down, knowing that he needed everything the ship had to keep from crashing and that a turn that sudden would black him out for a moment.

It did black him out.

And that was all. Now he was sitting in hot blue sand, stark naked but otherwise unhurt. No sign of his spaceship and—for that matter—no sign of space. That curve overhead wasn't a sky, whatever else it was.

He scrambled to his feet.

Gravity seemed a little more than Earth-normal. Not much more.

Flat sand stretching away, a few scrawny bushes in clumps here and there. The bushes were blue, too, but in varying shades, some lighter than the blue of the sand, some darker.

Out from under the nearest bush ran a little thing that was like a lizard, except that it had more than four legs. It was blue, too. Bright blue. It saw him and ran back again under the bush.

He looked up again, trying to decide what was overhead. It wasn't exactly a roof, but it was dome-shaped. It flickered and was hard to look at. But definitely, it curved down to the ground, to the blue sand, all around him.

He wasn't far from being under the center of the dome. At a guess, it was a hundred yards to the nearest wall, if it was a wall. It was as though a blue hemisphere of *something,* about two hundred and fifty yards in circumference, was inverted over the flat expanse of the sand.

And everything blue, except one object. Over near a far curving wall there was a red object. Roughly spherical, it seemed to be about a yard in diameter. Too far for him to see clearly through the flickering blueness. But, unaccountably, he shuddered.

He wiped sweat from his forehead, or tried to, with the back of his hand.

Was this a dream, a nightmare? This heat, this sand, that vague feeling of horror he felt when he looked toward the red thing?

A dream? No, one didn't go to sleep and dream in the midst of a battle in space.

Death? No, never. If there were immortality, it wouldn't be a senseless thing like this, a thing of blue heat and blue sand and a red horror.

Then he heard the voice—

Inside his head he heard it, not with his ears. It came from nowhere or everywhere.

"Through spaces and dimensions wandering," rang the words in his mind, *"and in this space and this time I find two peoples about to wage a war that would exterminate one and so weaken the other that it would retrogress and never fulfill its destiny, but decay and return to mindless dust whence it came. And I say this must not happen."*

"Who . . . what are you?" Carson didn't say it aloud, but the question formed itself in his brain.

"You would not understand completely. I am—" There was a pause as though the voice sought—in Carson's brain—for a word that wasn't there, a word he didn't know. *"I am the end of evolution of a race so old the time can not be expressed in words that have meaning to your mind. A race fused into a single entity, eternal—*

"An entity such as your primitive race might become"— again the groping for a word—*"time from now. So might the race you call, in your mind, the Outsiders. So I intervene in the battle to come, the battle between fleets so evenly matched that destruction of both races will result. One must survive. One must progress and evolve."*

"One?" thought Carson. "Mine, or—?"

"It is in my power to stop the war, to send the Outsiders back to their galaxy. But they would return, or your race would sooner or later follow them there. Only by remaining in this space and time to intervene constantly could I prevent them from destroying one another, and I cannot remain.

"So I shall intervene now. I shall destroy one fleet completely without loss to the other. One civilization shall thus survive."

Nightmare. This had to be nightmare, Carson thought. But he knew it wasn't.

It was too mad, too impossible, to be anything but real.

He didn't dare ask *the* question—*Which?* But his thoughts asked it for him.

"The stronger shall survive," said the voice. *"That I can not —and would not—change. I merely intervene to make it a complete victory, not"*—groping again—*"not Pyrrhic victory to a broken race.*

"From the outskirts of the not-yet battle I plucked two individuals, you and an Outsider. I see from your mind that in your early history of nationalisms battles between champions, to decide issues between races, were not unknown.

"You and your opponent are here pitted against one another, naked and unarmed, under conditions equally unfamiliar to you both, equally unpleasant to you both. There is no time limit, for here there is no time. The survivor is the champion of his race. That race survives."

"But—" Carson's protest was too inarticulate for expression, but the voice answered it.

"It is fair. The conditions are such that the accident of physical strength will not completely decide the issue. There is a barrier. You will understand. Brain-power and courage will be more important than strength. Most especially courage, which is the will to survive."

"But while this goes on, the fleets will—"

"No, you are in another space, another time. For as long as you are here, time stands still in the universe you know. I see you wonder whether this place is real. It is, and it is not. As I—to your limited understanding—am and am not real. My existence is mental and not physical. You saw me as a planet; it could have been as a dustmote or a sun.

"But to you this place is now real. What you suffer here will be real. And if you die here, your death will be real. If you die, your failure will be the end of your race. That is enough for you to know."

And then the voice was gone.

Again he was alone, but not alone. For as Carson looked up, he saw that the red thing, the red sphere of horror which he now knew was the Outsider, was rolling toward him.

Rolling.

It seemed to have no legs or arms that he could see, no features. It rolled across the blue sand with the fluid quickness of a drop of mercury. And before it, in some manner he could not understand, came a paralyzing wave of nauseating, retching, horrid hatred.

Carson looked about him frantically. A stone, lying in the sand a few feet away, was the nearest thing to a weapon. It wasn't large, but it had sharp edges, like a slab of flint. It looked a bit like blue flint.

He picked it up, and crouched to receive the attack. It was coming faster, faster than he could run.

No time to think out how he was going to fight it, and how anyway could he plan to battle a creature whose strength, whose characteristics, whose method of fighting he did not know? Rolling so fast, it looked more than ever like a perfect sphere.

Ten yards away. Five. And then it stopped.

Rather, it *was stopped*. Abruptly the near side of it flattened as though it had run up against an invisible wall. It bounced, actually bounced back.

Then it rolled forward again, but more slowly, more cautiously. It stopped again, at the same place. It tried again, a few yards to one side.

There was a barrier there of some sort. It clicked, then, in Carson's mind. That thought projected into his mind by the Entity who had brought them there: "—accident of physical strength will not completely decide the issue. There is a barrier.

A force-field, of course. Not the Netzian Field, known to Earth science, for that glowed and emitted a crackling sound. This one was invisible, silent.

It was a wall that ran from side to side of the inverted hemisphere; Carson didn't have to verify that himself. The Roller was doing that; rolling sideways along the barrier, seeking a break in it that wasn't there.

Carson took half a dozen steps forward, his left hand groping out before him, and then his hand touched the barrier. It felt smooth, yielding like a sheet of rubber rather than like glass. Warm to his touch, but no warmer than the sand underfoot. And it was completely invisible, even at close range.

He dropped the stone and put both hands against it, pushing.

It seemed to yield just a trifle. But no farther than that trifle, even when he pushed with all his weight. It felt like a sheet of rubber backed up by steel. Limited resiliency, and then firm strength.

He stood on tiptoe and reached as high as he could and the barrier was still there.

He saw the Roller coming back, having reached one side of the arena. That feeling of nausea hit Carson again, and he stepped back from the barrier as it went by. It didn't stop.

But did the barrier stop at ground level? Carson knelt down and burrowed in the sand. It was soft, light, easy to dig in. At two feet down the barrier was still there.

The Roller was coming back again. Obviously, it couldn't find a way through at either side.

There must be a way through, Carson thought. *Some* way we can get at each other, else this duel is meaningless.

But no hurry now, in finding that out. There was something to try first. The Roller was back now, and it stopped just across the barrier, only six feet away. It seemed to be studying him, although for the life of him, Carson couldn't find external evidence of sense organs on that thing. Nothing that looked like eyes or ears or even a mouth. There was though, he saw now, a series of grooves—perhaps a dozen of them altogether, and he saw two tentacles suddenly push out from two of the grooves and dip into the sand as though testing its consistency. Tentacles about an inch in diameter and perhaps a foot and a half long.

But the tentacles were retractable into the grooves and were kept there except when in use. They were retracted when the thing rolled and seemed to have nothing to do with its method of locomotion. That, as far as Carson could judge, seemed to be accomplished by some shifting—just *how* he couldn't even imagine —of its center of gravity.

He shuddered as he looked at the thing. It was alien, utterly alien, horribly different from anything on Earth or any of the life forms found on the other solar planets. Instinctively, somehow, he knew its mind was as alien as its body.

But he had to try. If it had no telepathic powers at all, the attempt was foredoomed to failure, yet he thought it had such powers. There had, at any rate, been a projection of something that was not physical at the time a few minutes ago when it had first started for him. An almost tangible wave of hatred.

If it could project that perhaps it could read his mind as well, sufficiently for his purpose.

Deliberately, Carson picked up the rock that had been his only weapon, then tossed it down again in a gesture of relinquishment and raised his empty hands palms up, before him.

He spoke aloud, knowing that although the words would be meaningless to the creature before him, speaking them would focus his own thoughts more completely upon the message.

"Can we not have peace between us?" he said, his voice sounding strange in the utter stillness. "The Entity who brought us here has told us what must happen if our races fight—extinction of one and weakening and retrogression of the other. The battle between them, said the Entity, depends upon what we do here. Why can not we agree to an external peace—your race to its galaxy, we to ours?"

Carson blanked out his mind to receive a reply.

It came, and it staggered him back, physically. He actually recoiled several steps in sheer horror at the depth and intensity of the hatred and lust-to-kill of the red images that had been projected at him. Not as articulate words—as had come to him the thoughts of the Entity—but as wave upon wave of fierce emotion.

For a moment that seemed an eternity he had to struggle against the mental impact of that hatred, fight to clear his mind of it and drive out the alien thoughts to which he had given admittance by blanking his own thoughts. He wanted to retch.

Slowly his mind cleared as, slowly, the mind of a man wakening from nightmare clears away the fear-fabric of which the dream was woven. He was breathing hard and he felt weaker, but he could think.

He stood studying the Roller. It had been motionless during the mental duel it had so nearly won. Now it rolled a few feet to one side, to the nearest of the blue bushes. Three tentacles whipped out of their grooves and began to investigate the bush.

"O.K.," Carson said, "so it's war then." He managed a wry

grin. "If I got your answer straight, peace doesn't appeal to you." And, because he was, after all, a quiet young man and couldn't resist the impulse to be dramatic, he added, "To the death!"

But his voice, in the utter silence, sounded very silly, even to himself. It came to him, then, that this *was* to the death. Not only his own death or that of the red spherical thing which he now thought of as the Roller, but death to the entire race of one or the other of them. The end of the human race, if he failed.

It made him suddenly very humble and very afraid to think that. More than to think it, to *know* it. Somehow, with a knowledge that was above even faith, he knew that the Entity who had arranged this duel had told the truth about its intentions and its powers. It wasn't kidding.

The future of humanity depended upon *him.* It was an awful thing to realize, and he wrenched his mind away from it. He had to concentrate on the situation at hand.

There had to be some way of getting through the barrier, or of killing through the barrier.

Mentally? He hoped that wasn't all, for the Roller obviously had stronger telepathic powers than the primitive, undeveloped ones of the human race. Or did it?

He had been able to drive the thoughts of the Roller out of his mind; could it drive out his? If its ability to project were stronger, might not its receptive mechanism be more vulnerable?

He stared at it and endeavored to concentrate and focus all his thoughts upon it.

"*Die,*" he thought. "*You are going to die. You are dying. You are—*"

He tried variations on it, and mental pictures. Sweat stood out on his forehead and he found himself trembling with the intensity of the effort. But the Roller went ahead with its investigation of the bush, as utterly unaffected as though Carson had been reciting the multiplication table.

So *that* was no good.

He felt a bit weak and dizzy from the heat and his strenuous effort at concentration. He was down on the blue sand to rest and gave his full attention to watching and studying the Roller. By close study, perhaps, he could judge its strength and detect its weaknesses, learn things that would be valuable to know when and if they should come to grips.

It was breaking off twigs. Carson watched carefully, trying to judge just how hard it worked to do that. Later, he thought, he could find a similar bush on his own side, break off twigs of equal thickness himself, and gain a comparison of physical strength between his own arms and hands and those tentacles.

The twigs broke off hard; the Roller was having to struggle with each one, he saw. Each tentacle, he saw, bifurcated at the tip into two fingers, each tipped by a nail or claw. The claws didn't seem to be particularly long or dangerous. No more so than his own fingernails, if they were let to grow a bit.

No, on the whole, it didn't look too tough to handle physically. Unless, of course, that bush was made of pretty tough stuff. Carson looked around him and, yes, right within reach was another bush of identically the same type.

He reached over and snapped off a twig. It was brittle, easy to break. Of course, the Roller might have been faking deliberately but he didn't think so.

On the other hand, where was it vulnerable? Just how would he go about killing it, if he got the chance? He went back to studying it. The outer hide looked pretty tough. He'd need a sharp weapon of some sort. He picked up the piece of rock again. It was about twelve inches long, narrow, and fairly sharp on one end. If it chipped like flint, he could make a serviceable knife out of it.

The Roller was continuing its investigations of the bushes. It rolled again, to the nearest one of another type. A little blue lizard, many-legged like the one Carson had seen on his side of the barrier, darted out from under the bush.

A tentacle of the Roller lashed out and caught it, picked it up. Another tentacle whipped over and began to pull legs off the lizard, as coldly and calmly as it had pulled twigs off the bush. The creature struggled frantically and emitted a shrill squealing sound that was the first sound Carson had heard here other than the sound of his own voice.

Carson shuddered and wanted to turn his eyes away. But he made himself continue to watch; anything he could learn about his opponent might prove valuable. Even this knowledge of its unnecessary cruelty. Particularly, he thought with a sudden vicious surge of emotion, this knowledge of its unnecessary cruelty. It would make it a pleasure to kill the thing, if and when the chance came.

He steeled himself to watch the dismembering of the lizard for that very reason.

But he felt glad when, with half its legs gone, the lizard quit squealing and struggling and lay limp and dead in the Roller's grasp.

It didn't continue with the rest of the legs. Contemptuously it tossed the dead lizard away from it, in Carson's direction. It arched through the air between them and landed at his feet.

It had come through the barrier! The barrier wasn't there any more!

Carson was on his feet in a flash, the knife gripped tightly in his hand, and leaped forward. He'd settle this thing here and now! With the barrier gone—

But it wasn't gone. He found that out the hard way, running head on into it and nearly knocking himself silly. He bounced back, and fell.

And as he sat up, shaking his head to clear it, he saw something coming through the air toward him, and to duck it, he threw himself flat again on the sand, and to one side. He got his body out of the way, but there was a sudden sharp pain in the calf of his left leg.

He rolled backward, ignoring the pain, and scrambled to his feet. It was a rock, he saw now, that had struck him. And the Roller was picking up another one now, swinging it back gripped between two tentacles, getting ready to throw again.

It sailed through the air toward him, but he was easily able to step out of its way. The Roller, apparently, could throw straight, but not hard nor far. The first rock had struck him only because he had been sitting down and had not seen it coming until it was almost upon him.

Even as he stepped aside from that weak second throw, Carson drew back his right arm and let fly with the rock that was still in his hand. If missiles, he thought with sudden elation, can cross the barrier, then two can play at the game of throwing them. And the good right arm of an Earthman—

He couldn't miss a three-foot sphere at only four-yard range, and he didn't miss. The rock whizzed straight, and with a speed several times that of the missiles the Roller had thrown. It hit dead center, but it hit flat, unfortunately, instead of point first.

But it hit with a resounding thump, and obviously it hurt. The Roller had been reaching for another rock, but it changed its mind and got out of there instead. By the time Carson could pick up and throw another rock, the Roller was forty yards back from the barrier and going strong.

His second throw missed by feet, and his third throw was short. The Roller was back out of range—at least out of range of a missile heavy enough to be damaging.

Carson grinned. That round had been his. Except—

He quit grinning as he bent over to examine the calf of his leg. A jagged edge of the stone had made a pretty deep cut, several inches long. It was bleeding pretty freely, but he didn't think it had gone deep enough to hit an artery. If it stopped bleeding of its own accord, well and good. If not, he was in for trouble.

Finding out one thing, though, took precedence over that cut. The nature of the barrier.

He went forward to it again, this time groping with his hands before him. He found it; then holding one hand against it, he tossed a handful of sand at it with the other hand. The sand went right through. His hand didn't.

Organic matter versus inorganic? No, because the dead lizard had gone through it, and a lizard, alive or dead, was certainly organic. Plant life? He broke off a twig and poked it at the barrier. The twig went through, with no resistance, but when his fingers gripping the twig came to the barrier, they were stopped.

He couldn't get through it, nor could the Roller. But rocks and sand and a dead lizard—

How about a live lizard? He went hunting, under bushes, until he found one, and caught it. He tossed it gently against the barrier and it bounced back and scurried away across the blue sand.

That gave him the answer, in so far as he could determine it now. The screen was a barrier to living things. Dead or inorganic matter could cross it.

That off his mind, Carson looked at his injured leg again.

The bleeding was lessening, which meant he wouldn't need to worry about making a tourniquet. But he should find some water, if any was available, to clean the wound.

Water—the thought of it made him realize that he was getting awfully thirsty. He'd *have* to find water, in case this contest turned out to be a protracted one.

Limping slightly now, he started off to make a full circuit of his half of the arena. Guiding himself with one hand along the barrier, he walked to his right until he came to the curving side-wall. It was visible, a dull blue-gray at close range, and the surface of it felt just like the central barrier.

He experimented by tossing a handful of sand at it, and the sand reached the wall and disappeared as it went through. The hemispherical shell was a force-field, too. But an opaque one, instead of transparent like the barrier.

He followed it around until he came back to the barrier, and walked back along the barrier to the point from which he'd started.

No sign of water.

Worried now, he started a series of zigzags back and forth between the barrier and the wall, covering the intervening space thoroughly.

No water. Blue sand, blue bushes, and intolerable heat. Nothing else.

It must be his imagination, he told himself angrily, that he was suffering *that* much from thirst. How long had he been here? Of course, no time at all, according to his own space-time frame. The Entity had told him time stood still out there, while he was here. But his body processes went on here, just the same. And according to his body's reckoning, how long had he been here? Three or four hours, perhaps. Certainly not long enough to be suffering seriously from thirst.

But he was suffering from it; his throat dry and parched. Probably the intense heat was the cause. It was *hot!* A hundred and thirty Fahrenheit, at a guess. A dry, still heat without the slightest movement of air.

He was limping rather badly, and utterly fagged out when he'd finished the futile exploration of his domain.

He stared across at the motionless Roller and hoped it was

as miserable as he was. And quite possibly it wasn't enjoying this, either. The Entity had said the conditions here were equally unfamiliar and equally uncomfortable for both of them. Maybe the Roller came from a planet where two-hundred degree heat was the norm. Maybe it was freezing while he was roasting.

Maybe the air was as much too thick for it as it was too thin for him. For the exertion of his explorations had left him panting. The atmosphere here, he realized now, was not much thicker than that on Mars.

No water.

That meant a deadline, for him at any rate. Unless he could find a way to cross that barrier or to kill his enemy from this side of it, thirst would kill him, eventually.

It gave him a feeling of desperate urgency. He *must* hurry.

But he made himself sit down a moment to rest, to think.

What was there to do? Nothing, and yet so many things. The several varieties of bushes, for example. They didn't look promising, but he'd have to examine them for possibilities. And his leg—he'd have to do something about that, even without water to clean it. Gather ammunition in the form of rocks. Find a rock that would make a good knife.

His leg hurt rather badly now, and he decided that came first. One type of bush had leaves—or things rather similar to leaves. He pulled off a handful of them and decided, after examination, to take a chance on them. He used them to clean off the sand and dirt and caked blood, then made a pad of fresh leaves and tied it over the wound with tendrils from the same bush.

The tendrils proved unexpectedly tough and strong. They were slender, and soft and pliable, yet he couldn't break them at all. He had to saw them off the bush with the sharp edge of a piece of the blue flint. Some of the thicker ones were over a foot long, and he filed away in his memory, for future reference, the fact that a bunch of the thick ones, tied together, would make a pretty serviceable rope. Maybe he'd be able to think of a use for rope.

Next, he made himself a knife. The blue flint *did* chip. From a foot-long splinter of it, he fashioned himself a crude but lethal weapon. And of tendrils from the bush, he made himself a rope-belt through which he could thrust the flint knife, to keep it with him all the time and yet have his hands free.

He went back to studying the bushes. There were three other types. One was leafless, dry, brittle, rather like a dried tumbleweed. Another was of soft, crumbly wood, almost like punk. It looked and felt as though it would make excellent tinder for a fire. The third type was the most nearly woodlike. It had fragile leaves that wilted at a touch, but the stalks, although short, were straight and strong.

It was horribly, unbearably hot.

He limped up to the barrier, felt to make sure that it was still there. It was.

He stood watching the Roller for a while. It was keeping a safe distance back from the barrier, out of effective stone-throwing range. It was moving around back there, doing something. He couldn't tell what it was doing.

Once it stopped moving, came a little closer, and seemed to concentrate its attention on him. Again Carson had to fight off a wave of nausea. He threw a stone at it and the Roller retreated and went back to whatever it had been doing before.

At least he could make it keep its distance.

And, he thought bitterly, a devil of a lot of good *that* did him. Just the same, he spent the next hour or two gathering stones of suitable size for throwing, and making several neat piles of them, near his side of the barrier.

His throat burned now. It was difficult for him to think about anything except water.

But he *had* to think about other things. About getting through that barrier, under or over it, getting *at* that red sphere and killing it before this place of heat and thirst killed him first.

The barrier went to the wall upon either side, but how high and how far under the sand?

For just a moment, Carson's mind was too fuzzy to think out how he could find out either of those things. Idly, sitting there in the hot sand—and he didn't remember sitting down—he watched a blue lizard crawl from the shelter of one bush to the shelter of another.

From under the second bush, it looked out at him.

Carson grinned at it. Maybe he was getting a bit punch-drunk, because he remembered suddenly the old story of the desert-colonists on Mars, taken from an older desert story of Earth—"Pretty soon you get so lonesome you find yourself talking to the lizards, and then not so long after that you find the lizards talking back to you—"

He should have been concentrating, of course, on how to kill the Roller, but instead he grinned at the lizard and said, "Hello, there."

The lizard took a few steps toward him. "Hello," it said.

Carson was stunned for a moment, and then he put back his head and roared with laughter. It didn't hurt his throat to do so, either; he hadn't been *that* thirsty.

Why not? Why should the Entity who thought up this nightmare of a place not have a sense of humor, along with the other powers he had? Talking lizards, equipped to talk back in my own language, if I talk to them—it's a nice touch.

He grinned at the lizard and said, "Come on over." But the lizard turned and ran away, scurrying from bush to bush until it was out of sight.

He was thirsty again.

And he had to *do* something. He couldn't win this contest by sitting here sweating and feeling miserable. He had to *do* something. But what?

Get through the barrier. But he couldn't get through it, or over it. But was he certain he couldn't get under it? And come to think of it, didn't one sometimes find water by digging? Two birds with one stone—

Painfully now, Carson limped up to the barrier and started digging, scooping up sand a double handful at a time. It was slow, hard work because the sand ran in at the edges and the deeper he got the bigger in diameter the hole had to be. How many hours it took him, he didn't know, but he hit bedrock four feet down. Dry bedrock; no sign of water.

And the force-field of the barrier went down clear to the bedrock. No dice. No water. Nothing.

He crawled out of the hole and lay there panting, and then raised his head to look across and see what the Roller was doing. It must be doing something back there.

It was. It was making something out of wood from the bushes, tied together with tendrils. A queerly shaped framework about four feet high and roughly square. To see it better, Carson climbed up onto the mound of sand he had excavated from the hole, and stood there staring.

There were two long levers sticking out of the back of it, one with a cup-shaped affair on the end of it. Seemed to be some sort of catapult, Carson thought.

Sure enough, the Roller was lifting a sizable rock into the cup-shaped outfit. One of his tentacles moved the other lever up and down for a while, and then he turned the machine slightly as though aiming it and the lever with the stone flew up and forward.

The stone arced several yards over Carson's head, so far away that he didn't have to duck, but he judged the distance it had traveled, and whistled softly. He couldn't throw a rock that weight more than half that distance. And even retreating to the rear of his domain wouldn't put him out of range of that machine, if the Roller shoved it forward almost to the barrier.

Another rock whizzed over. Not quite so far away this time.

That thing could be dangerous, he decided. Maybe he'd better do something about it.

Moving from side to side along the barrier, so the catapult couldn't bracket him, he whaled a dozen rocks at it. But that wasn't going to be any good, he saw. They had to be light rocks, or he couldn't throw them that far. If they hit the framework, they bounced off harmlessly. And the Roller had no difficulty, at that distance, in moving aside from those that came near it.

Besides, his arm was tiring badly. He ached all over from sheer weariness. If he could only rest awhile without having to duck rocks from that catapult at regular intervals of maybe thirty seconds each—

He stumbled back to the rear of the arena. Then he saw even that wasn't any good. The rocks reached back there, too, only there were longer intervals between them, as though it took longer to wind up the mechanism, whatever it was, of the catapult.

Wearily he dragged himself back to the barrier again. Several times he fell and could barely rise to his feet to go on. He was, he knew, near the limit of his endurance. Yet he didn't dare stop moving now, until and unless he could put that catapult out of action. If he fell asleep, he'd never wake up.

One of the stones from it gave him the first glimmer of an idea. It struck upon one of the piles of stones he'd gathered together near the barrier to use as ammunition, and it struck sparks.

Sparks. Fire. Primitive man had made fire by striking sparks, and with some of those dry crumbly bushes as tinder—

Luckily, a bush of that type was near him. He broke it off, took it over to the pile of stones, then patiently hit one stone against another until a spark touched the punklike wood of the bush. It went up in flames so fast that it singed his eyebrows and was burned to an ash within seconds.

But he had the idea now, and within minutes he had a little fire going in the lee of the mound of sand he'd made digging the hole an hour or two ago. Tindery bushes had started it, and other bushes which burned, but more slowly, kept it a steady flame.

The tough wirelike tendrils didn't burn readily; that made the fire-bombs easy to make and throw. A bundle of faggots tied about a small stone to give it weight and a loop of the tendril to swing it by.

He made half a dozen of them before he lighted and threw the first. It went wide, and the Roller started a quick retreat, pulling the catapult after him. But Carson had the others ready and threw them in rapid succession. The fourth wedged in the catapult's framework, and did the trick. The Roller tried desperately to put out the spreading blaze by throwing sand, but its clawed tentacles would take only a spoonful at a time and his efforts were ineffectual. The catapult burned.

The Roller moved safely away from the fire and seemed to concentrate its attention on Carson and again he felt that wave of hatred and nausea. But more weakly; either the Roller itself was weakening or Carson had learned how to protect himself against the mental attack.

He thumbed his nose at it and then sent it scuttling back to safety by throwing a stone. The Roller went clear to the back of its half of the arena and started pulling up bushes again. Probably it was going to make another catapult.

Carson verified—for the hundredth time—that the barrier was still operating, and then found himself sitting in the sand beside it because he was suddenly too weak to stand up.

His leg throbbed steadily now and the pangs of thirst were severe. But those things paled beside the utter physical exhaustion that gripped his entire body.

And the heat.

Hell must be like this, he thought. The hell that the ancients had believed in. He fought to stay awake, and yet staying awake seemed futile, for there was nothing he could do Nothing, while the barrier remained impregnable and the Roller stayed back out of range.

But there must be *something*. He tried to remember things he had read in books of archaeology about the methods of fighting used back in the days before metal and plastic. The stone missile, that had come first, he thought. Well, that he already had.

The only improvement on it would be a catapult, such as the Roller had made. But he'd never be able to make one, with the tiny bits of wood available from the bushes—no single piece longer than a foot or so. Certainly he could figure out a mechanism for one, but he didn't have the endurance left for a task that would take days.

Days? But the roller had made one. Had they been here days already? Then he remembered that the Roller had many tentacles to work with and undoubtedly could do such work faster than he.

And besides, a catapult wouldn't decide the issue. He had to do better than that.

Bow and arrow? No; he had tried archery once and knew his own ineptness with a bow. Even with a modern sportsman's durasteel weapon, made for accuracy. With such a crude, pieced-together outfit as he could make here, he doubted if he could shoot as far as he could throw a rock, and knew he couldn't shoot as straight.

Spear? Well, he *could* make that. It would be useless as a throwing weapon at any distance, but would be a handy thing at close range, if he ever got to close range.

And making one would give him something to do. Help keep his mind from wandering, as it was beginning to do. Sometimes now, he had to concentrate awhile before he could remember why he was here, why he had to kill the Roller.

Luckily he was still beside one of the piles of stones. He sorted through it until he found one shaped roughly like a spearhead. With a smaller stone he began to chip it into shape, fashioning sharp shoulders on the sides so that if it penetrated it would not pull out again.

Like a harpoon? There was something in that idea, he thought. A harpoon was better than a spear, maybe, for this crazy contest. If he could once get it into the Roller, and had a rope on it, he could pull the Roller up against the barrier and the stone blade of his knife would reach through that barrier, even if his hands wouldn't.

The shaft was harder to make than the head. But by splitting and joining the main stems of four of the bushes, and wrapping the joints with the tough but thin tendrils, he got a strong shaft about four feet long, and tied the stone head in a notch cut in the end.

It was crude, but strong.

And the rope. With the thin tough tendrils he made himself twenty feet of line. It was light and didn't look strong, but he knew it would hold his weight and to spare. He tied one end of it to the shaft of the harpoon and the other end about his right wrist. At least, if he threw his harpoon across the barrier, he'd be able to pull it back if he missed.

Then when he had tied the last knot and there was nothing more he could do, the heat and the weariness and the pain in his leg and the dreadful thirst were suddenly a thousand times worse than they had been before.

He tried to stand up, to see what the Roller was doing now, and found he couldn't get to his feet. On the third try, he got as far as his knees and then fell flat again.

"I've got to sleep," he thought. "If a showdown came now, I'd be helpless. He could come up here and kill me, if he knew. I've got to regain some strength."

Slowly, painfully, he crawled back away from the barrier. Ten yards, twenty—

The jar of something thudding against the sand near him waked him from a confused and horrible dream to a more confused and more horrible reality, and he opened his eyes again to blue radiance over blue sand.

How long had he slept? A minute? A day?

Another stone thudded nearer and threw sand on him. He got his arms under him and sat up. He turned around and saw the Roller twenty yards away, at the barrier.

It rolled away hastily as he sat up, not stopping until it was as far away as it could get.

He'd fallen asleep too soon, he realized, while he was still in range of the Roller's throwing ability. Seeing him lying motionless, it had dared come up to the barrier to throw at him. Luckily, it didn't realize how weak he was, or it could have stayed there and kept on throwing stones.

Had he slept long? He didn't think so, because he felt just as he had before. Not rested at all, no thirstier, no different. Probably he'd been there only a few minutes.

He started crawling again, this time forcing himself to keep going until he was as far as he could go, until the colorless, opaque wall of the arena's outer shell was only a yard away.

Then things slipped away again—

When he awoke, nothing about him was changed, but this time he knew that he had slept a long time.

The first thing he became aware of was the inside of his mouth; it was dry, caked. His tongue was swollen.

Something was wrong, he knew, as he returned slowly to full awareness. He felt less tired, the stage of utter exhaustion had passed. The sleep had taken care of that.

But that was pain, agonizing pain. It wasn't until he tried to move that he knew that it came from his leg.

He raised his head and looked down at it. It was swollen terribly below the knee and the swelling showed even halfway up his thigh. The plant tendrils he had used to tie on the protective pad of leaves now cut deeply into the swollen flesh.

To get his knife under that imbedded lashing would have been impossible. Fortunately, the final knot was over the shin bone, in front where the vine cut in less deeply than elsewhere. He was able, after an agonizing effort, to untie the knot.

A look under the pad of leaves told him the worst. Infection and blood poisoning both pretty bad and getting worse.

And without drugs, without cloth, without even *water,* there wasn't a thing he could do about it.

Not a thing, except *die,* when the poison had spread through his system.

He knew it was hopeless, then, and that he'd lost.

And with him humanity. When he died here, out there in the universe he knew, all his friends, everybody, would die too. And Earth and the colonized planets would be the home of the red, rolling, alien Outsiders. Creatures out of nightmare, things without a human attribute, who picked lizards apart for the fun of it.

It was the thought of that which gave him courage to start crawling, almost blindly in pain, toward the barrier again. Not crawling on hands and knees this time, but pulling himself along only by his arms and hands.

A chance in a million, that maybe he'd have strength left, when he got there, to throw his harpoon-spear just *once,* and with deadly effect, if—on another chance in a million—the Roller would come up to the barrier. Or if the barrier was gone, now.

It took him years, it seemed, to get there.

The barrier wasn't gone. It was as impassable as when he'd first felt it.

And the Roller wasn't at the barrier. By raising up on his elbows, he could see it at the back of its part of the arena, working on a wooden framework that was a half-completed duplicate of the catapult he'd destroyed.

It was moving slowly now. Undoubtedly it had weakened, too.

But Carson doubted that it would ever need the second catapult. He'd be dead, he thought, before it was finished.

If he could attract it to the barrier, now, while he was still alive—he waved an arm and tried to shout, but his parched throat would make no sound.

Or if he could get through the barrier—

His mind must have slipped for a moment, for he found himself beating his fists against the barrier in futile rage, and made himself stop.

He closed his eyes, tried to make himself calm.

"Hello," said the voice.

It was a small, thin voice. It sounded like—

He opened his eyes and turned his head. It *was* a lizard.

"Go away," Carson wanted to say. "Go away; you're not really there, or you're there but not really talking. I'm imagining things again."

But he couldn't talk; his throat and tongue were past all speech with the dryness. He closed his eyes again.

"Hurt," said the voice. "Kill. Hurt—kill. Come."

He opened his eyes again. The blue ten-legged lizard was still there. It ran a little way along the barrier, came back, started off again, and came back.

"Hurt," it said. "Kill. Come."

Again it started off, and came back. Obviously it wanted Carson to follow it along the barrier.

He closed his eyes again. The voice kept on. The same three meaningless words. Each time he opened his eyes, it ran off and came back.

"Hurt. Kill. Come."

Carson groaned. There would be no peace unless he followed the blasted thing. Like it wanted him to.

He followed it, crawling. Another sound, a high-pitched squealing, came to his ears and grew louder.

There was something lying in the sand, writhing, squealing. Something small, blue, that looked like a lizard and yet didn't—

Then he saw what it was—the lizard whose legs the Roller had pulled off, so long ago. But it wasn't dead; it had come back to life and was wriggling and screaming in agony.

"Hurt," said the other lizard. "Hurt. Kill. Kill."

Carson understood. He took the flint knife from his belt and killed the tortured creature. The live lizard scurried off quickly.

Carson turned back to the barrier. He leaned his hands and head against it and watched the Roller, far back, working on the new catapult.

"I could get that far," he thought, "if I could get through. If I could get through, I might win yet. It looks weak, too. I might—"

And then there was another reaction of black hopelessness, when pain snapped his will and he wished that he were dead. He envied the lizard he'd just killed. It didn't have to live on and suffer. And he did. It would be hours, it might be days, before the blood poisoning killed him.

If only he could use that knife on himself—

But he knew he wouldn't. As long as he was alive, there was the millionth chance—

He was straining, pushing on the barrier with the flat of his hands, and he noticed his arms, how thin and scrawny they were now. He must really have been here a long time, for days, to get as thin as that.

How much longer now, before he died? How much more heat and thirst and pain could flesh stand?

For a little while he was almost hysterical again, and then came a time of deep calm, and a thought that was startling.

The lizard he had just killed. *It had crossed the barrier, still alive.* It had come from the Roller's side; the Roller had pulled off its legs and then tossed it contemptuously at him and it had come through the barrier. He'd thought, because the lizard was dead.

But it hadn't been dead; it had been unconscious.

A live lizard couldn't go through the barrier, but an unconscious one could. The barrier was not a barrier, then, to living flesh, but to conscious flesh. It was a *mental* projection, a *mental* hazard.

And with that thought, Carson started crawling along the barrier to make his last desperate gamble. A hope so forlorn that only a dying man would have dared try it.

No use weighing the odds of success. Not when, if he didn't try it, those odds were infinitely to zero.

He crawled along the barrier to the dune of sand, about four feet high, which he'd scooped out in trying—how many days ago? —to dig under the barrier or to reach water.

The mound was right at the barrier, its farther slope half on one side of the barrier, half on the other.

Taking with him a rock from the pile nearby, he climbed up to the top of the dune and over the top, and lay there against the barrier, his weight leaning against it so that if the barrier were taken away he'd roll on down the short slope, into the enemy territory.

He checked to be sure that the knife was safely in his rope belt, that the harpoon was in the crook of his left arm and that the twenty-foot rope fastened to it and to his wrist.

Then with his right hand he raised the rock with which he would hit himself on the head. Luck would have to be with him on that blow; it would have to be hard enough to knock him out, but not hard enough to knock him out for long.

He had a hunch that the Roller was watching him, and would see him roll down through the barrier, and come to investigate. It would think he was dead, he hoped—he thought it had probably drawn the same deduction about the nature of the barrier that he had drawn. But it would come cautiously. He would have a little time—

He struck.

Pain brought him back to consciousness. A sudden, sharp pain in his hip that was different from the throbbing pain in his head and the throbbing pain in his leg.

But he had, thinking things out before he had struck himself, anticipated that very pain, even hoped for it, and had steeled himself against awakening with a sudden movement.

He lay still, but opened his eyes just a slit, and saw that he had guessed rightly. The Roller was coming closer. It was twenty feet away and the pain that had awakened him was the stone it had tossed to see whether he was alive or dead.

He lay still. It came closer, fifteen feet away, and stopped again. Carson scarcely breathed.

As nearly as possible, he was keeping his mind a blank, lest its telepathic ability detect consciousness in him. And with his mind blanked out that way, the impact of its thoughts upon his mind was nearly soul-shattering.

He felt sheer horror at the utter *alienness,* the *differentness* of those thoughts. Things that he felt but could not understand and could never express, because no terrestrial language had words, no terrestrial mind had images to fit them. The mind of a spider, he thought, or the mind of a praying mantis or a Martian sand-serpent, raised to intelligence and put in telepathic rapport with human minds, would be a homely familiar thing, compared to this.

He understood now that the Entity had been right: Man or Roller, and the universe was not a place that could hold them both. Farther apart than god and devil, there could never be even a balance between them.

Closer. Carson waited until it was only feet away, until its clawed tentacles reached out—

Oblivious to agony now, he sat up, raised and flung the harpoon with all the strength that remained to him. Or he thought it was all; sudden final strength flooded through him, along with a sudden forgetfulness of pain as definite as a nerve block.

As the Roller, deeply stabbed by the harpoon, rolled away, Carson tried to get to his feet to run after it. He couldn't do that; he fell, but kept crawling.

It reached the end of the rope, and he was jerked forward by the pull of his wrist. It dragged him a few feet and then stopped. Carson kept on going, pulling himself toward it hand over hand along the rope.

It stopped there, writhing tentacles trying in vain to pull out the harpoon. It seemed to shudder and quiver, and then it must have realized that it couldn't get away, for it rolled back toward him, clawed tentacles reaching out.

Stone knife in hand, he met it. He stabbed, again and again, while those horrid claws ripped skin and flesh and muscle from his body.

He stabbed and slashed, and at last it was still.

A bell was ringing, and it took him a while after he'd opened his eyes to tell where he was and what it was. He was strapped into the seat of his scouter, and the visiplate before him showed only empty space. No Outsider ship and no impossible planet.

The bell was the communications plate signal; someone wanted him to switch power into the receiver. Purely reflex action enabled him to reach forward and throw the lever.

The face of Brander, captain of the *Magellan,* mother-ship of his group of scouters, flashed onto the screen. His face was pale and his black eyes glowed with excitement.

"Magellan to Carson," he snapped. "Come on in. The fight's over. We've won!"

The screen went blank; Brander would be signaling the other scouters of his command.

Slowly, Carson set the controls for the return. Slowly, unbelievingly, he unstrapped himself from the seat and went back to get a drink at the cold-water tank. For some reason, he was unbelievably thirsty. He drank six glasses.

He leaned there against the wall, trying to think.

Had it happened? He was in good health, sound, uninjured. His thirst had been mental rather than physical; his throat hadn't been dry. His leg—

He pulled up his trouser leg and looked at the calf. There was a long white scar there, but a perfectly healed scar. It hadn't been there before. He zipped open the front of his shirt and saw that his chest and abdomen were criss-crossed with tiny, almost unnoticeable, perfectly healed scars.

It *had* happened.

The scouter, under automatic control, was already entering the hatch of the mother-ship. The grapples pulled it into its individual lock, and a moment later a buzzer indicated that the lock was air-filled. Carson opened the hatch and stepped outside, went through the double door of the lock.

He went right to Brander's office, went in, and saluted.

Brander still looked dizzily dazed. "Hi, Carson," he said. "What you missed! What a show!"

"What happened, sir?"

"Don't know, exactly. We fired one salvo, and their whole fleet went up in dust! Whatever it was jumped from ship to ship in a flash, even the ones we hadn't aimed at and that were out of range. The whole fleet disintegrated before our eyes, and we didn't get the paint of a single ship scratched!

'We can't even claim credit for it. Must have been some unstable component in the metal they used, and our sighting shot just set it off. Man, oh man, too bad you missed all the excitement."

Carson managed to grin. It was a sickly ghost of a grin, for it would be days before he'd be over the mental impact of his experience, but the captain wasn't watching, and didn't notice.

"Yes sir," he said. Common sense, more than modesty, told him he'd be branded forever as the worst liar in space if he ever said any more than that. "Yes, sir, too bad I missed all the excitement."

QUESTIONS

1 Discuss the plausibility of two rational creatures who are so utterly different that their only reaction upon meeting is to kill one another.

2 Does Brown mean for us to see the "eternal entity" which stages the fight as a futuristic deity? The implication is that age yields wisdom and concern for others. Is this a valid concept?

3 Brown could have used many other shapes for his alien creature. Is the "Roller," as he presents it, effective? Can you think of a more suitable description for his purpose?

4 What are the first three colors mentioned in the story? Are these colors there by accident or do you think Brown had a purpose in mind?

5 Brown uses the stylistic device of the "frame tale." What added dimensions does the "frame" give to the work as a whole?

6 The ending of "Arena" is highly conventional (i.e. the hero who must remain silent for fear of ridicule). What other parts of Brown's story can be labeled as conventions?

THE ILLUSTRATED MAN
Ray Bradbury

"Hey, the Illustrated Man!"

A calliope screamed, and Mr. William Philippus Phelps stood, arms folded, high on the summer-night platform, a crowd unto himself.

He was an entire civilization. In the Main Country, his chest, the Vasties lived—nipple-eyed dragons swirling over his fleshpot, his almost feminine breasts. His naval was the mouth of a slit-eyed monster—an obscene, in-sucked mouth, toothless as a witch. And there were secret caves where Darklings lurked, his armpits, adrip with slow subterranean liquors, where the Darklings, eyes jealously ablaze, peered out through rank creeper and hanging vine.

Mr. William Philippus Phelps leered down from his freak platform with a thousand peacock eyes. Across the sawdust meadow he saw his wife, Lisabeth, far away, ripping tickets in half, staring at the silver belt buckles of passing men.

Mr. William Philippus Phelps's hands were tattooed roses. At the height of his wife's interest, the roses shriveled, as with the passing of sunlight.

A year before, when he had led Lisabeth to the marriage bureau to watch her work her name in ink, slowly, on the form, his skin had been pure and white and clean. He glanced down at himself in sudden horror. Now he was like a great painted canvas, shaken in the night wind! How had it happened? Where had it all begun?

It had started with the arguments, and then the flesh, and then the pictures. They had fought deep into the summer nights, she like a brass trumpet forever blaring at him. And he had gone out to eat five thousand steaming hot dogs, ten million hamburgers, and a forest of green onions, and to drink vast red seas of orange juice. Peppermint candy formed his brontosaur bones, the hamburgers shaped his balloon flesh, and strawberry pop pumped in and out of his heart valves sickeningly, until he weighed three hundred pounds.

"William Philippus Phelps," Lisabeth said to him in the eleventh month of their marriage, "you're dumb and fat."

That was the day the carnival boss handed him the blue envelope. "Sorry, Phelps. You're no good to me with all that gut on you."

"Wasn't I always your best tent man, boss?"

"Once. Not any more. Now you sit, you don't get the work out."

"Let me be your Fat Man."

"I got a Fat Man. Dime a dozen." The boss eyed him up and down. "Tell you what, though. We ain't had a Tattooed Man since Gallery Smith died last year. . . ."

That had been a month ago. Four short weeks. From some-one, he had learned of a tattoo artist far out in the rolling Wisconsin country, an old woman, they said, who knew her trade. If he took the dirt road and turned right at the river and then left . . .

He had walked out across a yellow meadow, which was crisp from the sun. Red flowers blew and bent in the wind as he walked, and he came to the old shack, which looked as if it had stood in a million rains.

Inside the door was a silent, bare room, and in the center of the bare room sat an ancient woman.

Her eyes were stitched with red resin-thread. Her nose was sealed with black wax-twine. Her ears were sewn, too, as if a darning-needle dragonfly had stitched all her senses shut. She sat, not moving, in the vacant room. Dust lay in a yellow flour all about, unfootprinted in many weeks; if she had moved it would have shown, but she had not moved. Her hands touched each other like thin, rusted instruments. Her feet were naked and obscene as rain rubbers, and near them sat vials of tattoo milk— red, lightning-blue, brown, cat-yellow. She was a thing sewn tight into whispers and silence.

Only her mouth moved, unsewn: "Come in. Sit down. I'm lonely here."

He did not obey.

"You came for the pictures," she said in a high voice. "I have a picture to show you, first."

She tapped a blind finger to her thrust-out palm. "See!" she cried.

It was a tattoo-portrait of William Philippus Phelps.

"Me!" he said.

Her cry stopped him at the door. "Don't run."

He held to the edges of the door, his back to her. "That's me, that's me on your hand!"

"It's been there fifty years." She stroked it like a cat, over and over.

He turned. "It's an *old* tattoo." He drew slowly nearer. He edged forward and bent to blink at it. He put out a trembling finger to brush the picture. "Old. That's impossible! You don't know me. I don't know you. Your eyes, all sewed shut."

"I've been waiting for you." she said. "And many people." She displayed her arms and legs, like the spindles of an antique chair. "I have pictures on me of people who have already come here to see me. And there are other pictures of other people who are coming to see me in the next one hundred years. And you, you have come."

"How do you know it's me? You can't see!"

"You *feel* like the lions, the elephants, and the tigers to me. Unbutton your shirt. You need me. Don't be afraid. My needles are as clean as a doctor's fingers. When I'm finished with illustrating you, I'll wait for someone else to walk along out here and find me. And someday, a hundred summers from now, perhaps, I'll just go lie down in the forest under some white mushrooms, and in the spring you won't find anything but a small blue cornflower. . . ."

He began to unbutton his sleeves.

"I know the Deep Past and the Clear Present and the even Deeper Future," she whispered, eyes knotted into blindness, face lifted to this unseen man. "It is on my flesh. I will paint it on yours, too. You will be the only *real* Illustrated Man in the universe. I'll give you special pictures you will never forget. Pictures of the Future on your skin."

She pricked him with a needle.

He ran back to the carnival that night in a drunken terror and elation. Oh, how quickly the old dust-witch had stitched him with color and design. At the end of a long afternoon of being bitten by a silver snake, his body was alive with portraiture. He looked as if he had dropped and been crushed between the steel rollers of a print press, and come out like an incredible rotogravure. He was clothed in a garment of trolls and scarlet dinosaurs.

"Look!" he cried to Lisabeth. She glanced up from her cosmetic table as he tore his shirt away. He stood in the naked bulb-light of their car-trailer, expanding his impossible chest. Here, the Tremblies, half-maiden, half-goat, leaping when his biceps flexed. Here, the Country of Lost Souls, his chins. In so many accordion pleats of fat, numerous small scorpions, beetles, and mice were crushed, held, hid, darting into view, vanishing, as he raised or lowered his chins.

"My God," said Lisabeth. "My husband's a freak."

She ran from the trailer and he was left alone to pose before the mirror. Why had he done it? To have a job, yes, but most of all, to cover the fat that had larded itself impossibly over his bones. To hide the fat under a layer of color and fantasy, to hide it from his wife, but most of all from himself.

He thought of the old woman's last words. She had needled him two *special* tattoos, one on his chest, another for his back, which she would not let him see. She covered each with cloth and adhesive.

"You are not to look at these two," she had said.

"Why?"

"Later, you may look. The Future is in these pictures. You can't look now or it may spoil them. They are not quite finished. I put ink on your flesh and the sweat of you forms the rest of the picture, the Future—your sweat and your thought." Her empty mouth grinned. "Next Saturday night, you may advertise! The Big Unveiling! Come see the Illustrated Man Unveil his picture! You can make money in that way. You can charge admission to the Unveiling, like to an Art Gallery. Tell them you have a picture that even you never have seen, that *nobody* has seen yet. The most unusual picture ever painted. Almost alive. And it tells the Future. Roll the drums and blow the trumpets. And you can stand there and unveil at the Big Unveiling."

"That's a good idea," he said.

"But only unveil the picture on your chest," she said. "That is first. You must save the picture on your back, under the adhesive, for the following week. Understand?"

"How much do I owe you?"

"Nothing," she said. "If you walk with these pictures on you, I will be repaid with my own satisfaction. I will sit here for the next two weeks and think how clever my pictures are, for I make them to fit each man himself and what is inside him. Now walk out of this house and never come back. Good-by."

"Hey! The Big Unveiling!"

The red signs blew in the night wind: NO ORDINARY TATTOOED MAN! THIS ONE IS "ILLUSTRATED"! GREATER THAN MICHELANGELO! TONIGHT! ADMISSION 10 CENTS!

Now the hour had come. Saturday night, the crowd stirring their animal feet in the hot sawdust.

"In one minute—" the carny boss pointed his cardboard megaphone—"in the tent immediately to my rear, we will unveil the Mysterious Portrait upon the Illustrated Man's chest! Next Saturday night, the same hour, same location, we'll unveil the Picture upon the Illustrated Man's *back!* Bring your friends!"

There was a stuttering roll of drums.

Mr. William Philippus Phelps jumped back and vanished; the crowd poured into the tent, and, once inside, found him reestablished upon another platform, the band brassing out a jig-time melody.

He looked for his wife and saw her, lost in the crowd, like a stranger, come to watch a freakish thing, a look of contemptuous curiosity upon her face. For, after all, he was her husband, and this was a thing she didn't know about him herself. It gave him a feeling of great height and warmness and light to find himself the center of the jangling universe, the carnival world, for one night. Even the other freaks—the Skeleton, the Seal Boy, the Yoga, the Magician, and the Balloon—were scattered through the crowd.

"Ladies and gentlemen, the great moment!"

A trumpet flourish, a hum of drumsticks on tight cowhide.

Mr. William Philippus Phelps let his cape fall. Dinosaurs,

trolls, and half-women-half-snakes writhed on his skin in the stark light.

Ah, murmured the crowd, for surely there had never been a tattooed man like this! The beast eyes seemed to take red fire and blue fire, blinking and twisting. The roses on his fingers seemed to expel a sweet pink bouquet. The tyrannosaurus-rex reared up along his leg, and the sound of the brass trumpet in the hot tent heavens was a prehistoric cry from the red monster throat. Mr. William Philippus Phelps was a museum jolted to life. Fish swam in seas of electric-blue ink. Fountains sparkled under yellow suns. Ancient buildings stood in meadows of harvest wheat. Rockets burned across spaces of muscle and flesh. The slightest inhalation of his breath threatened to make chaos of the entire printed universe. He seemed afire, the creatures flinching from the flame, drawing back from the great heat of his pride, as he expanded under the audience's rapt contemplation.

The carny boss laid his fingers to the adhesive. The audience rushed forward silent in the oven vastness of the night tent.

"You ain't seen nothing yet!" cried the carny boss.

The adhesive ripped free.

There was an instant in which nothing happened. An instant in which the Illustrated Man thought that the Unveiling was a terrible and irrevocable failure.

But then the audience gave a low moan.

The carny boss drew back, his eyes fixed.

Far out at the edge of the crowd, a woman, after a moment, began to cry, began to sob, and did not stop.

Slowly, the Illustrated Man looked down at his naked chest and stomach.

The thing that he saw made the roses on his hands discolor and die. All of his creatures seemed to wither, turn inward, shrivel with the arctic coldness that pumped from his heart outward to freeze and destroy them. He stood trembling. His hands floated up to touch that incredible picture, which lived, moved and shivered with life. It was like gazing into a small room, seeing a thing of someone else's life, so intimate, so impossible that one could not believe and one could not long stand to watch without turning away.

It was a picture of his wife, Lisabeth, and himself.

And he was killing her.

Before the eyes of a thousand people in a dark tent in the center of a black-forested Wisconsin land, he was killing his wife.

His great flowered hands were upon her throat, and her face was turning dark and he killed her and he killed her and did not ever in the next minute stop killing her. It was real. While the crowd watched, she died, and he turned very sick. He was about to fall straight down into the crowd. The tent whirled like a monster bat wing, flapping grotesquely. The last thing he heard was a woman, sobbing, far out on the shore of the silent crowd.

And the crying woman was Lisabeth, his wife.

In the night, his bed was moist with perspiration. The carnival sounds had melted away, and his wife, in her own bed, was quiet now, too. He fumbled with his chest. The adhesive was smooth. They had made him put it back.

He had fainted. When he revived, the carny boss had yelled at him, "Why didn't you say what that picture was like?"

"I didn't know, I didn't," said the Illustrated Man.

"Good God!" said the boss. "Scare hell outa everyone. Scared hell outa Lizzie, scared hell outa me. Christ, where'd you get that damn tattoo?" He shuddered. "Apologize to Lizzie, now."

His wife stood over him.

"I'm sorry, Lisabeth," he said, weakly, his eyes closed. "I didn't know."

"You did it on purpose," she said. "To scare me."

"I'm sorry."

"Either it goes or I go," she said.

"Lisabeth."

"You heard me. That picture comes off or I quit this show."

"Yeah, Phil," said the boss. "That's how it is."

"Did you lose money? Did the crowd demand refunds!"

"It ain't the money, Phil. For that matter, once the word got around, hundreds of people wanted in. But I'm runnin' a clean show. That tattoo comes off! Was this your idea of a practical joke, Phil?"

He turned in the warm bed. No, not a joke. Not a joke at all. He had been as terrified as anyone. Not a joke. The little old dust-witch, what had she *done* to him and how had she done it? Had she put the picture there? No; she had said that the picture was unfinished, and that he himself, with his thoughts and perspiration would finish it. Well, he had done the job all right.

But what, if anything, was the significance? He didn't want to kill anyone. He didn't want to kill Lisabeth. Why should such a silly picture burn here on his flesh in the dark?

He crawled his fingers softly, cautiously down to touch the quivering place where the hidden portrait lay. He pressed tight, and the temperature of that spot was enormous. He could almost feel that little evil picture killing and killing and killing all through the night.

I don't wish to kill her, he thought, insistently, looking over at her bed. And then, five minutes later, he whispered aloud: "Or *do* I?"

"What?" she cried, awake.

"Nothing," he said, after a pause. "Go to sleep."

The man bent forward, a buzzing instrument in his hand. "This costs five bucks an inch. Costs more to peel tattoos off than to put 'em on. Okay, jerk the adhesive."

The Illustrated Man obeyed.

The skin man sat back. "Christ! No wonder you want that off! That's ghastly. I don't even want to look at it." He flicked his machine. "Ready? This won't hurt."

The carny boss stood in the tent flap, watching. After five minutes, the skin man changed the instrument head, cursing. Ten minutes later he scraped his chair back and scratched his head. Half an hour passed and he got up, told Mr. William Philippus Phelps to dress, and packed his kit.

"Wait a minute," said the carny boss. "You ain't done the job."

"And I ain't going to," said the skin man.

"I'm paying good money. What's wrong?"

"Nothing, except that damn picture just won't come off. Damn thing must go right down to the bone."

"You're crazy."

"Mister, I'm in business thirty years and never seen a tattoo like this. An inch deep, if it's anything."

"But I've got to get it off!" cried the Illustrated Man.

The skin man shook his head. "Only one way to get rid of that."

"How?"

"Take a knife and cut off your chest. You won't live long, but the picture'll be gone."

"Come back here!"

But the skin man walked away.

They could hear the big Sunday-night crowd, waiting.

"That's a big crowd," said the Illustrated man.

"But they ain't going to see what they came to see," said the carny boss. "You ain't going out there, except with the adhesive. Hold still now, I'm curious about this *other* picture, on your back. We might be able to give 'em an Unveiling on this one instead."

"She said it wouldn't be ready for a week or so. The old woman said it would take time to set, make a pattern."

There was a soft ripping as the carny boss pulled aside a flap of white tape on the Illustrated Man's spine.

"What do you see?" gasped Mr. Phelps, bent over.

The carny boss replaced the tape. "Buster, as a Tattooed Man, you're a washout, ain't you? Why'd you let that old dame fix you up this way?"

"I didn't know who she was."

"She sure cheated you on this one. No design to it. Nothing. No picture at all."

"It'll come clear. You wait and see."

The boss laughed. "Okay. Come on. We'll show the crowd part of you, anyway."

They walked out into an explosion of brassy music.

He stood monstrous in the middle of the night, putting out his hands like a blind man to balance himself in a world now tilted, now rushing, now threatening to spin him over and down into the mirror before which he raised his hands. Upon the flat, dimly lighted table top were peroxides, acids, silver razors, and squares of sandpaper. He took each of them in turn. He soaked the vicious tattoo upon his chest, he scraped at it. He worked steadily for an hour.

He was aware, suddenly, that someone stood in the trailer door behind him. It was three in the morning. There was a faint odor of beer. She had come home from town. He heard her slow breathing. He did not turn. "Lisabeth?" he said.

"You'd better get rid of it," she said, watching his hands move the sandpaper. She stepped into the trailer.

"I didn't want the picture this way," he said.

"You did," she said. "You planned it."

"I didn't."

"I know you," she said. "Oh, I know you hate me. Well, that's nothing. I hate you, I've hated you a long time now. Good God, when you started putting on the fat, you think anyone could love you then? I could teach you some things about hate. Why don't you ask me?"

"Leave me alone," he said.

"In front of that crowd, making a spectacle out of me!"

"I didn't know what was under the tape."

She walked around the table, hands fitted to her hips, talking to the beds, the walls, the table, talking it all out of her. And he thought: *Or did I know? Who made this picture, me or the witch? Who formed it? How? Do I really want her dead? No! And yet. . . .* He watched his wife draw nearer, nearer, he saw the ropy strings of her throat vibrate to her shouting. This and this and *this* was wrong with him! That and that and *that* was unspeakable about him! He was a liar, a schemer, a fat, lazy, ugly man, a child. Did he think he could compete with the carny boss of the tent-peggers? Did he think he was sylphine and graceful, did he think he was a framed El Greco? da Vinci, huh! Michelangelo, my eye! She brayed. She showed her teeth. "Well, you can't scare me into staying with someone I don't wan't touching me with their slobby paws!" she finished, triumphantly.

"Lisabeth," he said.

"Don't Lisabeth me!" she shrieked. "I know your plan. You had that picture put on to scare me. You thought I wouldn't *dare* leave you. Well!"

"Next Saturday night, the Second Unveiling," he said. "You'll be proud of me."

"Proud! You're silly and pitiful. God, you're like a whale. You ever see a beached whale? I saw one when I was a kid. There it was, and they came and shot it. Some lifeguards shot it. Jesus, a whale!"

"Lisabeth."

"I'm leaving, that's all, and getting a divorce."

"Don't."

"And I'm marrying a man, not a fat woman—that's what you are, so much fat on you there ain't no sex!"

"You can't leave me," he said.

"Just watch!"

"I love you," he said.

"Oh," she said. "Go look at your pictures."

He reached out.

"Keep your hands off," she said.

"Lisabeth."

"Don't come near me. You turn my stomach."

"Lisabeth."

All the eyes of his body seemed to fire, all the snakes to move, all the monsters to seethe, all the mouths to widen and rage. He moved toward her—not like a man, but a crowd.

He felt the great blooded reservoir of orangeade pump through him now, the sluice of cola and rich lemon pop pulse in sickening sweet anger through his wrists, his legs, his heart. All of it, the oceans of mustard and relish and all the million drinks he had drowned himself in the last year were aboil; his face was the color of a steamed beef. And the pink roses of his hands became those hungry, carnivorous flowers kept long years in tepid jungle and now let free to find their way on the night air before him.

He gathered her to him, like a great beast gathering in a struggling animal. It was a frantic gesture of love, quickening and demanding, which, as she struggled, hardened to another thing. She beat and clawed at the picture on his chest.

"You've got to love me, Lisabeth."

"Let me go!" she screamed. She beat at the picture that burned under her fists. She slashed at it with her fingernails.

"Oh, Lisabeth," he said, his hands moving up her arms.

"I'll scream," she said, seeing his eyes.

"Lisabeth." The hands moved up to her shoulders, to her neck. "Don't go away."

"Help!" she screamed. The blood ran from the picture on his chest.

He put his fingers about her neck and squeezed.

She was a calliope cut in mid-shriek.

Outside, the grass rustled. There was the sound of running feet.

Mr. William Philippus Phelps opened the trailer door and stepped out.

They were waiting for him. Skeleton, Midget, Balloon, Yoga, Electra, Popeye, Seal Boy. The freaks, waiting in the middle of the night, in the dry grass.

He walked toward them. He moved with a feeling that he must get away; these people would understand nothing, they were not thinking people. And because he did not flee, because he only walked, balanced, stunned, between the tents, slowly, the freaks moved to let him pass. They watched him, because their watching guaranteed that he would not escape. He walked steadily as long as he was visible, not knowing where he was going. They watched him go, and then they turned and all of them shuffled to the silent car-trailer together and pushed the door slowly wide . . .

The Illustrated Man walked steadily in the dry meadows beyond the town.

"He went that way!" a faint voice cried. Flashlights bobbled over the hills. There were dim shapes, running.

Mr. William Philippus Phelps waved to them. He was tired. He wanted only to be found now. He was tired of running away. He waved again.

"There he is!" The flashlights changed direction. "Come on! We'll get the bastard!"

When it was time, the Illustrated Man ran again. He was careful to run slowly. He deliberately fell down twice. Looking back, he saw the tent stakes they held in their hands.

He ran toward a far crossroads lantern, where all the summer night seemed to gather; merry-go-rounds of fireflies whirling, crickets moving their song toward that light, everything rushing, as if by some midnight attraction, toward that one high-hung lantern —the Illustrated Man first, the others close at his heels.

As he reached the light and passed a few yards under and beyond it, he did not need to look back. On the road ahead, in silhouette, he saw the upraised tent stakes sweep violently up, up, and then *down!*

A minute passed.

In the country ravines, the crickets sang. The freaks stood over the sprawled Illustrated Man, holding their tent stakes loosely.

Finally they rolled him over on his stomach. Blood ran from his mouth.

They ripped the adhesive from his back. They stared down for a long moment at the freshly revealed picture. Someone whispered. Someone else swore, softly. The Thin Man pushed back and walked away and was sick. Another and another of the freaks stared, their mouths trembling, and moved away, leaving the Illustrated Man on the deserted road, the blood running from his mouth.

In the dim light, the unveiled Illustration was easily seen.

It showed a crowd of freaks bending over a dying fat man on a dark and lonely road, looking at a tattoo on his back which illustrated a crowd of freaks bending over a dying fat man on a . . .

QUESTIONS

1   Is there any valid connection between Lisabeth and the dust-witch?
2   The circus has often been used by writers to represent "life." Is Bradbury commenting only upon a particular situation or does the meaning of his story go beyond the tiny, sordid world of the characters?
3   Discuss the crowd's fascination with Phelps. Why are so many people attracted to freaks?
4   Examine the unique descriptions of Phelps's soda-pop circulatory system and discuss their effectiveness.
5   When Phelps's boss tears away the bandage on his back he sees nothing. Does this imply that Phelps creates his own fate?

THE BIG FLASH

Norman Spinrad

T minus 200 days . . . and counting. . . .

They came on freaky for my taste—but that's the name of the game; freaky means a draw in the rock business. And if the Mandala was going to survive in LA, competing with a network-owned joint like The American Dream, I'd just have to hold my nose and outfreak the opposition. So after I had dug the Four Horsemen for about an hour, I took them into my office to talk turkey.

I sat down behind my Salvation Army desk (the Mandala is the world's most expensive shoestring operation) and the Horsemen sat down on the bridge chairs sequentially, establishing the group's pecking order.

First the head honcho, lead guitar and singer, Stony Clarke— blond shoulder-length hair, eyes like something in a morgue when he took off his steel-rimmed shades, a reputation as a heavy acid head and the look of a speed freak behind it. Then Hair, the drummer, dressed like a Hell's Angel, swastikas and all, a junkie, with fanatic eyes that were a little too close together, making me wonder whether he wore swastikas because he grooved behind the Angel thing or made like an Angel because it let him groove behind the swastika in public. Number three was a cat who called himself Super Spade and wasn't kidding—he wore earrings, natural hair, a Stokeley Carmichael sweatshirt, and on a thong around his neck a shrunken head that had been whitened with liquid shoe polish. He was the utility infielder: sitar, base, organ, flute, whatever. Number four, who called himself Mr. Jones, was about the creepiest cat I had ever seen in a rock group, and that is saying something. He was their visuals, synthesizer, and electronics man. He was at least forty, wore Early Hippy clothes that looked like they had been made by Sy Devore, and was rumored to be some kind of Rand Corporation dropout. There's no business like show business.

"Okay, boys," I said, "you're strange, but you're my kind of strange. Where you worked before?"

"We ain't, baby," Clarke said. "We're the New Thing. I've been dealing crystal and acid in the Haight. Hair was drummer for some plastic group in New York. The Super Spade claims it's the reincarnation of Bird and it don't pay to argue. Mr. Jones, he don't talk too much. Maybe he's a Martian. We just started putting our thing together."

One thing about this business, the groups that don't have square managers you can get cheap. They talk too much.

"Groovy," I said. "I'm happy to give you guys your start. Nobody knows you, but I think you got something going. So I'll take a chance and give you a week's booking. One A.M. to closing, which is two, Tuesday through Sunday, four hundred a week."

"Are you Jewish?" asked Hair.

"What?"

"Cool it," Clarke ordered. Hair cooled it. "What it means," Clarke told me, "is that four hundred sounds like pretty light bread."

"We don't sign if there's an option clause," Mr. Jones said.

"The Jones-thing has a good point," Clarke said. "We do the first week for four hundred, but after that it's a whole new scene, dig?"

I didn't feature that. If they hit it big, I could end up not being able to afford them. But on the other hand $400 was light bread, and I needed a cheap closing act pretty bad.

"Okay," I said. "But a verbal agreement that I get first crack at you when you finish the gig."

"Word of honor," said Stony Clarke.

That's this business—the word of honor of an ex-dealer and speed freak.

T minus 199 days . . . and counting. . . .

Being unconcerned with ends, the military mind can be easily manipulated, easily controlled, and easily confused. Ends are defined as those goals set by civilian authority. Ends are the conceded province of civilians; means are the province of the military, whose duty it is to achieve the ends set for it by the most advantageous application of the means at its command.

Thus the confusion over the war in Asia among my uniformed

clients at the Pentagon. The end has been duly set: eradication of the guerrillas. But the civilians have overstepped their bounds and meddled in means. The generals regard this as unfair, a breach of contract, as it were. The generals (or the faction among them most inclined to paranoia) are beginning to see the conduct of the war, the political limitation on means, as a ploy of the civilians for performing a putsch against their time-honored prerogatives.

This aspect of the situation would bode ill for the country were it not for the fact that the growing paranoia among the generals has enabled me to manipulate them into presenting both my scenarios to the President. The President has authorized implementation of the major scenario, provided that the minor scenario is successful in properly molding public opinion.

My major scenario is simple and direct. Knowing that the poor flying weather makes our conventional airpower, with its dependency on relative accuracy, ineffectual, the enemy has fallen into the pattern of grouping his forces into larger units and launching punishing annual offensives during the monsoon season. However, these larger units are highly vulnerable to tactical nuclear weapons, which do not depend upon accuracy for effect. Secure in the knowledge that domestic political considerations preclude the use of nuclear weapons, the enemy will once again form into division-sized units or larger during the next monsoon season. A parsimonious use of tactical nuclear weapons, even as few as twenty 100-kiloton bombs, employed simultaneously and in an advantageous pattern, will destroy a minimum of 200,000 enemy troops, or nearly two-thirds of his total force, in a twenty-four-hour period. The blow will be crushing.

The minor scenario, upon whose success the implementation of the major scenario depends, is far more sophisticated, due to its subtler goal: public acceptance of, or, optimally, even public clamor for, the use of tactical nuclear weapons. The task is difficult, but my scenario is quite sound, if somewhat exotic, and with the full if to-some-extent-clandestine support of the upper military hierarchy, certain civil government circles, and the decision makers in key aerospace corporations, the means now at my command would seem adequate. The risks, while statistically significant, do not exceed an acceptable level.

T minus 189 days . . . and counting. . . .

The way I see it, the network deserved the shafting I gave them. They shafted me, didn't they? Four successful series I produced for those bastards, and two bomb out after thirteen weeks and they send me to the salt mines! A discotheque, can you imagine they make me a producer at a lousy discotheque! A remittance man they make me, those schlockmeisters. Oh, those schnorrers made the American Dream sound like a kosher deal—twenty percent of the net, they say. And you got access to all our sets and contract players. It'll make you a rich man, Herm. And like a yuk, I sign, being broke at the time, without reading the fine print. I should know they've set up the American Dream as a tax loss? I should know that I've *gotta* use their lousy sets and stiff contract players and have it written off against my gross? I should know their shtick is to run the American Dream at a loss and then do a network TV show out of the joint from which I don't see a penny? So I end up running the place for them at a paper loss, living on salary, while the network rakes it off the TV show that I end up paying for out of my end.

Don't bums like that deserve to be shafted? It isn't enough they use me as a tax loss patsy, they gotta tell me who to book! "Go sign the Four Horsemen, the group that's packing them in at the Mandala," they say. "We want them on *A Night with the American Dream.* They're hot."

"Yeah, they're hot," I say, "which means they'll cost a mint. I can't afford it."

They show me more fine print—next time I read the contract with a microscope. I *gotta* book whoever they tell me to and I gotta absorb the cost on my books! It's enough to make a Litvak turn anti-semit.

So I had to go to the Mandala to sign up these hippies. I made sure I didn't get there till 12:30 so I wouldn't have to stay in that nuthouse any longer than necessary. Such a dive! What Bernstein did was take a bankrupt Hollywood-Hollywood club on the Strip, knock down all the interior walls, and put up this monster tent inside the shell. Just thin white screening over two-by-fours. Real shlock. Outside the tent, he's got projectors, lights, speakers, all the electronic mumbo-jumbo, and inside is like being surrounded by movie screens. Just the tent and the bare floor, not even a real stage, just a platform on wheels they shlepp in and out of the tent when they change groups.

So you can imagine he doesn't draw exactly a class crowd. Not with the American Dream up the street being run as a network tax loss. What they get is the smelly hard-core hippies I don't let in the door and the kind of j.d. high-school kids that think it's smart to hang around putzes like that. A lot of dope-pushing goes on. The cops don't like the place and the rousts draw professional troublemakers.

A real den of iniquity—I felt like I was walking onto a Casbah set. The last group had gone off and the Horsemen hadn't come on yet, so what you had was this crazy tent filled with hippies, half of them on acid or pot or amphetamine or for all I know Ajax, high-school would-be hippies, also mostly stoned and getting ugly, and a few crazy schwartzes looking to fight cops. All of them standing around waiting for something to happen, and about ready to make it happen. I stood near the door, just in case. As they say, "the vibes were making me uptight."

All of a sudden the house lights go out and it's black as a network executive's heart. I hold my hand on my wallet—in this crowd, tell me there are no pickpockets. Just the pitch black and dead silence for what, ten beats, and then I start feeling something, I don't know, like something crawling along my bones, but I know it's some kind of subsonic effect and not my imagination because all the hippies are standing still and you don't hear a sound.

Then from monster speakers so loud you feel it in your teeth, a heartbeat, but heavy, slow, half-time like maybe a whale's heart. The thing crawling along my bones seems to be synchronized with the heartbeat and I feel almost like I am that big dumb heart beating there in the darkness.

Then a dark red spot—so faint it's almost infrared—hits the stage which they have wheeled out. On the stage are four uglies in crazy black robes—you know, like the Grim Reaper wears—with that ugly red light all over them like blood. Creepy. Boom-ba-boom. Boom-ba-boom. The heartbeat still going, still that subsonic bone crawl, and the hippies are staring at the Four Horsemen like mesmerized chickens.

The bass player, a regular jungle-bunny, picks up the rhythm of the heartbeat. Dum-da-dum. Dum-da-dum. The drummer beats it out with earsplitting rim shots. Then the electric guitar, tuned like a strangling cat, makes with horrible heavy chords. Whang-ka-whang. Whang-ka-whang.

It's just awful, I feel it in my guts, my bones; my eardrums are just like some great big throbbing vein. Everybody is swaying to it, I'm swaying to it. Boom-ba-boom. Boom-ba-boom.

Then the guitarist starts to chant in rhythm with the heartbeat, in a hoarse, shrill voice like somebody dying: *"The big flash . . . the big flash. . . ."*

And the guy at the visuals console diddles around and rings of light start to climb the walls of the tent, blue at the bottom becoming green as they get higher, then yellow, orange, and finally, as they become a circle on the ceiling, eye-killing neon red. Each circle takes exactly one heartbeat to climb the walls.

Boy, what an awful feeling! Like I was a tube of toothpaste being squeezed in rhythm till the top of my head felt like it was gonna squirt up with those circles of light through the ceiling.

And then they start to speed it up gradually. The same heartbeat, the same rim shots, same chords, same circles of light, same *"The big flash . . . the big flash . . .,"* same base, same subsonic bone crawl, but just a little faster. . . . Then faster! Faster!

Thought I would die! Knew I would die! Heart beating like a lunatic. Rim shots like a machine gun. Circles of light sucking me up the walls, into that red neon hole.

Oy, incredible! Over and over faster and faster till the voice was a scream and the heartbeat a boom and the rim shots a whine and the guitar howled feedback and my bones were jumping out of my body—

Every spot in the place came on and I went blind from the sudden light—

An awful explosion sound came over every speaker, so loud it rocked me on my feet—

I felt myself squirting out of the top of my head and loved it. Then:

The explosion became a rumble—

The light seemed to run together into a circle on the ceiling, leaving everything else black.

And the circle became a fireball.

The fireball became a slow-motion film of an atomic bomb cloud as the rumbling died away. Then the picture faded into a moment of total darkness and the house lights came on.

What a number!

Gevalt, what an act!

So after the show, when I got them alone and found out they had no manager, not even an option to the Mandala, I thought faster than I ever had in my life.

To make a long story short and sweet, I gave the network the royal screw. I signed the Horsemen to a contract that made me their manager and gave me twenty percent of their take. Then I booked them into the American Dream at ten thousand a week, wrote a check as proprietor of the American Dream, handed the check to myself as manager of the Four Horsemen, then resigned as a network flunky, leaving them with a ten-thousand-dollar bag and me with twenty percent of the hottest group since the Beatles.

What the hell, he who lives by the fine print shall perish by the fine print.

T minus 148 days . . . and counting. . . .

"You haven't seen the tape yet, have you, B.D.?" Jake said. He was nervous as hell. When you reach my level in the network structure, you're used to making subordinates nervous, but Jake Pitkin was head of network continuity, not some office boy, and certainly should be used to dealing with executives at my level. Was the rumor really true?

We were alone in the screening room. It was doubtful that the projectionist could hear us.

"No, I haven't seen it yet," I said. "But I've heard some strange stories."

Jake looked positively deathly. "About the tape?" he said.

"About you, Jake," I said, deprecating the rumor with an easy smile. "That you don't want to air the show."

"It's true, B.D.," Jake said quietly.

"Do you realize what you're saying? Whatever our personal tastes—and I personally think there's something unhealthy about them—the Four Horsemen are the hottest thing in the country right now and that dirty little thief Herm Gellman held us up for a quarter of a million for an hour show. It cost another two hundred thousand to make it. We've spent another hundred thousand on promotion. We're getting top dollar from the sponsors. There's over a million dollars one way or the other riding on that show. That's how much we blow if we don't air it."

"I know that, B.D.," Jake said. "I also know this could cost me my job. Think about that. Because knowing all that, I'm still against airing the tape. I'm going to run the closing segment for you. I'm sure enough that you'll agree with me to stake my job on it."

I had a terrible feeling in my stomach. I have superiors too and The Word was that *A Trip with the Four Horsemen* would be aired, period. No matter what. Something funny was going on. The price we were getting for commercial time was a precedent and the sponsor was a big aerospace company which had never bought network time before. What really bothered me was that Jake Pitkin had no reputation for courage; yet here he was laying his job on the line. He must be pretty sure I would come around to his way of thinking or he wouldn't dare. And though I couldn't tell Jake, I had no choice in the matter whatsoever.

"Okay, roll it," Jake said into the intercom mike. "What you're going to see," he said as the screening room lights went out, "is the last number."

On the screen:

A shot of empty blue sky, with soft, lazy electric guitar chords behind it. The camera pans across a few clouds to an extremely long shot on the sun. As the sun, no more than a tiny circle of light, moves into the center of the screen, a sitar drone comes in behind the guitar.

Very slowly, the camera begins to zoom in on the sun. As the image of the sun expands, the sitar gets louder and the guitar begins to fade and a drum starts to give the sitar a beat. The sitar gets louder, the beat gets more pronounced and begins to speed up as the sun continues to expand. Finally, the whole screen is filled with unbearably bright light behind which the sitar and drum are in a frenzy.

Then over this, drowning out the sitar and drum, a voice like a sick thing in heat: *"Brighter . . . than a thousand suns. . . ."*

The light dissolves into a closeup of a beautiful dark-skinned girl with huge eyes and moist lips, and suddenly there is nothing on the sound track but soft guitar and voices crooning low: *"Brighter . . . Oh God, it's brighter . . . brighter . . . than a thousand suns. . . ."*

The girl's face dissolves into a full shot of the Four Horsemen in their Grim Reaper robes and the same melody that had played behind the girl's face shifts into a minor key, picks up whining, reverberating electric guitar chords and a sitar drone, and becomes a dirge: *"Darker . . . the world grows darker . . ."*

And a series of cuts in time to the dirge:

A burning village in Asia strewn with bodies—

"Darker . . . the world grows darker . . ."

The corpse heap at Auschwitz—

"Until it gets so dark . . ."

A gigantic auto graveyard with gaunt Negro children dwarfed in the foreground—

"I think I'll die . . ."

A Washington ghetto in flames with the Capitol misty in the background—

". . . before the daylight comes . . ."

A jump-cut to an extreme closeup on the lead singer of the Horsemen, his face twisted into a mask of desperation and ecstasy. And the sitar is playing double time, the guitar is wailing, and he is screaming at the top of his lungs: *"But before I die, let me make that trip before the nothing comes . . ."*

The girl's face again, but transparent, with a blinding yellow light shining through it. The sitar beat gets faster and faster with the guitar whining behind it and the voice is working itself up into a howling frenzy: *". . . the last big flash to light my sky . . ."*

Nothing but the blinding light now—

". . . and zap! The world is done . . ."

An utterly black screen for a beat that becomes black fading to blue at a horizon—

". . . but before we die let's dig that high that frees us from our binds . . . that blows all cool that ego-drool and burns us from our mind . . . the last big flash, mankind's last gas, the trip we can't take twice. . . ."

Suddenly, the music stops dead for half a beat. Then:

The screen is lit up by an enormous fireball—

A shattering rumble—

The fireball coalesces into a mushroom-pillar cloud as the roar goes on. As the roar begins to die out, fire is visible inside the monstrous nuclear cloud. And the girl's face is faintly visible superimposed over the cloud.

A soft voice, amplified over the roar, obscenely reverential now: *Brighter . . . great God, it's brighter . . . brighter than a thousand suns. . . ."*

And the screen went blank and the lights came on.

I looked at Jake. Jake looked at me.

"That's sick," I said. "That's really sick."

"You don't want to run a thing like that, do you, B.D.?" Jake said softly.

I made some rapid mental calculations. The loathsome thing ran something under five minutes . . . it could be done. . . .

"You're right, Jake," I said. "We won't run a thing like that. We'll cut it out of the tape and squeeze in another commercial at each break. That should cover the time."

"You don't understand," Jake said. "The contract Herm rammed down our throats doesn't allow us to edit. The show's a package—all or nothing. Besides, the whole show's like that."

"All like that? What do you mean, all like that?"

Jake squirmed in his seat. "Those guys are . . . well, perverts, B.D.," he said.

"Perverts?"

"They're . . . well, they're in love with the atom bomb or something. Every number leads up to the same thing."

"You mean . . . they're *all* like that?"

"You get the picture, B.D.," Jake said. "We run an hour of *that* or we run nothing at all."

"Jesus."

I knew what I wanted to say. Burn the tape and write off the million dollars. But I also knew it would cost me my job. And I knew that five minutes after I was out the door they would have someone in my job who would see things their way. Even my superiors seemed to be just handing down The Word from higher up. I had no choice. There was no choice.

"I'm sorry, Jake," I said. "We run it."

"I resign," said Jake Pitkin, who had no reputation for courage.

T minus 10 days . . . and counting. . . .

"It's a clear violation of the Test-Ban Treaty," I said.

The Under Secretary looked as dazed as I felt. "We'll call it a peaceful use of atomic energy, and let the Russians scream," he said.

"It's insane."

"Perhaps," the Under Secretary said. "But you have your orders, General Carson, and I have mine. From higher up. At exactly 8:58 P.M. local time on July fourth, you will drop a fifty-kiloton atomic bomb on the designated ground zero at Yucca Flats."

"But the people . . . the television crews. . . ."

"Will be at least two miles outside the danger zone. Surely, SAC can manage that kind of accuracy under 'laboratory conditions.' "

I stiffened. "I do not question the competence of any bomber crew under my command to perform this mission," I said. "I question the reason for the mission. I question the sanity of the orders."

The Under Secretary shrugged, smiled wanly. "Welcome to the club."

"You mean you don't know what this is all about either?"

"All I know is what was transmitted to me by the Secretary of Defense, and I got the feeling he doesn't know everything, either. You know that the Pentagon has been screaming for the use of tactical nuclear weapons to end the war in Asia—you SAC boys have been screaming the loudest. Well, several months ago, the President conditionally approved a plan for the use of tactical nuclear weapons during the next monsoon season."

I whistled. The civilians were finally coming to their senses. Or were they?

"But what does that have to do with—?"

"Public opinion," the Under Secretary said. "It was conditional upon a drastic change in public opinion. At the time the plan was approved, the polls showed that seventy-eight point eight percent of the population opposed the use of tactical nuclear weapons, nine point eight percent favored their use, and the rest were undecided or had no opinion. The President agreed to authorize the use of tactical nuclear weapons by a date, several months from now, which is still top secret, provided that by that date at least sixty-five percent of the population approved their use and no more than twenty percent actively opposed it."

"I see. . . . Just a ploy to keep the Joint Chiefs quiet."

"General Carson," the Under Secretary said, "apparently you are out of touch with the national mood. After the first Four Horsemen show, the polls showed that twenty-five percent of the population approved the use of nuclear weapons. After the second show, the figure was forty-one percent. It is now forty-eight percent. Only thirty-two percent are now actively opposed."

"You're trying to tell me that a rock group—"

"A rock group and the cult around it, General. It's become a national hysteria. There are imitators. Haven't you seen those buttons?"

"The ones with a mushroom cloud on them that say 'Do it'?"

The Under Secretary nodded. "Your guess is as good as mine whether the National Security Council just decided that the Horsemen hysteria could be used to mold public opinion, or whether the Four Horsemen were their creatures to begin with. But the results are the same either way—the Horsemen and the cult around them have won over precisely that element of the population which was most adamantly opposed to nuclear weapons: hippies, students, dropouts, draft-age youth. Demonstrations against the war and against nuclear weapons have died down. We're pretty close to that sixty-five percent. Someone—perhaps the President himself—has decided that one more big Four Horsemen show will put us over the top."

"The President is behind this?"

"No one else can authorize the detonation of an atomic bomb, after all," the Under Secretary said. "We're letting them do the show live from Yucca Flats. It's being sponsored by an aerospace company heavily dependent on defense contracts. We're letting them truck in a live audience. Of course the government is behind it."

"And SAC drops an A-bomb as the show-stopper?"

"Exactly."

"I saw one of those shows," I said. "My kids were watching it. I got the strangest feeling . . . I almost wanted that red telephone to ring. . . ."

"I know what you mean," the Under Secretary said. "Sometimes I get the feeling that whoever's behind this has gotten caught up in the hysteria themselves . . . that the Horsemen are now using whoever was using them . . . a closed circle. But I've been tired lately. The war's making us all so tired. If only we could get it all over with. . . ."

"We'd all like to get it over with one way or the other," I said.

T minus 60 minutes . . . and counting. . . .

I had orders to muster *Backfish*'s crew for the live satellite relay of *The Four Horsemen's Fourth.* Superficially, it might seem strange to order the whole Polaris fleet to watch a television show, but the morale factor involved was quite significant.

Polaris subs are frustrating duty. Only top sailors are chosen and a good sailor craves action. Yet if we are ever called upon to act, our mission will have been a failure. We spend most of our time honing skills that must never be used. Deterrence is a sound strategy but a terrible drain on the men of the deterrent forces— a drain exacerbated in the past by the negative attitude of our countrymen toward our mission. Men who, in the service of their country, polish their skills to a razor edge and then must refrain from exercising them have a right to resent being treated as pariahs.

Therefore the positive change in the public attitude toward us that seems to be associated with the Four Horsemen has made them mascots of a kind to the Polaris fleet. In their strange way they seem to speak for us and to us.

I chose to watch the show in the missile control center, where a full crew must always be ready to launch the missiles on five-minute notice. I have always felt a sense of communion with the duty watch in the missile control center that I cannot share with the other men under my command. Here we are not captain and crew but mind and hand. Should the order come, the will to fire the missiles will be mine and the act will be theirs. At such a moment, it will be good not to feel alone.

All eyes were on the television set mounted above the main console as the show came on and. . . .

The screen was filled with a whirling spiral pattern, metallic yellow on metallic blue. There was a droning sound that seemed part sitar and part electronic and I had the feeling that the sound was somehow coming from inside my head and the spiral seemed etched directly on my retinas. It hurt mildly, yet nothing in the world could have made me turn away.

Then two voices, chanting against each other:

"Let it all come in. . . ."

"Let it all come out. . . ."

"In . . . out . . . in . . . out . . . in . . . out . . ."

My head seemed to be pulsing—in-*out*, in-*out*, in-*out*,—and the spiral pattern began to pulse color changes with the words: yellow-on-blue (in) . . . green-on-red (*out*). . . . In-*out*-in-*out*-in-*out*-in-*out* . . ."

In the screen . . . *out* my head . . . I seemed to be beating against some kind of invisible membrane between myself and the screen as if something were trying to embrace my mind and I were fighting it. . . . But why was I fighting it?

The pulsing, the chanting, got faster and faster till in could not be told from *out* and negative spiral afterimages formed in my eyes faster than they could adjust to the changes, piled up on each other faster and faster till it seemed my head would explode—

The chanting and droning broke and there were the Four Horsemen, in their robes, playing on some stage against a backdrop of clear blue sky. And a single voice, soothing now: *"You are in . . ."*

Then the view was directly above the Horsemen and I could see that they were on some kind of circular platform. The view moved slowly and smoothly up and away and I saw that the circular stage was atop a tall tower; around the tower and completely encircling it was a huge crowd seated on desert sands that stretched away to an empty infinity.

"And we are in and they are in . . ."

I was down among the crowd now; they seemed to melt and flow like plastic, pouring from the television screen to enfold me . . .

"And we are all in here together. . . ."

A strange and beautiful feeling . . . the music got faster and wilder, ecstatic . . . the hull of the *Backfish* seemed unreal . . . the crowd was swaying to it around me . . . the distance between my-self and the crowd seemed to dissolve . . . I was there . . . they were here. . . . We were transfixed . . .

"Oh yeah, we are all in here together . . . together. . . ."

T minus 45 minutes . . . and counting. . . .

Jeremy and I sat staring at the television screen, ignoring each other and everything around us. Even with the short watches and the short tours of duty, you can get to feeling pretty strange down here in a hole in the ground under tons of concrete, just you and the guy with the other key, with nothing to do but think dark thoughts and get on each other's nerves. We're all supposed to be as stable as men can be, or so they tell us, and they must be right because the world's still here. I mean, it wouldn't take much— just two guys on the same watch over the same three Minutemen flipping out at the same time, turning their keys in the dual lock, pressing the three buttons. . . . Pow! World War III!

A bad thought, the kind we're not supposed to think or I'll start watching Jeremy and he'll start watching me and we'll get a paranoia feedback going. . . . But that can't happen; we're too stable, too responsible. As long as we remember that it's healthy to feel a little spooky down here, we'll be all right.

But the television set is a good idea. It keeps us in contact with the outside world, keeps it real. It'd be too easy to start thinking that the missile control center down here is the only real world and that nothing that happens up there really matters. . . . Bad thought!

The Four Horsemen . . . somehow these guys help you get it all out. I mean that feeling that it might be better to release all that tension, get it all over with. Watching the Four Horsemen, you're able to go with it without doing any harm, let it wash over you and then through you. I suppose they are crazy; they're all the human craziness in ourselves that we've got to keep very careful watch over down here. Letting it all come out watching the Horse-men makes it surer that none of it will come out down here. I guess that's why a lot of us have taken to wearing those "Do It" buttons off duty. The brass doesn't mind; they seem to understand that it's the kind of inside sick joke we need to keep us functioning.

Now that spiral thing they had started the show with—and the droning—came back on. Zap! I was right back in the screen again, as if the commercial hadn't happened.

"We are all in here together. . . ."

And then a closeup of the lead singer, looking straight at me, as close as Jeremy and somehow more real. A mean-looking guy with something behind his eyes that told me he knew where everything lousy and rotten was at.

A bass began to thrum behind him and some kind of electronic hum that set my teeth on edge. He began playing his guitar, mean and low down. And singing in that kind of drop-dead tone of voice that starts brawls in bars:

"I stabbed my mother and I mugged my paw . . ."

A riff of heavy guitar chords echoed the words mockingly as a huge swastika (red-on-black, black-on-red) pulsed like a naked vein on the screen—

The face of the Horseman, leering—

"Nailed my sister to the toilet door . . ."

Guitar behind the pulsing swastika—

"Drowned a puppy in a cement machine. . . . Burned a kitten just to hear it scream. . . ."

On the screen, just a big fire burning in slow motion, and the voice became a slow, shrill, agonized wail:

"Oh God, I've got this red-hot fire burning in the marrow of my brain. . . .

"Gotta get me a blowtorch . . . and set some naked flesh on flame. . . ."

The fire dissolved into the face of a screaming Oriental woman, who ran through a burning village clawing at the napalm on her back.

"I got this message . . . boiling in the bubbles of my blood. . . . A man ain't nothing but a fire burning . . . in a dirty glob of mud. . . ."

A film clip of a Nuremburg rally: a revolving swastika of marching men waving torches—

Then the leader of the Horsemen superimposed over the twisted flaming cross:

"Don't you hate me, baby, can't you feel somethin' scream-ing in your mind?

"Don't you hate me, baby, feel me drowning you in slime!"

Just the face of the Horseman howling hate—

"Oh yes, I'm a monster, mother. . . ."

A long view of the crowd around the platform, on their feet, waving arms, screaming soundlessly. Then a quick zoom in and a kaleidoscope of faces, eyes feverish, mouths open and howling—

"Just call me—"

The face of the Horseman superimposed over the crazed faces of the crowd—

"Mankind!"

I looked at Jeremy. He was toying with the key on the chain around his neck. He was sweating. I suddenly realized that I was sweating too and that my own key was throbbing in my hand alive. . . .

T minus 13 minutes . . . and counting. . . .

A funny feeling, the Captain watching the Four Horsemen here in the *Backfish*'s missile control center with us. Sitting in front of my console watching the television set with the Captain kind of breathing down my neck . . . I got the feeling he knew what was going through me and I couldn't know what was going through him . . . and it gave the fire inside me a kind of greasy feel I didn't like . . .

Then the commercial was over and that spiral thing came on again and whoosh! It sucked me right back into the television set and I stopped worrying about the Captain or anything like that . . .

Just the spiral going yellow-blue, red-green, and then starting to whirl and whirl, faster and faster, changing colors and whirling, whirling, whirling. . . . And the sound of a kind of Coney Island carousel tinkling behind it, faster and faster and faster, whirling and whirling and whirling, flashing red-green, yellow-blue, and whirling, whirling, whirling . . .

And this big hum filling my body and whirling, whirling,

whirling. . . . My muscles relaxing, going limp, whirling, whirling, whirling, all limp, whirling, whirling, whirling, oh so nice, just whirling, whirling . . .

And in the center of the flashing spiraling colors, a bright dot of colorless light, right at the center, not moving, not changing, while the whole world went whirling and whirling in colors around it, and the humming was coming from the dot the way the carousel music was coming from the spinning colors and the dot was humming its song to me. . . .

The dot was a light way down at the end of a long, whirling, whirling tunnel. The humming started to get a little louder. The bright dot started to get a little bigger. I was drifting down the tunnel toward it, whirling, whirling, whirling. . . .

T minus 11 minutes . . . and counting . . .

Whirling, whirling, whirling down a long, long tunnel of pulsing colors, whirling, whirling, toward the circle of light way down at the end of the tunnel. . . . How nice it would be to finally get there and soak up the beautiful hum filling my body and then I could forget that I was down here in this hole in the ground with a hard brass key in my hand, just Duke and me, down here in a cave under the ground that was a spiral of flashing colors, whirling, whirling toward the friendly light at the end of the tunnel, whirling, whirling. . . .

T minus 10 minutes . . . and counting. . . .

The circle of light at the end of the whirling tunnel was getting bigger and bigger and the humming was getting louder and louder and I was feeling better and better and the *Backfish*'s missile control center was getting dimmer and dimmer as the awful weight of command got lighter and lighter, whirling, whirling, and I felt so good I wanted to cry, whirling, whirling . . .

T minus 9 minutes . . . and counting. . . .

Whirling, whirling . . . I was whirling, Jeremy was whirling, the hole in the ground was whirling, and the circle of light at the end of the tunnel whirled closer and closer and—I was through! A place filled with yellow light. Pale metal-yellow light. Then pale metallic blue. Yellow. Blue. Yellow. Blue. Yellow-blue-yellow-blue-yellow-blue-yellow . . .

Pure light pulsing . . . and pure sound droning. And just the *feeling* of letters I couldn't read between the pulses—not-yellow and not-blue—too quick and too faint to be visible, but important, very important . . .

And then a voice that seemed to be singing from inside my head, almost as if it were my own:

"Oh, oh, oh . . . don't I really wanna know. . . . Oh, oh, oh . . . don't I really wanna know. . . ."

The world pulsing, flashing around those words I couldn't read, couldn't quite read, had to read, could *almost* read . . .

"Oh, oh, oh . . . great God I really wanna know. . . ."

Strange amorphous shapes clouding the blue-yellow-blue flickering universe, hiding the words I hated to read. . . . Dammit, why wouldn't they get out of the way so I could find out what I had to know!

"Tell me tell me tell me tell me tell me. . . . Gotta know gotta know gotta know gotta know. . . ."

T minus 7 minutes . . . and counting. . . .

Couldn't read the words! Why wouldn't the Captain let me read the words?

And that voice inside me: *"Gotta know . . . gotta know . . . gotta know why it hurts me so. . . ."* Why wouldn't it shut up and let me read the words? Why wouldn't the words hold still? Or just slow down a little? If they'd slow down a little, I could read them and then I'd know what I had to do. . . .

T minus 6 minutes . . . and counting. . . .

I felt the sweaty key in the palm of my hand. . . . I saw Duke stroking his own key. Had to know! Now—through the pulsing blue-yellow-blue light and the unreadable words that were building up an awful pressure in the back of my brain—I could see the Four Horsemen. They were on their knees, crying, looking up at something and begging: *"Tell me tell me tell me tell me . . ."*

Then soft billows of rich red and orange fire filled the world and a huge voice was trying to speak. But it couldn't form the words. It stuttered and moaned—

The yellow-blue-yellow flashing around the words I couldn't read—the same words, I suddenly sensed, that the voice of the fire was trying so hard to form—and the Four Horsemen on their knees begging: *"Tell me tell me tell me . . ."*

The friendly warm fire trying so hard to speak—

"Tell me tell me tell me tell me . . ."

T minus 4 minutes . . . and counting. . . .

What were the words? What was the order? I could sense my men silently imploring me to tell them. After all, I was their captain, it was my duty to tell them. It was my duty to find out!

"Tell me tell me tell me . . ." The robed figures on their knees implored through the flickering pulse in my brain and I could almost make out the words . . . almost . . .

"Tell me tell me tell me . . . ," I whispered to the warm orange fire that was trying so hard but couldn't quite form the words. The men were whispering it too: "Tell me tell me . . ."

T minus 3 minutes . . . and counting. . . .

The question burning blue and yellow in my brain: WHAT WAS THE FIRE TRYING TO TELL ME? WHAT WERE THE WORDS I COULDN'T READ?

Had to unlock the words! Had to find the key!

A key . . . *the* key? THE KEY! And there was the lock that imprisoned the words, right in front of me! Put the key in the lock . . . I looked at Jeremy. Wasn't there some reason, long ago and far away, why Jeremy might try to stop me from putting the key in the lock?

But Jeremy didn't move as I fitted the key into the lock. . . .

T minus 2 minutes . . . and counting. . . .

Why wouldn't the Captain tell me what the order was? The fire knew, but it wouldn't tell. My head ached from the pulsing, but I couldn't read the words.

"Tell me tell me tell me . . . ,"I begged.

Then I realized that the Captain was asking too.

T minus 90 seconds . . . and counting. . . .

"Tell me tell me tell me . . . ," the Horsemen begged. And the words I couldn't read were a fire in my brain.

Duke's key was in the lock in front of us. From very far away, he said: "We have to do it together."

Of course . . . our keys . . . our keys would unlock the words!

I put my key into the lock. One, two, three, we turned our keys together. A lid on the console popped open. Under the lid were three red buttons. Three signs on the console lit up in red letters: "ARMED."

T minus 60 seconds . . . and counting. . . .

The men were waiting for me to give some order. I didn't know what the order was. A magnificent orange fire was trying to tell me but it couldn't get the words out. . . . Robed figures were praying to the fire. . . .

Then, through the yellow-blue flicker that hid the words I had to read, I saw a vast crowd encircling a tower. The crowd was on its feet begging silently—

The tower in the center of the crowd became the orange fire that was trying to tell me what the words were—

Became a great mushroom of billowing smoke and blinding orange-red glare . . .

T minus 30 seconds . . . and counting. . . .

The huge pillar of fire was trying to tell Jeremy and me what the words were, what we had to do. The crowd was screaming at the cloud of flame. The yellow-blue flicker was getting faster and faster behind the mushroom cloud. I could almost read the words! I could see that there were two of them!

T minus 20 seconds . . . and counting. . . .

Why didn't the Captain tell us? I could almost see the words!

Then I heard the crowd around the beautiful mushroom cloud shouting: "DO IT! DO IT! DO IT! DO IT! DO IT!"

T minus 10 seconds . . . and counting. . . .
"DO IT! DO IT! DO IT! DO IT! DO IT! DO IT! DO IT!"
What did they want me to do? Did Duke know?

9

The men were waiting! What was the order? They hunched
over the firing controls, waiting. . . . The firing controls . . . ?
"DO IT! DO IT! DO IT! DO IT! DO IT!"

8

"DO IT! DO IT! DO IT! DO IT! DO IT!": The crowd
screaming.
"Jeremy!" I shouted. "I can read the words!"

7

My hands hovered over my bank of firing buttons. . . .
"DO IT! DO IT! DO IT! DO IT!" the words said.
Didn't the Captain understand?

6

"What do they want us to do, Jeremy?"

5

Why didn't the mushroom cloud give the order? My men
were waiting! A good sailor craves action.
Then a great voice spoke from the pillar of fire: "DO IT . . .
DO IT . . . DO IT . . ."

4

"There's only one thing we can do down here, Duke."

3

"The order, men! Action! Fire!"

2

Yes, yes, yes! Jeremy—

1

I reached for my bank of firing buttons. All along the console, the men reached for their buttons. But I was too fast for them! I would be first!

0

THE BIG FLASH

QUESTIONS

1 Discuss the primitive nature of hard rock music and the dancing associated with it. Is it possible that the music and dance incite one to violence?
2 What real-life comparisons can be made with the wide-spread blood lust and thirst for destruction in this story?
3 Is Spinrad suggesting that if humanity is susceptible to evil then it should be destroyed? Is this the theme of Revelations?
4 Discuss the interrelationship between actual violence in society and the ever increasing violence we are subjected to in movies, TV, and fiction.
5 Discuss the rapid shifts in perspective throughout the story. What effect, if any, does this have on the reader?

SUGGESTED READINGS

Bradbury, Ray: *The Martian Chronicles*. Garden City, N.Y.: Doubleday & Company, Inc., 1958.

Burgess, Anthony: *A Clockwork Orange*. New York: W. W. Norton & Company, Inc., 1963.

Daniels, D. N., F. M. Gilula, and F. M. Ochberg (eds.): *Violence and the Struggle for Existence*. Boston: Little, Brown and Company, 1973.

Farmer, Philip José: *Flesh*. New York: Signet Books, New American Library, Inc., 1969.

Golding, William: *Lord of the Flies*. New York: Coward-McCann, Inc., 1962.

Heinlein, Robert A.: *Stranger in a Strange Land*. New York: Berkeley Publishing Corporation, 1961.

————: *Methuselah's Children.* New York: Signet Books, New American Library, Inc., 1958.

Herbert, Frank: *Dune.* New York: Ace Books, 1955.

Huxley, Aldous: *Ape and Essence.* New York: Harper & Brothers, 1948.

Keyes, Daniel: *Flowers for Algernon.* New York: Bantam Books, Inc., 1967.

Lewis, C. S.: *An Experiment in Criticism.* New York: Cambridge, University Press, 1961.

Lorenz, K.: *On Aggression.* New York: Harcourt, Brace & World, Inc., 1966.

Miller, Walter M.: *A Canticle for Liebowitz.* Philadelphia: J. B. Lippincott Company, 1960.

Spinrad, Norman: *The Iron Dream.* New York: Avon Book Division, The Hearst Corporation, 1972.

Storr, A.: *Human Aggression.* New York: Atheneum Publishers, 1968.

Vonnegut, Kurt: *Slaughterhouse Five.* New York: Delacorte Press, Dell Publishing Co., Inc., 1969.

Weiner, Norbert: *The Human Use of Human Beings: Cybernetics and Society.* 2d ed. rev., Garden City, N.Y.: Anchor Books, Doubleday & Company, Inc., 1954.

Wells, H. G.: *War of the Worlds.* New York: Armont Publishing Co., Inc., Classic Series.

PART 4
Man and His Children: Generations of Change

In 1802 William Wordsworth composed a poem including the line, "The Child is father of the Man." Wordsworth and his contemporaries saw in the child an innocence uncorrupted by society, a natural, spontaneous acceptance of life. Children possessed that most important quality to a poet—*imagination.* The Romantics sought to lower the psychic barriers between child and adult, to assert the continuity and unity of the human experience. When man refuses to learn from his offspring, when the senses become callous and the voice of youth begins to die, disaster is close at hand.

The later decades of the nineteenth century brought the Victorian frame of consciousness and with it the repression of all those qualities lauded by earlier poets. Children were not encouraged to develop on their own. As in the Gradgrind School of Dicken's *Hard Times,* utilitarianism ruled their education. Fantasy and imagination were driven, shamed, and literally beaten out of young minds. Facts, applied science, and materialism were force fed and the most valued child was a perverse reflection of his tutors. Those few writers, such as Lewis Carroll, who seemed to recognize the lost world of childhood, spoke not of growth and integration but of a detachment and retreat from adult life; they created an immovable barrier of regret and nostalgia between youth and maturity.

The twentieth century is the age of psychology. The shelves of every book shop, the racks in markets and drugstores—all contain volumes on child-raising. Yet with all our accumulated wisdom, man and his children still exist in a paradox of love and hate. We both covet and fear our own flesh and blood. We still express those diametrically opposed attitudes of the Romantics and Victorians. Since death is certain, children are our only hope for immortality. Every man, consciously or unconsciously, feels a sense of ownership regarding his children. In the mistaken belief that we can extend our own brief existence by creating younger replicas, we attempt to dominate and mold our progeny. Most parents remain blissfully ignorant of the tense struggle for self-expression. They are taken unawares by the inevitable solution—*The king must die. The son must kill the father* or remain forever a child, denied the potential responses of adult life.

The subtitle of this section is "Generations of Change." Each story concerns a child with more than what we normally consider "human" abilities. Their names are Paul, Simon, Absalom, and Kaph. In different ways, all but Paul succeed in severing the parental bonds.

"The Rocking-Horse Winner" opens with the aura of a traditional fairy tale—"There was a woman ..." The beautiful, hard-hearted, materialistic mother is plagued by one thing. She believes herself to be unlucky and to her luck means money. Her son Paul craves affection from a mother "who could not feel love ... for anybody." Paul is convinced that God has told him he possesses luck; consequently he creates a simple equation in his mind: his luck will yield money and money must lead to his mother's love.

The theme of the story is related to an old cliché: "lucky in money, unlucky in love." The artistry is evident in the way Lawrence weaves this memorable work around such a simple premise. The rockinghorse, which Paul rides in such a mad frenzy, becomes symbolic of the futile, life-destroying nature of the boy's quest. Horses are everywhere in Lawrence's fiction. Dynamic, sensual sources of energy, they represent the natural life force that he finds lacking in most humans. To discover Lawrence's opinion of his characters, a reader need only observe how they act in the presence of the horse. However, Paul's case is unique. Here the horse is not alive; it is a thing of springs and wood. Just as Paul becomes a manic, twisted parody of a normal child, the horse is an inanimate perversion of Lawrencian nature. The mother's insatiable desire is heard in the whispers of the house: "There must be more money! Oh-h-h there must be more money." Like Faust, Paul trades his sanity and his life in an effort to buy happiness. Is his *luck* something God-given? We can hardly believe that as his uncle makes a last observation to Paul's mother: "You're eighty-odd thousand to the good and a poor devil of a son to the bad."

In his memorable novel, *Lord of the Flies,* William Golding collapses the myth of children's innocence. Left alone on a deserted island, his school boys quickly metamorphose into a band of bloodthirsty devil-worshiping savages. Obviously social and moral restrictions are less firmly implanted in the child. Is it possible that the Romantic concept was totally invalid? Could it be that indeed children are closer to raw humanity and that evil is more nearly akin to their nature? If there is a question as to the demonic involvement in Paul's case, it quickly disappears in "Thus I Refute Beelzy." Beelzy is a nickname for Beelzebub, who, in Luke 11:15, is called "the chief of the devils." "Lord of the flies" is a translation of Beelzebub into English.

Collier's description of the Carter's summer house establishes the tone of this piece. It was "passing

close by beauty on its way to complete decay." It
would seem that Collier wants us to see Small Simon
driven toward decay by an archetypal clash of wills.
The father, Big Simon (who wants his son to be a
mirror image of himself), is a compulsive believer in
reality who sadistically threatens his son with violence
unless little Simon is willing to admit that his games
are unreal. The father is completely oblivious to the
import of the marks Small Simon must make with his
stick to summon his friend, Mr. Beelzy. Fathers must
love and protect their children; Mr. Beelzy does just
that. When asked "What is the pretend?" Small Simon
answers, "Big Simon and Small Simon." Big Simon
will not recognize the fact that his relationship to his
son is a fantasy created by his own egotism. He has
always been dead to the boy. What had begun as a
game quickly changes to reality. Play becomes ritual;
the irrational becomes the overt. By forcing his child
to name Beelzy, the wrath of the devil is vested upon
all but Big Simon's foot. To use the word is to incite the
bearer. Beelzy protects his little boy in a way that
Paul's luck could not.

Simon and Absalom have much in common. They
both are faced with the unyielding conviction of a
father who knows what is best for his son. There are
no overt devils in "Absalom" but there are sinister
overtones concerning the boy's heightened mental
capacity. We are asked to accept the theory that a
transition is taking place "from Homo sapiens to Homo
superior." Absalom is a member of this new species
as are all of the children in the Quizkid Crèche.

The father's name, Joel Locke is a thinly disguised
variant of John Locke, the seventeenth-century
philosopher who stressed logic, reason, and empiricism.
The Hebrew name Absalom is ironically translated
as "father of peace." The biblical Absalom was the
third son of King David. Although next in line of succession for the crown, Absalom revolted against his
father. Absalom's fervent desire to become king and
the corruption of his counselor, Achitophel, caused
him to wrongly assess his father's military strategy and
he is killed by Loab.

The author includes lines from the Bible's version of the Absalom story and there is no doubt we are meant to compare the two. Should the young prince wait calmly for the old king to die? Kuttner's work suggests the complexity of this question. He implies that Joel Locke may be jealous of his son. We must determine for ourselves how much of Mr. Locke's statement, "Immature intelligence is dangerous," stems from love and how much from his own ego. It is quite possible that, as Ryan suggests, Joel Locke is unconsciously trying to kill his son. Absalom believes the function of parents should be to protect superior children, not interfere with their growth. Obsessed with the desire to prove his control, the frustrated father resorts to violence. And yet, this threat of physical assault does not seem to justify the final destruction of Locke's free will. We are left with the haunting sense of repetition—"Someday Absalom would have a son."

Freud claims that the compulsion to repeat overrides even the pleasure principle. Parents dominate children; children struggle to be free. In most cases the family tension does not erupt in the violence portrayed by our stories, but the extreme reactions focus our attention as the norm could not. Ursula Le Guin's "Nine Lives" presents us with a clone, ten human beings artificially created from a donor's intestinal cells, ten entities that work and think as one. Who is the parent of this genetic innovation? The donor, John Chow? Or might it be "Scientific Man" obsessed by his desire to eliminate the erratic, emotional qualities of the individual? The clone appears to be "the first truly stable self-reliant human being . . . sufficient to itself physically, sexually, emotionally, intellectually."

The crux of the story revolves around the true "mother," the planet itself—more specifically the mine called Hellmouth. The descent of the clone into the mine and the emergence of Kaph as the only survivor recall the mythic quest where the hero is engulfed by a beast whose stomach represents hell, or the underworld. Here he must undergo a symbolic death, a cleansing, in order to discover the secret necessary to revive his dying society. On a psychological level the underworld visitation represents an inner journey which is to annihilate the individual ego and reach true self-understanding. Kaph is born through death, not one death but nine. He repeats the death throes for each of his clone. He must then learn the hardest human lesson—how to be alone. Kaph's growth from dependence to true individuality is guided by the bickering "inferior" specimens, Pugh and Martin. They are not brilliant; they are not always logical; but they are wise enough to know the difference between domination or egotism and love.

INFANT SORROW

William Blake

My mother groan'd! my father wept.
Into the dangerous world I leapt;
Helpless, naked, piping loud:
Like a fiend hid in a cloud.

Struggling in my father's hands,
Striving against my swadling bands,
Bound and weary I thought best
To sulk upon my mother's breast.

THE ROCKING-HORSE WINNER
D. H. Lawrence

There was a woman who was beautiful, who started with all the advantages, yet she had no luck. She married for love, and the love turned to dust. She had bonny children, yet she felt they had been thrust upon her and she could not love them. They looked at her coldly, as if they were finding fault with her. And hurriedly she felt she must cover up some fault in herself. Yet what it was that she must cover up she never knew. Nevertheless, when her children were present, she always felt the centre of her heart go hard. This troubled her, and in her manner she was all the more gentle and anxious for her children, as if she loved them very much. Only she herself knew that at the centre of her heart was a hard little place that could not feel love, no, not for anybody. Everybody else said of her: "She is such a good mother. She adores her children." Only she herself, and her children themselves, knew it was not so. They read it in each other's eyes.

There were a boy and two little girls. They lived in a pleasant house, with a garden, and they had discreet servants, and felt themselves superior to anyone in the neighbourhood.

Although they lived in style, they felt always an anxiety in the house. There was never enough money. The mother had a small income, and the father had a small income, but not nearly enough for the social position which they had to keep up. The father went into town to some office. But though he had good prospects, these prospects never materialized. There was always the grinding sense of the shortage of money, though the style was always kept up.

At last the mother said: "I will see if I can't make something." But she did not know where to begin. She racked her brains, and tried this thing and the other, but could not find anything successful. The failure made deep lines come into her face. Her children were growing up, they would have to go to school. There must be more money, there must be more money. The father, who was always very handsome and expensive in his tastes, seemed as if he never would be able to do anything worth doing.

And the mother, who had a great belief in herself, did not succeed any better, and her tastes were just as expensive.

And so the house came to be haunted by the unspoken phrase: There must be more money! There must be more money! The children could hear it all the time, though nobody said it aloud. They heard it at Christmas, when the expensive and splendid toys filled the nursery. Behind the shining modern rocking horse, behind the smart doll's-house, a voice would start whispering: "There must be more money! There must be more money!" And the children would stop playing, to listen for a moment. They would look into each other's eyes, to see if they had all heard. And each one saw in the eyes of the other two that they too had heard. "There must be more money! There must be more money."

It came whispering from the springs of the still-swaying rocking horse, and even the horse, bending his wooden, champing head, heard it. The big doll, sitting so pink and smirking in her new pram, could hear it quite plainly, and seemed to be smirking all the more self-consciously because of it. The foolish puppy, too, that took the place of the Teddy bear, he was looking so extraordinarily foolish for no other reason but that he heard the secret whisper all over the house: "There must be more money!"

Yet nobody ever said it aloud. The whisper was everywhere, and therefore no one spoke it. Just as no one ever says: "We are breathing!" in spite of the fact that breath is coming and going all the time.

"Mother," said the boy Paul one day, "why don't we keep a car of our own? Why do we always use uncle's, or else a taxi?"

"Because we're the poor members of the family," said the mother.

"But why are we, mother?"

"Well—I suppose," she said slowly and bitterly, "it's because your father has no luck."

The boy was silent for some time.

"Is luck money, mother?" he asked, rather timidly.

"No, Paul. Not quite. It's what causes you to have money."

"Oh!" said Paul vaguely. "I thought when Uncle Oscar said filthy lucker, it meant money."

"Filthy lucre does mean money," said the mother. "But it's lucre, not luck."

"Oh!" said the boy. "Then what is luck, mother?"

"It's what causes you to have money. If you're lucky you have money. That's why it's better to be born lucky than rich. If you're rich, you may lose your money. But if you're lucky, you will always get more money."

"Oh! Will you? And is father not lucky?"

"Very unlucky, I should say," she said bitterly.

The boy watched her with unsure eyes.

"Why?" he asked.

"I don't know. Nobody ever knows why one person is lucky and another unlucky."

"Don't they? Nobody at all? Does nobody know?"

"Perhaps God. But He never tells."

"He ought to, then. And aren't you lucky either, mother?"

"I can't be, if I married an unlucky husband."

"But by yourself, aren't you?"

"I used to think I was, before I married. Now I think I am very unlucky indeed."

"Why?"

"Well—never mind! Perhaps I'm not really," she said.

The child looked at her, to see if she meant it. But he saw, by the lines of her mouth, that she was only trying to hide something from him.

"Well, anyhow," he said stoutly, "I'm a lucky person."

"Why?" said his mother, with a sudden laugh.

He stared at her. He didn't even know why he had said it.

"God told me," he asserted, brazening it out.

"I hope He did, dear!" she said, again with a laugh, but rather bitter.

"He did, mother!"

"Excellent!" said the mother, using one of her husband's exclamations.

The boy saw she did not believe him; or, rather, that she paid no attention to his assertion. This angered him somewhat, and made him want to compel her attention.

He went off by himself, vaguely, in a childish way, seeking

for the clue to "luck." Absorbed, taking no heed of other people, he went about with a sort of stealth, seeking inwardly for luck. He wanted luck, he wanted it, he wanted it. When the two girls were playing dolls in the nursery, he would sit on his big rocking horse, charging madly into space, with a frenzy that made the little girls peer at him uneasily. Wildly the horse careered, the waving dark hair of the boy tossed, his eyes had a strange glare in them. The little girls dared not speak to him.

When he had ridden to the end of his mad little journey, he climbed down and stood in front of his rocking horse, staring fixedly into its lowered face. Its red mouth was slightly open, its big eye was wide and glassy-bright.

"Now!" he would silently command the snorting steed. "Now, take me to where there is luck! Now take me!"

And he would slash the horse on the neck with the little whip he had asked Uncle Oscar for. He knew the horse could take him to where there was luck, if only he forced it. So he would mount again, and start on his furious ride, hoping at last to get there. He knew he could get there.

"You'll break your horse, Paul!" said the nurse.

"He's always riding like that! I wish he'd leave off!" said his elder sister Joan.

But he only glared down on them in silence. Nurse gave him up. She could make nothing of him. Anyhow he was growing beyond her.

One day his mother and his Uncle Oscar came in when he was on one of his furious rides. He did not speak to them.

"Hallo, you young jockey! Riding a winner?" said his uncle.

"Aren't you growing too big for a rocking horse? You're not a very little boy any longer, you know," said his mother.

But Paul only gave a blue glare from his big, rather close-set eyes. He would speak to nobody when he was in full tilt. His mother watched him with an anxious expression on her face.

At last he suddenly stopped forcing his horse into the mechanical gallop, and slid down.

"Well, I got there!" he announced fiercely, his blue eyes still flaring, and his sturdy long legs straddling apart.

"Where did you get to?" asked his mother.

"Where I wanted to go," he flared back at her.

"That's right, son!" said Uncle Oscar. "Don't you stop till you get there. What's the horse's name?"

"He doesn't have a name," said the boy.

"Gets on without all right?" asked the uncle.

"Well, he has different names. He was called Sansovino last week."

"Sansovino, eh? Won the Ascot. How did you know his name?"

"He always talks about horse races with Bassett," said Joan.

The uncle was delighted to find that his small nephew was posted with all the racing news. Bassett, the young gardener, who had been wounded in the left foot in the war and had got his present job through Oscar Cresswell, whose batman he had been, was a perfect blade of the "turf." He lived in the racing events, and the small boy lived with him.

Oscar Cresswell got it all from Bassett.

"Master Paul comes and asks me, so I can't do more than tell him, sir," said Bassett, his face terribly serious, as if he were speaking of religious matters.

"And does he ever put anything on a horse he fancies?"

"Well—I don't want to give him away—he's a young sport, a fine sport, sir. Would you mind asking him yourself? He sort of takes a pleasure in it, and perhaps he'd feel I was giving him away, sir, if you don't mind."

Bassett was serious as a church.

The uncle went back to his nephew, and took him off for a ride in the car.

"Say, Paul, old man, do you ever put anything on a horse?" the uncle asked.

The boy watched the handsome man closely.

"Why, do you think I oughtn't to?" he parried.

"Not a bit of it! I thought perhaps you might give me a tip for the Lincoln."

The car sped on into the country, going down to Uncle Oscar's place in Hampshire.

"Honour bright?" said the nephew.

"Honour bright, son!" said the uncle.

"Well, then Daffodil."

"Daffodil! I doubt it, sonny. What about Mirza?"

"I only know the winner," said the boy. "That's Daffodil."

"Daffodil, eh?"

There was a pause. Daffodil was an obscure horse comparatively.

"Uncle!"

"Yes, son?"

"You won't let it go any further, will you? I promised Bassett."

"Bassett be damned, old man! What's he got to do with it?"

"We're partners. We've been partners from the first. Uncle, he lent me my first five shillings, which I lost. I promised him, honour bright, it was only between me and him; only you gave me that ten-shilling note I started winning with, so I thought you were lucky. You won't let it go any further, will you?"

The boy gazed at his uncle from those big, hot, blue eyes, set rather close together. The uncle stirred and laughed uneasily.

"Right you are, son! I'll keep your tip private. Daffodil, eh? How much are you putting on him?"

"All except twenty pounds," said the boy. "I keep that in reserve."

The uncle thought it a good joke.

"You keep twenty pounds in reserve, do you, you young romancer? What are you betting, then?"

"I'm betting three hundred," said the boy gravely. "But it's between you and me, Uncle Oscar! Honour bright?"

The uncle burst into a roar of laughter.

"It's between you and me all right, you young Nat Gould," he said, laughing. "But where's your three hundred?"

"Bassett keeps it for me. We're partners."

"You are, are you! And what is Bassett putting on Daffodil?"

"He won't go quite as high as I do, I expect. Perhaps he'll go a hundred and fifty."

"What, pennies?" laughed the uncle.

"Pounds," said the child, with a surprised look at his uncle. "Bassett keeps a bigger reserve than I do."

Between wonder and amusement Uncle Oscar was silent. He

pursued the matter no further, but he determined to take his nephew with him to the Lincoln races.

"Now, son," he said, "I'm putting twenty on Mirza, and I'll put five for you on any horse you fancy. What's your pick?"

"Daffodil, uncle."

"No, not the fiver on Daffodil!"

"I should if it was my own fiver," said the child.

"Good! Good! Right you are! A fiver for me and a fiver for you on Daffodil."

The child had never been to a race meeting before, and his eyes were blue fire. He pursed his mouth tight, and watched. A Frenchman just in front had put his money on Lancelot. Wild with excitement, he flayed his arms up and down, yelling "Lancelot! Lancelot!" in his French accent.

Daffodil came in first, Lancelot second, Mirza third. The child, flushed and with eyes blazing, was curiously serene. His uncle brought him four five-pound notes, four to one.

"What am I to do with these?" he cried, waving them before the boy's eyes.

"I suppose we'll talk to Bassett," said the boy. "I expect I have fifteen hundred now; and twenty in reserve; and this twenty."

His uncle studied him for some moments.

"Look here, son!" he said. "You're not serious about Bassett and that fifteen hundred, are you?"

"Yes, I am. But it's between you and me, uncle. Honour bright!"

"Honour bright all right, son! But I must talk to Bassett."

"If you'd like to be a partner, uncle, with Bassett and me, we could all be partners. Only, you'd have to promise, honour bright, uncle, not to let it go beyond us three. Bassett and I are lucky, and you must be lucky, because it was your ten shillings I started winning with . . ."

Uncle Oscar took both Bassett and Paul into Richmond Park for an afternoon, and there they talked.

"It's like this, you see, sir," Bassett said. "Master Paul would get me talking about racing events, spinning yarns, you know, sir. And he was always keen on knowing if I'd made or if I'd lost. It's about a year since, now, that I put five shillings on Blush of

Dawn for him—and we lost. Then the luck turned, with that ten shillings he had from you, that we put on Singhalese. And since that time, it's been pretty steady, all things considering. What do you say, Master Paul?"

"We're all right when we're sure," said Paul. "It's when we're not quite sure that we go down."

"Oh, but we're careful then," said Bassett.

"But when are you sure?" smiled Uncle Oscar.

"It's Master Paul, sir," said Bassett, in a secret, religious voice. "It's as if he had it from heaven. Like Daffodil, now, for the Lincoln. That was as sure as eggs."

"Did you put anything on Daffodil?" asked Oscar Cresswell.

"Yes, sir, I made my bit."

"And my nephew?"

Bassett was obstinately silent, looking at Paul.

"I made twelve hundred, didn't I, Bassett? I told uncle I was putting three hundred on Daffodil."

"That's right," said Bassett, nodding.

"But where's the money?" asked the uncle.

"I keep it safe locked up, sir. Master Paul he can have it any minute he likes to ask for it."

"What, fifteen hundred pounds?"

"And twenty! And forty, that is, with the twenty he made on the course."

"It's amazing!" said the uncle.

"If Master Paul offers you to be partners, sir, I would, if I were you; if you'll excuse me," said Bassett.

Oscar Cresswell thought about it.

"I'll see the money," he said.

They drove home again, and sure enough, Bassett came round to the garden-house with fifteen hundred pounds in notes. The twenty pounds reserve was left with Joe Glee, in the Turf Commission deposit.

"You see, it's all right, uncle, when I'm sure! Then we go strong, for all we're worth. Don't we, Bassett?"

"We do that, Master Paul."

"And when are you sure?" said the uncle, laughing.

"Oh, well, sometimes I'm absolutely sure, like about Daffodil," said the boy, "and sometimes I have an idea; and sometimes I haven't even an idea, have I, Bassett? Then we're careful, because we mostly go down."

"You do, do you! And when you're sure, like about Daffodil, what makes you sure, sonny?"

"Oh well, I don't know," said the boy uneasily. "I'm sure, you know, uncle; that's all."

"It's as if he had it from heaven, sir," Bassett reiterated.

"I should say so!" said the uncle.

But he became a partner. And when the Leger was coming on, Paul was "sure" about Lively Spark, which was a quite inconsiderable horse. The boy insisted on putting a thousand on the horse, Bassett went for five hundred, and Oscar Cresswell two hundred. Lively Spark came in first, and the betting had been ten to one against him. Paul had made ten thousand.

"You see," he said, "I was absolutely sure of him."

Even Oscar Cresswell had cleared two thousand.

"Look here, son," he said, "this sort of thing makes me nervous."

"It needn't, uncle! Perhaps I shan't be sure again for a long time."

"But what are you going to do with your money?" asked the uncle.

"Of course," said the boy, "I started it for mother. She said she had no luck, because father is unlucky, so I thought if I was lucky, it might stop whispering."

"What might stop whispering?"

"Our house. I hate our house for whispering."

"What does it whisper?"

"Why—why"—the boy fidgeted—"why, I don't know. But it's always short of money, you know, uncle."

"I know it, son, I know it."

"You know people send mother writs, don't you, uncle?"

"I'm afraid I do," said the uncle.

"And then the house whispers, like people laughing at you behind your back. It's awful, that is! I thought if I was lucky . . ."

"You might stop it," added the uncle.

The boy watched him with big blue eyes that had an uncanny cold fire in them, and he said never a word.

"Well, then!" said the uncle. "What are we doing?"

"I shouldn't like Mother to know I was lucky," said the boy.

"Why not, son?"

"She'd stop me."

"I don't think she would."

"Oh!"—and the boy writhed in an odd way—"I don't want her to know, uncle."

"All right, son! We'll manage it without her knowing."

They managed it very easily. Paul, at the other's suggestion, handed over five thousand pounds to his uncle, who deposited it with the family lawyer, who was then to inform Paul's mother that a relative had put five thousand pounds into his hands, which sum was to be paid out a thousand pounds at a time, on the mother's birthday, for the next five years.

"So she'll have a birthday present of a thousand pounds for five successive years," said Uncle Oscar. "I hope it won't make it all the harder for her later."

Paul's mother had her birthday in November. The house had been "whispering" worse than ever lately, and, even in spite of his luck, Paul could not bear up against it. He was very anxious to see the effect of the birthday letter, telling his mother about the thousand pounds.

When there were no visitors, Paul now took his meals with his parents, as he was beyond the nursery control. His mother went into town nearly every day. She had discovered that she had an odd knack of sketching furs and dress materials, so she worked secretly in the studio of a friend who was the chief "artist" for the leading drapers. She drew the figures of ladies in furs and ladies in silk and sequins for the newspaper advertisements. This young woman artist earned several thousand pounds a year, but Paul's mother only made several hundred, and she was again dissatisfied. She so wanted to be first in something, and she did not succeed, even in making sketches for drapery advertisements.

She was down to breakfast on the morning of her birthday.

Paul watched her face as she read her letters. He knew the lawyer's letter. As his mother read it, her face hardened and became more expressionless. Then a cold, determined look came on her mouth. She hid the letter under the pile of others, and said not a word about it.

"Didn't you have anything nice in the post for your birthday, mother?" said Paul.

"Quite moderately nice," she said, her voice cold and absent.

She went away to town without saying more.

But in the afternoon Uncle Oscar appeared. He said Paul's mother had had a long interview with the lawyer, asking if the whole five thousand could be advanced at once, as she was in debt.

"What do you think, uncle?" said the boy.

"I leave it to you, son."

"Oh, let her have it, then! We can get some more with the other," said the boy.

"A bird in the hand is worth two in the bush, laddie!" said Uncle Oscar.

"But I'm sure to know for the Grand National; or the Lincolnshire; or else the Derby. I'm sure to know for one of them," said Paul.

So Uncle Oscar signed the agreement, and Paul's mother touched the whole five thousand. Then something very curious happened. The voices in the house suddenly went mad, like a chorus of frogs on a spring evening. There were certain new furnishings, and Paul had a tutor. He was really going to Eton, his father's school, in the following autumn. There were flowers in the winter, and a blossoming of the luxury Paul's mother had been used to. And yet the voices in the house, behind the sprays of mimosa and almond blossom, and from under the piles of iridescent cushions, simply trilled and screamed in a sort of ecstasy: "There must be more money! Oh-h-h, there must be more money. Oh, now, now-w! Now-w-w—there must be more money—more than ever! More than ever!"

It frightened Paul terribly. He studied away at his Latin and Greek with his tutors. But his intense hours were spent with Bassett. The Grand National had gone by: he had not "known," and had lost a hundred pounds. Summer was at hand. He was in agony for the Lincoln. But even for the Lincoln he didn't "know" and he lost fifty pounds. He became wild-eyed and strange, as if something were going to explode in him.

"Let it alone, son! Don't you bother about it!" urged Uncle Oscar. But it was as if the boy couldn't really hear what his uncle was saying.

"I've got to know for the Derby! I've got to know for the Derby!" the child reiterated, his big blue eyes blazing with a sort of madness.

His mother noticed how overwrought he was.

"You'd better go to the seaside. Wouldn't you like to go now to the seaside, instead of waiting? I think you'd better," she said, looking down at him anxiously, her heart curiously heavy because of him.

But the child lifted his uncanny blue eyes.

"I couldn't possibly go before the Derby, mother!" he said. "I couldn't possibly!"

"Why not?" she said, her voice becoming heavy when she was opposed. "Why not? You can still go from the seaside to see the Derby with your Uncle Oscar, if that's what you wish. No need for you to wait here. Besides, I think you care too much about these races. It's a bad sign. My family has been a gambling family, and you won't know till you grow up how much damage it has done. But it has done damage. I shall have to send Bassett away, and ask Uncle Oscar not to talk racing to you, unless you promise to be reasonable about it; go away to the seaside and forget it. You're all nerves!"

"I'll do what you like, mother, so long as you don't send me away till after the Derby," the boy said.

"Send you away from where? Just from this house?"

"Yes," he said, gazing at her.

"Why, you curious child, what makes you care about this house so much, suddenly? I never knew you loved it."

He gazed at her without speaking. He had a secret within a secret, something he had not divulged, even to Bassett or to his Uncle Oscar.

But his mother, after standing undecided and a little bit sullen for some moments, said:

"Very well, then! Don't go to the seaside till after the Derby, if you don't wish it. But promise me you won't let your nerves go to pieces. Promise you won't think so much about horse racing and events, as you call them!"

"Oh, no," said the boy casually. "I won't think much about them, mother. You needn't worry. I wouldn't worry, mother, if I were you."

"If you were me and I were you," said his mother, "I wonder what we should do!"

"But you know you needn't worry, mother, don't you?" the boy repeated.

"I should be awfully glad to know it," she said wearily.

"Oh, well, you can, you know. I mean, you ought to know, you needn't worry," he insisted.

"Ought I? Then I'll see about it," she said.

Paul's secret of secrets was his wooden horse, that which had no name. Since he was emancipated from a nurse and a nursery-governess, he had had his rocking horse removed to his own bedroom at the top of the house.

"Surely, you're too big for a rocking horse!" his mother had remonstrated.

"Well, you see, mother, till I can have a real horse, I like to have some sort of animal about," had been his quaint answer.

"Do you feel he keeps you company?" she laughed.

"Oh, yes! He's very good, he always keeps me company, when I'm there," said Paul.

So the horse, rather shabby, stood in an arrested prance in the boy's bedroom.

The Derby was drawing near, and the boy grew more and more tense. He hardly heard what was spoken to him, he was very frail, and his eyes were really uncanny. His mother had sudden seizures of uneasiness about him. Sometimes, for half-an-hour, she would feel a sudden anxiety about him that was almost anguish. She wanted to rush to him at once, and know he was safe.

Two nights before the Derby, she was at a big party in town, when one of her rushes of anxiety about her boy, her first-born, gripped her heart till she could hardly speak. She fought with the feeling, might and main, for she believed in common sense. But it was too strong. She had to leave the dance and go downstairs to telephone to the country. The children's nursery-governess was terribly surprised and startled at being rung up in the night.

"Are the children all right Miss Wilmot?"

"Oh, yes, they are quite all right."

"Master Paul? Is he all right?"

"He went to bed as right as a trivet. Shall I run up and look at him?"

"No," said Paul's mother reluctantly. "No! Don't trouble. It's all right. Don't sit up. We shall be home fairly soon." She did not want her son's privacy intruded upon.

"Very good," said the governess.

It was about one o'clock when Paul's mother and father drove up to their house. All was still. Paul's mother went to her room and slipped off her white fur coat. She had told her maid not to wait up for her. She heard her husband downstairs, mixing a whisky-and-soda.

And then, because of the strange anxiety at her heart, she stole upstairs to her son's room. Noiselessly she went along the upper corridor. Was there a faint noise? What was it?

She stood, with arrested muscles, outside his door, listening. There was a strange, heavy, and yet not loud noise. Her heart stood still. It was a soundless noise, yet rushing and powerful. Something huge, in violent, hushed motion. What was it? What in God's name was it? She ought to know. She felt that she knew the noise. She knew what it was.

Yet she could not place it. She couldn't say what it was. And on and on it went, like a madness.

Softly, frozen with anxiety and fear, she turned the door handle.

The room was dark. Yet in the space near the window, she heard and saw something plunging to and fro. She gazed in fear and amazement.

Then suddenly she switched on the light, and saw her son, in his green pyjamas, madly surging on the rocking horse. The blaze of light suddenly lit him up, as he urged the wooden horse, and lit her up, as she stood, blonde, in her dress of pale green and crystal, in the doorway.

"Paul" she cried. "Whatever are you doing?"

"It's Malabar!" he screamed, in a powerful, strange voice. "It's Malabar."

His eyes blazed at her for one strange and senseless second, as he ceased urging his wooden horse. Then he fell with a crash to the ground, and she, all her tormented motherhood flooding upon her, rushed to gather him up.

But he was unconscious, and unconscious he remained, with some brain fever. He talked and tossed, and his mother sat stonily by his side.

"Malabar! It's Malabar! Bassett, Bassett, I know it! It's Malabar!"

So the child cried, trying to get up and urge the rocking horse that gave him his inspiration.

"What does he mean by Malabar?" asked the heart-frozen mother.

"I don't know," said the father stonily.

"What does he mean by Malabar?" she asked her brother Oscar.

"It's one of the horses running for the Derby," was the answer.

And, in spite of himself, Oscar Cresswell spoke to Bassett, and himself put a thousand on Malabar: at fourteen to one.

The third day of the illness was critical: they were waiting for a change. The boy, with his rather long, curly hair, was tossing ceaselessly on the pillow. He neither slept nor regained consciousness, and his eyes were like blue stones. His mother sat, feeling her heart had gone, turned actually into a stone.

In the evening, Oscar Cresswell did not come, but Bassett sent a message, saying could he come up for one moment, just one moment? Paul's mother was very angry at the intrusion, but on second thought she agreed. The boy was the same. Perhaps Bassett might bring him to consciousness.

The gardener, a shortish fellow with a little brown moustache, and sharp little brown eyes, tiptoed into the room, touched his imaginary cap to Paul's mother, and stole to the bedside, staring with glittering, smallish eyes, at the tossing, dying child.

"Master Paul!" he whispered. "Master Paul! Malabar come in

first all right, a clean win. I did as you told me. You've made over seventy thousand pounds, you have; you've got over eighty thousand. Malabar came in all right, Master Paul."

"Malabar! Malabar! Did I say Malabar, mother? Did I say Malabar? Do you think I'm lucky, mother? I knew Malabar, didn't I? Over eighty thousand pounds! I call that lucky, don't you mother? Over eighty thousand pounds! I knew, didn't I know I knew? Malabar came in all right. If I ride my horse till I'm sure, then I tell you, Bassett, you can go as high as you like. Did you go for all you were worth, Bassett?"

"I went a thousand on it, Master Paul."

"I never told you, mother, that if I can ride my horse, and get there, then I'm absolutely sure—oh, absolutely! Mother, did I ever tell you? I'm lucky."

"No, you never did," said the mother.

But the boy died in the night.

And even as he lay dead, his mother heard her brother's voice saying to her: "My God, Hester, you're eighty-odd thousand to the good and a poor devil of a son to the bad. But, poor devil, poor devil, he's best gone out of a life where he rides his rocking horse to find a winner."

QUESTIONS

1 Does the fairy-tale quality of Lawrence's story detract from its seriousness?

2 Discuss the possibility that the story is not "fantasy" and that Paul's hallucinations are simply indicative of mental illness.

3 How does Lawrence want us to feel about Paul's uncle? Is he partially responsible for the boy's death?

4 Consider the quality of "luck." What does the word imply? Is a person born with it? Is it somehow earned or bestowed upon people? Do you feel that it comes from either God or the devil?

5 Discuss the character of Paul's mother. Does she merely exist as a stimulant for Paul's activity or do you feel that she becomes a well-developed, convincing person?

THUS I REFUTE BEELZY
John Collier

"There goes the tea bell," said Mrs. Carter. "I hope Simon hears it."

They looked out from the window of the drawing-room. The long garden, agreeably neglected, ended in a waste plot. Here a little summer-house was passing close by beauty on its way to complete decay. This was Simon's retreat. It was almost completely screened by the tangled branches of the apple tree and the pear tree, planted too close together, as they always are in the suburbs. They caught a glimpse of him now and then, as he strutted up and down, mouthing and gesticulating, performing all the solemn mumbo-jumbo of small boys who spend long afternoons at the forgotten ends of long gardens.

"There he is, bless him!" said Betty.

"Playing his game," said Mrs. Carter. "He won't play with the other children any more. And if I go down there—the temper! And comes in tired out!"

"He doesn't have his sleep in the afternoons?" asked Betty.

"You know what Big Simon's ideas are," said Mrs. Carter. " 'Let him choose for himself,' he says. That's what he chooses, and he comes in as white as a sheet."

"Look! He's heard the bell," said Betty. The expression was justified, though the bell had ceased ringing a full minute ago. Small Simon stopped in his parade exactly as if its tinny dingle had at that moment reached his ear. They watched him perform certain ritual sweeps and scratchings with his little stick, and come lagging over the hot and flaggy grass toward the house.

Mrs. Carter led the way down to the play-room, or garden-room, which was also the tea-room for hot days. It had been the huge scullery of this tall Georgian house. Now the walls were cream-washed, there was coarse blue net in the windows, canvas-covered armchairs on the stone floor, and a reproduction of Van Gogh's *Sunflowers* over the mantelpiece.

Small Simon came drifting in, and accorded Betty a perfunctory greeting. His face was an almost perfect triangle, pointed at the chin, and he was paler than he should have been. "The little elf-child!" cried Betty.

Simon looked at her. "No," said he.

At that moment the door opened, and Mr. Carter came in, rubbing his hands. He was a dentist, and washed them before and after everything he did. "You!" said his wife. "Home already!"

"Not unwelcome, I hope," said Mr. Carter, nodding to Betty. "Two people cancelled their appointments: I decided to come home. I said, I hope I am not unwelcome."

"Silly!" said his wife. "Of course not."

"Small Simon seems doubtful," continued Mr. Carter. "Small Simon, are you sorry to see me at tea with you?"

"No, Daddy."

"No, what?"

"No, Big Simon."

"That's right. Big Simon and Small Simon. That sounds more like friends, doesn't it? At one time little boys had to call their father 'sir.' If they forgot—a good spanking. On the bottom, Small Simon! On the bottom!" said Mr. Carter, washing his hands once more with his invisible soap and water.

The little boy turned crimson with shame or rage.

"But now, you see," said Betty, to help, "you can call your father whatever you like."

"And what," asked Mr. Carter, "has Small Simon been doing this afternoon? While Big Simon has been at work."

"Nothing," muttered his son.

"Then you have been bored," said Mr. Carter. "Learn from experience, Small Simon. Tomorrow, do something amusing, and you will not be bored. I want him to learn from experience, Betty. That is my way, the new way."

"I have learned," said the boy, speaking like an old, tired man, as little boys so often do.

"It would hardly seem so," said Mr. Carter, "if you sit on your behind all afternoon, doing nothing. Had *my* father caught me doing nothing, I should not have sat very comfortably."

"He played," said Mrs. Carter.

"A bit," said the boy, shifting on his chair.

"Too much," said Mrs. Carter. "He comes in all nervy and dazed. He ought to have his rest."

"He is six," said her husband. "He is a reasonable being. He must choose for himself. But what game is this, Small Simon, that is worth getting nervy and dazed over? There are very few games as good as all that."

"It's nothing," said the boy.

"Oh, come," said his father. "We are friends, are we not? You can tell me. I was a Small Simon once, just like you, and played the same games you play. Of course there were no aeroplanes in those days. With whom do you play this fine game? Come on, we must all answer civil questions, or the world would never go round. With whom do you play?"

"Mr. Beelzy," said the boy, unable to resist.

"Mr. Beelzy?" said his father, raising his eyebrows inquiringly at his wife.

"It's a game he makes up," said she.

"Not makes up!" cried the boy. "Fool!"

"That is telling stories," said his mother. "And rude as well. We had better talk of something different."

"No wonder he is rude," said Mr. Carter, "if you say he tells lies, and then insist on changing the subject. He tells you his fantasy: you implant a guilt feeling. What can you expect? A defence mechanism. Then you get a real lie."

"Like in *These Three*," said Betty. "Only different, of course. *She* was an unblushing little liar."

"I would have made her blush," said Mr. Carter, "in the proper part of her anatomy. But small Simon is in the fantasy stage. Are you not, Small Simon? You just make things up."

"No, I don't," said the boy.

"You do," said his father. "And because you do, it is not too late to reason with you. There is no harm in a fantasy, old chap. There is no harm in a bit of make-believe. Only you have to know the difference between day dreams and real things, or your brain will never grow. It will never be the brain of a Big Simon. So come on. Let us hear about this Mr. Beelzy of yours. Come on. What is he like?"

"He isn't like anything," said the boy.

"Like nothing on earth?" said his father. "That's a terrible fellow."

"I'm not frightened of him," said the child, smiling. "Not a bit."

"I should hope not," said his father. "If you were, you would be frightening yourself. I am always telling people, older people than you are, that they are just frightening themselves. Is he a funny man? Is he a giant?"

"Sometimes he is," said the little boy.

"Sometimes one thing, sometimes another," said his father. "Sounds pretty vague. Why can't you tell us just what he's like?"

"I love him," said the small boy. "He loves me."

"That's a big word," said Mr. Carter. "That might be better kept for real things, like Big Simon and Small Simon."

"He is real," said the boy, passionately. "He's not a fool. He's real."

"Listen," said his father. "When you go down the garden there's nobody there. Is there?"

"No," said the boy.

"Then you think of him, inside your head, and he comes."

"No," said Small Simon. "I have to make marks. On the ground. With my stick."

"That doesn't matter."

"Yes, it does."

"Small Simon, you are being obstinate," said Mr. Carter. "I am trying to explain something to you. I have been longer in the world than you have, so naturally I am older and wiser. I am explaining that Mr. Beelzy is a fantasy of yours. Do you hear? Do you understand?"

"Yes, Daddy."

"He is a game. He is a let's-pretend."

The little boy looked down at his plate, smiling resignedly.

"I hope you are listening to me," said his father. "All you have to do is to say, 'I have been playing a game of let's-pretend. With someone I make up, called Mr. Beelzy.' Then no one will say you tell lies, and you will know the difference between dreams and reality. Mr. Beelzy is a day dream."

The little boy still stared at his plate.

"He is sometimes there and sometimes not there," pursued Mr. Carter. "Sometimes he's like one thing, sometimes another. You can't really see him. Not as you see me. I am real. You can't touch him. You can touch me. I can touch you." Mr. Carter stretched out his big, white dentist's hand, and took his little son by the nape of the neck. He stopped speaking for a moment and tightened his hand. The little boy sank his head still lower.

"Now you know the difference," said Mr. Carter, "between a pretend and a real thing. You and I are one thing; he is another. Which is the pretend? Come on. Answer me. What is the pretend?"

"Big Simon and Small Simon," said the little boy.

"Don't!" cried Betty, and at once put her hand over her mouth, for why should a visitor cry "Don't!" when a father is explaining things in a scientific and modern way? Besides, it annoys the father.

"Well, my boy," said Mr. Carter, "I have said you must be allowed to learn from experience. Go upstairs. Right up to your room. You shall learn whether it is better to reason, or to be perverse and obstinate. Go up. I shall follow you."

"You are not going to beat the child?" cried Mrs. Carter.

"No," said the little boy. "Mr. Beelzy won't let him."

"Go on up with you!" shouted his father.

Small Simon stopped at the door. "He said he wouldn't let anyone hurt me," he whimpered. "He said he'd come like a lion, with wings on, and eat them up."

"You'll learn how real he is!" shouted his father after him. "If you can't learn it at one end, you shall learn it at the other. I'll have your breeches down. I shall finish my cup of tea first, however," said he to the two women.

Neither of them spoke. Mr. Carter finished his tea, and unhurriedly left the room, washing his hands with his invisible soap and water.

Mrs. Carter said nothing. Betty could think of nothing to say. She wanted to be talking for she was afraid of what they might hear.

Suddenly it came. It seemed to tear the air apart. "Good

God!" she cried. "What was that? He's hurt him." She sprang out of her chair, her silly eyes flashing behind her glasses. "I'm going up there!" she cried, trembling.

"Yes, let us go up," said Mrs. Carter. "Let us go up. That was not Small Simon."

It was on the second floor landing that they found the shoe, with the man's foot still in it, like that last morsel of a mouse which sometimes falls unnoticed from the side of the jaws of the cat.

QUESTIONS

1 The name Simon has Biblical connotations (i.e., Simon called Peter) as well as recalling the fairy-tale character Simple Simon. Can either or both of these associations be helpful in interpreting the story?

2 Discuss the relationships between games, ritual, and overt violence.

3 Is it necessary to believe in devils to derive any meaning from this story?

4 Do parents who advocate physical violence to assert their authority always run a marked risk of instilling hatred in their children?

5 Are children less shocked and appalled by blood and violence because they are not conditioned by conventional morality?

6 Explain Small Simon's behavior. Are his activities unusual for a child his age? If you have ever pretended to have an invisible friend, what was your parents' reaction?

ABSALOM
Henry Kuttner

At dusk Joel Locke came home from the university where he held the chair of psychonamics. He came quietly into the house, by a side door, and stood listening, a tall, tight-lipped man of forty with a faintly sardonic mouth and cool grey eyes. He could hear the precipitron humming. That meant that Abigail Schuler, the housekeeper, was busy with her duties. Locke smiled slightly and turned toward a panel in the wall that opened at his approach.

The small elevator took him noiselessly upstairs.

There, he moved with curious stealth. He went directly to a door at the end of the hall and paused before it, his head bent, his eyes unfocused. He heard nothing. Presently he opened the door and stepped into the room.

Instantly the feeling of unsureness jolted back, freezing him where he stood. He made no sign, though his mouth tightened. He forced himself to remain quiet as he glanced around.

It could have been the room of a normal twenty-year-old, not a boy of eight. Tennis racquets were heaped in a disorderly fashion against a pile of book records. The thiaminizer was turned on, and Locke automatically clicked the switch over. Abruptly he turned. The televisor screen was blank, yet he could have sworn that eyes had been watching him from it.

This wasn't the first time it had happened.

After a while Locke turned again and squatted to examine the book reels. He picked out one labeled "BRIAFF ON EN-TROPIC LOGIC" and turned the cylinder over in his hands, scowling. Then he replaced it and went out of the room, with a last, considering look at the televisor.

Downstairs Abigail Schuler was fingering the Mastermaid switchboard. Her prim mouth was as tight as the severe bun of gray-shot hair at the back of her neck.

"Good evening," Locke said. "Where's Absalom?"

"Out playing, Brother Locke," the housekeeper said formally. "You're home early. I haven't finished the living room yet."

"Well, turn on the ions and let 'em play," Locke said. "It won't take long. I've got some papers to correct, anyway."

He started out, but Abigail coughed significantly.

"Well?"

"He's looking peaked."

"Then outdoor exercise is what he needs," Locke said shortly. "I'm going to send him to a summer camp."

"Brother Locke," Abigail said, "I don't see why you don't let him go to Baja California. He's set his heart on it. You let him study all the hard subjects he wanted before. Now you put your foot down. It's none of my affair, but I can tell he's pining."

"He'd pine worse if I said yes. I've my reasons for not wanting him to study entropic logic. Do you know what it involves?"

"I don't—you know I don't. I'm not an educated woman, Brother Locke. But Absalom is bright as a button."

Locke made an impatient gesture.

"You have a genius for understatement," he said. "Bright as a button!"

Then he shrugged and moved to the window, looking down at the play court below, where his eight-year-old son played handball. Absalom did not look up. He seemed engrossed in his game. But Locke, watching, felt a cool, stealthy terror steal through his mind, and behind his back his hands clenched together.

A boy who looked ten, whose maturity level was twenty, and yet who was still a child of eight. Not easy to handle. There were many parents just now with the same problem—something was happening to the graph curve that charted the percentage of child geniuses born in recent times. Something had begun to stir lazily far back in the brains of the coming generations, and a new species, of a sort, was coming slowly into being. Locke knew that well. In his own time he, too, had been a child genius.

Other parents might meet the problem in other ways, he thought stubbornly. Not himself. He *knew* what was best for Absalom. Other parents might send their genius children to one of the crèches where they could develop among their own kind. Not Locke.

"Absalom's place is here," he said aloud. "With me, where

I can—" He caught the housekeeper's eye and shrugged again, irritably, going back to the conversation that had broken off. "Of course he's bright. But not bright enough yet to go to Baja California and study entropic logic. Entropic logic: It's too advanced for the boy. Even you ought to realize that. It isn't like a lollypop you can hand the kid—first making sure there's castor oil in the bathroom closet. Absalom's immature. It would actually be dangerous to send him to the Baja California University now to study with men three times his age. It would involve mental strain he isn't fit for yet. I don't want him turned into a psychopath."

Abigail's prim mouth pursed up sourly.

"You let him take calculus."

"Oh, leave me alone." Locke glanced down again at the small boy on the play court. "I think," he said slowly, "that it's time for another rapport with Absalom."

The housekeeper looked at him sharply, opened her thin lips to speak, and then closed them with an almost audible snap of disapproval. She didn't understand entirely, of course, how a rapport worked or what it accomplished. She only knew that there were ways in which it was possible to enforce hypnosis, to pry open a mind willy-nilly and search it for contraband thoughts. She shook her head, lips pressed tight.

"Don't try to interfere in things you don't understand," Locke said. "I tell you, I know what's best for Absalom. He's in the same place I was thirty-odd years ago. Who could know better? Call him in, will you? I'll be in my study."

Abigail watched his retreating back, a pucker between her brows. It was hard to know what was best. The mores of the day demanded rigid good conduct, but sometimes a person had trouble deciding in her own mind what was the right thing to do. In the old days, now, after the atomic wars, when license ran riot and anybody could do anything he pleased, life must have been easier. Nowadays, in the violent backswing to a Puritan culture, you were expected to think twice and search your soul before you did a doubtful thing.

Well, Abigail had no choice this time. She clicked on the wall microphone and spoke into it.

"Absalom?"

"Yes, Sister Schuler?"

"Come in. Your father wants you."

In his study Locke stood quiet for a moment, considering. Then he reached for the house microphone.

"Sister Schuler, I'm using the televisor. Ask Absalom to wait."

He sat down before his private visor. His hands moved deftly.

"Get me Dr. Ryan, the Wyoming Quizkid Crèche. Joel Locke calling."

Idly as he waited he reached out to take an old-fashioned cloth-bound book from a shelf of antique curiosa. He read:

But Absalom sent spies throughout all the tribes of Israel, saying, As soon as ye hear the sound of the trumpet, then ye shall say, Absolom reigneth in Hebron.

"Brother Locke?" the televisor asked.

The face of a white-haired, pleasant-featured man showed on the screen. Locke replaced the book and raised his hand in greeting.

"Dr. Ryan. I'm sorry to keep bothering you."

"That's all right," Ryan said. "I've plenty of time. I'm supposed to be supervisor at the crèche, but the kids are running it to suit themselves." He chuckled. "How's Absalom?"

"There's a limit," Locke said sourly. "I've given the kid his head, outlined a broad curriculum, and now he wants to study entropic logic. There are only two universities that handle the subject, and the nearest's in Baja California."

"He could commute by 'copter, couldn't he?" Ryan asked, but Locke grunted disapproval.

"Take too long. Besides, one of the requirements is in-boarding, under a strict regime. The discipline, mental and physical, is supposed to be necessary in order to master entropic logic. Which is spinach. I got the rudiments at home, though I had to use the tri-disney to visualize it."

Ryan laughed.

"The kids here are taking it up. Uh—are you sure **you** understood it?"

"Enough, yeah. Enough to realize it's nothing for a kid to study until his horizons have expanded."

"We're having no trouble with it," the doctor said. Don't forget that Absalom's a genius, not an ordinary youngster."

"I know. I know my responsibility too. A normal home environment has to be maintained to give Absalom some sense of security—which is one reason I don't want the boy to live in Baja California just now. I want to be able to protect him."

"We've disagreed on that point before. All the quizkids are pretty self-sufficient, Locke."

"Absalom's a genius, and a child. Therefore he's lacking in a sense of porportion. There are more dangers for him to avoid. I think it's a grave mistake to give the quizkids their heads and let them do what they like. I refused to send Absalom to a crèche for an excellent reason. Putting all the boy geniuses in a batch and letting them fight it out—completely artificial environment."

"I'm not arguing," Ryan said. "It's your business. Apparently you'll never admit that there's a sine curve of geniuses these days. A steady increase. In another generation—"

"I was a child genius myself, but I got over it," Locke said irritably. "I had enough trouble with my father. He was a tyrant, and if I hadn't been lucky, he'd have managed to warp me psychologically way out of line. I adjusted, but I had trouble. I don't want Absalom to have that trouble. That's why I'm using psychonamics."

"Narcosynthesis? Enforced hypnotism?"

"It's not enforced," Locke snapped. It's a valuable mental catharsis. Under hypnosis, he tells me everything that's on his mind, and I can help him."

"I didn't know you were doing that," Ryan said slowly. "I'm not at all sure it's a good idea."

"I don't tell you how to run your crèche."

No. But the kids do. A lot of them are smarter than I am."

"Immature intelligence is dangerous. A kid will skate on thin ice without making a test first. Don't think I'm holding

Absalom back. I'm just running tests for him first. I make sure the ice will hold him. Entropic logic I can understand, but he can't —yet. So he'll have to wait on that."

"Well?"

Locke hesitated. "Uh—do you know if your boys have been communicating with Absalom?"

"I don't know," Ryan said. "I don't interfere with their lives."

"All right, I don't want them interfering with mine, or with Absalom's. I wish you'd find out if they're getting in touch with him."

There was a long pause. Then Ryan said slowly:

"I'll try. But if I were you, Brother Locke, I'd let Absalom go to Baja California if he wants to."

"I know what I'm doing," Locke said, and broke the beam. His gaze went toward the Bible again.

Entropic logic!

Once the boy reached maturity, his somatic and physiological symptoms would settle toward the norm, but meanwhile the pendulum still swung wildly. Absalom needed strict control, for his own good.

And, for some reason, the boy had been trying to evade the hypnotic rapports lately. There was something going on.

Thoughts moved chaotically through Locke's mind. He forgot that Absalom was waiting for him, and remembered only when Abigail's voice, on the wall transmitter, announced the evening meal.

At dinner Abigail Schuler sat like Atropos between father and son, ready to clip the conversation whenever it did not suit her. Locke felt the beginnings of a long-standing irritation at Abigail's attitude that she had to protect Absalom against his father. Perhaps conscious of that, Locke himself finally brought up the subject of Baja California.

"You've apparently been studying the entropic logic thesis." Absalom did not seem startled. "Are you convinced yet that it's too advanced for you?"

"No, Dad," Absalom said, "I'm not convinced of that."

"The rudiments of calculus might seem easy to a youngster.

But when he got far enough into it—I went over that entropic logic, Son, through the entire book, and it was difficult enough for me. And I've a mature mind."

"I know you have. And I know I haven't—yet. But I still don't think it would be beyond me."

"Here's the thing," Locke said. "You might develop psychotic symptoms if you studied that thing, and you might not be able to recognize them in time. If we could have a rapport every night, or every other night, while you were studying—"

"But it's in Baja California!"

"That's the trouble. If you want to wait for my sabbatical, I can go there with you. Or one of the nearer universities may start the course. I don't want to be unreasonable. Logic should show you my motive."

"It does," Absalom said. "That part's all right. The only difficulty's an intangible, isn't it? I mean, you think my mind couldn't assimilate entropic logic safely, and I'm convinced that it could."

"Exactly," Locke said. "You've the advantage of knowing yourself better than I could know you. You're handicapped by immaturity, lack of a sense of proportion. And I've had the advantage of more experience."

"Your own, though, Dad. How much would such values apply to me?"

"You must let me be the judge of that, Son."

"Maybe," Absalom said. "I wish I'd gone to a quizkid crèche, though."

"Aren't you happy here?" Abigail asked, hurt, and the boy gave her a quick, warm look of affection.

"Sure I am, Abbie. You know that."

"You'd be a lot less happy with dementia praecox," Locke said sardonically. "Entropic logic, for instance, presupposes a grasp of temporal variations being assumed for problems involving relativity."

"Oh, that gives me a headache," Abigail said. "And if you're so worried about Absalom's overtraining his mind, you shouldn't talk to him like that." She pressed buttons and slid the cloisonné metal dishes into the compartment. "Coffee, Brother Locke . . . milk, Absalom . . . and I'll take tea."

Locke winked at his son, who merely looked solemn. Abigail rose with her teacup and headed toward the fireplace. Seizing the little hearth broom, she whisked away a few ashes, relaxed amid cushions, and warmed her skinny ankles by the wood fire. Locke patted back a yawn.

"Until we settle this argument, Son, matters must stand. Don't tackle that book on entropic logic again. Or anything else on the subject. Right?"

There was no answer.

"Right?" Locke insisted.

"I'm not sure," Absalom said after a pause. "As a matter of fact, the book's already given me a few ideas."

Looking across the table, Locke was struck by the incongruity of that incredibly developed mind in the childish body.

"You're still young," he said. "A few days won't matter. Don't forget that legally I exercise control over you, though I'll never do that without your agreement that I'm acting justly."

"Justice for you may not be justice for me," Absalom said, drawing designs on the tablecloth with his fingernail.

"We'll discuss it again until we've thrashed it out right. Now I've some papers to correct."

He went out.

"He's acting for the best, Absalom," Abigail said.

"Of course he is, Abbie," the boy agreed. But he remained thoughtful.

The next day Locke went through his classes in an absent-minded fashion, and at noon he televised Dr. Ryan at the Wyoming Quizkid Crèche. Ryan seemed entirely too casual and noncommittal. He said he had asked the quizkids if they had been communicating with Absalom, and they had said no.

"But they'll lie at the drop of a hat, of course, if they think it advisable," Ryan added, with inexplicable amusement.

"What's so funny?" Locke inquired.

"I don't know," Ryan said. "The way the kids tolerate me. I'm useful to them at times, but originally I was supposed to be supervisor here. Now the boys supervise me."

"Are you serious?"

Ryan sobered.

"I've a tremendous respect for the quizkids. And I think

you're making a very grave mistake in the way you're handling your son. I was in your house once, a year ago. It's *your* house. Only one room belongs to Absalom. He can't leave any of his possessions around anywhere else. You're dominating him tremendously."

"I'm trying to help him."

"Are you sure you know the right way?"

"Certain," Locke snapped. "Even if I'm wrong, does that mean I'm committing fl—filio—"

"That's an interesting point," Ryan said casually. "You could have thought of the right words for matricide, parricide, or fratricide easily enough. But it's seldom one kills his own son. The word doesn't come to the tongue quite as instantly."

Locke glared at the screen. "What the devil do you mean?"

"Just be careful," Ryan said. "I believe in the mutant theory, after running this crèche for fifteen years."

"I was a child genius myself," Locke repeated.

"Uh-huh," Ryan said, his eyes intent. "I wonder if you know that the mutation's supposed to be cumulative? Three generations ago two per cent of the population were child geniuses. Two generations ago, five per cent. One generation—a sine curve, Brother Locke. And the I.Q. mounts proportionately. Wasn't your father a genius too?"

"He was," Locke admitted. "But a maladjusted one."

"I thought so. Mutations take time. The theory is that the transition is taking place right now, from homo sapiens to homo superior."

"I know. It's logical enough. Each generation of mutations—this dominant mutation at least—taking another step forward till Homo superior is reached. What that will be—"

"I don't think we'll ever know," Ryan said quietly. "I don't think we'd understand. How long will it take, I wonder? The next generation? I don't think so. Five more generations, or ten or twenty? And each one taking another step, realizing another buried potentiality of homo, until the summit is reached. Superman, Joel."

"Absalom isn't a superman," Locke said practically. "Or a superchild, for that matter."

"Are you sure?"

"Good Lord! Don't you suppose I know my own son?"

"I won't answer that," Ryan said. "I'm certain that I don't know all there is to know about the quizkids in my crèche. Beltram, the Denver Crèche supervisor, tells me the same thing. These quizkids are the next step in the mutation. You and I are members of a dying species, Brother Locke."

Locke's face changed. Without a word he clicked off the televisor.

The bell was ringing for his next class. But Locke stayed motionless, his cheeks and forehead slightly damp.

Presently, his mouth twisted in a curiously unpleasant smile; he nodded and turned from the televisor . . .

He got home at five. He came in quietly, by the side entrance, and took the elevator upstairs. Absalom's door was closed, but voices were coming through it faintly. Locke listened for a time. Then he rapped sharply on the panel.

"Absalom. Come downstairs. I want to talk to you."

In the living room he told Abigail to stay out for a while. With his back to the fireplace, he waited until Absalom came.

*The enemies of my lord the king, and all
that rise against thee to do thee hurt,
be as that young man is.*

The boy entered without obvious embarrassment. He came forward and he faced his father, the boy's face calm and untroubled. He had poise, Locke saw, no doubt of that.

"I overheard some of your conversation, Absalom," Locke said.

"It's just as well," Absalom said coolly. "I'd have told you tonight anyway. I've got to go on with that entropic logic course."

Locke ignored that. "Who were you vising?"

"A boy I know. Malcolm Roberts, in the Denver Quizkid Crèche."

"Discussing entropic logic with him, eh? After what I told you?"

"You'll remember that I didn't agree."

Locke put his hands behind him and interlaced his fingers.

"Then you'll also remember that I mentioned that I had legal control over you."

"Legal," Absalom said, "yes. Moral, no."

"This has nothing to do with morals."

"It has, though. And with ethics. Many of the youngsters—younger than I—at the quizkid crèches are studying entropic logic. It hasn't harmed them. I must go to a crèche, or to Baja California. I must."

Locke bent his head thoughtfully.

"Wait a minute," he said. "Sorry, Son. I got emotionally tangled for a moment. Let's go back on the plane of pure logic."

"All right," Absalom said, with a quiet, imperceptible withdrawal.

"I'm convinced that that particular study might be dangerous for you. I don't want you to be hurt. I want you to have every possible opportunity, especially the ones I never had."

"No," Absalom said, a curious note of maturity in his high voice. "It wasn't lack of opportunity. It was incapability."

"What?" Locke said.

"You could never allow yourself to be convinced I could safely study entropic logic. I've learned that. I've talked to other quizkids."

"Of private matters?"

"They're of my race," Absalom said. "You're not. And please don't talk about filial love. You broke that law yourself long ago."

"Keep talking," Locke said quietly, his mouth tight. "But make sure it's logical."

"It is. I didn't think I'd ever have to do this for a long time, but I've got to now. You're holding me back from what I've got to do."

"The step mutation. Cumulative. I see."

The fire was too hot. Locke took a step away from the hearth. Absalom made a slight movement of withdrawal. Locke looked at him intently.

"It *is* a mutation," the boy said. "Not the complete one, but Grandfather was one of the first steps. You are farther along than he was. And I'm farther than you. My children will be closer toward the ultimate mutation. The only psychonamic experts worth anything are the child geniuses of your generation."

"Thanks."

"You're afraid of me," Absalom said. "You're afraid of me and jealous of me."

Locked started to laugh. "What about logic now?"

The boy swallowed. "It *is* logic. Once you were convinced that the mutation was cumulative, you couldn't bear to think I'd displace you. It's a basic psychological warp in you. You had the same thing with Grandfather, in a different way. That's why you turned to psychonamics, where you were a small god, dragging out the secret minds of your students, molding their brains as Adam was molded. You're afraid that I'll outstrip you. And I will."

"That's why I let you study anything you wanted, I suppose?" Locke asked. "With this exception."

"Yes, it is. A lot of child geniuses work so hard they burn themselves out and lose their mental capacities entirely. You wouldn't have talked so much about the danger if—under these circumstances—it hadn't been the one thing paramount in your mind. Sure you gave me my head. And, subconsciously, you were hoping I *would* burn myself out, so I wouldn't be a possible rival any more."

"I see."

"You let me study math, plane geometry, calculus, non-Euclidean, but you kept pace with me. If you didn't know the subject already, you were careful to bone up on it, to assure yourself that it was something you *could* grasp. You made sure I couldn't outstrip you, that I wouldn't get any knowledge you couldn't get. And that's why you wouldn't let me take entropic logic."

There was no expression on Locke's face.

"Why?" he asked coldly.

"You couldn't understand it yourself," Absalom said. "You tried it, and it was beyond you. You're not flexible. Your logic isn't flexible. It's founded on the fact that a second hand registers sixty seconds. You've lost the sense of wonder. You've translated too much from abstract to concrete. I *can* understand entropic logic. I can understand it!"

"You've picked this up in the last week," Locke said.

"No. You mean the rapports. A long time ago I learned to keep part of my mind blanked off under your probing."

"That's impossible!" Locke said, startled.

"It is for you. I'm a further step in the mutation. I have a lot of talents you don't know anything about. And I know this—I'm not far enough advanced for my age. The boys in the crèches are ahead of me. Their parents followed natural laws—it's the role of homo sapiens to protect homo superior, as it's the role of any parent to protect its young. Only the immature parents are out of step—like you."

Locke was still quite impassive.

"I'm immature? And I hate you? I'm jealous of you? You're quite settled on that?"

"Is it true or not?"

Locke didn't answer. "You're still inferior to me mentally," he said, "and you will be for some years to come. Let's say, if you want it that way, that your superiority lies in your—flexibility and your homo superior talents. Whatever they are. Against that, balance the fact that I'm a physically mature adult and you weigh less than half of what I do. I'm legally your guardian. And I'm stronger than you are."

Absalom swallowed again, but said nothing. Locke rose a little higher, looking down at the boy. His hand went to his middle, but found only a lightweight zipper.

He walked to the door. He turned.

"I'm going to prove to you that you're my inferior," he said coldly and quietly. "You're going to admit it to me."

Absalom said nothing.

Locke went upstairs. He touched the switch on his bureau, reached into the drawer, and withdrew an elastic lucite belt. He drew its cool, smooth length through his fingers once. Then he turned to the dropper again.

His lips were white and bloodless by now.

At the door of the living room he stopped, holding the belt. Absalom had not moved, but Abigail Schuler was standing beside the boy.

"Get out, Sister Schuler," Locke said.

"You're not going to whip him," Abigail said, her head held high, her lips purse-string tight.

"Get out."

"I won't. I heard every word. And it's true, all of it."

"Get out, I tell you!" Locke screamed.

He ran forward, the belt uncoiled in his hand. Absalom's nerve broke at last. He gasped with panic and dashed away, blindly seeking escape where there was none.

Locke plunged after him.

Abigail snatched up the little hearth broom and thrust it at Locke's legs. The man yelled something inarticulate as he lost his balance. He came down heavily, trying to brace himself against the fall with stiff arms.

His head struck the edge of a chair seat. He lay motionless.

Over his still body, Abigail and Absalom looked at each other. Suddenly the woman dropped to her knees and began sobbing.

"I've killed him," she forced out painfully. "I've killed him —but I couldn't let him whip you, Absalom—I couldn't!"

The boy caught his lower lip between his teeth. He came forward slowly to examine his father.

"He's not dead."

Abigail's breath came out in a long, shuddering sigh.

"Go on upstairs, Abbie," Absalom said, frowning a little. "I'll give him first aid. I know how."

"I can't let you—"

"Please, Abbie," he coaxed. "You'll faint or something. Lie down for a bit. It's all right, really."

At last she took the dropper upstairs. Absalom, with a thoughtful glance at his father, went to the televisor.

He called the Denver Crèche. Briefly he outlined the situation. "What had I better do, Malcolm?"

"Wait a minute." There was a pause. Another young face showed on the screen. "Do this," an assured, high-pitched voice said, and there followed certain intricate instructions. "Got that straight, Absalom?"

"I have it. It won't hurt him?"

"He'll live. He's psychotically warped already. This will just give it a different twist, one that's safe for you. It's projection. He'll externalize all his wishes, feelings, and so forth. On you. He'll get his pleasure only out of what *you* do, but he won't be able to control you. You know the psychonamic key to his brain. Work with the frontal lobe chiefly. Be careful of Broca's area. We don't want aphasia. He must be made harmless to you, that's all. Any killing would be awkward to handle. Besides, I suppose you wouldn't want that."

"No," Absalom said. "H-he's my father."

"All right," the young voice said, "Leave the screen on. I'll watch and help."

Absalom turned toward the unconscious figure on the floor.

For a long time the world had been shadowy now. Locke was used to it. He could still fulfill his ordinary functions, so he was not insane, in any sense of the word.

Nor could he tell the truth to anyone. They had created a psychic bloc. Day after day he went to the university and taught psychonomics and came home and ate and waited in hopes that Absalom would call him on the televisor.

And when Absalom called, he might condescend to tell something of what he was doing in Baja California. What he had accomplished. What he had achieved. For those things mattered now. They were the only things that mattered. The projection was complete.

Absalom was seldom forgetful. He was a good son. He called daily, though sometimes, when work was pressing, he had to make the call short. But Joel Locke could always work at his immense scrapbooks filled with clippings and photographs about Absalom. He was writing Absalom's biography too.

He walked otherwise through a shadow world, existing in flesh and blood, in realized happiness, only when Absalom's face appeared on the televisor screen. But he had not forgotten anything. He hated Absalom, and hated the horrible, unbreakable bond that would forever chain him to his own flesh—the flesh that was not quite his own, but one step farther up the ladder of the new mutation.

Sitting there in the twilight of unreality, his scrapbooks

spread before him, the televisor set never used except when Absalom called but standing ready before his chair, Joel Locke nursed his hatred and a quiet, secret satisfaction that had come to him.

Someday Absalom would have a son. Someday. Someday.

QUESTIONS

1   The creation of new words is an extremely important part of writing science fiction. The sound of a new word and any association between it and other similar words determine a reader's reaction. Examine this story and discuss the quality of Kuttner's additions to your vocabulary.
2   Would the story have been equally effective without any reference to the Bible?
3   What debt do you feel parents owe to children and children to parents?
4   Kuttner mentions a "violent backswing to a Puritan culture," with a rigid code of conduct. Do you foresee this eventually coming about in this country?
5   Do you feel that the generation gap would close if parents and children were able to have Kuttnerlike "rapport" sessions?
6   Compare Joel Locke with Big Simon Carter. What are their similarities and differences?
7   Absalom suggests that "justice" may have different meanings. Is there any "justice" in this story?

NINE LIVES

Ursula K. Le Guin

She was alive inside but dead outside, her face a black and dun net of wrinkles, tumors, cracks. She was bald and blind. The tremors that crossed Libra's face were mere quiverings of corruption: Underneath, in the black corridors, the halls beneath the skin, there were crepitations in darkness, ferments, chemical nightmares that went on for centuries. "Oh the damned flatulent planet," Pugh murmured as the dome shook and a boil burst a kilometer to the southwest, spraying silver pus across the sunset. The sun had been setting for the last two days. "I'll be glad to see a human face."

"Thanks," said Martin.

"Yours is human to be sure," said Pugh, "but I've seen it so long I can't see it."

Radvid signals cluttered the communicator which Martin was operating, faded, returned as face and voice. The face filled the screen, the nose of an Assyrian king, the eyes of a samurai, skin bronze, eyes the color of iron: young, magnificent. "Is that what human beings look like?" said Pugh with awe. "I'd forgotten."

"Shut up, Owen, we're on."

"Libra Exploratory Mission Base, come in please, this is *Passerine* launch."

"Libra here. Beam fixed. Come on down, launch."

"Expulsion in seven E-seconds. Hold on." The screen blanked and sparkled.

"Do they all look like that? Martin, you and I are uglier men than I thought."

"Shut up, Owen. . . ."

For twenty-two minutes Martin followed the landing craft down by signal and then through the cleared dome they saw it, small star in the blood-colored east, sinking. It came down neat and quiet, Libra's thin atmosphere carrying little sound. Pugh and Martin closed the headpieces of their imsuits, zipped out of the dome airlocks, and ran with soaring strides, Nijinsky and Nureyev, toward the boat. Three equipment modules came floating down at four-minute intervals from each other and hundred-meter intervals east of the boat. "Come on out," Martin said on his suit radio, "we're waiting at the door."

"Come on in, the methane's fine," said Pugh.

The hatch opened. The young man they had seen on the screen came out with one athletic twist and leaped down onto the shaky dust and clinkers of Libra. Martin shook his hand, but Pugh was staring at the hatch, from which another young man emerged with the same neat twist and jump, followed by a young woman who emerged with the same neat twist, ornamented by a wriggle, and the jump. They were all tall, with bronze skin, black hair, high-bridged noses, epicanthic fold, the same face. They all had the same face. The fourth was emerging from the hatch with a neat twist and jump. "Martin bach," said Pugh, "we've got a clone."

"Right," said one of them, "we're a tenclone. John Chow's the name. You're Lieutenant Martin?"

"I'm Owen Pugh."

"Alvaro Guillen Martin," said Martin, formal, bowing slightly. Another girl was out, the same beautiful face; Martin stared at her and his eye rolled like a nervous pony's. Evidently he had never given any thought to cloning and was suffering technological shock. "Steady," Pugh said in the Argentine dialect, "it's only excess twins." He stood close by Martin's elbow. He was glad himself of the contact.

It is hard to meet a stranger. Even the greatest extrovert meeting even the meekest stranger knows a certain dread, though he may not know he knows it. Will he make a fool of me wreck my image of myself invade me destroy me change me? Will he be different from me? Yes, that he will. There's the terrible thing: the strangeness of the stranger.

After two years on a dead planet, and the last half year isolated as a team of two, oneself and one other, after that it's even harder to meet a stranger, however welcome he may be. You're out of the habit of difference, you've lost the touch; and so the fear revives, the primitive anxiety, the old dread.

The clone, five males and five females, had got done in a couple of minutes what a man might have got done in twenty:

greeted Pugh and Martin, had a glance at Libra, unloaded the boat, made ready to go. They went, and the dome filled with them, a hive of golden bees. They hummed and buzzed quietly, filled up all silences, all spaces with a honey-brown swarm of human presence. Martin looked bewildered at the long-limbed girls, and they smiled at him, three at once. Their smile was gentler than that of the boys, but no less radiantly self-possessed.

"Self-possessed," Owen Pugh murmured to his friend, "that's it. Think of it, to be oneself ten times over. Nine seconds for every motion, nine ayes on every note. It would be glorious! But Martin was asleep. And the John Chows had all gone to sleep at once. The dome was filled with their quiet breathing. They were young, they didn't snore. Martin sighed and snored, his Hershey-bar-colored face relaxed in the dim afterglow of Libra's primary, set at last. Pugh had cleared the dome and stars looked in, Sol among them, a great company of lights, a clone of splendors. Pugh slept and dreamed of a one-eyed giant who chased him through the shaking halls of Hell.

From his sleeping bag Pugh watched the clone's awakening. They all got up within one minute except for one pair, a boy and a girl, who lay snugly tangled and still sleeping in one bag. As Pugh saw this there was a shock like one of Libra's earthquakes inside him, a very deep tremor. He was not aware of this and in fact thought he was pleased at the sight; there was no other such comfort on this dead hollow world, more power to them, who made love. One of the others stepped on the pair. They woke and the girl sat up flushed and sleepy, with bare golden breasts. One of her sisters murmured something to her; she shot a glance at Pugh and from another direction a fierce stare, from still another direction a voice: "Christ, we're used to having a room to ourselves. Hope you don't mind, Captain Pugh."

"It's a pleasure," Pugh said half truthfully. He had to stand up then wearing only the shorts he slept in, and he felt like a plucked rooster, all white scrawn and pimples. He had seldom envied Martin's compact brownness so much. The United Kingdom had come through the Great Famines well, losing less than half its population: a record achieved by rigorous food control. Black marketeers and hoarders had been executed. Crumbs had been shared. Where in richer lands most had died and a few had thriven, in Britain fewer died and none throve. They all got lean. Their sons were lean, their grandsons lean, small, brittle-boned, easily infected. When civilization became a matter of standing in lines, the British had kept queue and so had replaced the survival of the fittest with the survival of the fair-minded. Owen Pugh was a scrawny little man. All the same, he was there.

At the moment he wished he wasn't.

At breakfast a John said, "Now if you'll brief us, Captain Pugh—"

"Owen, then."

"Owen, we can work out our schedule. Anything new on the mine since your last report to your Mission? We saw your reports when *Passerine* was orbiting Planet V, where they are now."

Martin did not answer, though the mine was his discovery and project, and Pugh had to do his best. It was hard to talk to them. The same faces, each with the same expression of intelligent interest, all leaned toward him across the table at almost the same angle. They all nodded together.

Over the Exploitation Corps insigne on their tunics each had a nameband, first name John and last name Chow of course, but the middle names different. The men were Aleph, Kaph, Yod, Gimel, and Samedh; the women Sadhe, Daleth, Zayin, Beth, and Resh. Pugh tried to use the names but gave it up at once; he could not even tell sometimes which one had spoken, for all the voices were alike.

Martin buttered and chewed his toast, and finally interrupted: "You're a team. Is that it?"

"Right," said two Johns.

"God, what a team! I hadn't seen the point. How much do you each know what the others are thinking?"

"Not at all, properly speaking," replied one of the girls, Zayin. The others watched her with the proprietary, approving look they had. "No ESP, nothing fancy. But we think alike. We have exactly the same equipment. Given the same stimulus, the same problem, we're likely to be coming up with the same reactions and solutions at the same time. Explanations are easy—don't even have to make them, usually. We seldom misunderstand each other. It does facilitate our working as a team."

"Christ yes," said Martin. "Pugh and I have spent seven hours out of ten for six months misunderstanding each other. Like most people. What about emergencies, are you as good at meeting the unexpected problem as a nor . . . an unrelated team?"

"Statistics so far indicate that we are," Zayin answered readily. Clones must be trained, Pugh thought, to meet questions, to reassure and reason. All they said had the slightly bland and stilled quality of answers furnished to the Public. "We can't brainstorm as singletons can, we as a team don't profit from the interplay of varied minds; but we have a compensatory advantage. Clones are drawn from the best human material, individuals of IQ ninety-ninth percentile, Genetic Constitution alpha double A, and so on. We have more to draw on than most individuals do."

"And it's multiplied by a factor of ten. Who is—who was John Chow?"

"A genius surely," Pugh said politely. His interest in cloning was not so new and avid as Martin's.

"Leonardo Complex type," said Yod. "Biomath, also a cellist and an undersea hunter, and interested in structural engineering problems and so on. Died before he'd worked out his major theories."

"Then you each represent a different facet of his mind, his talents?"

"No," said Zayin, shaking her head in time with several others. "We share the basic equipment and tendencies, of course, but we're all engineers in Planetary Exploitation. A later clone can be trained to develop other aspects of the basic equipment. It's all training; the genetic substance is identical. We *are* John Chow. But we are differently trained."

Martin looked shell-shocked. "How old are you?"

"Twenty-three."

"You say he died young—had they taken germ cells from him beforehand or something?"

Gimel took over: "He died at twenty-four in an air car crash. They couldn't save the brain, so they took some intestinal cells and cultured them for cloning. Reproductive cells aren't used for cloning, since they have only half the chromosomes. Intestinal cells happen to be easy to despecialize and reprogram for total growth."

"All chips off the old block," Martin said valiantly. "But how can . . . some of you be women . . .?"

Beth took over: "It's easy to program half the clonal mass back to the female. Just delete the male gene from half the cells and they revert to the basic, that is, the female. It's trickier to go the other way, have to hook in artificial Y chromosomes. So they mostly clone from males, since clones function best bisexually."

Gimel again: "They've worked these matters of technique and function out carefully. The taxpayer wants the best for his money, and of course clones are expensive. With the cell manipulations, and the incubation in Ngama Placantae, and the maintenance and training of the foster-parent groups, we end up costing about three million apiece."

"For your next generation," Martin said, still struggling, "I suppose you . . . you breed?"

"We females are sterile," said Beth with perfect equanimity. "You remember that the Y chromosome was deleted from our original cell. The males can interbreed with approved singletons, if they want to. But to get John Chow again as often as they want, they just reclone a cell from this clone."

Martin gave up the struggle. He nodded and chewed cold toast. "Well," said one of the Johns, and all changed mood, like a flock of starlings that change course in one wingflick, following a leader so fast that no eye can see which leads. They were ready to go. "How about a look at the mine? Then we'll unload the equipment. Some nice new models in the roboats; you'll want to see them. Right?" Had Pugh or Martin not agreed they might have found it hard to say so. The Johns were polite but unanimous; their decisions carried. Pugh, Commander of Libra Base 2, felt a qualm. Could he boss around this superman-woman-entity-of-ten? and a genius at that? He stuck close to Martin as they suited for outside. Neither said anything.

Four apiece in the three large airjets, they slipped off north from the dome, over Libra's dun rugose skin, in starlight.

"Desolate," one said.

It was a boy and girl with Pugh and Martin. Pugh wondered if these were the two that had shared a sleeping bag last night. No doubt they wouldn't mind if he asked them. Sex must be as handy as breathing to them. Did you two breathe last night?

"Yes," he said, "it is desolate."

"This is our first time off, except training on Luna." The girl's voice was definitely a bit higher and softer.

"How did you take the big hop?"

"They doped us. I wanted to experience it." That was the boy; he sounded wistful. They seemed to have more personality, only two at a time. Did repetition of the individual negate individuality?

"Don't worry," said Martin, steering the sled, "you can't experience no-time because it isn't there."

"I'd just like to once," one of them said. "So we'd know."

The Mountains of Merioneth showed leprotic in starlight to the east, a plume of freezing gas trailed silvery from a vent-hole to the west, and the sled tilted groundward. The twins braced for the stop at one moment, each with a slight protective gesture to the other. Your skin is my skin, Pugh thought, but literally, no metaphor. What would it be like, then, to have someone as close to you as that? Always to be answered when you spoke; never to be in pain alone. Love your neighbor as you love yourself. . . . That hard old problem was solved. The neighbor was the self: the love was perfect.

And here was Hellmouth, the mine.

Pugh was the Exploratory Mission's ET geologist, and Martin his technician and cartographer; but when in the course of a local survey Martin had discovered the U-mine, Pugh had given him full credit, as well as the onus of prospecting the lode and planning the Exploitation Team's job. These kids had been sent out from Earth years before Martin's reports got there and had not known what their job would be until they got here. The Exploitation Corps simply sent out teams regularly and blindly as a dandelion sends out its seed, knowing there would be a job for them on Libra or the next planet out or one they hadn't even heard about yet. The government wanted uranium too urgently to wait while reports drifted home across the light-years. The stuff was like gold, old-fashioned but essential, worth mining extraterrestrially and shipping interstellar. Worth its weight in people, Pugh thought sourly, watching the tall young men and women go one by one, glimmering in starlight, into the black hole Martin had named Hellmouth.

As they went in their homeostatic forehead-lamps brightened. Twelve nodding gleams ran along the moist, wrinkled walls. Pugh heard Martin's radiation counter peeping twenty to the dozen up ahead. "Here's the drop-off," said Martin's voice in the suit intercom, drowning out the peeping and the dead silence that was around them. "We're in a side-fissure, this is the main vertical vent in front of us." The black void gaped, its far side not visible in the headlamp beams. "Last volcanism seems to have been a couple of thousand years ago. Nearest fault is twenty-eight kilos east, in the Trench. This area seems to be as safe seismically as anything in the area. The big basalt-flow overhead stabilizes all these substructures, so long as it remains stable itself. Your central lode is thirty-six meters down and runs in a series of five bubble caverns northeast. It is a lode, a pipe of very high-grade ore. You saw the percentage figures, right? Extraction's going to be no problem. All you've got to do is get the bubbles topside."

"Take off the lid and let 'em float up." A chuckle. Voices began to talk, but they were all the same voice and the suit radio gave them no location in space. "Open the thing right up —Safer that way. —But it's a solid basalt roof, how thick, ten meters here? —Three to twenty, the report said. —Blow good ore all over the lot. —Use this access we're in, straighten it a bit and run slider rails for the robos. —Import burros. —Have we got enough propping material? —What's your estimate of total pay-load mass, Martin?"

"Say over five million kilos and under eight."

"Transport will be here in ten E-months. —It'll have to go pure. —No, they'll have the mass problem in NAFAL shipping licked by now, remember it's been sixteen years since we left Earth last Tuesday. —Right, they'll send the whole lot back and purify it in Earth orbit. —Shall we go down, Martin?"

"Go on. I've been down."

The first one—Aleph? (Heb, the ox, the leader)—swung onto the ladder and down; the rest followed. Pugh and Martin stood at the chasm's edge. Pugh set his intercom to exchange only with Martin's suit, and noticed Martin doing the same. It was a bit wearing, this listening to one person think aloud in ten voices, or was it one voice speaking the thoughts of ten minds?

"A great gut," Pugh said, looking down into the black pit, its veined and warted walls catching stray gleams of headlamps far below. "A cow's bowel. A bloody great constipated intestine."

Martin's counter peeped like a lost chicken. They stood inside the dead but epileptic planet, breathing oxygen from tanks, wearing suits impermeable to corrosives and harmful radiations, resistant to a 200-degree range of temperatures, tearproof, and as shock-resistant as possible given the soft vulnerable stuff inside.

"Next hop," Martin said, "I'd like to find a planet that has nothing whatever to exploit."

"You found this."

"Keep me home next time."

Pugh was pleased. He had hoped Martin would want to go on working with him, but neither of them was used to talking much about their feelings, and he had hesitated to ask. "I'll try that," he said.

"I hate this place. I like caves, you know. It's why I came in here. Just spelunking. But this one's a bitch. Mean. You can't ever let down in here. I guess this lot can handle it, though. They know their stuff."

"Wave of the future, whatever," said Pugh.

The wave of the future came swarming up the ladder, swept Martin to the entrance, gabbled at and around him: "Have we got enough material for supports?—If we convert one of the extractor servos to anneal, yes.—Sufficient if we miniblast?—Kaph can calculate stress—" Pugh had switched his intercom back to receive them; he looked at them, so many thoughts jabbering in an eager mind, and at Martin standing silent among them, and at Hellmouth and the wrinkled plain.—"Settled! How does that strike you as a preliminary schedule, Martin?"

"It's your baby," Martin said.

Within five E-days the Johns had all their material and equipment unloaded and operating and were starting to open up the mine. They worked with total efficiency. Pugh was fascinated and frightened by their effectiveness, their confidence, their independence. He was no use to them at all. A clone, he thought, might indeed be the first truly stable, self-reliant human being. Once adult it would need nobody's help. It would be sufficient to itself physically, sexually, emotionally, intellectually. Whatever he did, any member of it would always receive the support and approval of his peers, his other selves. Nobody else was needed.

Two of the clone stayed in the dome doing calculations and paperwork, with frequent sled trips to the mine for measurements and tests. They were the mathematicians of the clone, Zayin and Kaph. That is, as Zayin explained, all ten had had thorough mathematical training from age three to twenty-one, but from twenty-one to twenty-three she and Kaph had gone on with math while the others intensified other specialties, geology, mining, engineering, electronic engineering, equipment robotics, applied atomics, and so on. "Kaph and I feel," she said, "that we're the element of the clone closest to what John Chow was in his singleton lifetime. But of course he was principally in biomath, and they didn't take us far in that."

"They needed us most in this field," Kaph said, with the patriotic priggishness they sometimes evinced.

Pugh and Martin soon could distinguish this pair from the others, Zayin by gestalt, Kaph only by a discolored left fourth fingernail, got from an ill-aimed hammer at the age of six. No doubt there were many such differences, physical and psychological, among them; nature might be identical, nurture could not be. But the differences were hard to find. And part of the difficulty was that they really never talked to Pugh and Martin. They joked with them, were polite, got along fine. They gave nothing. It was nothing one could complain about; they were very pleasant, they had the standardized American friendliness. "Do you come from Ireland, Owen?"

"Nobody comes from Ireland, Zayin."

"There are lots of Irish-Americans."

"To be sure, but no more Irish. A couple of thousand in all

the island, the last I knew. They didn't go in for birth control, you know, so the food ran out. By the Third Famine there were no Irish left at all but the priesthood, and they all celibate, or nearly all."

Zayin and Kaph smiled stiffly. They had no experience of either bigotry or irony. "What are you then, ethnically?" Kaph asked, and Pugh replied, "A Welshman."

"Is it Welsh that you and Martin speak together?"

None of your business, Pugh thought, but said, "No, it's his dialect not mine: Argentinean. A descendant of Spanish."

"You learned it for private communication?"

"Whom had we here to be private from? It's just that sometimes a man likes to speak his native language."

"Ours is English," Kaph said unsympathetically. Why should they have sympathy? That's one of the things you give because you need it back.

"Is Wells quaint?" asked Zaylin.

"Wells? Oh, Wales, it's called. Yes, Wales is quaint." Pugh switched on his rock-cutter, which prevented further conversation by a synapse-destroying whine, and while it whined he turned his back and said a profane word in Welsh.

That night he used the Argentine dialect for private communication. "Do they pair off in the same couples or change every night?"

Martin looked surprised. A prudish expression, unsuited to his features, appeared for a moment. It faded. He too was curious. "I think it's random."

"Don't whisper, man, it sounds dirty. I think they rotate."

"On a schedule?"

"So nobody gets omitted."

Martin gave a vulgar laugh and smothered it. "What about us? Aren't we omitted?"

"That doesn't occur to them."

"What if I proposition one of the girls?"

"She'd tell the others and they'd decide as a group."

"I am not a bull," Martin said, his dark, heavy face heating up. "I will not be judged—"

"Down, down, *machismo*," said Pugh. "Do you mean to proposition one?"

Martin shrugged, sullen. "Let 'em have their incest."

"Incest is it, or masturbation?"

"I don't care, if they'd do it out of earshot!"

The clone's early attempts at modesty had soon worn off, unmotivated by any deep defensiveness of self or awareness of others. Pugh and Martin were daily deeper swamped under the intimacies of its constant emotional-sexual-mental interchange: swamped yet excluded.

"Two months to go," Martin said one evening.

"To what?" snapped Pugh. He was edgy lately, and Martin's sullenness got on his nerves.

"To relief."

In sixty days the full crew of their Exploratory Mission were due back from their survey of the other planets of the system. Pugh was aware of this.

"Crossing off the days on your calendar?" he jeered.

"Pull yourself together, Owen."

"What do you mean?"

"What I say."

They parted in contempt and resentment.

Pugh came in after a day alone on the Pampas, a vast lava plain the nearest edge of which was two hours south by jet. He was tired but refreshed by solitude. They were not supposed to take long trips alone but lately had often done so. Martin stopped under bright lights, drawing one of his elegant masterly charts: This one was of the whole face of Libra, the cancerous face. The dome was otherwise empty, seeming dim and large as it had before the clone came. "Where's the golden horde?"

Martin grunted ignorance, cross-hatching. He straightened his back to glance round at the sun, which squatted feebly like a great red toad on the eastern plain, and at the clock, which said 18:45. "Some big quakes today," he said, returning to his map. "Feel them down there? Lots of crates were falling around. Take a look at the seismo."

The needle jigged and wavered on the roll. It never stopped dancing here. The roll had recorded five quakes of major intensity back in midafternoon; twice the needle had hopped off the roll. The attached computer had been activated to emit a slip reading, "Epicenter 61' N by 42'4" E."

"Not in the Trench this time."

"I thought it felt a bit different from usual. Sharper."

"In Base One I used to lie awake all night feeling the ground jump. Queer how you get used to things."

"Go spla if you didn't. What's for dinner?"

"I thought you'd have cooked it."

"Waiting for the clone."

Feeling put upon, Pugh got out a dozen dinnerboxes, stuck two in the Instobake, pulled them out. "All right, here's dinner."

"Been thinking," Martin said, coming to table. "What if some clone cloned itself? Illegally. Made a thousand duplicates—ten thousand. Whole army. They could make a tidy power grab, couldn't they?"

"But how many millions did this lot cost to rear? Artificial placentae and all that. It would be hard to keep secret, unless they had a planet to themselves. . . . Back before the Famines when Earth had national governments, they talked about that: Clone your best soldiers, have whole regiments of them. But the food ran out before they could play that game."

They talked amicably, as they used to do.

"Funny," Martin said, chewing. "They left early this morning, didn't they?"

"All but Kaph and Zayin. They thought they'd get the first payload above ground today. What's up?"

"They weren't back for lunch."

"They won't starve, to be sure."

"They left at seven."

"So they did." Then Pugh saw it. The air tanks held eight hours' supply.

"Kaph and Zayin carried out spare cans when they left. Or they've got a heap out there."

"They did, but they brought the whole lot in to recharge."

Martin stood up, pointing to one of the stacks of stuff that cut the dome into rooms and alleys.

"There's an alarm signal on every imsuit."

"It's not automatic."

Pugh was tired and still hungry. "Sit down and eat, man. That lot can look after themselves."

Martin sat down but did not eat. "There was a big quake, Owen. The first one. Big enough it scared me."

After a pause Pugh sighed and said, "All right."

Unenthusiastically, they got out the two-man sled that was always left for them and headed it north. The long sunrise covered everything in poisonous red jello. The horizontal light and shadow made it hard to see, raised walls of fake iron ahead of them which they slid through, turned the convex plain beyond Hellmouth into a great dimple full of bloody water. Around the tunnel entrance a wilderness of machinery stood, cranes and cables and servos and wheels and diggers and robocarts and sliders and control huts, all slanting and bulking incoherently in the red light. Martin jumped from the sled, ran into the mine. He came out again, to Pugh. "Oh God, Owen, it's down," he said. Pugh went in and saw, five meters from the entrance, the shiny moist, black wall that ended the tunnel. Newly exposed to air, it looked organic, like visceral tissue. The tunnel entrance, enlarged by blasting and double-tracked for robocarts, seemed unchanged until he noticed thousands of tiny spiderweb cracks in the walls. The floor was wet with some sluggish fluid.

"They were inside," Martin said.

"They may be still. They surely had extra air cans—"

"Look, Owen, look at the basalt flow, at the roof, don't you see what the quake did, look at it."

The low hump of land that roofed the caves still had the unreal look of an optical illusion. It had reversed itself, sunk down, leaving a vast dimple or pit. When Pugh walked on it he saw that it too was cracked with many tiny fissures. From some a whitish gas was seeping, so that the sunlight on the surface of the gas pool was shafted as if by the waters of a dim red lake.

"The mine's not on the fault. There's no fault here!"

Pugh came back to him quickly. "No, there's no fault, Martin. —Look, they surely weren't all inside together."

Martin followed him and searched among the wrecked machines dully, then actively. He spotted the airsled. It had come down heading south, and stuck at an angle in a pothole of colloidal dust. It had carried two riders. One was half sunk in the dust, but his suit meters registered normal functioning; the other hung strapped onto the tilted sled. Her imsuit had burst open on the broken legs, and the body was frozen hard as any rock. That was all they found. As both regulation and custom demanded, they cremated the dead at once with the laser guns they carried by regulation and had never used before. Pugh, knowing he was going to be sick, wrestled the survivor onto the two-man sled and sent Martin off to the dome with him. Then he vomited and flushed the waste out of his suit, and finding one four-man sled undamaged, followed after Martin, shaking as if the cold of Libra had got through to him.

The survivor was Kaph. He was in deep shock. They found a swelling on the occiput that might mean concussion, but no fracture was visible.

Pugh brought two glasses of food concentrate and two chasers of aquavit. "Come on," he said. Martin obeyed, drinking off the tonic. They sat down on crates near the cot and sipped the aquavit.

Kaph lay immobile, face like beeswax, hair bright black to the shoulders, lips stiffly parted for faintly gasping breaths.

"It must have been the first shock, the big one," Martin said. "It must have slid the whole structure sideways. Till it fell in on itself. There must be gas layers in the lateral rocks, like those formations in the Thirty-first Quadrant. But there wasn't any sign—" As he spoke the world slid out from under them. Things leaped and clattered, hopped and jigged, shouted Ha! Ha! Ha! —"It was like this at fourteen hours," said Reason shakily in Martin's voice, amidst the unfastening and ruin of the world. But Unreason sat up, as the tumult lessened and things ceased dancing, and screamed aloud.

Pugh leaped across his spilt aquavit and held Kaph down. The muscular body flailed him off. Martin pinned the shoulders down. Kaph screamed, struggled, choked; his face blackened. "Oxy," Pugh said, and his hand found the right needle in the medical kit as if by homing instinct; while Martin held the mask he struck the needle home to the vagus nerve, restoring Kaph to life.

"Didn't know you knew that stunt," Martin said, breathing hard.

"The Lazarus Jab, my father was a doctor. It doesn't often work," Pugh said. "I want that drink I spilled. Is the quake over? I can't tell."

"Aftershocks. It's not just you shivering."

"Why did he suffocate?"

"I don't know, Owen. Look in the book."

Kaph was breathing normally and his color was restored; only the lips were still darkened. They poured a new shot of courage and sat down by him again with their medical guide. "Nothing about cyanosis or asphyxiation under 'shock' or 'concussion.' He can't have breathed in anything with his suit on. I don't know. We'd get as much good out of *Mother Mog's Home Herbalist*. . . . 'Anal Hemorrhoids,' fy!" Pugh pitched the book to a crate table. It fell short, because either Pugh or the table was still unsteady.

"Why didn't he signal?"

"Sorry?"

"The eight inside the mine never had time. But he and the girl must have been outside. Maybe she was in the entrance and got hit by the first slide. He must have been outside, in the control hut maybe. He ran in, pulled her out, strapped her onto the sled, started for the dome. And all that time never pushed the panic button in his imsuit. Why not?"

"Well, he'd had that whack on his head. I doubt he ever realized the girl was dead. He wasn't in his senses. But if he had been I don't know if he'd have thought to signal us. They looked to one another for help."

Martin's face was like an Indian mask, grooves at the mouth corners, eyes of dull coal. "That's so. What must he have felt, then, when the quake came and he was outside, alone—"

In answer Kaph screamed.

He came off the cot in the heaving convulsions of one suffocating, knocked Pugh right down with his flailing arm, staggered into a stack of crates and fell to the floor, lips blue, eyes white. Martin dragged him back onto the cot and gave him a whiff of oxygen, then knelt by Pugh, who was sitting up, and wiped at his cut cheekbone. "Owen, are you all right, are you going to be all right, Owen?"

"I think I am," Pugh said. "Why are you rubbing that on my face?"

It was a short length of computer tape, now spotted with Pugh's blood. Martin dropped it. "Thought it was a towel. You clipped your cheek on that box there."

"Is he out of it?"

"Seems to be."

They stared down at Kaph lying stiff, his teeth a white line inside dark parted lips.

"Like epilepsy. Brain damage maybe?"

"What about shooting him full of meprobamate?"

Pugh shook his head. "I don't know what's in that shot I already gave him for shock. Don't want to overdose him."

"Maybe he'll sleep it off now."

"I'd like to myself. Between him and the earthquake I can't seem to keep on my feet."

"You got a nasty crack there. Go on, I'll sit up a while."

Pugh cleaned his cut cheek and pulled off his shirt, then paused.

"Is there anything we ought to have done—have tried to do—"

"They're all dead," Martin said heavily, gently.

Pugh lay down on top of his sleeping bag and one instant later was wakened by a hideous, sucking, struggling noise. He staggered up, found the needle, tried three times to jab it in correctly and failed, began to massage over Kaph's heart. "Mouth-to-mouth," he said, and Martin obeyed. Presently Kaph drew a harsh breath, his heartbeat steadied, his rigid muscles began to relax.

"How long did I sleep?"

"Half an hour."

They stood up sweating. The ground shuddered, the fabric

of the dome sagged and swayed. Libra was dancing her awful polka again, her *Totentanz*. The sun, though rising, seemed to have grown larger and redder; gas and dust must have been stirred up in the feeble atmosphere.

"What's wrong with him, Owen?"

"I think he's dying with them."

"Them—but they're all dead, I tell you."

"Nine of them. They're all dead, they were crushed or suffocated. They were all him, he is all of them. They died, and now he's dying their deaths one by one."

"Oh, pity of God," said Martin.

The next time was much the same. The fifth time was worse, for Kaph fought and raved, trying to speak but getting no words out, as if his mouth were stopped with rocks or clay. After that the attacks grew weaker, but so did he. The eighth seizure came at about four-thirty; Pugh and Martin worked till five-thirty doing all they could to keep life in the body that slid without protest into death. They kept him, but Martin said, "The next will finish him." And it did; but Pugh breathed his own breath into the inert lungs, until he himself passed out.

He woke. The dome was opaqued and no light on. He listened and heard the breathing of two sleeping men. He slept, and nothing woke him till hunger did.

The sun was well up over the dark plains, and the planet had stopped dancing. Kaph lay asleep. Pugh and Martin drank tea and looked at him with proprietary triumph.

When he woke Martin went to him: "How do you feel, old man?" There was no answer. Pugh took Martin's place and looked into the brown, dull eyes that gazed toward but not into his own. Like Martin he quickly turned away. He heated food concentrate and brought it to Kaph. "Come on, drink."

He could see the muscles in Kaph's throat tighten. "Let me die," the young man said.

"You're not dying."

Kaph spoke with clarity and precision: "I am nine-tenths dead. There is not enough of me left alive."

That precision convinced Pugh, and he fought the conviction. "No," he said, peremptory. "They are dead. The others. Your brothers and sisters. You're not them, you're alive. You are John Chow. Your life is in your own hands."

The young man lay still, looking into a darkness that was not there.

Martin and Pugh took turns taking the Exploitation hauler and a spare set of robos over to Hellmouth to salvage equipment and protect it from Libra's sinister atmosphere, for the value of the stuff was, literally, astronomical. It was slow work for one man at a time, but they were unwilling to leave Kaph by himself. The one left in the dome did paperwork, while Kaph sat or lay and stared into his darkness and never spoke. The days went by silent.

The radio spat and spoke: the Mission calling from ship. "We'll be down on Libra in five weeks, Owen. Thirty-four E-days nine hours I make it as of now. How's tricks in the old dome?"

"Not good chief. The Exploit team were killed all but one of them, in the mine. Earthquake. Six days ago."

The radio crackled and sang starsong. Sixteen seconds' lag each way; the ship was out around Planet II now. "Killed, all but one? You and Martin were unhurt?"

"We're all right, chief."

Thirty-two seconds.

Passerine left an Exploit team out here with us. I may put them on the Hellmouth project then, instead of the Quadrant Seven project. We'll settle that when we come down. In any case you and Martin will be relieved at Dome Two. Hold tight. Anything else?"

"Nothing else."

Thirty-two seconds.

"Right then. So long, Owen."

Kaph had heard all this, and later on Pugh said to him, "The chief may ask you to stay here with the other Exploit team. You know the ropes here." Knowing the exigencies of Far Out life, he wanted to warn the young man. Kaph made no answer. Since he had said, "There is not enough of me left alive," he had not spoken a word.

"Owen," Martin said on suit intercom, "he's spla. Insane. Psycho."

"He's doing very well for a man who's died nine times."

"Well? Like a turned-off android is well? The only emotion he has left is hate. Look at his eyes."

"That's not hate, Martin. Listen, it's true that he has, in a sense, been dead. I cannot imagine what he feels. But it's not hatred. He can't even see us. It's too dark."

"Throats have been cut in the dark. He hates us because we're not Aleph and Yod and Zayin."

"Maybe. But I think he's alone. He doesn't see us or hear us, that's the truth. He never had to see anyone else before. He never was alone before. He had himself to see, talk with, live with, nine other selves all his life. He doesn't know how you go it alone. He must learn. Give him time."

Martin shook his heavy head. "Spla," he said. "Just remember when you're alone with him that he could break your neck one-handed."

"He could do that," said Pugh, a short, soft-voiced man with a scarred cheekbone; he smiled. They were just outside the dome airlock, programming one of the servos to repair a damaged hauler. They could see Kaph sitting inside the great half-egg of the dome like a fly in amber.

"Hand me the insert pack there. What makes you think he'll get any better?"

"He has a strong personality, to be sure."

"Strong? Crippled. Nine-tenths dead, as he put it."

"But he's not dead. He's a live man: John Kaph Chow. He had a jolly queer upbringing, but after all every boy has got to break free of his family. He will do it."

"I can't see it."

"Think a bit, Martin bach. What's this cloning for? To repair the human race. We're in a bad way. Look at me. My IIQ and GC are half this John Chow's. Yet they wanted me so badly for the Far Out Service that when I volunteered they took me and fitted me out with an artificial lung and corrected my myopia. Now if there were enough good sound lads about would they be taking one-lunged short-sighted Welshmen?"

"Didn't know you had an artificial lung."

"I do then. Not tin, you know. Human, grown in a tank from a bit of somebody; cloned, if you like. That's how they make replacement organs, the same general idea as cloning, but bits and pieces instead of whole people. It's my own lung now, whatever. But what I am saying is this, there are too many like me these days and not enough like John Chow. They're trying to raise the level of the human genetic pool, which is a mucky little puddle since the population crash. So then if a man is cloned, he's a strong and clever man. It's only logic, to be sure."

Martin grunted; the servo began to hum.

Kaph had been eating little; he had trouble swallowing his food, choking on it, so that he would give up trying after a few bites. He had lost eight or ten kilos. After three weeks or so, however, his appetite began to pick up, and one day he began to look through the clone's possessions, the sleeping bags, kits, papers which Pugh had stacked neatly in a far angle of a packing-crate alley. He sorted, destroyed a heap of papers and oddments, made a small packet of what remained, then relapsed into his walking coma.

Two days later he spoke. Pugh was trying to correct a flutter in the tape-player and failing; Martin had the jet out, checking their maps of the Pampas. "Hell and damnation!" Pugh said, and Kaph said in a toneless voice, "Do you want me to do that?"

Pugh jumped, controlled himself, and gave the machine to Kaph. The young man took it apart, put it back together, and left it on the table.

"Put on a tape," Pugh said with careful casualness, busy at another table.

Kaph put on the topmost tape, a chorale. He lay down on his cot. The sound of a hundred human voices singing together filled the dome. He lay still, his face blank.

In the next days he took over several routine jobs, unasked. He undertook nothing that wanted initiative, and if asked to do anything he made no response at all.

"He's doing well," Pugh said in the dialect of Argentina.

"He's not. He's turning himself into a machine. Does what he's programmed to do, no reaction to anything else. He's worse off than when he didn't function at all. He's not human any more."

Pugh sighed. "Well, good night," he said in English. "Good night, Kaph."

"Good night," Martin said; Kaph did not.

Next morning at breakfast Kaph reached across Martin's plate for the toast. "Why don't you ask for it," Martin said with the geniality of repressed exasperation. "I can pass it."

"I can reach it," Kaph said in his flat voice.

"Yes, but look. Asking to pass things, saying good night or hello, they're not important, but all the same when somebody says something a person ought to answer. . . ."

The young man looked indifferently in Martin's direction; his eyes still did not seem to see clear through to the person he looked toward. "Why should I answer?"

"Because somebody has said something to you."

"Why?"

Martin shrugged and laughed. Pugh jumped up and turned on the rock-cutter.

Later on he said, "Lay off that, please, Martin."

"Manners are essential in small isolated crews, some kind of manners, whatever you work out together. He's been taught that, everybody in Far Out knows it. Why does he deliberately flout it?"

"Do you tell yourself good night?"

"So?"

"Don't you see Kaph's never known anyone but himself?"

Martin brooded and then broke out. "Then by God this cloning business is all wrong. It won't do. What are a lot of duplicate geniuses going to do for us when they don't even know we exist?"

Pugh nodded. "It might be wiser to separate the clones and bring them up with others. But they make such a grand team this way."

"Do they? I don't know. If this lot had been ten average inefficient E.T. engineers, would they all have got killed? What if, when the quake came and things started caving in, what if all those kids ran the same way, farther into the mine, maybe, to save the one that was farthest in? Even Kaph was outside and went in. . . . It's hypothetical. But I keep thinking, out of ten ordinary confused guys, more might have got out."

"I don't know. It's true that identical twins tend to die at about the same time, even when they have never seen each other. Identity and death, it is very strange ..."

The days went on, the red sun crawled across the dark sky, Kaph did not speak when spoken to, Pugh and Martin snapped at each other more frequently each day. Pugh complained of Martin's snoring. Offended, Martin moved his cot clear across the dome and also ceased speaking to Pugh for some while. Pugh whistled Welsh dirges until Martin complained, and then Pugh stopped speaking for a while.

The day before the Mission ship was due, Martin announced he was going over to Merioneth.

"I thought at least you'd be giving me a hand with the computer to finish the rock analyses," Pugh said, aggrieved.

"Kaph can do that. I want one more look at the Trench. Have fun," Martin added in dialect, and laughed, and left.

"What is that language?"

"Argentinean. I told you that once, didn't I?"

"I don't know." After a while the young man added, "I have forgotten a lot of things, I think."

"It wasn't important, to be sure," Pugh said gently, realizing all at once how important this conversation was. "Will you give me a hand running the computer, Kaph?"

He nodded.

Pugh had left a lot of loose ends, and the job took them all day. Kaph was a good coworker, quick and systematic, much more so than Pugh himself. His flat voice, now that he was talking again, got on the nerves; but it didn't matter, there was only this one day left to get through and then the ship would come, the old crew, comrades and friends.

During tea break Kaph said, "What will happen if the Explore ship crashes?"

"They'd be killed."

"To you, I mean."

"To us? We'd radio SOS signals and live on half rations till the rescue cruiser from Area Three Base came. Four and a half E-Years away it is. We have life support here for three men for let's see, maybe between four, and five years. A bit tight, it would be."

"Would they send a cruiser for three men?"

"They would."

Kaph said no more.

"Enough cheerful speculations," Pugh said cheerfully, rising to get back to work. He slipped sideways and the chair avoided his hand; he did a sort of half-pirouette and fetched up hard against the dome hide. "My goodness," he said, reverting to his native idiom, "what is it?"

"Quake," said Kaph.

The teacups bounced on the table with a plastic cackle, a litter of papers slid off a box, the skin of the dome swelled and sagged. Underfoot there was a huge noise, half sound, half shaking, a subsonic boom.

Kaph sat unmoved. An earthquake does not frighten a man who died in an earthquake.

Pugh, white-faced, wiry black hair sticking out, a frightened man, said, "Martin is in the Trench."

"What trench?"

"The big fault line. The epicenter for the local quakes. Look at the seismograph." Pugh struggled with the stuck door of a still-jittering locker.

"Where are you going?"

"After him."

"Martin took the jet. Sleds aren't safe to use during quakes. They go out of control."

"For God's sake man, shut up."

Kaph stood up, speaking in a flat voice as usual. "It's unnecessary to go out after him now. It's taking an unnecessary risk."

"If his alarm goes off radio me," Pugh said, shut the headpiece of his suit, and ran to the lock. As he went out Libra picked up her ragged skirts and danced belly dance from under his feet clear to the red horizon.

Inside the dome, Kaph saw the sled go up, tremble like a meteor in the dull red daylight, and vanish to the northeast. The hide of the dome quivered, the earth coughed. A vent south of the dome belched up a slow-flowing bile of black gas.

A bell shrilled and a red light flashed on the central control board. The sign under the light read Suit 2 and scribbled under that, A. G. M. Kaph did not turn the signal off. He tried to radio Martin, then Pugh, but got no reply from either.

When the aftershocks decreased he went back to work and finished up Pugh's job. It took him about two hours. Every half hour he tried to contact Suit 1 and got no reply, then Suit 2 and got no reply. The red light had stopped flashing after an hour.

It was dinnertime. Kaph cooked dinner for one and ate it. He lay down on his cot.

The aftershocks had ceased except for faint rolling tremors at long intervals. The sun hung in the west, oblate, pale red, immense. It did not sink visibly. There was no sound at all.

Kaph got up and began to walk about the messy, half-packed-up, overcrowded, empty dome. The silence continued. He went to the player and put on the first tape that came to hand. It was pure music, electronic, without harmonies, without voices. It ended. The silence continued.

Pugh's uniform tunic, one button missing, hung over a stack of rock samples. Kaph stared at it a while.

The silence continued.

The child's dream: There is no one else alive in the world but me. In all the world.

Low, north of the dome a meteor flickered.

Kaph's mouth opened as if he were trying to say something, but no sound came. He went hastily to the north wall and peered out into the gelatinous red light.

The little star came in and sank. Two figures blurred the airlock. Kaph stood close beside the lock as they came in. Martin's imsuit was covered with some kind of dust so that he looked raddled and warty like the surface of Libra. Pugh had him by the arm.

"Is he hurt?"

Pugh shucked his suit, helped Martin peel off his. "Shaken up," he said, curt.

"A piece of cliff fell onto the jet," Martin said, sitting down at the table and waving his arms. "Not while I was in it though. I was parked, see, and poking about that carbon-dust area when I felt things humping. So I went out onto a nice bit of early igneous I'd noticed from above, good footing and out from under the cliffs. Then I saw this bit of the planet fall off onto the flyer, quite a sight it was, and after a while it occurred to me the spare aircans were in the flyer, so I leaned on the panic button. But I didn't get any radio reception, that's always happening here during quakes, so I didn't know if the signal was getting through either. And things went on jumping around and pieces of the cliff coming off. Little rocks flying around, and so dusty you couldn't see a meter ahead. I was really beginning to wonder what I'd do for breathing in the small hours, you know, when I saw old Owen buzzing up the Trench in all that dust and junk like a big ugly bat—"

"Want to eat?" said Pugh.

"Of course I want to eat. How'd you come through the quake here, Kaph? No damage? It wasn't a big one actually, was it, what's the seismo say? My trouble was I was in the middle of it. Old Epicenter Alvaro. Felt like Richter fifteen there—total destruction of planet—"

"Sit down," Pugh said. "Eat."

After Martin had eaten a little his spate of talk ran dry. He very soon went off to his cot, still in the remote angle where he had removed it when Pugh complained of his snoring. "Good night, you one-lunged Welshman," he said across the dome.

"Good night."

There was no more out of Martin. Pugh opaqued the dome, turned the lamp down to a yellow glow less than a candle's light, and sat doing nothing, saying nothing, withdrawn.

The silence continued.

"I finished the computations."

Pugh nodded thanks.

"The signal from Martin came through, but I couldn't contact you or him."

Pugh said with effort, "I should not have gone. He had two hours of air left even with only one can. He might have been heading home when I left. This way we were all out of touch with one another. I was scared."

The silence came back, punctuated now by Martin's long, soft snores.

"Do you love Martin?"

Pugh looked up with angry eyes: "Martin is my friend. We've worked together, he's a good man." He stopped. After a while he said, "Yes, I love him. Why did you ask that?"

Kaph said nothing, but he looked at the other man. His face was changed, as if he were glimpsing something he had not seen before; his voice too was changed. "How can you. . . . How do you . . ."

But Pugh could not tell him. "I don't know," he said, "it's practice, partly. I don't know. We're each of us alone, to be sure. What can you do but hold your hand out in the dark?"

Kaph's strange gaze dropped, burned out by its own intensity.

"I'm tired," Pugh said. "That was ugly, looking for him in all that black dust and muck, and mouths opening and shutting in the ground. . . . I'm going to bed. The ship will be transmitting to us by six or so." He stood up and stretched.

"It's a clone," Kaph said. "The other Exploit Team they're bringing with them."

"Is it then?"

"A twelveclone. They came out with us on the *Passerine.*"

Kaph sat in the small yellow aura of the lamp seeming to look past it at what he feared: the new clone, the multiple self of which he was not part. A lost piece of a broken set, a fragment, inexpert at solitude, not knowing even how you go about giving love to another individual, now he must face the absolute, closed self-sufficiency of the clone of twelve; that was a lot to ask of the poor fellow, to be sure. Pugh put a hand on his shoulder in passing. "The chief won't ask you to stay here with a clone. You can go home. Or since you're Far Out maybe you'll come on farther out with us. We could use you. No hurry deciding. You'll make out all right."

Pugh's quiet voice trailed off. He stood unbuttoning his coat, stooped a little with fatigue. Kaph looked at him and saw the thing he had never seen before: saw him: Owen Pugh, the other, the stranger who held his hand out in the dark.

"Good night," Pugh mumbled, crawling into his sleeping bag and half asleep already, so that he did not hear Kaph reply after a pause, repeating, across darkness, benediction.

QUESTIONS

1 Discuss the possibility that too much efficiency may be undesirable.
2 Sociologists are concerned about the weakening family structure and its effect on children. If human beings can be grown without benefit of parents (as we know them), what might the families of the future look like?
3 Would the reader's attitude toward the clone's incestuous behavior be altered if the women were not sterile?
4 How do the descriptions of the planet set the tone of the story?
5 Does Le Guin actually want us to believe that Pugh and Martin are superior to the clone?
6 We all search for group identity and a certain amount of conformity. Sigmund Freud claims that if it were possible we would make love only to ourselves. If conformity and egotism are such strong drives, then why would it be undesirable to be surrounded by people who looked, thought, and acted as you did?

SUGGESTED READINGS

Ardrey, Robert: *African Genesis.* New York: Atheneum Publishers, 1961.
Blish, James: *The Seedling Stars.* New York: Signet Books, New American Library, Inc., 1957.
Bradbury, Ray: *The Martian Chronicles.* Garden City, N. Y.: Doubleday & Company, Inc., 1958.
Cheetham, Anthony (ed.): *Science against Man.* New York: Avon Book Division, The Hearst Corporation, 1970.
Chermayeff, Serge, and Christopher Alexander: *Community and Privacy: Toward a New Architecture of Humanism.* Garden City, N. Y.: Anchor Books, Doubleday & Company, Inc., 1965.
Dubos, René: *Man Adapting.* New Haven and London: Yale University Press, 1965.
Golding, William: *Lord of the Flies.* New York: Coward-McCann, Inc., 1962.
Heinlein, Robert A.: *I Will Fear No Evil.* New York: G. P. Putnam's Sons, 1970.
————: *Methuselah's Children.* New York: Signet Books, New American Library, Inc., 1958.
Herbert, Frank: *Dune.* New York: Ace Books, 1965.
Hillegas, Mark R.: *The Future as Nightmare: H. G. Wells and the Anti-Utopians.* New York: Oxford University Press, 1967.

Kahn, Herman, and Anthony J. Wiener (eds.): *The Year 2000: A Framework for Speculation on the Next Thirty-Three Years.* New York: The Macmillan Company, 1967.

Keith, Sir Arthur: *Evolution and Ethics.* New York: G. P. Putnam's Sons, 1947.

Lewis, C. S.: *An Experiment in Criticism.* New York: Cambridge University Press, 1961.

Penzoldt, Peter: *The Supernatural in Fiction.* New York: Humanities Press, 1965.

Rank, Otto: *The Myth of the Birth of the Hero.* New York: Alfred A. Knopf, Inc., 1959.

Shelley, Mary: *Frankenstein.* New York: Collier Books, The Macmillan Company, 1966.

Sturgeon, Theodore: *More Than Human.* New York: Ballantine Books, Inc., 1953.

Taylor, Gordon Rattray: *The Biological Time Bomb.* New York: Signet Books, The New American Library, Inc., 1968.

Toffler, Alvin: *Future Shock.* New York: Random House, Inc., 1970.